DAUGHTER
OF ASHES

Books by the author

——⟨∞⟩——

Flowers Over the Inferno
The Sleeping Nymph

DAUGHTER OF ASHES

ILARIA TUTI

translated from the Italian by Ekin Oklap

First published in Italian under the title *Figlia della cenere*.
Copyright © 2021 by Longanesi & C. S.r.l.
—Milano, Gruppo editoriale Mauri Spagnol.

English translation copyright © 2022 by Ekin Oklap

Published by
Soho Press, Inc.
227 W 17th Street
New York, NY 10011

Library of Congress Cataloging-in-Publication Data
Names: Tuti, Ilaria, author. | Oklap, Ekin, translator.
Title: Daughter of ashes / Ilaria Tuti ; translated from the Italian by Ekin Oklap.
Other titles: Figlia della cenere. English
Description: New York, NY : Soho Crime, [2023]
Series: A Teresa Battaglia novel ; [3] | Identifiers: LCCN 2023018595

ISBN 978-1-64129-619-9
eISBN 978-1-64129-418-8

Subjects: LCGFT: Detective and mystery fiction. | Novels.
Classification: LCC PQ4920.U86 F5413 2023 | DDC 853'.92—dc23/
eng/20230502
LC record available at https://lccn.loc.gov/2023018595

Interior design by Janine Agro, Soho Press, Inc.

Printed in the United States of America

10 9 8 7 6 5 4 3 2 1

To the women who've been hurt

I know nothing is decided in the heavens
or on earth—yet still I knead my firm breast
as the farmer with the heifer's womb.
I, too, will deliver a new heart
it will slip between my legs with useless pain
and I will not know what to do with it.

—Elisa Ruotolo, Body of Bread

DAUGHTER OF ASHES

PROLOGUE

Twenty-seven years ago
At the end of everything

SHE WASN'T MUCH OLDER than thirty and she felt like she had turned to dust. What could she make out of dust? A second life, but she would have to knead it with blood and tears, and the sweat of a creature clinging to the edge of an abyss.

When she lay down on the bed for another round of the treatment that was supposed to relieve her pain and rebuild what had shattered inside of her, Teresa had initially dreaded the feel of a stranger's hands on her body, but realized she found it soothing. The doctor's practiced touch took her back to her childhood, to the cradle, as if her whimpers might be the cries of an infant.

"We die and we are reborn many times over the course of a single existence, Teresa. This has already happened. It will happen again, and it will hurt, but look at who you've *become*."

Teresa shifted her gaze from the ceiling to the woman's face. She felt like an empty vessel, incapable of welcoming anything at all.

The doctor leaned over the bed where that arid emptiness lay.

Every word that came out of the doctor's mouth was molded by the inflections of her mother tongue, nestled in the space between her palate and her teeth, and curled across the back of the fêng huang phoenix embroidered on her robe of red silk. Red like the fruit of the strawberry tree whose color blazed through misty winters in Teresa's grandparents' garden.

"Everyone is talking about what you managed to do."

It was disturbingly easy to wind your memories back, when all seemed lost. The end was a tilted plane where everything slipped back to the point of origin. Teresa was falling slowly into a black hole.

The ritual incense sticks released plumes of twisting smoke. In the background, bamboo flutes mimicked whispering winds from faraway lands.

The doctor inserted a second needle into Teresa's skin.

"This energy point is called *Da Ling*, meaning 'great hill.' It represents burial mounds . . ."

Teresa closed her eyes, her body a living grave.

"But every tomb carries a secret; that is why *Da Ling* is known by other names, too. To reveal, and to restore." Another needle into the skin. "*Gui Xin*, ghost of the heart. *Zhu Xin*, governor of the heart. It is the past and your guilt that you must bury, Teresa, not your talent."

Teresa parted her lips. Even talking was painful. Her jaw, pierced with screws from her operation, was still in a brace.

"I'm d-d-dust," she managed.

Anyone could have blown on her and swept her away. A man she had once loved had flung her bones across a black altar. Teresa could feel them now spinning, swirling in the breath of life, as if reassembling the skeleton upon which a new beginning might rest. They crackled with the sound of the fears that woke her in the middle of the night. The snap of breaking bones. *Her* bones.

The panic attacks always ambushed her after dark, in the silence, her arms and legs tangled in the sheets, an offering to ruin. They rode on a herd of black horses galloping across the slopes of her ravaged flesh. The horses would pummel their way across her stitches, their hooves digging into her knees and the inner curve of her elbows, pounding against her collarbones and her ankles. They pulverized what Teresa could barely keep together, breaking the woman she had become, a woman reduced to bare bones, her skin flayed off. They reduced her to tiny fragments, and a little piece of her was lost every time.

Behind her, Mei Gao put her acupuncture equipment away. Then she held her patient's face in her hands and gave it a gentle pull until Teresa's chin lifted.

Teresa felt her body opening up to the pain and to a deeper breathing, handing itself over to a force that came with a price—to be paid in the currency of hurt.

"You were dust, but your suffering has turned into fire," the woman whispered. "You are incandescent. And from the ashes of your previous life, you are reborn. Such is the fate of commanders, Superintendent Battaglia. Don't ever bow your head again, not to anything or anyone. Not even to yourself."

1

Today

THE TAXI STOPPED OUTSIDE the gates of the maximum security prison.

The woman made no move to open the door. Her expression seemed to suggest that freedom lay on the other side, just past the watchtowers and the ramparts made of reinforced concrete.

The driver turned around, resting his elbow on the passenger seat.

"Is this the right address?"

It was, and her destination was right there: "beyond," where any certainty would disappear.

"Ma'am?"

The woman hesitated, wary of taking another step forward in this life she should have bid farewell to long ago, and feeling self-conscious about the person she no longer was—though everyone else insisted on treating her as such. Bit by bit, that mirror image was peeling off her body, consigning the woman she had once been to the past. She was nearly sixty years old; her body creaked as if she were eighty, and her soul ached as if she'd lived for a century. She felt like a ghost in a world that was no longer her own.

"Ma'am, is this where you wanted to go?"

Ghosts have no voice. From the pavement outside, someone replied in her stead.

"Yes, it is."

Massimo Marini opened the door. The heavy afternoon light of spring shone behind him, illuminating the quiver of a muscle down the side of his jaw. Inspector Marini was nervous, as nervous, perhaps, as the woman before him, who recognized in that twitch of his jaw the signs of barely contained emotion. They hadn't seen each other in two weeks, not since the day they had both nearly died.

The inspector took his wallet out from the inside pocket of his jacket, paid for the ride, and put his arm out to help the passenger out of the car.

"Shall we go, Superintendent?"

Teresa Battaglia tightened her grip on her walking stick, deliberately holding it aloft between them.

Is this how you want me? she was silently asking him, the savage irony in her gesture aimed really at herself. Her disabilities, both the visible one and the one that was still hidden, were an uncomfortable presence they both needed to come to terms with.

Marini leaned a little closer.

"Shall I just pick you up? I could, you know."

"You'd break your back."

Marini grabbed her stick.

"You'll have to whack me with this thing before I let you change your mind."

She tugged at the stick but couldn't wrest it back.

"I might just do that."

"Come on, get out of the car."

"I'm only getting out because I have chosen to do so."

The driver started the engine.

"Lady, please just get out."

Teresa took Marini's arm. It wasn't only her muscles that ached, but her pride, too, pilloried by her own body's clumsy slowness. Fragile and exposed, Teresa felt like she had surrendered her weapons, but somehow, this had not brought her the anguish she had expected. On the contrary, the weight on her shoulders seemed to have eased. Feather by feather, she had relieved herself of the wings she'd so often had to patch together to overcome her latest obstacle, and had donned instead the delicate robe of courage.

Now that they were finally face to face again, they took a moment to study each other. It had scarcely been twenty days since they'd closed the case of the *Sleeping Nymph*, and they both still bore its scars: a bout of sciatica for her, a few burns and bruises for Inspector Marini. But how his eyes blazed. Teresa saw in him the young officer she had once been, sleep-deprived and desperately eager to prove herself. He was already primed to dive into a fresh case, and he wanted Teresa to go with him—unaware that she had already fallen into this particular vortex before, nearly thirty years ago.

"How are you?"

Teresa was afraid. She felt cornered, uneasy, a laughing stock, yet still alive in spite of it all. But life was so exhausting.

"I'm tired."

Marini smiled, and all of a sudden, he looked like a little boy. All the shadows gone, every need swept away by the sheer joy of the moment.

"I know. Thanks for being here."

Teresa watched as a poplar seed came to rest on the inspector's shoulder, a ball of fluff that caught the light.

"And how are you?" she asked, without meeting his eyes.

"I've missed you."

She wondered whether the tiny seed could feel the warmth of the sun through the fine white hairs that surrounded it—and if in that ligneous darkness where nothing seemed to move, life might already be planning a million different ways to be reborn, each path older than humanity itself. That same warmth had just touched her, too.

"Did you hear what I said?"

Teresa forced herself to ignore the tenderness in his words.

"Careful, Marini. Someone might get the wrong idea."

He burst out laughing.

"That would be an interesting diversion for Lona to deal with."

At this mention of the district attorney, Teresa became serious again. She took a few labored steps forward. The painkillers and anti-inflammatories weren't helping much.

"How are Elena and your daughter doing?"

"They're well, thank you. Elena always asks after you, and our *son* grows with every ultrasound."

"It's going to be a girl."

"That's not the feeling I'm getting. There must be something to be said for paternal instinct."

"I wouldn't be so sure about yours, Marini . . ."

"Oh, drop it."

"Welcome back, boss."

Teresa looked up.

Officers de Carli and Parisi were standing by the watchman's cabin, smiling at her. In their jeans and polo shirts, they looked like puppies—not the ruthless hunters she had trained. Like Inspector Marini, they were around half her age, and would forever be her "boys."

Teresa was accustomed to gauging other people's reactions as part of her work, studying their body language for the words they refused to let themselves speak, and for the lies they withheld. But she was not used to doing the same solely for her own benefit. She felt a little unmoored now, eyes roaming from one face to the next in search of the truth.

All she found there was affection. She was forced to lower her gaze, feigning an unusual interest in the unevenness of the asphalt beneath her feet.

"I don't know why I'm here," she muttered. Her discomfort caused the walking stick to slip out of her hand. Marini bent down to retrieve it, then took one of her hands and placed it in the crook of his arm.

"You're here to take back the place that's yours by right, aren't you?"

Limping forward, and with her back hunched, Teresa swallowed a joke she would previously not have hesitated to make. But she did not want to seem too bitter. Or was it far too late for that?

"I'm not taking back anything," she murmured. "I won't have you spreading these rumors; Lona might have a stroke."

De Carli cleared his throat, failing to stifle an involuntary chuckle.

"Actually, the district attorney is waiting for you, Superintendent."

Parisi looked at his watch.

"Has been for an hour, in fact, though he seems to be keeping his cool for now."

Teresa felt her back straighten. She glared at each of them in turn.

"Have I not made myself clear to you all?"

Marini gestured at the guard on duty to open the prison gates.

"Crystal clear, Superintendent, and it's clear to the district attorney, too. Specifically the fact that a convicted serial killer has requested to speak to you and you alone. There was nothing else Lona could do but take note."

The cage doors opened with a clanging of locks and a flurry of sliding gates, the echoes reaching where the eye couldn't see. Like a machine designed to devour tormented souls, it quickly swallowed them whole.

2

Today

THE PRISON WAS A labyrinth where the mind could easily lose its way, tangling in the sharp corners and intersecting paths of the hundreds of lives held within its walls. There was nothing natural about its unembellished geometry, designed to keep inmates forever confined to an existence that contrasted starkly with the unbridled, capricious rush of life. It was not a place of rehabilitation, but only of punishment; crossing its threshold willingly meant letting its shadow cloak your own, and breathing in its feral, metallic, masculine scent. It meant consenting to being locked up—if only temporarily.

Teresa would never get used to the feeling of those captive lives pressing against hers. Even from behind the bars, the thick walls, and the gates that kept them at bay, they still found a way to touch her. They were furious—or, more simply, they were desperate.

But there was another presence now, one whose ways were indecipherable, and who was waiting for her, in the flesh, at the end of the corridor.

Albert Lona seemed completely unmoved as he watched her stagger toward him, and did not take a single step to shorten the distance between them.

Teresa was unperturbed. The district attorney had vowed to ruin her, and he was a man of his word, imprisoned by his past and by his own noxious pride. Yet only a few days earlier, that same man had leapt into a fire to save her.

By the time she finally reached him, Teresa's muscles were shaking with the effort. She was flushed and out of breath, and more certain than ever before that she would never be able to return to work. She cut an incongruous figure next to him, with his freshly pressed tailored suit and a sophisticated cologne that reminded Teresa of some expensive brand. The strand of Englishness that still inflected his Italian half lent him a somewhat gentlemanly air. Yet nothing could ever truly hide his predatory nature. They were the same age and had joined the police force at the same time, but Albert had moved so much faster, his climb to the top taking him far from Teresa at first before bringing him right back into her life.

It hadn't been long since she had turned in her badge and gun. Albert had gotten Marini to deliver them right back to her house the next day—without so much as a word or an accompanying note.

They remained where Teresa had left them. Her life was precisely at that stage of a rollercoaster ride where the car, having cranked its way to the top of the ramp, hangs suspended over the void for a few terrifying seconds before plunging forward into a mad descent.

"Doctor Lona," she said, by way of greeting.

"Teresa . . ." said Albert, seemingly in search of the right words. "How is your recovery going?"

"Swimmingly. Can't you tell?"

Whatever thought might have caused the district attorney's brow to furrow, he kept it to himself. Not for the first time, Teresa wondered if there was a single person in the world who could truly claim they knew him.

The prison warden, who had been standing beside Albert all this time, proceeded to greet Teresa with a warm handshake, managing with some difficulty to navigate his way around the walking stick she was leaning on, and which she now clumsily switched to her other hand. They had known each other for a long time, and the warden was tactful enough not to let his eyes linger on her infirmity.

"I did as you suggested, Superintendent. We have provided him with everything he requested."

Teresa hadn't doubted that they would. The warden was a man of intellectual integrity who always did everything in his power to mitigate the more punitive aspects of prison life.

Teresa's eyes scanned the bare walls in search of a chair she could finally sit on.

"So now we wait . . ."

Albert interrupted her.

"Deputy Prosecutor Gardini will be here soon. He said we should begin. As for *him*," he said, motioning toward the closed door behind them, "his only condition is that you two be left alone. He doesn't even want his lawyer there."

Teresa pulled her notebook out of her shoulder bag. Its charred cover told the tale of its owner's latest adventure, and of the flames Albert had faced in order to rescue her. Teresa looked up to find the district attorney staring at the notebook's blackened edges. Perhaps he, too, was thinking what Teresa was thinking: they could have both so easily turned to ash.

She put the notebook back inside her bag. .

"Inspector Marini is coming with me. And *he* will just have to deal with it."

Albert snapped out of his reverie, a hint of menace back in his face.

"You will follow your orders, Teresa. You will go alone."

"That's not the correct procedure."

Any remaining pretense of formality vanished immediately.

"I don't give a damn about procedure. Follow your orders."

"And I don't give a damn about your whims, Albert. If you want me to go in there, I'll do it my way. Otherwise you'll have to find some other fix."

The district attorney was fuming, but he did not react to her insubordination. Teresa let several moments pass, but no alternative seemed forthcoming. Their clash of wills was another unresolved issue between them, one that Albert was bound to add to her account eventually—but by now Teresa had very little left to lose, and everything to put behind her.

Teresa pulled Marini aside so that they would not be heard.

"Listen carefully. I will do the talking. Try not to look at him, and if you really must, be as neutral as you can."

Marini glanced over his shoulder. He looked astonished.

"Did I imagine it, or did you just basically tell the district attorney to fuck off?"

"Listen to me!"

"I'm listening."

"Don't give him any reason to take an interest in you."

Inspector Marini lowered his voice.

"You talk about him as if he were some kind of animal . . ."

"He is, and he belongs to a particularly dangerous species. He's a serial killer, Marini. The fewer opportunities you give him to work you out, the better."

She made as if to straighten his jacket, though what she was really trying to convey was reassurance. This young man was going to be a father soon. Teresa wanted to protect him, but she also knew that the time for her to pass the torch on was fast approaching.

"Whatever he says, do not show any signs of irritation—or worse, your characteristic horror. He will toy with us, and try to shock us. He will probably attempt to confuse us. People like him are master manipulators. Don't miss a word he says. This is a priceless learning opportunity. Above all, you must be respectful."

"*Respectful?*"

Teresa pulled his jacket hard, as if to tug at his attention.

"When he was conducting his research on criminal personalities, Robert Ressler interviewed countless serial killers on behalf of the FBI's Behavioral Science Unit. They were all cruel, deadly psychopaths. Do you know what he wrote about Charles Manson?"

"That he respected him?"

"He wrote that he was fully prepared when he went to see him, and genuinely interested in hearing his story—his *real* story. He hadn't gone there to judge him, but to try to understand. Manson appreciated this approach, and opened up to Ressler as he hadn't done with anyone else before. It is only thanks to that neutral—one might even call it *scientific*—approach that today, more than forty years on, we can say we have an inkling of how the mind of a killer works."

Marini looked instinctively at the closed door they were supposed to walk through together.

"And is that what you plan to do now?"

"I'll do what I'm best at. I'll listen to his story: the one he decides to tell us, and especially the one he chooses not to tell. Are you ready?"

"No."

"Let's go."

3

Twenty-seven years ago

THE LIPS HAD RETRACTED, exposing gums which glistened with dew. White and turgid, they resembled exotic mushrooms that had sprouted in the night. A blade of grass curled over the man's open mouth, a droplet hanging from its tip like a tiny lantern illuminating the darkness of the throat. There would be no breath to shake it off before it was ready to fall on its own.

Teresa leaned over the victim, her knees sinking into the waterlogged earth. The scent of spring mixed with the exhaust fumes from the cars passing by just a few meters from the crime scene—a small park in a residential district.

It was eight o'clock on a warm, gloomy morning. The sirocco had blown all night. The city was awake now, and the workers and students on its tree-lined streets all had places to be—but even so, the ambulance and police cars had begun to catch their eyes. The screen that had been put up to shield the old man's body kept curious onlookers at bay. Every now and then someone would work up the courage to ask what had happened, only to be ushered away by one of the attending officers. The prevailing rumor spoke of a heart attack. But the people who believed this rumor hadn't seen the body.

Teresa was still crouching down beside it. In this realm dominated by men, she had learned the subtle art of making herself invisible, taking up whatever space was freed up by others' neglect. In the meantime, she watched and learned, roaming freely where no one else bothered to go.

The photographs had been taken; the coroner had concluded his inspection and was busy filling out forms. Unlike the others, he was perfectly aware of the silent dance Teresa had been performing around the body. Every now and then she would catch him watching her with a grave look in his eyes. He was studying her, measuring her every move, and making no attempt to hide it.

In truth, she was somewhat in awe of Antonio Parri. She'd heard him talking to the public prosecutor and to the superintendent in charge of the investigation in a tone that could be described as brusque, if not downright disrespectful. A lunatic.

Teresa turtled into her shoulders, pulled the collar of her parka up, and shifted her focus back to the body.

It wouldn't be long before it was removed, so she only had a few minutes left to try and picture its last living moments. They were inscribed in the bones of its fractured skull, laid out like primitive portents for the eyes of the seer—Teresa—who was tasked with interpreting their meaning.

The victim had been found facedown on a grassy flowerbed close to the edge of the road. His walking stick lay beside him, its handle stained with blood. It had already been identified as the likely murder weapon. Teresa pictured the murderer gripping it around the tip and smashing it against the back of the old man's head until his skull cracked open.

The coroner had turned the body over to reveal a crater in the middle of the victim's chest, a deep gash in which his purplish heart lay exposed in his rib cage. You had to let your gaze rest there, and you had to breathe in that smell, in order to take the first steps toward understanding the meaning of what had unfolded here.

The man was not wearing any trousers. His shirt and thin cardigan were pulled open like stage curtains, the hems barely covering his underwear. His atrophied legs bore three cruciform incisions.

Swallowing her nausea and her pity, Teresa brought her face close to the victim's.

The head was tilted sideways, the eyes wide open and already clouded. The mouth was open, too, and rigid, as if the jaw joints had popped. There were no teeth; it was like looking inside a baby's mouth. She saw faint traces of blood on the tongue and on the mucus membrane.

The killer had removed seven phalanges from the victim's hands. The police were still looking for them, though Teresa didn't think they'd find them. The killer must have taken them away. There was bound to be some significance to the mutilation.

Her gaze fell once again on the disfiguring incisions on the man's legs.

"Battaglia!"

Teresa leapt to her feet like a puppet yanked by a hostile hand.

Albert grabbed her elbow and pulled her away. Ever since he'd been made superintendent, his behavior toward her had become openly aggressive.

"Have you gone mad? That's a dead body you were about to drape yourself over. That's evidence."

"I wasn't about to . . ."

Teresa fell silent. The public prosecutor was standing behind Albert and staring right at her. Teresa looked down, following Prosecutor Pace's gaze. The wet grass had stained her jeans around her knees. One of her shoelaces had come undone, and her parka had slipped from her shoulder. She quickly pulled it up. A single lock of dark hair fell across her face, defying her attempts at order.

"I just wanted to take a closer look. Those cuts . . ."

But they'd already stopped listening to her. They were talking to each other now with their backs turned. Once again, Teresa had become invisible, though this because others were choosing not to see her. She should have been used to it by now, but it still stung every time.

Albert was giving the public prosecutor a summary of what they had discovered so far.

"The victim is a local who lives a ten-minute walk away. Giovanni Bordin. Seventy-one years old, retired. His wife is already here."

Teresa gathered the errant lock in a fresh ponytail and peered past the shielding screen to look for the widow. She was cradling a miniature pinscher in her arms, and sobbing uncontrollably. Her hair still carried the traces of a back comb, but half her head bore the imprint of her pillow.

Albert was still talking when he took one step back and tread on Teresa's foot. He made no attempt to apologize. "Watch out, Battaglia." He didn't even turn around.

"The widow confirms her husband left the house very early, around five-thirty, to take the dog out. He had been using a walking stick after a recent operation, but he had no other notable physical or mental impairments. The dog returned an hour later in a state of anxiety, dragging its leash behind it. Around that same time, someone in the neighborhood came across the body. He must have been killed between five-thirty and six-thirty."

The prosecutor pointed at the body with the fountain pen she was always holding—whether she was in her office or at the most secluded of crime scenes—but which Teresa had never seen her use. Elvira Pace took all of her notes in her mind, and so far, she had never been caught unprepared.

"We need to figure out where the murder took place, though I would assume not far from here." She tilted her head. "What happened to the teeth?"

"Dentures. They ended up over there, flung away by the impact on the body, perhaps . . . His neighbors told us he would spend his afternoons at the café on the corner at the end of the road. It seems he had become involved in soccer betting. Maybe he won something at the wrong people's expense; maybe he was in debt. His wife had no clue any of it was going on."

Teresa cleared her throat.

"The lacerations on his legs. I think they're significant."

Albert and the prosecutor had already started walking toward the magistrate's car.

Teresa stifled the urge to grab their coats and pull them back. Her arms remained hanging at her sides, but rage whirled in her stomach like a lump she could not digest. She shoved it deep into her belly.

If Albert was determined to stick to more traditional leads, nothing Teresa could say or do would ever dissuade him.

But once he'd exhausted those, he would have little left to go on—for the story imprinted on the victim's body pointed to a path that led in an altogether different direction.

The moment its owner's body was lifted from the ground and placed inside a steel box, the pinscher began to howl, even though it couldn't see what was happening behind the screen.

Teresa picked up the moccasin that had slipped off the victim's foot and handed it to a couple of officers who were cataloging evidence nearby. The mud coating the sole of the shoe soiled her gloves.

"Take a sample from this."

She had given the order instinctively, and became suddenly aware of how firm she had sounded. The two officers looked at her as if she'd made a terrible joke but took the shoe anyway.

The poor dog was inconsolable, its barking so shrill it hurt the ears.

Teresa pulled the screen to one side. A newly formed and still nebulous idea prompted her to step toward the dog. She looked inside her shoulder bag for her packet of wet wipes, and pulled one out.

She had no words of consolation to offer the widow.

"May I?"

She examined the dog's paws. Mud.

She rubbed the wet wipe over the animal's dark fur several times, then examined the material. It was covered in red smears.

The widow screamed.

Teresa turned around to call for Albert, but couldn't find him among the officers still working at the scene. No one was paying any attention to her, or to the widow, who was in a state of shock, or to the dog, who was barking hysterically.

No one except Antonio Parri.

4

Today

GIACOMO MAINARDI WAS FIFTY years old, with a lean figure, and shaved, graying hair that gleamed under the fluorescent lights. A hint of what might have been a smile hovered on his lips like a snarl, magnified by a pair of extraordinarily eloquent eyebrows. He would have been able to convey any emotion with just those—irritation, anger, incredulity, wonder, even a kind of amusement. He would have been able to shift the expression on his face from one of seraphic calm to that of an avenging angel, all with the slightest of twitches.

Now those same eyebrows traced a contemptuous arc across his furrowed brow.

"Who's this?"

He had spoken in a hiss, looking down at his own restless fingers all the while.

Teresa leaned her hands on the back of one of the visitor

chairs, but although she was in a lot of pain, she made no move to sit down.

"This is Inspector Massimo Marini. He works with me."

Mainardi absorbed the information with a blink.

"They did not take my requests seriously. Neither the warden nor that asshole, the district attorney. I recognized him, you know. Is he still torturing you?"

Teresa let her eyes roam over his muscular torso, emphasized by the T-shirt he was wearing. Giacomo had kept up his training all this time. He had nurtured the beast inside.

"I was the one who insisted that Inspector Marini be present."

"That's disappointing. You might as well leave now, and take your lapdog with you."

"Look at me, Giacomo."

He did, prompted, perhaps, by the vulnerability in her voice, or by their enduring bond.

"I'm a frail old lady. Whatever it is you want from me, I can assure you I won't be able to do it without the inspector's assistance. I trust him. Otherwise I would not have brought him in to see you."

He lowered his gaze back to his work tools.

"Sit, Teresa. Not you, Inspector."

Teresa sighed as she sat down.

"What's wrong?" asked the killer.

"It would be quicker to tell you what *isn't* wrong."

Giacomo's hands paused their work, hovering in place.

"Thank you for getting my tools to me. I know that was your doing."

"And I know how much they mean to you."

From the moment they had walked into the meeting room

turned workshop, Giacomo Mainardi had not stopped
maneuvering colored tiles across the table, using a hammer and tile nippers to sculpt them into his desired shape.
The mosaic was beginning to exhibit the features of a face
whose final form was still difficult to picture, though the
artist's skill could already be glimpsed in his painstaking
workmanship, and in the expert way he brought an ever-
changing variety of colors together to craft a face that
looked made of real skin. He had been refining his technique for twenty-seven years, and no longer even needed
an image to work from. It all came from his mind, which
was just as capable of creating aberrations as it was of pro-
ducing rapturous visions.

Teresa could feel Marini's eyes upon her. She could
imagine his expression—a picture of incredulity mixed with
annoyance.

"What did you want to talk to me about, Giacomo?"

Mainardi cut an ivory-colored tile with his clippers and
held it up to the light, his expression hungry, his lips wet
with saliva. Teresa suddenly felt nauseous. Aberration and
ecstasy.

"They're just pale imitations. Just pale imitations," she
heard him mutter.

"Giacomo, why did you hand yourself in to the police?
After you managed to break out . . ."

"After you caught me and had me locked me up. I spent
twenty-seven years in a cage because of you."

Marini flinched. Teresa pretended not to notice, but Giacomo's eyes were on him like a pointer.

Teresa rested her hand next to the tiles on the table and
tried to come up with a quick riposte that might draw his

attention back to her. Things hadn't exactly gone as he'd described, but she didn't contradict him.

"It's my job."

Giacomo went back to his hammering, though he had briefly glanced at her fingers as if they might be able to satiate his hunger.

"I know, and I don't blame you. It wasn't an accusation."

Marini leaned against the table, and one of his clenched fists accidentally brushed against the tiles.

Teresa cursed internally. Giacomo's expression shifted. It was black now, black like his dilated pupils and his feral excitement. Overcome with tension, Marini had made forbidden contact with the symbols scattered across the table, with those tiles that were so sacred to the killer's sensibilities.

Teresa pushed Marini's hand away, but the damage had already been done.

"Leave us alone, Inspector."

He gave her a puzzled look. He was not aware of the reaction he had so nearly sparked in Giacomo, and which still lurked beneath the surface. "You want me to go?"

"Yes."

He stood still, his face flushed, and Teresa had no choice but to reluctantly put him in his place.

"Don't make me repeat myself, Marini."

Their confrontation had quietly shifted terrain—to one where Giacomo was in charge.

He studied them both for a moment, then burst into laughter.

"So you hadn't told him? Poor little inspector, you must be *really* important." He pointed at the empty chair. "You can sit."

Giacomo's placid expression had returned, his excitement extinguished. His jealousy erased. Marini was no longer prey, and neither was he a rival.

Teresa gestured at Marini to take the proffered seat, and focused on Giacomo again.

"Why did you turn yourself in?"

A hammer blow broke one of the tiles in half.

"You should be glad I did. I won't be killing anyone in here."

"Your cellmate died last night."

"Drowned in a toiled bowl."

"So I'm told."

"You think I killed him?"

Teresa shook her head.

"No, Giacomo. You'd never do that."

The killer smiled, a real smile, which erased his snarl, if only for a moment.

"You've always understood me. That's why you were able to stop me."

Teresa felt sorry for him. There was a whole life enclosed in those two sentences. Her own, and Giacomo's. Two lives that had crossed paths and crashed into each other, some parts disintegrating on contact—while others had been strengthened.

"So what happened, Giacomo?"

He put his hammer down. The ties around his wrists made it tricky for him to wipe the dust off his fingers.

"Whoever killed him was after me. I was supposed to be cleaning the guards' toilets yesterday, not him."

Teresa and Marini watched him impassively.

"If I turned myself in, it's not because I changed my mind."

Teresa leaned across the table, ignoring the safety protocols.

"You mean someone's trying to hunt you down?"

"Yes."

"Who is it, and why are they doing it?"

"You're the one who's supposed to figure that out, Superintendent Battaglia."

Teresa glanced at Marini; he looked as perplexed as she was. She took her diary out of her bag, opened it to a fresh page, and put her reading glasses on.

"At least give me a motive," she told him.

"You're not going to like it."

"Don't be shy now, Giacomo. Tell me what happened when you were on the run."

He was examining his own fingers, rubbing them slowly against each other. Perhaps he was thinking about what it had felt like to brush them against a human heart.

"I was asked to commit a murder."

Teresa stopped taking notes and peered at him over the frame of her glasses.

"And you agreed?"

He raised an eyebrow, while the other stayed put. The movement lifted one of his shoulders, too.

"Obviously, Teresa."

"Of course," she murmured.

"It was all . . . perfect."

"When you say *perfect*, you mean that the victim . . ."

"Fulfilled my fantasies, yes."

"So an older man. Sixty, seventy years old."

A blink.

"More or less."

"Can you give me a name?"

"No."

Teresa took her glasses off and started chewing at one of the temple tips.

"Where did you meet him?"

"Near the stadium. I don't know what he was doing there. Maybe he was looking for prostitutes."

"Did the person who gave you the job tell you you'd find him there?"

"Yes. Bang on time. And I hit him bang on the head."

"Then what?"

"Then I took him to where I had decided to dispose of the body. Using a stolen car."

"And did you also . . . ?"

"Yes."

"Where did you put what you took from him?"

He didn't reply. There was no point in pushing.

"And the car?"

"I got rid of it. Don't ask me where." He turned to Marini. "God knows this city has changed in the past twenty-seven years."

Teresa spoke more firmly.

"How were you contacted? How did they find you?"

Giacomo lowered his voice. Teresa took note: he must feel threatened.

"They had my number, Teresa. Even I didn't know what it was yet; I'd only got myself a phone a few hours before."

Now the stabbing pain was back, and though Teresa tried to ignore it, her concentration was suffering, kept afloat only by her dogged determination to leave no stone unturned.

"I need every piece of information you can give me. Can

you estimate the age from the voice? Did you hear any background noises you recognized?"

Giacomo seemed lost in his gloomy thoughts. He had turned away, his eyes fixed on some distant point beyond the wall, beyond the chains of the prison.

"They knew everything about me. *Everything.* They knew how to convince me."

It was all too easy for Teresa to follow the path he was on.

"You were offered what you most desired."

Giacomo's lips parted. It was as if he could taste the victim's blood on his tongue.

"Oh yes. That's right," he whispered. "The perfect prey."

"How did you communicate?"

"Just a couple of phone calls; that was enough. The caller's number was hidden. They told me where to go. Nothing else needed. They said do what you want with him. Do *whatever* you want."

"And now you think they're trying to kill you."

"They came so close to doing it, Teresa. They were within reach. Whoever it is, they have influence in here, too."

Teresa tilted her head to one side as she considered him. A new thought was making its way through her failing mind.

"You turned yourself in for safety."

"Big mistake."

"Which means that . . . someone had already tried to kill you while you were still outside?"

"Twice. The first time, I almost got run over. The car accelerated toward me just as I was crossing the street. And the night I turned myself in, the shed I had been sleeping in caught fire."

"And the mobile phone you mentioned?"

"Melted away."

Teresa rubbed her eyes.

"Giacomo . . ."

"It's the truth."

"When did this happen? When did you kill him?"

A pause. Not one of hesitation, nor of doubt.

"The evening of May 20."

Teresa could feel Giacomo's blood-soaked hands pressing against her chest, even though he hadn't moved them, even though they were clean. They were pressing to take her back—back to life or to the past again.

She looked into the killer's eyes for the answer to the question she didn't have the courage to ask.

He had picked the date himself. It wasn't an accident. It was her birthday.

Teresa glanced at Marini, then back at Giacomo.

"We'll have to look into this. The man you say you killed, where is he now? We can't open a case if we don't have a body."

Giacomo flung himself across the table and grabbed her hand. Marini shouted at him to stay back, and was about to lunge when Teresa stopped him.

"It's nothing, Marini. It's nothing." Perhaps she was trying to convince herself, too.

Giacomo's grip was tight, but all it did was convey his need. The need to be believed, and to be saved. Yet the warmth of his skin on hers chilled Teresa to the bone.

"I left the body in that spot where you and I had our second meeting—remember? In the usual way. But it's not there anymore." His voice sounded like a squeak now, evoking shadows and underground realms that were best avoided.

"Someone moved it, and now they want to bury me, too. You have to stop them, Teresa. Stop them just like you stopped me."

Marini opened the door and called for the guards.

The killer's eyes were wide open as they led him away, and when Teresa looked at them, she saw a living paradox.

What could possibly frighten fear itself?

Teresa opened her hand. The answer might just be written in the note she found scrunched up inside her palm.

5

Today

"WHEN WERE YOU GOING to tell me?"

Marini's face was tilted toward the sun, eyes shielded by Ray-Bans, shirtsleeves rolled up, jacket hanging off the back of the bench behind him. They were sitting in the prison courtyard, waiting for the district attorney and the deputy prosecutor to arrive.

"You're the one who caught him," Marini said.

It sounded almost like an accusation, though only a mild one. Marini actually looked quite relaxed, perhaps even a little drowsy.

Teresa gazed up at the mountains surrounding the verdant valley in which the prison was situated. Emerald-green slopes and meadows covered every inch of the districts of Fondovalle and Prealpi. Every breath filled the lungs with the sweet scent of linden trees in bloom, their leaves rustled by darting sparrows. Someone was operating a chainsaw nearby. The air smelled of resin and freshly cut grass.

"I thought you'd read the file," said Teresa. She felt inside her pockets. "Do you have any sweets?"

"I didn't have time to read it. I was still recovering when they called me, just like you were."

"Don't make excuses. They never sound good, and they hardly ever work as one would hope."

The inspector stretched his arms and put his hands in the pockets of his trousers, from which he retrieved a piece of sugar-free candy and offered it to Teresa.

"I came across like an incompetent fool."

"You did well, actually. You made the right choice. You entertained him, which is why Giacomo allowed you to sit down, and why he started talking to us. He wouldn't have said a word, otherwise. I didn't tell you before we went in because I wanted you both to be caught by surprise."

Marini slid his sunglasses down with a finger.

"A surprise. For your colleague. During an interrogation."

"You're always quibbling. What happened back there is that Giacomo gave you permission to join the game. He's not afraid of you, nor is he interested in you as a potential victim, but he does feel gratified by the dynamic between us. You came across as fiery, which he appreciates. That means he'll let you sit in on our future meetings. I'd count that as a victory."

"It doesn't feel very honorable to me."

"Maybe so, but you're not some kind of samurai. Try to look at the bigger picture."

"I could have gotten there some other way."

"Some more sophisticated way, you mean? Let me clear

that up for you: absolutely not. Giacomo wouldn't have let you. If you think you can dupe him, you've already made your first mistake. We were honest with him. If we keep going down this path, he'll do the same for us."

"It feels like there's something between the two of you. I mean, beyond the fact that you've already met before. Will you ever tell me what happened? And I don't mean the details of the case."

"Maybe I will someday."

"How's it going with the insulin pump?"

Teresa felt for it under her top. She'd forgotten she was even wearing the device.

"Not too bad."

"You'll never let me win, will you?"

"What do you want me to say?"

"That my suggestion has improved your life, for instance, and that you should have followed my advice sooner."

Teresa burst out laughing. Marini still thought her biggest problem was diabetes, when really, it was Teresa's mind that no longer worked as it used to. Her memories were breaking apart, fragments already lost forever.

She had to say something, she had to tell him that she could not go back to leading the team. But she kept postponing the moment.

"Marini, after this period of sick leave . . ."

He planted his elbows on his knees. His wristwatch caught the light, and for a moment, Teresa was blinded.

"Lona will make things difficult, I know that, but if we stick together—and we will—we can keep him in check. He'll get tired of stepping on your toes eventually, Superintendent. He can't keep it up forever."

"I'm afraid you're deluding yourself there. Anyway, the problem isn't Lona."

"You're tired. I get it."

"I *am* tired. My body is tired, and my mind, Marini . . ."

The inspector turned to her with a wry, knowing smile.

"You've still got so much to teach us, Superintendent, and we can't wait to get going again." He stood up, filled with renewed vigor. "You're not the kind of cop who thrives on the field, anyway."

"Oh, really. And you are?"

"Your hunting ground is the human mind. Your own as well as the killers'. You're able to reconstruct their stories; you can see what they intend to do before it even happens. You can keep doing that, and you *will* keep doing that." He gestured toward the prison. "What happened in there? I can't even explain it. You could put your hand inside a tiger's mouth and it would start licking your fingers and purring for you."

Teresa didn't know what to say. It was comforting to think that she could retire soon. Perhaps she would never have to explain anything to anyone, except the doctor who issued her next sick note.

"You have no investigative instincts when it comes to me, Marini. Did you know that?"

He frowned.

"What do you mean?"

"My point exactly."

Marini carefully rolled his sleeves down, smoothing the creases, and put his jacket back on.

"So Giacomo Mainardi denies murdering his cellmate, but confesses to a different murder. How long was he out of jail for?"

"The time it takes you to pick an outfit."

"Just over ten days. Enough for the bloodlust to return."

There was a note of contempt in his statement of the facts.

Teresa bent down to poke at a dandelion that had sprung up through a gap in the pavement. When she was little, she used to pick their tufted heads and wave them around like magic wands.

"Giacomo was a lively, active boy, full of physical energy. He wanted to become an athlete; any sport would do. He dreamed of races, medals, applause. That's what all his teachers said."

"Why are you telling me this?"

Her head was still bowed. She could see the tips of his shoes.

"As we discovered after he was caught, he has a higher than average IQ, yet he never did well in school. To say that he didn't excel at any subject would be an understatement. His classmates ostracized him—at best. At worst, they bullied him. Giacomo suffered from a congenital deformity that made him visibly different. *Pectus excavatum*. His sternum was caved in. They would call him 'the heartless one.'" Teresa let out a bitter laugh. "Eventually he convinced himself he really didn't have a heart."

"He had a sunken chest?"

"Yes, a veritable chasm. It's a kind of malformation that can be fixed with surgery, but in his case, the operation was delayed. By the time he finally got one, it was already too late. The deformity had taken root in his soul. I already mentioned, didn't I, that as a little boy—and in spite of everything—Giacomo had always been full of energy and life?"

"Yes."

Teresa looked up.

"Well, they managed to snuff that life right out of him. One day he confessed to me that he started harboring his first cannibalistic fantasies at the age of twelve. So, who is this monster you find so repugnant, Marini? You know nothing about Giacomo. Nothing at all."

Marini had gone quiet.

"Giacomo quickly learned the meaning of loneliness and rage. And it wasn't long before he learned to hate. Perhaps the depression in his body ended up seeping into his soul."

"What about his family?"

"Ah, yes, his family. A sensitive topic. All you had to do, Inspector, was ask yourself: What was this man's past like? The answer might have surprised you, for his story is not so different from yours." Teresa felt sad now. "His story is no different from yours, except that you managed to save yourself. He did not."

He winced, and she felt so sorry for him, for the little boy he had once been—betrayed by the world of adults. But although she hated herself for it, she knew she had no choice: she'd had to deliver that blow, because sometimes the only way to understand someone else's pain was to relive your own—like summoning a phantom whose presence still has the power to make your skin crawl.

Marini gathered himself.

"I found someone who could save me, Superintendent."

"Giacomo, on the other hand, had no one at all."

"I suspect someone did eventually come along, just like someone did for me. The same person, in fact. You."

They looked at each other without another word until Albert and Deputy Prosecutor Gardini arrived.

Teresa stood up, trying to mask the pain that hunched her shoulders.

Gardini was just closing the briefcase that held the case file.

"I've obtained a recording of the interview, so that will be all for now. The prisoner will be placed in solitary confinement, of course."

Teresa flinched.

"Solitary confinement would be ill-advised. It might even prove counterproductive; we've seen that with him before. His paranoid inclinations . . ."

"I understand your point of view, Teresa, but this is a serial murderer who has already escaped once before, and has just confessed to another homicide. Not to mention, his cellmate has been killed, and he is the primary suspect."

"It's not a point of view, and there is no evidence against Giacomo. He didn't kill his cellmate."

Albert took the opportunity to mount his attack.

"I find your confidence in his innocence to be unwarranted, if not downright dangerous. The investigation is ongoing."

Teresa did not balk.

"Then we will see what the outcome is, though I am sure it will prove me right."

"How presumptuous, Superintendent."

Teresa turned to Gardini.

"Giacomo would never have killed his cellmate. Not like that. He has his own rituals, phases to observe—even certain motives, if we really must get down to the specifics."

Albert looked her up and down.

"Giacomo. So you're on a first-name basis now? How intimate. If we really must get down to the specifics, you shouldn't even be here."

"You were willing to tolerate my presence because you knew you wouldn't get anywhere with him if you tried to do it yourself. Just like you couldn't the first time."

Albert's expression darkened.

"Careful, Teresa."

Marini opened his mouth to say something, but Teresa put a placating hand on his arm. It was Gardini who took it upon himself to restore some calm.

"I can't spare him solitary confinement, Teresa, but at least his tools won't be taken away. I can guarantee you that, though I know it's not much."

"It's very important, actually. Thank you."

"That's unacceptable. We mustn't reward him," Lona said.

"It's not about rewarding him, Doctor Lona," Teresa snapped. She tried to count to ten, but only made it to three. "Do you know the difference between artists and serial killers? The medium they use to express themselves. They are both visual thinkers, in dialogue with internal images and communicating their own psychic realms. They estrange themselves from reality in order to create something, and only return when it is time to give their creation concrete form—when it is time to *act*, in other words."

"Is that what *you* think?"

"No. But even if I were to cite Jung's technique of active imagination, the ego and the id, or de Luca's theories, I don't suppose it would make any difference to you."

"Teresa . . ." said Gardini, calling her to order.

She closed her eyes for a moment, trying to collect herself before she continued.

"Look, Giacomo Mainardi is both a killer and an artist, and that's not something we can ignore, because that's just what he is. His imagination plays a crucial role. We must allow him to channel his fantasies into more harmless modes of expression. Believe me when I tell you that the psychological phases a serial killer goes through have been proven to be the same as the phases of artistic creation. The aura phase, excitement, seduction, the creative phase, the totemic . . ."

"Oh please, Teresa!"

"And finally the depressive phase, *Albert*. All of which is to say, if we take his tiles and his tools away, Giacomo will soon be desperate to kill again, to pull a bone out of someone's body, cut it into seven little pieces, and stick them somewhere other than a mosaic. And he will find a way to do it, whether or not he's in isolation. He'll be looking for an opportunity every waking moment of his life, for he needs it to survive just as much as the air he breathes."

Albert averted his eyes, and in that subtle gesture of concession, Teresa saw her chance to consolidate her point.

"Separating him from his art would cause him anxiety and depression. Chronic stress causes hypertrophy of the amygdala and increased activity in the limbic system. Children who are abused or abandoned have larger amygdalae compared to their peers."

"Get to the point, Teresa."

"Oh, I'll get to the point. What I mean is that the reptilian brain we still share with animals, and which we've been carrying around for millions of years, is always ready to pounce, and it would be rather unwise to allow that to happen in a man who *needs* to kill in order to feel better. It's like goading a bear, you see? But if we eliminate all sources of stress, the beast will retreat to its den."

Gardini cleared his throat.

"Great, well, I think we're all persuaded now that it would be best to let Mainardi have his mosaics."

Albert would not give her the satisfaction of agreeing.

"Mainardi has confessed to a murder for which we don't even have a body," he noted. "Perhaps we should concern ourselves with finding it. Assuming it exists, that is. I've dispatched a team to the location he described. They haven't found anything."

"Not yet," Teresa pointed out. "And he did tell us that someone had moved the body. I would suggest we gather the profiles of his previous targets and use those to draw up a possible profile of the latest victim. If someone presented this man to Giacomo as a sacrificial offering, and he accepted their offer, it must mean that the victim fit perfectly with his fantasies—as Giacomo himself has already confirmed. We need to compare the information we have with a list of people who disappeared on the night of May 20, the date Giacomo claims to have committed the murder. It's already been ten days; any disappearances will have been reported by now."

Gardini opened his briefcase again and took out a digital planner.

"What about before the twentieth?"

"No. He's never held anyone captive, and homeless people disgust him. His hunting grounds were always elsewhere."

"So we should trust a serial killer?"

"When it comes to death, serial killers take matters extremely seriously."

Albert lit a cigarette and took a deep drag.

"The tale he's told us just doesn't hold water. They're all paranoid delusions, that's what I think. And this story about being told to kill—do we really believe it?"

Teresa would have loved to strike him with her walking stick.

"It's been twenty-seven years, and you still don't realize how much you're underestimating him?"

Gardini ended the debate.

"In any event, we have no choice but to consider his allegations," said Gardini, ending the debate. "There is no alternative. If there ever was a body in that location, we'll find traces of DNA, though it will take time and resources. It was a fallow field outside the city, as I recall."

"It is quite an extensive area," Albert confirmed.

They began to discuss the next steps in the investigation. Teresa walked away, motioning at Marini to stay and listen to their conversation. She wasn't going to be the one to lead the team anyway.

She looked for a sweet in her pocket, then remembered she had done so earlier to no avail. Someday soon, she was going to start asking the same questions over and over again, and making the same gestures, unable to remember that she had already spoken the same words and made the very same movements just moments before. Her mind kept skipping like a broken record.

It was a dangerous game she was trying to play.

She looked at the three men, each of whom—for better or for worse—represented an important part of her personal and professional life.

What better moment, then, to finally reveal the truth that was bound to have people talking about her for a long time? Not that she cared much about that. She would soon forget all about it.

She was just clearing her throat to speak when her fingers brushed against a piece of paper buried in her pocket. She took the note out and unfolded it.

It was a single word, inscribed in nervous handwriting, the letters lopsided and stuck together as if for support, or else thrusting and elbowing against each other. They were written in blood. Teresa pictured Giacomo cutting into his skin, collecting a drop of blood, and using it to write the word out.

She had no idea how the note had ended up in her pocket, though it was definitely meant for her, and she had no doubt about the identity of its author. Yet she still couldn't remember.

"Are you with us, Superintendent?" said Albert, his tone brimming with irritation.

Teresa looked up. How was she supposed to tell him?

In the only way she could: directly, and without the slightest attempt at conciliation.

"I know where to find at least part of the victim's body. Or whatever's left of it."

6

Twenty-seven years ago

THE PUBLIC PROSECUTOR AND Superintendent Lona left the coroner's office after the conclusion of the postmortem examination.

Teresa watched them walk down the corridor toward the exit, talking as they went, and as soon as they had disappeared behind the swinging doors, she returned to the autopsy room.

At the threshold, she hesitated for a moment. Antonio Parri was still inside, sterilizing the tools he had just been using. The assistant on shift had already left.

They did not know each other well, for although she was always there during crime scene investigations and present at autopsies related to cases she was involved in, she never contributed any questions or comments.

Instead, she observed everything from a distance. She had learned that death was not always black, as classic iconography might suggest, but that it came in many different colors. Not just blood red or bone white, but every shade of yellow, turquoise, and blue, all the way to purple and green when the cause of death was poisoning; or transparent—even luminescent—when it was a case of contamination.

Death released a smell that no industrial product or natural scent could possibly cloak.

Now it lay on the steel autopsy bed, in human form, residing in the victim's corpse and its deepest recesses like the oily fumes of a ritual sacrifice.

Antonio Parri knew how to read the stiffened lips of the dead, presiding over the mysteries of their viscera like an ancient Egyptian *hery seshta*.

"Could the cruciform cuts on his legs be hiding bite marks?" Teresa asked without preamble.

"Hello, Inspector Battaglia. I think this is the first time I've heard you speak in here."

He hadn't even looked up. He must have been aware of her presence from the start.

She took a halting step forward.

"I think there are bite marks down there."

Parri turned to look at her in silent scrutiny.

Teresa wrung her hands and flushed with discomfort. She knew she must either find the courage to keep talking, or turn around and leave.

"People like him do that kind of thing. They bite."

Parri's eyes narrowed, as if to bring her ramblings into focus.

"People like what?"

Teresa surrendered to her nerves and pulled a cigarette out of the wrinkled packet she carried in her pocket, but as soon as she placed it between her lips, she remembered she wasn't supposed to smoke. She tried to put it back, but her gestures were clumsy, and the cigarette broke. Tobacco spilled onto the floor.

The doctor put another one of his tools away. Teresa was the one who needed dissecting now.

"You're always one step ahead of your colleagues, yet you never speak. You take notes on everything I say, and on what the others say, too. Are you trying to be top of the class? You're the only woman on the team. I suppose you feel you constantly need to prove how good you are." He pointed at her face. "But it must be hard to do, with that bruise on your jaw that you're trying to cover up with makeup." He let his eyes linger on the wedding band Teresa wore on her ring finger. He'd already figured out what her story must be—and he wasn't wrong.

She covered her hand, as if to deny the connection that the coroner's intuition had led him to make. Her anger was beginning to make her feel uncharacteristically aggressive—though it was herself she despised, not Parri.

"I imagine you must be exhausted too, Doctor, from always having to mask the smell of alcohol with breath mints."

They stared at each other, both equally incredulous. Parri burst out laughing.

"Is it that bad?"

Teresa couldn't believe what she had just said.

"I don't . . . I'm sorry. I'm mortified. I didn't mean to be so rude."

"Rude? You only gave as good as you got. Don't make excuses. They never sound good, and they hardly ever work as one would hope."

Teresa touched her face. It felt unbearably sore.

"Is it very obvious?"

He played it down.

"No, not really. I'm just used to picking up on these things." He took a dermatoscope from one of the shelves and returned to the autopsy table. He placed the instrument on the gleaming, scuff-marked surface. "But you should fix the problem and send him off to live somewhere else. Though now you're going to say I could fix my problem too, if I wanted to—and you would be right."

Teresa smiled, even though she felt sad.

"If it were that easy, we would have both sorted out our problems already, wouldn't we?"

"Amen to that. Come on then, take your coat off and come here so we can look for these bite marks you keep going on about. And there's no need to call me Doctor, by the way; Antonio is just fine."

Teresa didn't need asking twice. She got rid of her parka and hung it on the coat rack, then rolled her sleeves up and tucked her hair behind her ears. But she couldn't bring herself to step any closer.

Parri turned the lamp back on and pointed it at the corpse.

"I noticed you were there during the postmortem. Don't be afraid to take a closer look next time. Otherwise you're bound to miss things."

"It's not that I'm shy. I just find corpses really gross."

She realized as soon as she'd spoken that perhaps it wasn't the most appropriate admission to make to a coroner. It was like telling him she thought he wallowed in filth.

Parri gave her a sideways look.

"Put the gloves on."

Teresa closed her eyes.

"I've been having stomach troubles recently. I'd really rather . . ."

"Put the gloves on."

Though Parri's tone was gentle, Teresa knew that this was a conditio sine qua non. If she wanted the coroner's help, she would have to do this. She slipped on a pair of latex gloves from a box that stood on the tray with all his tools.

"Is this even legal?"

Parri took her hand and placed it over the victim's chest. Teresa felt the taste of bile rising up her throat and into her mouth. The doctor stared right into her eyes.

"Can you feel it—this unnatural rigidity? That's what's scaring you; that's all. Touching death. But death *wants* to be touched. It is precious, and it has a complicated back-story to disclose. This body demands justice and begs for compassion. Treat it with respect, if only for the pain that it has endured. Care for it, even. And if you do, it will tell you more than you can imagine."

Parri let go of her hand, but Teresa didn't remove it. She kept it there, resting upon the story of the living, breathing human that this corpse used to be. Somewhere in that room, its heart was still beating, enclosed in a ruptured life. Slowly, Teresa's nausea began to recede.

"Look at the wrists, Teresa. Traces of the glue I was talking about earlier. The killer tied him up, and took the tape off later."

Teresa studied the marks, etching them into her memory. The glue had caught some dirt, leaving behind the occasional faint streak.

It was the kind of thing she'd read about in textbooks but had never seen in real life. She ran her hands all the way down to the victim's wrists, then turned them around. When she spoke, she was surprised by her own confidence.

"The killer was organized to a certain extent, but the murder weapon was chosen at random."

Parri brought out the walking stick from inside an evidence bag.

"Here's the weapon. Traces of blood, skin, and hair on the handle—almost certainly the victim's. I managed to isolate a partial fingerprint. The killer may have wiped it down. He would have held it around the tip and struck downward. Three times."

Teresa could picture him doing it.

"I suspect two of the three blows must have been comparatively weak."

Parri put his report down.

"That's right. How did you know?"

Teresa leaned over the corpse again.

"Because he was rehearsing. He'd planned to kill him with his bare hands, then changed his mind and used whatever weapon he happened to find. He was worried he wouldn't be able to handle him, which explains the use of tape, and the fact that he struck from behind."

"But he used a blade to make the cuts, and to remove the phalanges."

"He brought the knife along to mutilate the body—not to kill with."

"Does it make a difference?"

"It makes a huge difference."

"And in fact the chest was carved open after death."

"We're looking for a young Caucasian male."

"How can you tell?"

Teresa studied the victim's face. The loose skin of his cheeks was covered in abrasions.

"Statistically speaking, the older the victims are, the younger the killer tends to be. It's all about having control over their prey."

"*Victims.* You're using the plural. And earlier you said, 'People like him.'"

Teresa looked at him.

"There is hesitation written all over this murder, and signs of the perpetrator's insecurity. It's likely to be his first, but it certainly won't be his last."

The doctor whistled.

"You'd better not sound so sure of yourself when you speak to Superintendent Lona. You'll give him quite a shock. Could you please lift the right leg up, so we don't have to turn him over?"

Teresa did so, though it was by no means an easy task.

"Make sure you don't rotate it, now. He's got a prosthetic hip. I wouldn't want it to get stuck."

Teresa felt like she was sinking under the weight she held in her arms. It was absence of life in its most carnal manifestation—rigid and absolute.

Parri began studying the cruciform cuts through his dermatoscope.

"These cuts are postmortem, too, no doubt about it. No sign of clotting."

Teresa followed his line of thinking.

"Lona will never listen to me. He's determined to follow other leads."

"I have the feeling he might be barking up the wrong tree—don't you?"

"It would be better if he were right."

Parri pointed at the evidence bag containing the old man's clothes.

"The killer took the trouble to remove the victim's trousers, yet there are no signs of sexual violence. Perhaps he ran out of time, or perhaps what he did was enough to satisfy him. In any event, I haven't found any traces of ejaculation."

"No, that's not why he took the victim's trousers off. At least I don't think so; I can't see any sexual motive behind any of this. There must be some other message for us to decipher."

Parri was looking at her as if she had gone mad.

Teresa's determination wavered. She must have seemed crazy—or worse, naive. The nausea returned. Would she ever be capable of sounding authoritative, of being and feeling like a true professional? Sometimes she felt like she was trying to sense her way around in the dark, with her ability to improvise her only trump card. And that was far too little to secure the respect of her more established colleagues.

Parri returned to the cuts with greater conviction.

"So what you're saying is that he tried to commit a controlled murder, but something still got out of hand?"

He sounded genuinely interested. That was new.

"Yes . . . yes. He tried his best, but he was unable to complete his work as he had originally conceived it. He succumbed to his animal instincts. He bit the victim and tried to hide the tooth marks with these cuts. He knew that a dental impression could get him into trouble, while carving crosses into the victim's skin could easily put us on the wrong track."

"Is that what they teach you lot these days?"

"I've taught myself."

"It's fascinating stuff. The other leg, please. Anyway, don't worry, I'll look for your bite mark. If he really did bite, it must have been after the victim was already dead. I can't see any bruising beneath the incisions."

Teresa let her gaze roam over the body. She was ready to heed its siren call, and let herself be dragged into the vortex of its last living moments.

She was nearly tempted to caress him. He seemed like a kind man. The gap between his eyebrows did not bear the furrowed marks of a mean spirit.

"The killer panicked." Teresa spoke in a whisper now, as if to avoid rousing death. "He couldn't keep his excitement in check. He moved the body more than once, as indicated by the scratches on the victim's face. May I?" she said, pointing at the mouth.

Parri seemed enraptured.

"Of course."

Teresa lowered the leg back onto the table.

"The phalanges have not been removed in a professional manner. It's almost like a butcher's work. He must have used an ordinary knife, maybe even a box cutter," Parri warned her. "Same with the gash on the chest—though there isn't anything missing in there."

But that wasn't what Teresa was looking at; the cavity that had caught her attention was a different one. She took a flashlight from the tool tray and shone it onto the mucus membrane inside the mouth.

"Gravel."

"Yes . . . I was just about to point that out to you. We haven't washed him yet."

"He moved the body. Several times." She mimicked the action. "Dragged it by the arms. This contact with the body stimulated him. And in the end he just left it lying there in plain sight. He took a pretty big risk. He's only just getting started. He'll get braver, and more confident, but more careful, too."

"He did it all in an hour."

Teresa had thought about that, too.

"He didn't kill him too far from where he left him to be found. And he didn't have much difficulty getting the victim to follow him—perhaps even into his car. They must have known each other. Let's not forget about the dog: he was covered in blood. He's a boisterous little creature, yet he doesn't seem to have given the killer any trouble. There was no duress."

Parri was watching her.

"I saw how you wiped that cloth over its fur. I must admit I was impressed."

"Oh, right!"

Teresa went to retrieve the two bags she had put in the pocket of her parka and handed them to the coroner: wet wipes covered in blood and mud.

"You should run some tests on these, if you don't mind. There might be something in the chemical composition that can lead us to a more precise location. If the blood matches the victim's, then we can confirm the dog was with them when it happened. One way or another, the three of them must have gone off together. That's not exactly a minor detail; it suggests a completely different kind of behavior than what you might see during a kidnapping."

"Of course. I'll get those analyzed right away."

"I've been reading about these new laboratory tests; they say it's possible now to extract DNA code from blood samples and use that to identify whose blood it is."

"Yes, but don't get too carried away, Inspector. It's still an experimental technique, and I wouldn't bet on it coming to our little lab anytime soon."

Teresa hid her disappointment. She looked at the victim's pale hands.

"The widow said that there was something missing from his personal possessions, a golden ring he wore on the little finger of his right hand and never took off. It was his mother's wedding ring."

"Indeed. You can see the mark here."

Teresa held the mutilated hand in her own and peered at the thin strip of lighter skin where the ring used to be.

"The bones he removes are a trophy and may even become his signature for future murders. The modus operandi might change, it might be perfected, but the signature will remain the same. It's like a trademark. The ring is a sort of talisman that will help him relive the different phases of the murder and feel that sense of power and fulfillment all over again. A simple object taken from the victim and which the killer may one day even find a way to return to the victim's relatives—or gift to someone he feels close to."

"Really? That's horrifying."

Teresa smiled at him.

"That's the killer's story, Doctor. You told me yourself: this man's death is telling us all about it."

"A munificent death, indeed. I might have found something of interest. Here, look, just on the outer edge of the calf." The doctor pointed a pair of tweezers at a patch of loose skin. "There's something there."

"What is it?"

"The faintest of shadows, really, but I would go so far as to say it is the beginnings of a premortem bruise in a familiar shape." He took his glasses off. He looked incredulous, or perhaps just approving. "Death rewards you, Inspector."

Teresa took note of the designation. Parri was the only one who'd ever called her that. He put the tweezers down.

"The heart had already stopped, but it must have managed with its last beat to direct a final stream of blood into this bit of flesh right as it was being attacked. There it is: the bite mark you were looking for."

7

Today

"AQUILEIA. OF COURSE. WHERE else?"

Marini was inspecting the columns of the forum. Teresa
noticed how the initial hint of disbelief in his voice had been
quickly replaced with the understanding that there was no
setting on earth more fitting for the tale of death that Giacomo's own story told.

The sky was tinged with red, as if the wrath of a surviving
god had set the millennial ruins on fire. This place had been
desecrated. By Giacomo.

Aquileia: that was the word the killer had written in his
note to Teresa. Aquileia submerged, and forever lost. The
ancient Roman city surfaced now in the long shadows of
the evening. Teresa was reminded of the translucent skin of
a sacred serpent. No scales to cover it, but blocks of marble
springing out of the black earth.

The city had welcomed them with the vestiges of an

ancient realm, with the mineral scent of Istrian stone, with the ruins of the circus and the thermae, and the inland port that had once connected it to the Adriatic Sea—before the river had deserted its bed and poured itself elsewhere with even greater vigor.

We are walking over countless layers of life, thought Teresa, *a thousand souls to every step, retracing the paths of the greats.* Julius Caesar, the first Christians to arrive from Alexandria of Egypt, Attila and his wrath. Legend had it that even Saint Mark had once passed through here.

Today the town consisted of a handful of houses clustered in the flat countryside, almost within sight of the coastal lagoon. That first furrow that the triumvirate had dug to mark the perimeter of the city as an eagle floated above their heads had been turned over again and again across the centuries until it had finally faded away. The names and feats of its Patriarchs were chiseled into Aquileia, but when you looked at the city now, there was little sign of that mighty past.

Teresa's eyes scanned the horizon. It was like looking at a peasant girl for signs of an empress. And yet the ground beneath those crops and fields was teeming with fallen capitals, amphorae, and golden treasures, all yet to be discovered. The city's ornaments kept pushing up against the surface of the earth, bearing witness to what it had once been.

Aquileia the forgotten, Aquileia the unknown. Not by all, perhaps, but certainly by most.

Behind the columns of the forum, the thousand-year-old belfry built with marble blocks taken from the amphitheater soared above the lancing silhouettes of a row of fragrant cypress trees. Right beside it, lit up in the encroaching evening, and on a scale incongruous with the settlement itself, stood the church, a cathedral constructed by means of identical blocks of stone that made clear its ancient origins. The layers of plaster and the various adornments that had been added in subsequent periods had all since been removed, returning the building to its original beauty. The basilica of Aquileia was the grand and primordial house of God that Theodore I had envisaged, erected over the *domus ecclesiae* that had welcomed martyrs and the persecuted, nearly two thousand years' worth of sanctity and blood mixed into its foundations.

Teresa and Marini began heading in its direction, Teresa leaning on him as they walked. They had been waiting for hours for the forensics team to finish gathering evidence. Hanging in the air was the fragrance of night-time blooms, of salty sea spray carried in the wind blowing from the south, and—as hidden as it was portentous—the sepulchral smell of the dust that all men were destined to become. Aquileia was an open tomb, exposed anew.

Teresa had already gulped down a couple of painkillers. But her aches kept gnawing at her, and wouldn't let go.

As they walked toward the basilica, following the path of ancient furrows, stepping over countless other relics that lay forgotten beneath the surface of the earth, she became aware once more that there was nothing novel about her suffering, nothing especially valuable about it that might make it somehow more worthy of note. It was simply one of many tremors of pain crossing the fabric of space and time, yet lacking the force to curve it. She caught herself wondering if it was human misery that held the universe together, a kind of gravity keeping the stars bound to its axis.

Nothing was being asked of her that others had not already endured.

The silence in this place seemed unreal. The security tape around the cathedral had kept most curious onlookers away. Even the boldest bystanders had tired of waiting, leaving with the early shadows of the evening and the first enticing smells from freshly laid dinner tables.

Teresa stopped before the stretch of burnished bricks that led to the entrance of the basilica.

"Leaving something behind is a little like dying."

She was gazing at a statue of the Capitoline She-Wolf suckling a pair of infants. Perched atop an ancient column, on a carved capital that had come straight from the Roman past, her teats provided nourishment for a dream of long-faded grandeur.

Teresa sat at the base of the column. She could have sworn that her comment had made Marini's blood pump faster; his wrist felt warm under her fingers. Or perhaps it was her own blood that was rushing to her ears in protest. A cacophony of emotions, of leaps and falls—densely packed into a single moment, and all while she stood completely still. She was like a black hole now.

"Don't say that, Superintendent. Sometimes leaving something behind just means making a new beginning."

He was in agony, too. It was as if the night were summoning darker nights inside them.

Teresa stopped him with the tough love she'd accustomed him to.

"Don't you say another word, Marini."

By the basilica door, a team of experts was rolling up cables and packing tools away. The police vans were turning their engines back on. There was no time to rest. She had to get back on her feet.

She let go of Marini's arm.

"Give me a push."

He helped her up, then put his hands back in his pockets and stood watching as the other officers prepared to leave the scene.

"So I guess we're done for the day, and with nothing much to show for it."

"*They're* done. We haven't even started."

"You don't mean . . . ?"

"Of course I do. I've not been waiting here for hours, twiddling my thumbs, only to go home now."

"I thought we were only supposed to intervene if any traces were found."

"I've already made other arrangements."

"With whom? When?"

"When you went to the toilet."

He threw up his hands.

"You're not ill at all, are you? I can't have been gone for longer than five minutes. How did you even manage to . . . ?"

Teresa turned to look at the car that was coming to a stop just behind the tape marking the search zone. The headlights blinded her for a moment. Shortly thereafter, de Carli and Parisi got out of the car. Then the back door opened, and out came a mutt with black and gray fur, followed by a skinny young woman with long blue hair and ripped jeans. The woman opened a folding cane with one hand and twisted the other until the dog's leash was wrapped tight around her wrist.

Teresa smiled. Her search team was here.

"Great. We have the full squad now."

The Basilica of St. Mary of the Assumption had been built along the axis of the sun, its altar aligning with the east to symbolize the light of Christianity, which was supposed to illuminate the darkness of the human soul. Its consecrated heart held the oldest and largest paleo-Christian mosaic pavement in the Western world. Millions of tiles to be examined one by one, in search of the scent of death.

When she stepped across its threshold not long thereafter, Teresa was overwhelmed by a tangible weight, the air inside steeped in the humors of centuries of history. It seemed to be breathing over her. It was the past in all its solemnity, a past with a soul and a skeleton made of stone, its joints set around the cardinal points of humanity. And some kind of ineffable force.

Now that they had confirmed there was no whole body in there, what was left to look for was the thing Teresa had most feared. Hidden somewhere among the millions of mosaic tiles inside the cathedral were seven fragments of human bone.

8

---❧---

IV Century

CERES'S HOUR WAS NIGH. *Thus spoke the alignment of celestial bodies.*

It was the night the goddess breathed life into the stars and the oracles. The clipei of the soldiers of the ancient regio X drummed against the bowels of the earth, all for her.

The torches in the military encampment outside the urbe aquileiensis were already alight. Fires crackled and burned in the twilight, their flames mirrored in the calm waters of the Natiso. Boats hung as if suspended over the gleaming surface of the river port. A breeze carried the scent of seashells and salt-washed timber over the fields. A few leagues to the south swirled the Mare Superum, the upper sea, while the bountiful shores of Histria and Illyricum unfurled in a black ribbon reaching for the horizon. Spread out at regular intervals, the vast braziers of the castra and of the trading ports across the sea started to light up one after the other.

Aquileia had shrugged off the bustle of the day and donned in its place the peaceful cloak of night. Only in the tabernae, tucked away among narrow streets, could the sound of animated chatter still be heard. Many were the languages spoken, and in the reviving light of the flickering lanterns, every face was a different color.

The legionnaire was a shadow among shadows. He passed the forum, the circus, the amphitheater with its limestone dolphins, and the baths, until he reached the muggy gloom of the former palatium. Its foundations now supported the basilica commissioned by Bishop Theodore.

The era of the Christians had begun. Some had begun to whisper that the age of the great legions had come to an end. The world would no longer be ruled by sharpened blades, but by the cross. Like an eclipse, the banner of Christ would soon obscure the emperor's eagle and the face of Jove.

The voices of women and men could be heard singing from the Christian temple. They were not hiding, though perhaps they should be. For even within their own faith, the cracks were beginning to turn into ruptures. Christians were turning against Christians.

Wrapped in his cape the color of the night sky, the legionnaire paused.

The wind had changed direction, bringing a different scent from that of fields and soft rush. He had learned to recognize it by now. It was the sacred essence of the temple of Edfu, resin of terebinth and olibanum, myrrh and balm of Gilead.

Two Ethiopian servants with shaven heads emerged from the darkness, their necks and wrists girdled in copper and bronze. It was hard to distinguish where the ornaments ended and the slave chains began.

The legionnaire recognized their faces.

"Tell your mistress that I am unarmed."

Calida Lupa did not wait a moment longer. She revealed herself like the moon from behind the clouds, her robe of white gauze embroidered with the two hundred and three resting scarabs of the priestess of Isis, and her shoes adorned with golden sprigs of ivy. Her skin was gleaming and fragrant with ointments.

"Why do you follow me, daughter of Isis?"

The vestal swept the palm of her hand in front of the legionnaire's face. Her eyes, made up with powdered lapis, showed signs of disquiet.

"Do not speak her name, Lusius. The night has ears as sharp as a fox's. I am following you to save your life. Go back to where you came from; join your fellow soldiers in the evening rites. Stay away from the Christians."

The legionnaire looked toward the basilica. Its windows shone with a tremulous light. The flames of a new creed burned within its walls, while they who stood out here were the last repositories of a dying faith. There were only embers left of it now, and soon the winds of Christianity would blow them into ash.

"Isis sings her anguish," he told her. "Even Rome seems to have declared war on the goddess. It has happened before, but this defeat will be her last. You will not be safe, either."

The eyes of the priestess filled with tears.

"I pray every day that it may not be so, yet the statues continue to fall, and the temples to crumble. They wish to erase her. They fear the love that people still hold for her and which feeds the power of her priests. What makes you think the Christians will show her worshippers any mercy? They call their own brothers heretics."

"They know what it means to be persecuted."

The suffering etched upon the woman's face transformed into fury.

"They know what it means, and they will do the same! This

is a land where the cartouches of the gods of the pyramids coexist with the symbols of Rome, and the Menorah lamps of the Hebrew people are lit with the same flame that illuminates the effigies of Mithras and of the god Antinous. What can be the fate of a world so confused?" She grabbed his arm. "Don't go. I fear the Christian priest's invitation may be a trap."

"Have you cast your astragali, Calida Lupa?"

"I have seen your future in the flames of the holy fire, soldier. The gods have spoken."

The legionnaire wished he were carrying an amulet with the power to repel such an inauspicious pronouncement, but he had long since renounced the hand of Sabazios. He freed himself from her gentle hold.

"If it really is my destiny that the gods have shown you, there is nothing I can do but face it."

He walked backward, not letting her out of his sight. When she slipped back into the shadows, he surrendered to the night and to whatever fate lay for him therein.

The basilica welcomed him with the singing he had heard earlier, songs of hope and of divine invocation. In the vestibule, some attendants made him remove his cloak and shoes. When he handed them his helmet and his armor with the glittering phalera fashioned in the imperial forges of Antioch, he felt as if he had relinquished his own self.

They washed his hands and feet in a basin of gilded bronze. Finally, the man who had promised him an audience emerged from behind a purple curtain shielding the great hall where the eucharistic synaxis was taking place. Cyriac, as he liked to be known, pulled him into a fraternal embrace before introducing him to the mysteries of the new religion.

Barefoot and clad only in his tunic, the legionnaire ventured forward into the worldly paradise unfolding beneath his feet in the form of uncommonly beautiful mosaics. Meek-eyed beasts, thriving plants, and radiant shepherds directed him to the baptismal font the Christians used for a ritual of rebirth whose workings he had yet to understand. There, immersed in the mystery of faith, they were anointed with the chrism that consecrated kings, prophets, and priests. The light of dawn would soon shine upon the vibrant paintings that decorated the walls, and the rays of the rising sun would reflect off the crystalline water. The new convert would feel that light illuminating him from the inside.

But Lusius was no such man. He had only come to that place to understand how far this new faith could embrace his own. He had heard rumors about the mysterious rituals that were said to take place inside this temple, and whose secrets were not entirely unknown to him. They were rituals that had come from far away, from the distant past. They were more ancient than any man who had walked these lands. Even among the Christians themselves were those who did not know them, and others who abhorred them. There was bound to be a rift soon.

Cyriac led him into the second chamber, forbidden to most. Only initiates were allowed in here, but Lusius had shown that he was already acquainted with some of its secrets. Cyriac the Christian had been astonished by this, and had wanted to see with his own eyes how well the Roman pagan would be able to find his way through the path of initiation set out beneath his feet.

Incense burned in the second room, and lamps hung from chains anchored to the ceiling, illuminating the mosaic tiles.

Stupefaction and wonderment. The brilliance of the heavens reflected upon the earth.

The followers of Christ stood waiting to one side, dressed in white just as he was, and as the priests of Calida Lupa were.

Children cradled small fish-shaped vials of scented oil in their hands, in containers of the finest glass colored like precious stones. A young woman held a basket woven from rush. Inside, coiled up among loaves of bread fresh from the oven, there was a snake.

9

Today

OVER THE COURSE OF her adult life, Teresa had set foot inside a church only a handful of times—most recently the previous winter, in a little mountain village where the evil that breathed softly within the four walls of people's homes was just as bad as the kind that howled through the woods.

The basilica of Aquileia greeted her arrival with an echo that reverberated through the formidable expanse of the building and swelled inside her chest. At their feet, beneath suspended walkways made of glass and steel, the mosaic pavement was suffused with a white light, and seemed to reflect a faraway world—no longer buried in the earth, as it had been until a century ago, but connected to another, higher realm.

"*Per aspera ad astra.*"

Through hardships to the stars. As she uttered the words, Teresa's gaze followed the church's towering columns all the way up to the shadows of its vaulted ceiling. The timber roof trusses and pointed arches were testament to the vertiginous heights humanity had scaled. Women and men had always sought the face of God in the beauty of art, and had searched, by extension, for a trace of the divine spark within themselves. Nobody could say for sure whether that spark really existed, but Teresa had always been moved by the unceasing devotion of those who pursued it, no matter how painful the search might turn out to be. Human beings had constructed this immortal temple with their bare and unwashed hands, drawing splendor all around them and handing their creation over to posterity. Mired, as they were, in earthly mud, they had managed nonetheless to erect the gates of heaven.

Teresa, too, sometimes looked for that spark in the mirror. She couldn't bring herself to believe that everything would be over once her body perished—or perhaps even sooner, once her memories were gone. She would stare into her own eyes and sink into herself. Recently, she had begun to glimpse the spark in the pain she had endured, in the sense of dignity she held tight against her chest, in the effort it took to straighten her back and stand up straight. Roused in part by an anger befitting the betrayal of a great love, she had concluded that not even a god could have come as far as she had—for although godlike perfection might not allow for failure, neither could it experience rebirth.

She looked up at the crucifix at the far end of the nave, which seemed at once to bless and judge everything and everyone around it.

Perhaps only a god-made human could truly comprehend the value of fallen souls. Perfection never accustoms itself to sacrifice because no sacrifice is ever asked of it. And so, as eternity wears on, it is condemned not only to the silence of suffering, but also of the heart.

Someone quietly slipped their hand into hers.

It was Blanca, who had come to assist them in their search. She was holding Smoky by the leash. Like Teresa, she, too, carried a stick, but hers was a slender cane clicking along the walkway like a clock, a probing device the young woman used to shape and order the darkness that surrounded her.

Blanca had become an increasingly familiar presence in Teresa's life. Teresa still hoped that the girl and her dog—armed with their matchless ability to track the olfactory traces of human remains—might someday permanently join the roster of experts employed by the prosecutor's office. They would certainly inject new life into the department. But after a first attempt, Blanca had seemed reluctant to continue, and for a while, it had even looked like she might disappear altogether. Teresa squeezed her hand, then let go again.

"Are you ready?"

The young woman tilted her face up as if in search of Teresa's voice.

"Yes. Just say when."

Inspector Marini crouched down and helped her put on the special footwear used by professional restorers. Smoky's paws needed covering, too. Marini got to work with a roll of sticky tape and a set of rubber-soled dog boots. Smoky swiped his tongue across the inspector's face.

"Stop that, you drool-dispenser." He pushed the dog away, only to receive two more licks in return.

Teresa gave the dog a pat.

"Come now, Marini, he's starting to like you."

"Not at all. He does it because he knows how much I hate it."

"Hold on a second. Are you saying he's licking you out of spite?"

"Obviously."

Marini put his hand out to pet him, but Smoky bared his teeth and started growling.

Blanca called the dog to her feet.

"He's still making his mind up on whether or not to trust you."

Teresa wondered if Blanca felt the same way about Marini, too.

The director of the region's cultural heritage department, in charge of preserving its archaeological and artistic legacy, was waiting for them at the entrance. Teresa called out to her, and the woman came over to verify that they were operating in accordance with the instructions they had been given.

"I must urge you once again to take the greatest possible care. Our charge has endured more than enough strain for the day. We must protect it from any further shocks."

She kept referring to the mosaic pavement as if it were a living thing, moving her hands as she spoke and caressing the tiles from afar. She seemed afraid that it might be injured in some way. So far she had not hesitated to help the police, but now that her good intentions were about to lead to more action, she seemed suddenly doubtful.

Teresa placed her hand on Blanca's shoulder. The girl and her dog would be the only ones to set foot on the mosaics.

"I brought these two here precisely to avoid dragging things on. Don't worry about them; they're professionals."

The director looked them up and down: a blind girl and a mangy mutt with lopsided fangs and crazed, ice-blue eyes.

"I trust . . . you, Superintendent."

"Not so much the rest of us, then."

Blanca's comment had come out as a whisper. Teresa took her aside.

"Don't let it get to you, now. Just go down there with Smoky and do what you know best. Nothing else matters right now."

Blanca almost seemed to be looking at Teresa, searching in the shadows of her vision for the features of this woman she had come to consider a friend. But the universe that swirled in Blanca's clouded eyes remained a mystery to Teresa.

"If District Attorney Lona comes by and finds us here . . ."

"That won't happen, and if it does, I'll deal with it." She put her arm over Blanca's shoulders. "You and Smoky are the best we have, and you've already proven that. Who cares if you're not part of the police force? It's your CV that counts. Understood?"

"Understood."

"Come on then."

Teresa nudged her toward the walkway. One of the side panels had been removed to give the investigators better access to the pavement.

Marini helped Blanca down. Smoky followed with a graceful leap. The forensics team had already divided the nearly eight hundred square meters of mosaic art into equal sections, each measuring ten by ten meters, and marked out with rope.

The dog and his human began their search for traces of biological matter.

"To start with, I'll let him loose around the perimeter. If he doesn't find anything there, we'll start scanning each sector individually."

She called Smoky to heel, then issued the command: "Sniff!"

The department director approached Teresa.

"I didn't mean to offend her. I should have expressed myself more clearly. It's just that it's such a delicate, unusual operation." She turned toward the nave. "I simply cannot believe this place could have been violated like that, that someone could have come in here and . . . done what you think they did. It would mean that the guards haven't been watchful enough, that the security ring around the site hasn't worked. This will need to be investigated, CCTV recordings will need to be examined, shift managers will need to be questioned . . ."

"We're already doing all of that, Professor." But if Giacomo had told the truth—and Teresa had no reason to doubt that he had—they would not discover anything he hadn't already confessed to.

"We'll need to launch an internal investigation to identify those responsible for allowing this breach to happen."

Teresa would have liked to explain that there was no way anyone could divert a serial killer from his objective, not once the psychological mechanisms that eventually led to the ritual of murder—and the liturgical practices that followed it—had been triggered. But there simply wasn't enough time for all that, and neither did she have the strength to summarize the results of years of psychiatric and behavioral evaluations Giacomo Mainardi had undergone.

"Trust me, it's a good thing it happened the way it did."

The woman gave her a look of disbelief.

"Are you saying it's a good thing this work of art was defiled and the basilica desecrated?"

"I'm saying it's a good thing no one crossed his path." Teresa motioned at Marini. "You'll have to excuse me now. The inspector and I will be following the search from a distance, up here on the walkway. It would be best not to have anyone else in the vicinity."

The director nodded.

"I'll be waiting by the entrance."

Smoky was still searching for the scent cone that would lead him to the human remains concealed within the mosaic. According to Giacomo, the fragments of bone from his latest victim were hidden somewhere in there, embedded among those beautiful figurations.

Teresa and Marini moved down the walkway, their footsteps calm, their souls in a state of turmoil. Teresa could sense the agitation hidden beneath the inspector's apparent composure. She would have loved to be able to comfort him, but she couldn't give him what he needed.

Under their feet, the splendors of the earthly paradise began to reveal the biblical story of the prophet Jonah, cast into the sea by the Phoenicians and resurfacing three days later, alive, from the belly of a monstrous fish. An allegory of resurrection. The mosaics, which dated from the era of Theodore I, had first been discovered in the early 1900s; for the 1,500 years before that, they had remained in the shadows, covered by a surface layer of marble.

Blanca and Smoky had reached the foot of the altar, flanked by Renaissance-era pulpits. Smoky did not show any signs of excitement. He had yet to catch the scent of human death.

Teresa and Marini, meanwhile, headed for the basilica's frescoed crypt, which was next to the apse commissioned by the patriarch Maxentius. In the fresco that adorned the dome of the apse, the Mother of God looked at her Son with aching tenderness as she offered him to humanity.

Walking down the steps that led to the crypt was like crossing a threshold in time and reemerging at the other end in the low light and warm hues of twelfth-century medieval soils and ochers. The walls and the low vaulted roof were covered in frescoes depicting salient episodes from Christian history and from the birth of Christianity in Aquileia. In the alcoves, scenes from the crucifixion of Christ and the passion of the early martyrs were reminiscent of the canons of Byzantine art.

"Who are they?" asked Marini, his face right up against a fresco showing two men getting beheaded.

Teresa pointed at the urns stored in a nearby cabinet.

"It's them, probably. Martyrs."

"This place is astonishing."

Teresa wasn't sure whether he was referring to life and death, or to the artistic treasures that had survived the passage of time.

A curtain situated at hip height showed two battling knights spurring their horses to a gallop. One of the two seemed to be wearing the robes of a Templar. He was the one doing the chasing, while the other knight was turning around to shoot an arrow at his enemy.

It wasn't the first time Teresa had seen this kind of image, but at this new stage of her life, she found something of herself in it, too. She had hunted. She had chased. Now the arrow was about to be fired at her, even as she doggedly clung to the saddle and insisted on continuing the chase.

Teresa looked for the fresco of the Dormition of the Virgin, a scene which had become increasingly rare in the history of religious iconography. Few were interested in the death of the Mother. The fresco showed her Son watching over her body and cradling her soul in his arms, swaddled like a newborn. To Teresa, it all seemed almost painfully tender.

When the moment arrived, who would hold *her* in a comforting embrace?

"Shall we go, Superintendent?"

Teresa managed with some difficulty to tear herself away from her musings.

They emerged from the crypt and returned to the floor of the basilica. The girl and her dog had nearly completed their first circuit of the perimeter. Teresa had always been impressed by how perfectly coordinated they were, how very few words (never stern and always kind) they seemed to need in order to communicate, and by the instinctive understanding that bound them.

She leaned against the balustrade, her eyes fixed on the young woman.

"She says she wants nothing to do with Lona. He makes her anxious."

Marini followed Teresa's gaze.

"It would be a shame if she gave up because of that, though I suppose it's not my place to try and dissuade her.

You two have become friends over these past few weeks, haven't you?"

Teresa felt the beginnings of a laugh bubbling inside her chest.

"Are you jealous?"

"It wasn't easy winning you over, Superintendent. You gave me a rough ride."

"Who says you've won me over?"

Marini gave her a playful nudge with his elbow.

"I know you're fond of me, deep down."

Teresa's smile faltered.

"You know an awful lot, but there's one thing you still don't. Listen, Marini . . ."

"Is something up with that girl?" he said, leaning against the balustrade, too. "The way you've been looking at her, recently—it's different."

"Different?"

"Don't act surprised. I do know you a little bit by now. You've been staring at her as if there's something about her you can't quite work out. You used to look at me the same way, too."

Teresa shrugged.

"I've started calling her Blue."

"Like her hair."

Teresa pulled her cardigan tight around her shoulders. The dampness of the crypt seemed to be rising through the foundations of the building and seeping through her very pores.

"Blue like the mix of emotions she carries, Marini. She says she dyes her hair indigo because that's what she feels inside. It's the only color she can pick out from among the shadows."

"But of course that explanation isn't enough to satisfy you."

"Americans use the word *blue* to refer to an emotional state of delicate and inexplicable melancholy. Did you know that the blues are named after the blue devils? That's what they used to call depression and delirium tremens, back in the 1800s."

"You really care about her."

"I'm happy I met her."

"But . . . ? I can hear a 'but' in there somewhere."

"But, she's *blue*: from what she's told me about her life, there seems to be no obvious cause for the melancholy that besets her, and yet it seems it can't be warded off."

"*From what she's told me about her life?*" Marini shook his head. "Oh, no. Don't do that again."

"Do what?"

"*Suspect* things. And try to save everyone you cross paths with. Maybe Blue is fine the way she is."

"Maybe, Marini. Maybe."

"She's visually impaired. No one would be happy about that, especially not a twenty-year-old."

Teresa seemed to weigh up his words.

"Do you really think a disability can determine how happy or otherwise a person's entire existence may be?"

"I would say so."

"You only think that because you don't have a disability yourself. That's why the thought scares you so much."

"Of course it scares me."

Teresa stood up a little straighter—or tried to, at least.

"Human beings are designed to survive, Marini. Magnificently so. Even the absence of one of the senses, even the loss of a limb, even . . . *this*. Here I am, barely able to stand, having to relinquish my independence, my self-sufficiency. Here you are, giving me a push up the backside to help me up."

"Don't be silly. It wasn't your backside."

They were dancing around the real problem. Teresa turned to look at him.

"The spirit replaces what is missing, and fills the void. That's what's happened inside of Blue."

"And inside of you, Superintendent," he said, stepping away from the balustrade and standing in front of her.

Teresa tapped her walking stick against his leg to nudge him aside, and started making her way back toward Blanca and Smoky.

"You've become far too sentimental, Marini."

He stayed where he was, his back to her.

"You can't give up now, Superintendent. Don't say good-bye before it's time."

Teresa hesitated, but only for the briefest moment. She tightened her grip on the walking stick.

"It's never the right time for whoever's watching, Marini. But someone has to say when enough is enough."

"Superintendent . . ."

Just then, Blanca called out to them from the far end of the basilica. She had searched the whole perimeter and come right back round to the entrance. Smoky began to bark at a sealed door on the left-hand side of the wall, close to the entrance and to a medieval-era reconstruction of the Holy Sepulchre made from Greek marble. He seemed altogether disinclined to stop barking, despite his human's best attempts to calm him down.

Teresa and Marini made their way toward them. The director had already rushed over, alarmed by the barking.

"That's the entrance to the Crypt of the Excavations," she explained. "But it has been closed to tourists for several months now. It's the most primitive section of the basilica, containing the northern hall's surviving mosaic fragment, and the original *domus ecclesiae* upon which everything else was built. I can assure you that no one could have accessed the mosaics in there."

The dog barked louder. Blanca crouched down to soothe him, one hand reaching out for Teresa.

"Whatever it is that Smoky can smell, it's made of blood and bones."

Teresa looked at the director.

"Open the door."

10

Twenty-seven years ago

TERESA SET ABOUT ARRANGING the perfect life in the perfect home. She had taken off her T-shirt and her soiled jeans, rolled them up into a ball, and thrown them in the washing machine. She had put away her parka and her boots in the wardrobe by the front door, changed into her kimono, and donned the mask that all defeated creatures wear—the kind that alters your features until you think you no longer know who you truly are.

Dinner was warming up in the oven. On the table, porcelain plates and crystal tumblers—wedding gifts. It had only been a year, but they'd already lost their luster. The kitchen door was shut so that the other rooms of the house would not become contaminated with the smell of food. Sebastiano couldn't stand it when that happened.

She walked around the house barefoot, checking that everything was in order, more perfect than perfection itself. The study was her refuge. She shared it with Sebastiano, but he was never there, and only used it as a storage space for the books that didn't fit in the office the university had given him: volumes that had long since fallen out of print, some with so many passages underlined that the pages had creased up; and others completely untouched—unopened, forgotten gifts from equally forgettable colleagues.

The section of the library set aside for Teresa had increasingly come to resemble her husband's. The manuals on criminal procedure and forensic medicine had gradually been displaced by books on psychopathology and clinical psychology, cognitive neuroscience, and mood disorders, while hidden in the shadows on the lower shelves were volumes in English that had yet to be translated, written by authors Sebastiano regarded as eccentric shamans rather than serious scientists. Teresa crouched down and brushed her fingers against their spines: criminology, a new science based on intricate connections with statistics and psychology, and more a matter of observation than watertight theory. Across the Atlantic, where it had first emerged, it had enjoyed some degree of success, but here it was still mostly unknown. These books had become Teresa's new bible. She opened one now, a vast, unpublished volume no library in the world would stock, as it was a collection of teaching materials from a training course. There was a dedication on the first page, in English, inscribed with the same vigor the lecturer injected into his classes.

To Teresa,
from a hunter to a huntress.
May the darkness have mercy on you.

R.

Teresa ran her fingers over the words. A huntress of free-falling souls. As she gathered them from the ground where they had crashed and shattered into pieces, Teresa had to believe there was something in a killer's heart, and in the tribe of Cain, that was still worth saving. Otherwise the darkness would overcome her, too.

She stared at the library, thousands of pages brimming with theories, analyses, data. And conjecture. Right from the start of this latest case, Teresa had argued for the central importance of ritual, and raised the possibility that they might be dealing with a serial murderer. But she had no proof. None of the clues they had found so far was enough to remove all traces of doubt.

Was the killer really motivated by a range of deep-seated and equally deviant psychological mechanisms, or was Teresa detecting patterns in the old man's murder only because she was so adamant they were there? Maybe Albert was right, and the true motive lay elsewhere.

Maybe.

She sat on the floor, under the soft light of a lamp, and started leafing through various books, dossiers, faxes, and course packets. She laid everything out on the parquet and began combing through the academic correspondence she had kept up over the past few months with criminal investigation units in the United Kingdom and the United States.

Teresa herself could scarcely believe she might be dealing with the kind of textbook case she had been studying for years now. Yet that had been her hunch right from the very start.

She opened her notebook and began to draw up a criminal profile.

Triggering factor? → *some specific event has broken the equilibrium and sparked a violent spiral (romantic rejection? eviction? firing?) ANGER–FRUSTRATION–URGE TO KILL*

Killer's age: around 25 (first violent fantasies beginning in adolescence)
Probable paranoid schizophrenia (most common form of psychosis)

Victim: male role model, mature in age (I don't expect that to change, though the victims may get younger—if not by much—as the killer gains confidence in his abilities)

Body found in exposed, high-risk location. The key question to understanding the killer is the following: what kind of danger does the victim represent?

Her pen paused midair. Teresa had begun to feel a little foolish. Or perhaps she was just too many steps ahead.

The sound of actual footsteps echoed down the corridor.

She turned around, her heart in her throat. There was a shadow blackening the shadows. Teresa scrambled to her feet, stepping over the papers she had spread out on the floor.

"I didn't hear you come in."

Sebastiano had already taken his coat off; his wheeled suitcase stood by the door. He had been watching her. He was still watching her.

"You were busy."

A simple observation? Or a criticism that was the prelude

to another argument? Everything he said, every word he uttered, was an enigma to be solved.

He took a few steps toward her, his hands in his pockets, and no evidence of travel weariness to be found on the hard line of his jaw. Not the trace of a beard, not the slightest dent in his starched collar. Only a graying around his temples alluded to his transience. Nothing else. His eyes were pebbles from a riverbed, wet black rock.

"Dinner's ready, you've made it back in time. I'll go get . . ."

He grabbed her wrist. His thumb caressed the soft skin there, while his other fingers held her in place and measured the ripples of her heartbeat.

"Did you really make it yourself?"

It was no use lying. He would have checked the bins and found the boxes from the deli.

"No, I bought it."

What would happen now? A perfunctory rebuke, perhaps, or something sterner, accusations, his voice raised, maybe even his hand raised.

Teresa had no idea how things had gotten to this point.

She had not glimpsed the signs of the creature that lived inside of him. Yet there they were: etched into his face, and whenever he cracked his knuckles and clenched his fists. Fists he could turn into punches, and which he once had, leaving a mark on the wardrobe and a bruise on her skin.

Now all that suppressed energy was visible in the fire that reddened his ears, the purpureal tinge of the bulging vein in his neck.

What use were the sharpened scalpels of her accumulated knowledge when Sebastiano was the one who needed dissecting? When faced with his exculpatory defenses, they were merely crude, blunt instruments, powerless to dismantle the falsehoods he told himself.

Sebastiano traced his finger over her jaw, then cupped his hand over her face, leaving it half free and half imprisoned—which was exactly how Teresa felt. She couldn't tell whether he was about to caress her or tighten his grip. The gesture was embryonic and unspecific, carrying the potential to turn into anything at all, just like the man who stood before her.

It wasn't the threat of a blow that scared her, so much as the awareness that Sebastiano was practicing the art of torment, sizing up the extent of his dominion.

In that moment, that male hand, like so many other male hands, was shaping a woman's destiny. And within Teresa, as within countless other women who had been in her position, the urge to flee wrestled with the impulse to attack, to bend that wrist until it broke, and shatter the chain that bound her to Sebastiano. Violence purging violence. But the thought remained as such, and soon the vision faded.

Sebastiano ran his fingers through her hair, his hand brushing her neck where her ponytail had left it bare.

"You know I like it better when you wear your hair down. You know that."

"It gets in my way at work."

He twisted a lock around his finger and pulled it loose.

"It's a good thing you changed your mind about the color. This darker tone makes you look more sophisticated. If you want people to take you seriously, red won't do; it gives the wrong impression."

He stepped away from her, as if he'd become irritated at the contact. He sat on the armrest of the couch and undid his tie, sliding the fabric down the palm of his hand like a lion tamer's whip.

Teresa instinctively tucked the lock behind her ear.

"It's just a color."

"And you're just an inspector." He rolled up his tie and threw it onto the table. "Were you really going to turn up at the superintendents' exam with your hair dyed a color that says 'I'm available'?"

It wasn't a genuine question. They never were. They were boreholes where Sebastiano placed the explosive seeds of doubt, humiliating her in order to undermine her confidence.

By the time Teresa had realized this, it was already too late. Sebastiano hadn't always been so transparent. But then something seemed to accelerate inside of him, like a shadow that fed on her fear and insecurity. It was greedy, and it no longer felt the need to hide.

He was just a jealous boyfriend. And how special his jealousy had made her feel.

He was just a jealous and demanding husband, a distinguished professional for whom the human mind seemed to hold no secrets, and who expected his wife to be just as perfect.

And soon that shadow had tightened around her and sucked all the air out from her. It had revealed its true colors: possession, obsession, destruction. Bit by bit, Sebastiano's mask had crumbled, and she had seen his thirst for violence. Sebastiano didn't want her love: he wanted her heart, so that he might devour it.

Why have I stayed this long?

Perhaps because the man who stood before her was one

of the sons of Cain, and she had to believe—had *wanted* to believe—that she could save him. He killed her every single day, one piece of her soul at a time. And every single day she would pick up the broken piece and stitch it back on. By sacrificing herself, perhaps she might bring forth his redemption.

"Come here." Sebastiano patted the couch. "Sit down and give me a hug."

Teresa acquiesced, her stomach convulsing against the heat of his belly like enemy lines intersecting. She could hear Sebastiano's breath marking the rhythm of her own. For a brief moment, she really did pull him close, intoxicated by the memory of what they had once been. But the fissures in her soul, pushed nearly to breaking point, creaked loud enough to bring her back to reason. Within seconds, Teresa was back to analyzing every twitch of his muscles and preparing for the worst. The crack had opened; the edges were crumbling.

"Are you still angry?" Sebastiano asked.

Angry. That was all it was, to him.

"No, I'm not angry."

Anger had nothing to do with it. Anger—and whatever else it was mixed with—belonged to Sebastiano alone.

He pushed her away a little and studied the bruise he'd made, pressing lightly against it.

"I was tired, and you provoked me."

"Yes."

She hated herself for the tear that rolled down her cheek.

"Say you're sorry, Teresa."

"I'm sorry."

Sebastiano smiled.

11

Today

THE DIRECTOR OF THE region's cultural heritage department inserted her key into the bronze door of the crypt, struggling a little with the stiff lock.

"There was a time when there were two basilicas in Aquileia, one in the north and one in the south, erected next to each other above the original *domus ecclesiae*. We do not know why this was the case, nor what they were for. One theory is that the southern basilica was used for catechumenal purposes. The northern basilica, on the other hand, was used for the synaxis, and reserved exclusively to initiates. In its early days, Christianity was of course very much a mystery cult."

She seemed to be having second thoughts. The key remained in the lock, unmoving.

"Halfway through the fourth century, the northern hall was demolished, and the Constantinian basilica was built in the southern section. The new temple was consecrated by Bishop Athanasius, who had been exiled from Egypt for excessive orthodoxy. The remains of the mosaic floor of the northern hall slumbered under a blanket of earth for one thousand five hundred years. It was only in 1906 that a team of archaeologists brought them to light and opened this crypt."

She turned to look at them.

"We may be surrounded by marble, but History is made of glass. I beg you once again to take the greatest possible care."

Finally, she pushed the door open, letting out a sigh that hinted at her conflicting emotions. The breath of cold air that greeted them, heavy with mineral scents, promised not a leap back into History, but something closer to a descent.

The crypt was a treasure chest, enclosed between the looming presence of a modern black ceiling and the pavement, whose astonishingly three-dimensional quality was emphasized by the spotlights positioned throughout the chamber.

The director led the way, walking a few steps ahead of them.

"You will note that there are three visible layers. The deepest dates back to the imperial public buildings and *domus* of the first century. The second layer is a floor made from *opus signinum*, which may be what survives of a Gnostic sacellum leading to the main hall. And in the third layer, you can admire mosaics from the era of Theodore I."

Teresa was picking up a low drone, a kind of background noise that was making her already heightened senses thrum in response. If this was where the bone fragments really were, it meant the killer had wanted to take her along with him into the depths of human history. But why?

"Is something wrong, Superintendent?"

As always, the ever-vigilant Marini was standing right by her side, head tilted toward her. Teresa tugged at his jacket, her eyes firmly fixed on the myriad figures depicted by the mosaic tiles that lay just a few meters from where they stood. She hadn't yet moved a muscle.

"Don't let Blue out of your sight, not even for a moment."

Marini took note.

"What do you think we'll find down there?"

Teresa kept staring ahead, wondering what it was that her intuition had detected.

"I'm not sure. Probably nothing that would be of any immediate danger, but if Giacomo brought us here, it wasn't to show us how beautiful the mosaics are, or merely to lead us to where we might find a few pieces of the victim's body. There has to be a deeper message hidden somewhere within what he's told us and what he's done. But there's no guarantee we'll be able to understand it. I certainly won't."

"But you're the only one who . . ."

Teresa let go of his jacket and looked at him.

"It's your turn now, Inspector."

A tremor passed over his face.

"No. We're doing this *together*. Just like last time."

Blanca and Smoky caught up with them. The dog sat still while his human used her cane to measure out the walkway.

Marini offered her his arm.

"We're on a suspended walkway," he explained. "It runs along the wall that marks the perimeter of the basilica. Underneath us are some spectacular mosaics which I pray to

God you and Smoky won't mess up, as well as the ruins of various ancient buildings. Want me to step down with you?"

"Nope."

"All right, no need to get tetchy."

The seeker of blood and bones zipped her sweatshirt up and pulled her hood over the waves of her indigo hair. The bracelets she wore on her wrists tinkled at the motion.

"I'm sorry, but you would just end up confusing Smoky. There'd be too many false traces to sift through."

The director joined them.

"The mosaic is interrupted by the foundations of the belfry. They were not exactly careful, back in the eleventh century. The tower's stairs cut into tiles, and part of the mosaic is confined within its walls. I *do* hope," she said, taking a deep breath, "that whatever you're looking for isn't in there."

Teresa stroked Blanca's back. She could almost feel the tension there.

"I doubt it, Professor."

The director stepped aside, handing over that most fragile and invaluable of legacies.

Marini helped Blanca off the walkway and onto the mosaic pavement. When he picked Smoky up, the dog bared his teeth at him and growled.

"Will he ever get used to me?"

Teresa ruffled Smoky's fur.

"He's already used to you."

Within moments, the girl and her search dog had gone off to scour the depths of the crypt.

Teresa and Marini followed their slow progress from the walkway, an inverted L that ended behind the foundations of the belfry.

Having spent fifteen long centuries shielded from any sources of light, the colors of the mosaics in the crypt were more vivid compared to those inside the basilica. The figures they depicted looked like they were raring to go, leaping and growling before Teresa and Marini's eyes. The tale unfolding beneath their feet was a convoluted one, without the clear, linear narrative they had been able to admire in the basilica's depiction of the earthly paradise and of the story of Jonah.

Marini leaned over the balustrade.

"Slightly unusual decorations, for a Christian church. What does it all mean?"

Teresa trawled through her memories of the school trips that every child born in this region had made to this basilica, but failed to retrieve anything of substance. Had it all been too long ago? Was her illness progressing? The answer was yes to both questions, though nowadays the past seemed to loom closer by the minute, while the future crumbled like a vanishing mirage. It was often easier for her to remember the particulars of some event from way back in time than it was to recall something that had happened the day before.

But there was one thing she was sure of.

"They're not just decorations. Decorations don't require interpretation. These are not simple ornaments. Not in a place this holy. Not when you consider the sheer amount of wealth embedded within them. Look closer. There tiles are made of lapis lazuli. They would have cost a fortune, at the time. And it's not just about color, but workmanship, too: these mosaics are far more elaborate and sophisticated than the ones we saw earlier. I do remember one thing about them: it's almost certain that the craftsmen were from the Middle East." Her gaze took in the whole of the underground chamber. "Something of great significance was celebrated inside this hall, and these mosaics are telling us its story."

"Yes, but how?"

Teresa gestured toward a raring goat.

"Look, it's wearing episcopal vestments."

"You seem well-informed, Superintendent."

There was more: a black donkey up on its hind legs, black corvids, the eight-pointed star, a lobster, and a billy goat perched on what looked like palm trees, a ray fish, and Solomon's knots everywhere, symbolizing eternal life but also the orthodoxy of the one true faith.

They reached a corner of the bell tower. Marini pointed at an image of a rooster and a turtle locked in combat.

"I would have thought there'd be more crosses and less fauna."

"The turtle is an archaic symbol, a denizen of Tartarus—the underworld. It lives in darkness, while the rooster heralds the dawn of a new day."

"What does it say in the image next to it, just above the ram?"

They bent down to peer at the writing.

"CYRIACE VIBAS. 'Long live Cyriac,' or something like that."

Smoky barked. A single note. They both stood bolt upright; they knew what the signal meant.

Blanca turned toward them.

"He's found something."

The dog lay on the floor, waiting. His stance spoke for him: *What you're looking for is right here, on the floor.*

Marini climbed gingerly over the railing.

"Are we insured for any possible damage to the priceless archaeological treasure I'm about to jump onto?"

"No. Don't jump."

"I thought so."

He slowly lowered himself into the crypt. Blanca stood to one side while Marini crouched down to examine the spot. Smoky could be astonishingly precise. Leaning further over the walkway railing than seemed physically possible, Teresa hoped that Smoky's olfactory gifts had once again provided the solution to the enigma they were dealing with.

When Marini looked up toward her, the expression in his face gave her the answer she needed. There among that handful of mosaic tiles, bathed in a pool of white light that cut through the shadows, was what had been severed from the victim's body.

"I have to see!"

Teresa dropped her bag to the floor, removed her shoes, and took her jacket off, as if she were about to dive into the darkness of Giacomo's mind. He had brought her here; he had wanted her here. She had to be the first to pore over the message he had left there—for as she had once learned and never forgotten, the placement of the victim's body or of any of its parts is a profoundly intimate act, and always a function of the killer's most private needs.

"What are you doing?"

Marini lunged forward and grabbed her just as she was about to throw herself over the railing, her aches and the weight of her own body all but forgotten. He managed to catch her, though he nearly fell over in the process.

"Have you lost your mind?"

Perhaps she had, her illness stripping her of all reason

and allowing some kind of savage impulse to take over in its stead.

Barefoot and beyond embarrassment, Teresa approached the pool of light and managed with some effort to lower herself onto her knees.

The tiles chiseled from the victim's bones had been inserted into the figure of a white hare with red eyes, surrounded by a perfect octagon situated right where the massive steps that led to the belfry began to eat away at the mosaic floor. Some of the original tiles had been removed from the animal's snout and replaced by those made of human bone to form the Greek letter Tau, just like the one on the brow of the ram they had seen earlier.

But it wasn't just those seven tiles cut from bone that Giacomo had put there. Right at the center of the Tau, there was a tooth.

Teresa was confused. She muttered a few stuttering words even she couldn't understand. She counted the tiles again, filled with growing disbelief.

The killer's signature had changed. It was a detail that might have seemed irrelevant to the uninitiated.

"The signature stays the same because the personality remains unchanged. The signature stays the same."

She felt Marini place his arm gently around her shoulders.

"Come on, Superintendent."

His voice was shaking. She grabbed hold of his jacket, ignoring Blanca's worried interjection and the alarm voiced by the director, who had just rushed over to see what was going on.

"The signature has changed. No longer seven tiles made of bone, but eight."

"We need to get out of here and bring the forensics team in."

Teresa stretched out her hand, and he wasn't quick enough to stop her.

A rookie mistake she was only half aware of, stirred by some ineffable, slippery sense of urgency that had tipped her over the edge.

She touched the tooth and the bone fragments with her bare hands.

12

Today

GIACOMO'S HANDS WERE AS adept at fashioning beauty as they were death. He considered himself a craftsman, and saw the realms of his imagination reflected in the mosaics he created. He would hammer methodically at his tiles until he had shaped them into hexagons, the structure deemed by Nature herself to be most resilient. The engineers, architects, and builders who had erected humanity's greatest creations had all copied her.

"Even soap bubbles will group together in hexagonal patterns."

The guard who had come to check on him did not respond.

Giacomo looked up from his work.

"Though I bet someone right now is taking a great interest in octagons, too." His expression soured. He felt genuinely sorry for Teresa, but this was his language, the alphabet naturally suited to creatures like him.

"You're insane."

The guard looked impassive, but by now Giacomo had become proficient at spotting that frisson of head-to-toe terror that petrified everyone who came face-to-face with him. He could almost feel the shallow, quickened breathing of their terrified little lives blowing onto his cheeks. Every one of his senses was attuned to that kind of reaction.

He paused his work.

"*I'm* insane? Because of the things I say? Because of the things I can do with these hands that you can't?"

He jerked his arms up. The cable ties that bound them to the table went taut, scattering tiles and tools around. The guard flinched. Giacomo quieted down, talking now as if he were catching up with an old friend, when all he wanted to do was to tear the man's chest open and do what needed to be done. "Or do you think I'm insane because I came back? I'm exactly where I want to be. *You*, on the other hand, are wishing you could run as far away from me as possible."

The guard took a step forward and spat on the mosaic, then turned around and walked away, the haste and awkwardness in his movements betraying the fear he had tried to disguise as daring.

Giacomo picked up a cloth and wiped the mosaic in circular motions. Half of his work surface was still blank paper, without even a sketch to guide his hand; the picture was fully formed in his mind, as was the order in which every tile must be set into the cement mortar, in keeping with the ancient Greek and Roman traditions.

He breathed in the smell of the paste and picked up a piece of travertine—so pale, so hallowed—with worshipful care, using a pair of tongs to place it beside its peers by gradation. The pieces had all arrived together with red Pettery marble and *pasta vitrea* in a shipment from the Mosaic School of Spilimbergo—an institution that was unique in the world, and trained artisans like him. Except that Giacomo was an autodidact, his expertise fueled by obsession. He had also asked for river stones from the bed of the Tagliamento, whose clear, frigid waters imbued rocks with a specific shade of green that Giacomo had looked for elsewhere to no avail. But he knew that the school used river stones sometimes, and its director had heeded Giacomo's request.

Such was Teresa's power over people. The power of those who can see beyond the surface, of those who understand. There was nothing for anyone else to do but to follow her lead.

Giacomo kept working, stimulated by the smell that rose from the tiles.

"One day we will meet outside of here," he vowed.

But in the meantime, his retinae had caught signs of furtive movement at the edges of his field of vision. There was someone in the corridor. Someone without the heavy tread of the guards. Someone who was only a gray smudge silhouetted against the wall.

Once upon a time, Giacomo used to be monster; now he was the prey, already encaged.

Gripping the hammer in one hand and the tongs in the other, he began to beat his fists on the table.

He did not say a word; the only sound was that beat. Rhythmic, ancient, full of belligerent power. *Come and watch me rip your heart out. Come and see how even these cable ties can't keep you safe.*

He looked at the shadow, and the shadow stared back. Then, it vanished.

13

Today

PARRI WAS SWABBING THE inside of Teresa's mouth, rubbing the pad clockwise over her tongue, mucus membrane, and palate.

"Nearly done now."

They had to isolate her DNA as soon as possible so that they could separate it from the biological traces found on the tooth and bone fragments, all of which had already been tagged as evidence. It was a painstaking and unexpected task that would needlessly divert time and resources from the investigation. Teresa felt herself burning with shame. Her face, her chest, her viscera, every part of her blazed in sympathy, a fire without flames—not particularly glorious, and not at all heroic. One backward somersault and she had returned to being the rookie she'd been thirty years ago, the one who made life harder for her colleagues, the one you always had to keep an eye on if you wanted to avert major disasters. The one who needed restraining.

As she sat there, head tilted to the sky and mouth wide open, Teresa imagined that she was screaming.

Above her, a white ceiling, spiky fluorescent lights, and a distant god.

"Done. I'll check your insulin pump while I'm at it." He lifted the hem of her shirt and felt around for a few seconds. "All good. You're fit for service."

Teresa's gaze was like a frightened bird, constantly crashing into objects and faces until it finally plummeted to the gray floor and into a pair of well-worn shoes, down where a defeated human sat—Teresa herself.

She could hardly even hear what Parri was saying. He was doing it on purpose, dazing her with idle chatter and stories that might not even be true. He *knew*, and he was trying to pick her up and put her somewhere safe.

Marini was sitting by the wall opposite her. He hadn't left her side for a moment, even though Teresa had tried to send him away. He hadn't requested an explanation, either, nor had he tried to minimize what had happened. He had acted with the maximum efficiency, limiting the damage and initiating the chain of custody process for her DNA that had first alerted their colleagues in the forensics department and brought her here to the coroner's office. He had behaved impeccably.

Teresa looked toward him. He was watching her. *See me,* she would have liked to say, *really see me. Let your eyes bore through me.*

He seemed so serious. It was the first time since they'd met that the somberness on his face did not seem out of place. Massimo was growing up, while she was reverting to a small and fragile form.

"Are you two listening to me?" Parri intervened. "I expect to be done with the fingerprint analysis by tomorrow morning, and to have some initial samples ready for genetic analysis."

Teresa tried to muster the concentration she needed for this case. There were instructions that needed issuing.

Marini beat her to it.

"Come on, Doctor Parri, we know there's a lot more you can tell us."

Parri removed his lab coat and began turning the lights off.

"Based on my initial observations, I am confident that the bone the fragments did not belong to someone young. It is difficult to go much further, though, and we cannot know for sure which specific bone is involved. In fact it is practically impossible to establish that right now, as I still need to scrape much of the cement mortar off. But what I can say is that the tissue is porous and fragile. One sample still has pieces of cartilage attached to it. I am far from certain about its origins, and I cannot say more than that. As for the tooth, I will need to perform a transillumination and take a caliper measurement."

Teresa looked at the evidence laid out on the autopsy table. The bone fragments, which had been immersed in a solution of ethanol and sodium chloride, were pale, pinkish grains lying at the bottom of a sealed glass container.

"Most people think of Giacomo as a sadist, but I never got that impression." She hadn't spoken at all for the last two hours, not since her blunder at the crypt—a moment which, like all decisive acts, had proven to be revelatory. Her voice sounded hoarse, and guilty. She cleared her throat. "The amputations always occurred after the victim's death; the aim was never to cause suffering, but to take the life of those who were deemed—symbolically—not to deserve life at all."

Marini stood up.

"Except for this case. This time, he was instructed to commit the murder. Or at least that's what he claims. We mustn't forget that, even though the modus operandi is the same and the approach identical."

Teresa repeated the statement, absorbed in her thoughts.

"Except for this case."

A brief and seemingly banal statement, which nevertheless opened a chasm before their feet. Following the usual trails wouldn't take them far.

She felt for her walking stick and grabbed it as she got to her feet, helped on by Parri. How she had almost managed to climb over the walkway railing earlier would forever remain a mystery. Right now she could hardly move, despite being pumped full of painkillers.

"I've got a book at home that might help, Marini." She brushed her hand against her forehead, swiping at the hair that had fallen over her eyes. "I really can't remember the title, though."

"A book?"

He looked bewildered. Parri helped Teresa with her cardigan. Before they stepped out, she turned around to look at Marini again.

"*Serial Killers by Proxy*—that's the title."

Marini seemed wary, now.

"I don't understand, Superintendent."

He didn't *want* to understand, but soon he would have no choice. Teresa handed her bag to Parri, feeling depleted. She took one step toward Marini—just the one. With great effort, she stopped herself from going any closer. "Serial killers by proxy don't kill their victims, Inspector, but wield their influence to make others kill for them."

"A murderer using another murderer to kill on his behalf?"

"I'll make sure you get the book."

Marini leapt to his feet.

"You'll *make sure I get the book*? Do you mean when I come round to pick you up tomorrow? Because I can't see what the alternative would be."

He kept asking questions, but they were always the wrong ones. Teresa gave him the one answer he didn't want to hear.

"I'm not coming back from sick leave, Inspector Marini. Lona will soon assign a new superintendent to take charge of the team, though I'm sure that by the time they arrive, you'll have made good progress with the investigation. Actually, when do you plan on taking that superintendents' exam?"

She turned around; he forced her to look at him.

There was panic in his eyes, and not because he'd just lost his boss. Until a few months ago, Teresa could never have imagined that the thing that would hurt most about her farewell to arms was not *what* she was saying goodbye to—her vocation—but *who*.

"Are you ready, Teresa?" said Parri, coming to her rescue. He approached with a wheelchair he had procured from one of the departments he liked to refer to as "the world above." "Hospital procedure, I'm afraid—at least until you're out the front door."

"You've got nothing but corpses down here, Antonio."

"And a lady who thought she'd give hurdling a try."

Teresa gave the contraption a dirty look, but if she

wanted Marini to get the message, she might as well give him an unequivocal signal.

"Will you give me a hand, Antonio?"

Her friend helped her up and patiently lowered her into the chair, crouching down to place her feet on the footrests. Teresa let him do it, too exhausted to resist. She heard Parri exchange a few remarks with Marini—words of reassurance that would be of no comfort to the young man, but only served to cut him out. She opted for brevity.

"Give my best to Elena."

The blue resin floor of the hallway rolled away beneath the wheels, but it was the fibers of her own heart that Teresa could feel unspooling. One end of the thread that had held it all together was now caught inside that room where Marini had stood and watched her leave with an expression on his face that even Alzheimer's disease would never be able to wipe from her memories.

A sharp bend, then another. Parri was pushing fast, as eager as she was to leave behind the anguish he had just witnessed. He placed one hand on her shoulder, and Teresa gave it a grateful squeeze. At least she wasn't doing this alone.

All of a sudden, the wheelchair reared up, pushed forward with excessive vigor. Parri's curse was drowned out by Teresa's surprised shriek. She soon realized that the sound of her friend's voice was getting farther and farther away.

She turned around, gripping the armrests.

"Marini! What the fuck are you doing?"

"I won't allow this, Superintendent. You can't drop me like this."

"Don't be an idiot! Stop!"

"Did you *really* think you could just dump me like that?"

"Yes!"

"Is that so? Then safe travels to you, Superintendent Battaglia."

He let go of the handles and launched the wheelchair down the hallway, grabbing hold of it again just in time to avoid a collision with the wall.

When the world finally stopped moving, Teresa cradled her forehead in her hands. She was shaking.

"You're an imbecile, did you know that?"

He went down on one knee in front of her.

"Yes, an imbecile who happens to be desperate. And angry, too. I'm going to take you home now, and tomorrow I'll come by to see how you're doing."

Teresa barely registered Parri's reappearance.

"*No*, Marini."

"Superintendent, please let me—"

Teresa placed her hand over his. She couldn't recall having ever done that before—not like this, not the way she meant it now. They had always been so close, and yet so careful never to touch.

"Are you sure you want to know what's going on?"

Her eyes were staring right into his. *See me, really see me, let your bloodshot eyes bore through me.*

"No, you don't; I can tell from the way you're looking at me." She let go of his hand. "You know that nothing would ever be the same again. And you're right, Massimo. You're absolutely right."

14

Twenty-seven years ago

ON THE NIGHT OF June 3, he killed again, keeping the appointment Teresa felt they had made ever since he'd first drawn blood.

The second murder surprised her colleagues and disoriented Albert, but to Teresa, it was nothing more than a confirmation of her theories.

The body had been spotted by the lens of a helicopter which had been collecting orthophotographs of the area, for use in a study of urban sprawl. The flight's low altitude had allowed the camera to immortalize the pallid X-shaped form silhouetted in a patch of grass just outside the city, where ancient stone-hewn towns remained perfectly preserved, and old villas rose well-hidden behind crumbling walls.

Teresa pushed aside the water-soaked branches of a weeping cedar, causing dewdrops and accumulated rainwater to splash onto her neck. The garden was sweating into the early morning air saturated with verdant moisture, the ground sticking to the soles of their feet and making a sucking noise at every step. A jasmine plant in bloom sprawled over the steps that led up to the entrance of the building, still emitting its nocturnal fragrance.

The villa was an abandoned treasure from the early 1800s, and an open grave. It had gone to auction several times and was now under the ownership of the municipal government, awaiting the start of repair and restoration works that would probably come too late to save it.

There was an enormous entrance gate, corroded with rust and sealed with a lock and chain, but with a gap just wide enough to allow them to slip through.

They had already found the tire tracks. They ran along the uphill driveway edged by two rows of linden trees, and reached all the way to the clearing in front of the gate, where the killer and his victim must have gotten out of the car. There were two sets of footprints, but only one of those two people had walked back out.

While her colleagues took photographs and measurements, Teresa scrutinized the footprints, reenacting the long strides that matched the larger prints, taking notes, and trying to estimate the height of the strong young man they must have belonged to—if her theory was right. The second set of footprints, on the other hand, had forced her to narrow her stride. Here were the hesitant steps of an older, frailer man, but also the trusting gait of a person who had unwittingly handed himself over to his executioner. In the first set, the typical pattern of rubber soles; in the second, the smooth imprint of leather. Sneakers versus traditional shoes. No signs of dragging. They must have walked side by side up to the metal gate, where the more imposing of the two men had stepped aside to let the second through.

There was a story here, etched in the mud. Teresa kept letting her gaze run over it, caught unwillingly in its spell.

He had not erased it. The killer had not erased it.

Teresa began to follow the trail of interrupted footsteps. She walked along the inside of the perimeter wall, whose faded frescoes enclosed the mansion like a treasure chest. The paintings showed scenes from Greek mythology, all veiled with flowing curtains of thick, fleshy ivy, so dense in parts that it completely obscured the images underneath. In mythology, ivy crowned Dionysius's head and encircled immortal lovers as they embraced; here, it was the embodiment of neglect.

The garden was just over one hectare in size, and dotted with purplish clusters of surviving gladiolas. Freed of its human yoke, untamed nature still displayed traces of the sober beauty of organized cultivation, but it had also reclaimed spaces that had previously been forbidden, slithering to encroach on gravel paths, and generating adventitious roots that ate away at mold-blackened statues.

At the western edge of the perimeter wall, a decaying nymphaeum caught by the first light of day showed reflections of the sky in the gaps among the heart-shaped leaves and indigo-hued corollas of its water lilies. The pool had survived through years of neglect, feeding off rainwater and dew. Rippling under the wings of low-flying dragonflies, its surface shivered with the evanescent blues, greens, and pinks favored by Monet. Ensconced in a vaulted alcove flanked with crumbling columns, and missing one of her arms, was a statue of the pond's resident nymph. Her marble surface was beginning to gleam in the morning sun, the light climbing over her thighs and already reaching up toward her navel.

Teresa looked away, turning toward the scene opposite.

The place where the body had been found had been marked off in the early hours of the night, as soon as the people who had been developing the aerial photographs of the area had raised the alarm.

The forensics team was already at work, Parri crouching over the body. The victim had already been identified thanks to his ID, which had been left in his clothes. He was a seventy-two-year-old man who lived across the city from the first victim. His name was Alberto Rupil. His daughter had reported him missing when he had failed to return from an afternoon spent at the bocce club.

He was lying on his back, his naked arms and legs spread out over the ground to form the X which had been spotted from the skies, like a fallen, wilted Vitruvian Man. The pallor of human corpses was a color Teresa had never been able to describe. It had a physical consistency, belonging to the realms of fear and mystery.

No funeral dirge for him that morning—only the chirping of sparrows in the dissolving mist.

Teresa zigzagged her way through her fellow officers, some busy taking measurements and looking for stray items that might turn out to be evidence, others standing around and chatting in small groups. She studiously avoided Albert and squatted on the other side of the security tape, getting as close as she could to Parri.

The coroner acknowledged her presence with a sidelong glance.

"Are you ready, Inspector?" he said.

Teresa turned to a fresh page in her notebook, misshapen from use.

"I'm ready."

"The victim was not tied up. I haven't found any ligature marks."

This was not good news. It meant the killer hadn't felt the need to restrain his prey, unlike in the first murder. He must have felt more confident in his abilities. The fact that they had walked in there together suggested that the killer had used other methods to subdue his mark—words, perhaps, or even just his physical presence. He had established a personal rapport with the victim.

"He killed with a clean cut across the neck this time, from one ear to the other." Parri indicated the nymphaeum. "He did it over there, then brought the body here, stripped him naked, and laid him out like this, folding the clothes in a neat pile at the corpse's feet. Then, he opened his chest up."

The gash was right there in front of Teresa's eyes—an obscene crimson chasm, a gaping hole in the body. She felt at once repulsed and attracted by it. She knew she had to look at it if she wanted to understand.

"Did he drag him across?"

"No. He carried him over and placed him down exactly as you see here."

Teresa felt her insides churning.

"He *carried* him?"

"Among all the other things Lona is trying to keep from reaching your ears, there is a single set of footprints between the pond and here, and they are deeper because of the weight being carried." Teresa searched for Albert in the crowd. He hadn't spotted her yet. She turned again toward the victim, resting her chin on her knees.

"It feels almost like a compassionate act. Same goes for the way he folded the clothes up so carefully. As if to make amends for what he'd done. We haven't found the weapon yet."

The coroner pointed at the cut on the neck, just above the Adam's apple.

"You're looking for two again, just like last time. The murder weapon is not the same as the one he used for the ritual amputation. My guess is that for the actual killing, he employed a double-edged blade at least fifteen centimeters in length. Definitely not an ordinary kitchen knife, but something more professional."

"He brought it with him. He chose it especially."

"You seem shaken."

"I am. It seems to me his modus operandi is evolving rapidly, and we're struggling to keep up. It's been eighteen days since the first murder, a very brief cooling-off period, and we've achieved nothing, while he's been doing all *this*," she said, gesturing at the scene before them, the placement of the victim's naked body, the way his clothes had been folded up rather than simply tossed away. "If the weapon he used was not an improvised one, that means he must have chosen it, mulled it over, *fantasized* about it. The level of violence has intensified; he feels more assured, and takes greater pleasure from the act. At this point his fantasies have taken center stage, and from now on, everything, absolutely everything in his life, will revolve around this."

"There are seven phalanges missing, naturally, though this time he's taken them from the feet. The amputation is much cleaner, almost flawless. He took all the time he needed to execute it to perfection."

"Could he have used a knife?"

"A butcher's knife, perhaps, maybe a scalpel, or a fine surgical saw. It's an instrument similar to a scalpel, small and easy to handle."

"Fuck. Sorry."

It was clear by now that removal of the phalanges was the killer's signature, but the fact that the bones had been taken from a different part of the body this time was a troubling detail. Why not always the hands?

For the killer, these were symbols steeped in meaning, but Teresa was perturbed. Why the phalanx specifically—a bone devoid of iconography, absent from the literature of semiotics, and without any veiled cultural or historical connotations? Why had he carved the victims' chests open but left their hearts completely untouched—even when they were right there at his disposal, still warm, powerful symbols of life, and a ubiquitous presence in the cosmology of humanity's collective imagination?

But of course this was no ordinary criminal. His choice of signature indicated a link to some deeply personal experience.

The enigma Teresa was trying to solve was like a thread knotted around those few grams of missing bone, a thread the killer had pulled until he had released the bones from the life they had belonged to and delivered them to a realm of potent symbolism. That same thread, once unraveled, would lead her right to the hidden meaning of these human sacrifices.

Parri continued to list some basic facts the team had discovered, lowering his voice as two officers walked past.

"The wallet was in the pocket of his trousers. The photo from his driver's license is missing."

Teresa pretended to look for something in the grass.

"I'm sure we will find it when we catch him, as well as the wedding ring he took from the first victim, and a collection of newspaper cuttings about the case."

"Once again, there are no apparent signs of sexual violence."

"This is not a sexually motivated crime. We're not looking for a pervert."

Parri planted his hands on his knees, then stood up straight.

"So who *are* we looking for? Exactly which horrifying variety of human is it?"

Teresa offered her face up to the first rays of the rising sun—that same sun which showed up every morning, unvanquished by the night. Yet darkness still lingered in the gardens of the villa. It may have retreated to its lair for the time being, but it was still very much present, seeped into the green hues of the plants and the purple of the flower petals, blackening the victim's blood and the earth that had absorbed it.

Which horrifying variety of human was it? Someone who was thrashing about in that pool of blood trying to quench his thirst for an unattainable peace. It reminded her of Lucifer's words in Milton's *Paradise Lost*. "What though the field be lost? All is not lost; the unconquerable Will, and study of revenge, immortal hate, and courage never to submit or yield. And what is else not to be overcome?"

She stood up.

"A creature who has stumbled, who has fallen, but is not yet defeated."

Chasing that creature meant following it right into the Abyss, the darkest, deepest part of the biblical inferno.

Teresa walked to the nymphaeum, retracing the killer's footsteps from the opposite direction. Her colleagues had completed their search, placing numbered tags next to each footprint and all the way to the traces of blood, which Teresa had previously been too far away to see.

The actual murder had taken place close to the edge of the water. The markers left by the forensics team indicated the positions the killer and his victim had assumed. The grass was dirty. Had the killer looked his victim in the eyes as he lay dying? If it was true that he no longer knew fear, that must mean he didn't experience shame, either, and any hint of unease would have been suppressed by that feeling of omnipotence he aspired to as a way to cancel out his own self-loathing.

Teresa pictured him sitting in his lair right now. He was probably thinking about the death he had caused, basking in the enjoyment of the totems he had collected, the trophies he had torn from his victims. But soon the euphoria would fade, and his need would come roaring back.

What kind of need, Teresa?

She answered her own question.

"The need for power—absolute power over another human being."

She crouched down. The pond glistened with reflected light. The water lilies were unfurling their cerulean corollas. A pair of dragonflies—entirely unperturbed by Teresa's presence—kept orbiting the statue, brushing the surface of the water and displacing clouds of midges at their passage.

Teresa watched the smaller of the two as it settled on a

budding flower right where the pond lapped at a cluster of mossy limestone rocks. In the murky depths of the pond she noticed an arm cut off at the humerus, its sheer whiteness revealing its presence. It was the missing piece from the statue. There were no traces of mud on it, not even a light coating on the surface. It can't have been down there for more than a few hours.

Teresa leaned forward, her heart on edge. The dragonfly fled. Something glimmered around the arm's index finger, which was pointing gracefully at a tangle of aquatic roots. An unnatural, metallic glint.

Teresa rolled up her sleeve and plunged her hand into the pool of diluted slime.

Someone gave her hood a sharp tug, and she lost her balance, falling onto her back.

Albert was towering over her. He pulled her up unceremoniously.

"I told you to keep off the villa grounds."

Teresa gasped with rage.

"You told me to keep *off*? Off the case, I suppose."

"You need to deal with the evidence."

"You mean the evidence they finished cataloging hours ago?"

"Don't make me repeat myself, Teresa. Do not challenge me."

He turned his back to her.

Teresa tried to collect herself. Albert was as incandescent with rage as she was, but for a different reason: Teresa had shown that she had been right about the case all along, while his theories had been washed away by the blood of a second victim. But he was still her boss, and the superintendent in charge of the investigation.

"Albert, wait. Please."

The conciliatory note in her voice persuaded him to acquiesce, but his expression remained furious.

Teresa took a step toward him.

"Do you want to solve the case? Then listen to me."

"So much arrogance . . . Whatever it is you have to say, say it quickly."

"This isn't the type of homicide you'll find in our usual handbooks. There are profound motives at play here, Albert. This isn't about money, or jealousy, and it isn't just an outburst of anger, either. Every *single* detail in our surroundings is telling us the killer's story; we just have to figure out how to read it."

Albert had kept quiet, which was something. Teresa continued, her tone solemn.

"He's using his own language to talk to us," she began, waving her hands in the air as if to grasp for the right words. "It's kind of like a Ouija board. Letter by letter, he's telling us where to look."

"A Ouija board."

"It's just an example . . ."

"*Out.* Get out of here. Go back to where I told you to be. And stay there this time."

Teresa opened her hand, still slick with silt, to reveal a wedding ring twinkling in the light. She offered it to him.

"It was in the nymphaeum. I am sure it must be the one that was taken from the first victim. It's a message, Albert. He knew we would come here."

He grabbed her wrist, and the ring fell to the ground.

"You picked up a piece of evidence with your bare hands?"

Teresa's breath hitched. That was exactly what she had

done, her judgment clouded by the hunt. But it wasn't the realization of her mistake that was crushing her chest until she felt her heart might burst.

It was the masculine violence in Albert's hold, a reminder of what awaited her when she got home that night. The weak oppressed; the strong triumphant, and drunk on her fear.

"Are you even aware of what you've done?"

Albert tightened his grip, tightened the noose around his prey.

It was too much.

Teresa twisted her arm, trying to wrest it from his grasp. She let out a hysterical scream.

"Don't touch me! Don't you dare touch me again!"

She freed herself.

Albert gaped at her, outraged. Everyone was staring now. All those men who did not understand, could never understand. And her: the only woman there.

Someone else came up behind her, guiding her purposefully toward the gates of the garden. In the gentleness of his gestures, Teresa recognized Parri's hands.

15

Today

FOR THE PAST FEW months, the hours of darkness had been a torment for Teresa, but that night the specter of loneliness took pity on her and let her rest, rather than curling up on her chest and forcing her eyes wide open.

Teresa woke up to find the sun warming up the room. The sky outside held the promise of summer. Her muscles felt looser, and her pain levels had finally receded to something more bearable. She hadn't even been able to climb the stairs to her bedroom the previous evening, yet now, as she lay on the sofa, she was suffused with a feeling of lightness. She hadn't realized how intolerably heavy the mask she'd worn and the subterfuges she'd employed had been until she had finally been able to shrug them off.

She'd left her job, and doing so hadn't killed her after all. Who would've thought?

And who could say for sure that the future would only

bring despair? Perhaps forgetting was a recipe for happiness, and this was her journey to the end of the night.

She stretched her hand out into a patch of light and swirled the dust motes that hung suspended in the air. She used to do the same when she was little, pretending it was magic.

All of that would stay, really—that childlike, physical awareness and enjoyment of the world. Her body would figure out a way to sidestep her short-circuiting mind and find solace curled up in some comfortable nook. But she would never know. All she could do right now was hope, and that was no longer something she was used to doing. Just as she wasn't used to the kinds of sounds that animated her house that morning: the buzz of chatter hinting at shared confidences, the sudden bursts of laughter, the tinkling of crockery, a dog shaking its fur.

She sat up just as Smoky leapt up onto to cushions to nudge her cheek with his damp nose—his version of a kiss. He barked excitedly, whipping the air with his tail. Teresa ruffled his head.

"I'm coming, I'm coming, give me a minute."

She stood up gingerly—every part of her, visible and invisible, seemed to be holding firm so far—and followed him into the kitchen, her feet dragging on the floor. She pushed the door slightly ajar, but remained half-hidden.

Blanca and Antonio were busy putting lids on several boxes of food. She would seal them shut and he would label them, noting their contents in his spiky handwriting. As soon as they spotted Teresa, they stopped chatting and welcomed her inside.

Come, Teresa, sit, Teresa. Are you feeling better? Are you hungry?

Oh, this little feast? It's for you, of course. You mustn't worry about cooking. We'll put everything in the freezer. It'll be ready for you.

Teresa let them get on with it, feeling a little bewildered.

They'd stayed with her through the night, filling that space that had always been devoid of any other human presence with so much tenderness that all her anxieties had been soothed. They were the reason for the peace Teresa had felt upon waking up that morning.

They had lunch together, speaking the language of family. Sitting across from them at the table and holding a piece of bread in her hand, it seemed to Teresa that there was nothing holier than to be able to share it with those who persevered at her bedside.

But there was someone missing, and everyone was aware of it. Nobody mentioned Massimo, but his absence was like a presence. And the *reason* for his absence was even more obvious: he must be kept out of harm's way, away from the heart and away from her impending decline, he who was the most beloved of them all.

Nobody mentioned the mishap, either: when they had opened her front door the night before, they had been engulfed by the smell of gas. Teresa had forgotten to turn off her old-fashioned stovetop.

They spent the rest of the afternoon in a state of uncharacteristic inertia, though she could sense some kind of important restoration work going on inside of her. Sprawled across the cushions, they listened to music and talked about celebrity gossip, Antonio made popcorn, and they watched old movies.

They did not talk about her illness much. Antonio brought it up when he walked past a mirror.

"You need to get the house ready."

Teresa looked around. It felt like preparing for a siege. And perhaps that was what she was doing, in a way. The possibility of a nursing home hadn't even been raised.

"I suppose I do. Lots of things will change. Some already have."

"We'll help you."

Oh, those plural pronouns.

When evening fell, Antonio was the first to leave, stretching his back as he got up. He had to go to work. He promised he'd come back as soon as his shift was over. Teresa fixed the collar of his jacket.

"Go home and rest, Antonio."

"I'll go where I feel good. And this *is* home."

He kissed her on the cheek. Before she even knew it, he'd closed the door behind him and walked past the end of the driveway.

Blanca was still on the sofa.

"My father will be here soon. He wants to take me out for pizza."

She said it as if to excuse herself, or as if she were asking to be saved.

Teresa sat down beside her.

"Why don't you tell him to come inside? Just for five minutes. It would be nice to meet him."

"Maybe next time."

"Next time I might already have forgotten about it."

Blanca did not reply. She distanced herself with secrecy, in a manner Teresa had understood by now to be her usual way. Blanca's silence was her way of avoiding having to say no again, and Teresa wasn't particularly interested in forcing her to do so. This father, then, who was present in Blanca's life but whom the young woman kept hidden away, would have to remain faceless for a little longer—too long, perhaps.

Teresa watched Blanca feel around for the bag she had left on the floor, pick out a hairbrush, and start unraveling the tangle of knots generated by their afternoon of idleness. Her bracelets tinkled, and the piercing in her eyebrow shone when it caught the light.

"May I?"

Teresa took the brush and slowly ran it through the waves of Blanca's silky blue hair.

"I have always believed I was going to have a son," she murmured. "I still think of him that way, though I don't know for sure. I never wanted to know."

The cause of this admission also remained unknown. Blanca handed her a hairband and a clip.

"Have you told him about your illness?"

"Told who?"

"Massimo."

"That's a strange association to make. No, I haven't told him yet. He was too upset. He would not have taken it well."

"Teresa . . ."

"I know, I know. I'm making all this fuss, but I would have had to downshift anyway once I reached retirement age."

Blanca was biting her lips, a nervous tic that seemed to be getting worse recently, leaving the skin there in tatters.

"Are you really going to stop solving cases?"

"It won't be long before the only case I have to solve is how to put a pair of trousers on and tie my shoelaces."

"You're not just giving work up. You're giving *him* up."

"He has a partner. He's about to become a father. I'm not giving him up. I'm freeing him."

"I bet Massimo wouldn't agree."

"When does Marini ever agree?"

"You always refer to him by his surname."

She tried, she really did try to keep him at arm's length.

"You should trust him, Teresa."

"I do trust him."

"You've told me, and I'm still here."

Teresa stroked her face.

"It's more complicated with him."

"What is?"

"Everything."

"Have you ever wondered why that is?"

Teresa tied her braid and gave her the brush back.

"You're a friend, and good friends are there to hear about our catastrophes."

"And what about him? What is he?"

Teresa was too tired to keep circling around the matter. She had no time left for lies.

"He's a son. But I'm not his mother. He already has a mother. God, I could keep a therapist busy for days."

"I think that's beautiful. And people don't go to therapy for loving someone."

"They should if it's the wrong person, or if the emotion is all-consuming."

Blanca smiled, but she looked sad.

"I don't think that's how it is with you two, Teresa."

Blanca's phone pinged. An automated voice read out the message she had just received. Her father was waiting for her outside.

"I should go. Do you mind if I go?"

"Of course not. Don't worry about me."

"I'll be back soon."

"Come whenever you want. There's no rush."

"Please don't turn the stovetop on. Just use the microwave."

Teresa laughed. Apparently she was still capable of laughing at her own misfortune. An excellent sign.

"Don't worry about me, I'll be fine. Enjoy your evening with your father."

Blanca stretched her arms out to envelop her in an embrace that smelled of hair conditioner and peppermint sweets. When she let go, Teresa held her for a moment longer.

"You know you can trust me, right?"

Their smiles vanished. A car sounded its horn.

"I need to go. Talk to Massimo. Don't put it off any longer."

Teresa went up to the window and pulled the curtain aside. Blanca was getting in her father's car, an old runabout which looked like it had just been deep-cleaned—perhaps in honor of the occasion, or perhaps because of the care that people of limited means generally dedicate to important items. He was holding the door open for her. His tweed blazer had lost its shape around the shoulders and elbows. Smoky was already on the back seat, observing Teresa with his head cocked to one side and those funny little clumps of hair sticking out of his upright ears.

Teresa watched them leave with a feeling of loss she had not been prepared for.

The house surrendered to its usual silences—brimming with books, with professional publications, with objects she'd gathered along the way and photographs she herself never appeared in. A joyous mess of memories.

Teresa ran her hands across her manuals and the many files of notes she had collected over decades of work. She had studied hard, she had learned from the best, she had learned from the victims and their executioners, and now all of it was destined to disappear with her.

She took her diary out of her bag and held it in her hands for some time before putting it in her desk drawer. That part of her life was over now.

She needed to start thinking about how to move her furniture around, how to organize her belongings. Post-it notes on kitchen utensils wouldn't be enough. The "after" was already here and there was no time to waste. Sooner or later she would get to the point where she couldn't cook for herself anymore, or shower, or get dressed. No longer a woman, but a little girl without memories, with no heart (or perhaps with too big a heart), stripped once more of all experience. Who would be there to gather her dignity when it slipped off, and drape it back over her shoulders?

She placed her hand over her chest. In spite of it all, the urge to keep living in the world was beating in there, and with such vehemence, too. There was no anger there anymore, nor commiseration—only the will to live, pure and simple. She looked out at the dark sky outside the window.

What now?

The confusion didn't last long, and was soon supplanted by other questions: What was she doing? Why were all these books open on her desk? Old notes on yellowed pages—and faxes. Who was the person sending them from Chicago and signing off with an R? What a mess.

She pulled the curtains shut against the night, went to the kitchen, and turned on the stove.

16

Twenty-seven years ago

THE NAUSEA HAD BEEN bothering her all morning. Teresa had been forced to skip lunch, though she'd made up for it in the late afternoon with some Chinese takeout she had wolfed down in the office. She had thrown it up afterward, then felt hungry again, polishing off a pack of cookies that she kept in a drawer in the filing cabinet. The nausea had passed, replaced by heartburn.

She was exhausted, and it was only the beginning.

There were two large files on her desk full of material on the case of the "killer of the pensioners," but the investigation was languishing. Although the situation was obvious enough, if not yet fully clarified, Albert refused to take any of the necessary steps, insisting instead on lengthy witness interrogations, which were getting them nowhere.

Maybe she should be the one to take the initiative, but at what cost?

It wasn't the risk of being ridiculed or rebuffed by the rest of the team that she was worried about, but the possibility that her ideas might be dismissed by the person who had been her one guiding light in the blizzard she was forging through. A mentor figure who had inspired her both as a human being, and as a professional.

At what cost? she asked herself once more.

She grabbed a piece of paper, staring at it as if the fate of many—including her own—could be glimpsed on its blank surface, and finally began to write. A few sentences in English: only those that were strictly necessary, and would be enough for her correspondent to determine the presence or absence of evil.

She read through the note several times, made a few corrections, scrunched it up into a ball, and wrote a fresh one.

It was now or never.

She faxed the sheet to a number in Chicago, though she wasn't even sure whether it was still working, or if there was anyone there at the other end—ideally him—who would receive her plea for help. She wasn't hoping for a swift response; any answer would do, if it could reassure her that she hadn't completely lost her mind.

The machine's rollers swallowed the sheet up and churned it back out with a series of sounds heralding an invisible transmission that would cross thousands of kilometers in just a few seconds.

Teresa pushed back the taste of bile rising from her stomach. It was done; now she just had to be patient.

She opened her notebook and read through what she had written so far, jotting down some additional thoughts. Putting things in writing helped her to think and to ask herself new questions.

She was chewing the cap of her pen, pondering the mysterious ritual the killer performed with every murder. Each gesture, every detail was a powerful symbol that required correct interpretation. Nothing was done by accident, for the perpetrator's hand—like thousands before it—was guided by the principle of economy. As long as his emotional needs are fulfilled, the killer will tend toward the same modus operandi every time.

His emotional needs. What were they, in this case? It wasn't enough to search for footprints and traces of blood, unlikely eyewitnesses, and—even more unlikely—a standard motive behind the crimes. What they needed to do was to chase down a shadow and ask it following question: "What do you get from the death of an innocent man?"

She was startled by the sound of an incoming fax, and leapt to her feet. She watched in disbelief as the machine produced its answer, one line at a time. She nearly ripped the sheet out. The ideas it outlined were clear, and Teresa had no trouble translating them.

Dear Teresa, I have seen this happen before, with different signatures.

You must ask yourself: what kind of danger does the victim represent? Understanding that is fundamental to understanding *him*.

The killer undressed the victim so that you would not find fibers or other traces on his clothes. He knows the process: he has either been in prison before, or he follows crime news. He might be a reader of detective stories.

When he strikes again—and he will—you must
make sure your mind is a clean slate when you
arrive at the crime scene: it will be a scene he's
prepared especially for you all.

                                                              R.

True to form, Robert had not indulged in any unnecessary flourishes. But he was there across the ocean, he
believed her, and he was telling her what to do next. He
hadn't cast the slightest doubt on the validity of her assumptions. She felt a little less alone.

She couldn't sit still and wait for some fortuitous development that would help move the investigation forward—that
is, if it even arrived in time.

The light from the hallway dimmed. Her colleagues must
be going home, but Teresa knew that Albert would not have
left his office yet. He was furious about the impasse they
were in, thrashing about in the cage he himself had built.
It was up to her to release him, even at the risk of getting
bitten.

It cost her a hefty chunk of pride to knock on his door,
and an even greater amount to utter the words with which
she announced her arrival.

"I'm sorry to disturb you, Superintendent, but could I
have a minute of your time? I need to talk to you."

She saw him motion at her to come inside. As she stood
there, he kept his head bent over the papers and folders he
had been perusing, and let several minutes pass before he
finally spoke.

"Have you come to apologize?"

"What?"

"That ridiculous tantrum you threw earlier. You embarrassed me in front of the whole team."

Paternalism. A toxic paternalism Teresa had realized she was being forced to inhale wherever she went. She had nothing to apologize for. He was the one who had grabbed her in that brutish manner she wouldn't have dreamed of inflicting on anyone, treating her as if he had power over her—a power transcending anything to do with office hierarchies.

"I didn't like it, Teresa. I didn't like it at all."

She didn't like it, either—the way she was constantly being pushed aside, leapfrogged, her work diminished and undermined. Now he'd had the temerity to touch her; it must never happen again.

"I'm not here to apologize, Albert."

He finally deigned to look at her.

"We have no use for hysterical little women, here. How do you expect to have even the slightest shred of credibility after this? Do you know what they've been saying about you?"

"No, and I'm not interested."

"That the whole investigation hinges on your hormonal oscillations. How very authoritative you are, Inspector Battaglia. A *lady* inspector—good God, even the sound of it is ridiculous."

Teresa could feel herself flushing, as if she were the one who ought to feel ashamed—not him and all those others just like him. Before she spoke again, she bit her lip until she could feel the hardness of her teeth. If she wanted to survive, both in there and in the wider world, she had to make that hardness her own.

"Albert, the killer bit into his victim's body, then covered up the marks with cuts so that we wouldn't be able to take a dental impression."

"I've read Parri's report, obviously. Are you now *both* convinced that I should be looking for an aspiring cannibal?"

"I'm trying to show you how his mind works."

"How you *think* it works."

"It's just statistics. The analysis of hundreds of cases has shown that criminals with similar traits end up committing similar crimes. Bite marks are typical signs of uncontrollable rage. He literally wanted to feed on the violence he was meting out. He was hungry, and greedy. But crucially, there are no bite marks on the second victim."

"Perhaps he wasn't quite to the killer's taste."

"Could you try to take this seriously?"

"I was about to ask you to do the same, Teresa."

"The body of the first victim was left where it would be most easily noticed, while the second was concealed. This indicates that the perpetrator is in the process of perfecting his modus operandi. He is showing himself to be an organized killer, Albert. He is clearly of sound mind—and that is terrible news. He's learning, he is controlling his urges, and he has also become more violent. And more dangerous too, because . . ."

"Because he kills and has already done so twice? Thank you for the superlative insight; I'm sure it will prove invaluable to the progress of the investigation."

Teresa planted her palms on the cluttered surface of his desk, brushing manners and convention aside. Inside she was vibrating with energy, and she had to make sure he felt it, too, if she was going to persuade him to follow her lead.

"*No.* He is dangerous because he makes plans. From his

perspective, he is channeling his aggression in a more constructive fashion. He knows our methods, and knows how to trick us, nudging us further and further away from the truth and from himself."

Albert stood up and walked around the desk. Exhaustion had fallen like a gray shadow across his face, but there was also a growing anger there, which—as was his wont—he would mold around the shape of others, turning it into a trap.

"You say he knows how to trick us, but what you mean is me. *I'm* the one getting tricked. Is that it? You're questioning my abilities, and by extension my leadership of this unit, too."

"That is not what I meant."

Albert raised his hand to silence her. It hovered between them for a moment, but Teresa felt as if it were physically pressing against her mouth. Quiet. Shut up.

"Yes it is. But what you should really be asking yourself is: Are *you* part of this squad? Does this squad need you? Does it even want you? You're not a team player; everyone can see that."

Her breath caught.

"That's not true. I'm trying."

"But you're not getting anywhere. On a personal level, you're a failure. On a strictly professional level, your contribution is negligible. I can see you're fascinated by psychological profiling. Great, I'll give you one. Yours." He leaned toward her with his arms crossed over his chest, though he probably wanted to shake her instead. "A woman with obvious self-esteem issues, held hostage by her own frailties and obsessions, itching to prove herself, yet totally incapable of turning her intentions into concrete results. These fantasies of yours are nothing but the delusions of grandeur of someone who's read far too many murder mysteries and convinced themselves they are the hero. But this is *my* investigation, Teresa. *I'm* the one running it. If you want to be the hero, take the superintendents' exam, pass it, and lead your own team."

Teresa shook her head as if to brush off any dangerous thoughts. She mustn't let them take hold and start growing roots.

"*He's* the one who's been reading murder mysteries. The killer! He's well-informed. He follows the crime bulletins, he reads specialist publications. He knows that traces of evidence can stick to a victim's clothes, for instance. That's why he stripped them."

Albert narrowed his eyes. He pulled a handkerchief from the pocket of his jacket and swiped it over her cheek. Teresa backed away, but it was too late.

Her foundation was gone, revealing a new bruise. It hadn't been caused by a slap this time, but by a book thrown across the room in a fit of rage.

"Teresa . . ."

As he spoke her name—which, in that moment, meant something else altogether, and carried with it a whole host of unsaid words—his voice sounded almost tender, so much so that she was tempted to give in, one human being to another.

"Let me help you, Teresa."

She was shaking. He ran his finger over those parts of her skin that had turned purple. Her discomfort morphed into nausea.

"Come to me, and I promise I will help you."

Teresa looked up, confused. The unspoken "if" in his offer implied that whatever his intentions might be, they were contingent on something else.

"Come to you?"

"You seem surprised."

"That's not the word I would have used."

"There are many ways of loving, Teresa."

On hearing this admission, Teresa took a step backward. Albert noticed, and looked displeased.

"I thought you'd realized. Or perhaps you have, but think it inappropriate." He twitched. "I'm fed up with seeing scorn in your eyes every time you look at me."

Teresa wasn't sure whether he really meant the things he was saying.

"Albert . . ."

As he returned to his seat, Superintendent Lona was a picture of composure, and seemed to have already moved on from their exchange, but Teresa could have sworn she could feel the blazing heat of the anger he was emitting. He pretended to concentrate once more on the files he had been looking at when Teresa had interrupted him earlier.

"Albert, what will it take for you to understand that the killer is going to strike again—and very soon, judging by his behavior so far?"

He pointed at the door.

"I could say the same about your husband, Inspector Battaglia, and yet you seem disinclined to do anything to stop him. Now get out of my sight."

17

Today

THE GARLIC HAD BEGUN to sizzle, browning in the olive oil Parisi had brought her from Calabria. Teresa chopped the cherry tomatoes up and threw them in the pan. She added salt and pepper, and stirred a few times. She sautéed them and let them soften until they released their juices. From the table, her mobile phone alerted her to another message from Blanca, who was checking in on Teresa while she was out having dinner with her father. Perhaps she wasn't having a particularly enjoyable evening.

Teresa added oregano, chili, and roughly chopped Taggiasca olives, then turned off the gas. A pot of spaghetti was simmering beside it, releasing a cloud of fragrant steam that seemed to carry the aroma of all the herbs and spices she was using.

Her doorbell rang, announcing a visitor. Teresa glanced at the clock. No one ever came to see her at dinner time. She wiped her hands on her apron, and as she walked through the living room, she tidied up some magazines and plumped up the cushions.

She parted the curtains and peered out of the window. The man had his back to her, and was crouching down to tie up his shoelaces, but she would have recognized that troublesome backside anywhere; it had drawn more than a stray glance ever since it had first turned up at headquarters, and she'd been tempted—once or twice—to give it a well-placed kick.

She leaned with her shoulders against the wall. What did he want now?

In truth she knew exactly what he wanted, and was familiar with the need that had brought him here. She wasn't ready, she never would be, and yet he kept insisting, pushing her all the way to her limit at a time in her life when corralling and ordering her emotions was proving to be an impossible task. Teresa exploded with rage every time she felt sad, and with sadness when she was overcome with love. This illness was toying with her like a breeze with a dry leaf; torn from its branch, it was at the mercy of the weather, of the heavens, and of God.

She took off her apron and swung the door open.

"Marini!"

The inspector sprung upright with a sheepish smile.

"Superintendent."

Teresa gave him a once over. He looked like he was ready for a date, his hair still damp, his shirt fresh from the hanger, that scent of rain and leather Teresa had learned to recognize, and which encapsulated him so perfectly. It filled their office even when she left the windows wide open, and in the evenings she would find it lingering on her clothes, sticking there just as its human source stuck to her during the day. Soon it would become the scent of a stranger.

Marini was holding a bag.

"Any news on Giacomo?"

She saw him tense up.

"No. No news."

"Then why . . . ?"

Marini stammered as he spoke.

"I thought we could . . . I thought we might talk about the case. Tonight. You . . . and me."

He'd practically breathed the last two words in.

Teresa was feeling increasingly bewildered.

"I told you I'm not coming back to work. I thought I'd been clear enough."

He flushed.

"Should I leave?"

She felt a wave of tenderness for him. He seemed to have gone back to being that insecure young man who had first walked toward her one snowy, icy day, up to his knees in mud, dressed to the nines in an outfit that was wholly ill-suited to both location and weather—and running late, to boot.

He must have been so terrified of her, and yet he had never given up.

They'd come so far together in just a few months.

And it had taken so little, now, to send him into a tailspin—because emotions made you fragile, and left you exposed to your opponent's blows. But she had no intention of hurting him.

"You're blushing, Marini. What've you got there?"

"Ice cream."

She took the bag.

"Come on in."

WHEN MASSIMO CROSSED the threshold, his first thought was that after tonight, there would be no going back. Teresa Battaglia had already warned him: nothing would ever be the same again.

It was a little untidy inside, enough to show that the house was lived in, but not neglected. This was the clutter of a creative personality, lively, receptive, needing the objects around it to be in perpetual motion, always at hand, never static and tucked away. It was a house teeming with colors and scents, exotic items, modern art on the walls, and ancient-looking carpets. He could see dozens of books scattered across the living room. Some were open, others had bookmarks peeking out from between ruffled pages, which must have been read and reread countless times. This was the cozy den of a creature who led a solitary yet curious existence, open to all the discoveries the world had to offer.

But to those who had not been lucky enough to get to know her hidden qualities, or who had the misfortune of having to face her as an adversary, Superintendent Battaglia would have appeared to be the antithesis of her home. Massimo never ceased to be impressed by the aura of authority she radiated. It contrasted starkly with her appearance—soft, wide, maternal. She would give him a tongue-lashing if she heard him call her "wide," yet in that loose, distended figure, Massimo identified an ability to exist fully and powerfully in the world, with every cell and fiber of her being. Her body was emotion made of matter.

"I put the ice cream in the freezer. I haven't had dinner yet," Teresa said.

He stood there in a daze, staring at her red bob whose locks kept falling over her face—free of any makeup—and nearly brushing her eyes. The first time they had met, he'd described them to himself as her "little eyes," picturing her as some strange lady who was hanging around disrupting the investigation, but not a minute later, those same little eyes had pierced through him with brutal force and revealed her true nature: a ruthless huntress of murderers.

From that moment on, he had learned never to underestimate her. From that moment on, he had adored and loathed her in equal measure.

"Oh. You haven't had dinner," Massimo said.

He watched her thin eyebrows knit into a frown. A terrible sign. He had better be careful.

"What's wrong with you, Marini? Is Elena all right?"

"Yes, yes, she's fine, thank you. The pregnancy is going perfectly smoothly."

The silence that followed made him wish he'd never rung that doorbell.

Massimo ran a hand over his face, then tucked it back in his pocket. This woman knew how to read body language. She could dissect him and his insecurities with unsparing observations, and by God, she hit the target every time.

He decided to play his last remaining card.

"I haven't had dinner, either."

He had managed to shock her. He could tell from her expression, no longer belligerent, but now somewhat alarmed.

"You're not inviting yourself over for dinner, are you, Marini?"

He made as if to smile, when in fact he would have liked to disappear forever, right into the ground perhaps.

"Yes."

She burst out laughing.

"If I were thirty years younger, I would think you might be hitting on me, Inspector."

It would be all right after all.

"So I can stay?"

"Put some music on, then come and give me a hand."

Massimo acquiesced. The CD in the hi-fi was a Dire Straits album. He joined her in the kitchen, a spacious room with yellow lacquered cabinets. He noticed that the spice, pasta, and cereal jars had each been carefully labeled, as had every drawer. Near the stove was a sign written in red ink and with three exclamation marks, reminding her to shut the gas off. He looked away.

Teresa drained the pasta and poured it into the pan. The smell allowed Massimo to forget his embarrassment at being an unexpected guest.

Teresa looked bemused.

"I've made too much," she murmured. "You're lucky."

He felt a tug at his heart.

"Yes, I'm lucky."

"Get some plates and cutlery. They're in that drawer. Napkins are in the one underneath. Ah . . . well, it's all written down, as you can see."

He paid little attention to that remark, and gladly allowed her to boss him around, marveling at how little he seemed to mind.

They ate in the living room, on a pockmarked table he

referred to as "old." She immediately corrected him, declaring it an antique.

"It used to belong to a tavern. People played cards on it for a whole century, all the way through two world wars. Look: these markings are where they would use their penknives to keep track of their points."

"And how did it end up here?"

"I rescued it. The tavern belonged to my grandfather, and some of those scores are his."

It smelled of wood, beeswax, and olden times.

They paired their pasta with a young, perfectly chilled white, and kept their conversation casual—hardly ever talking about themselves, and even less so about the case they were dealing with. They rarely had the chance to talk like this, as there was always some investigation to follow, or Parisi and de Carli hanging around—if not Lona himself. This was new territory they were carving out, and he was surprised to find it so instantly comfortable.

At a certain point, she became untalkative, and Massimo realized that she was no longer listening.

"I'll clear up, it's the least I can do."

She let him do so.

"Dessert?" he called from the kitchen.

"Later."

Massimo returned to the living room and found her lying on the sofa, her feet curled up beneath her body. She was watching him as if she were waiting to pounce.

"I know I shouldn't ask, Marini, but have you been to see Giacomo again?"

He took a chair and sat in front of her, elbows planted on his knees.

"You can ask me anything you want. No, I've not met him yet, but I suppose it'll happen soon enough."

Teresa looked at him through narrowed eyes, chewing at the temples of her reading glasses.

"Does he make you uneasy?"

"Does he make me uneasy? He's a homicidal beast. Of course he makes me uneasy."

"You do know, don't you, that personal prejudices won't help you in the long run, if you don't figure out how to control them?"

Massimo was taken aback.

"What exactly are you scolding me for?"

"You're about to become a father. Don't bring thoughts of death into your and Elena's lives."

"What are you worried about?"

"Leaving you on your own."

Massimo opened his mouth, then closed it again, unable to find the right words. He swallowed, his throat constricting.

"I'll be careful."

"Don't be alone with him, Marini."

"That's not exactly reassuring."

She touched her forehead.

"*This* is where you mustn't let him in. And if you want to understand what happened, if you want to see what he sees and *how* he sees it, then *this* is what you must use." She pointed at his heart, and Massimo felt as if she had actually touched him right there, on his chest. Her lowered voice, that closeness he had worked so hard to foster and which had never felt so deep as in that moment, her meekness—it all made her every gesture reverberate inside of him.

"Do you know his story, Marini?"

"I've caught up. I've read his file."

"That's not enough. Do you know his story?"

Massimo slowly shook his head, telling himself no over and over again.

"I'm not like you, Superintendent. I will never understand people like him. I can't feel anything for them. Certainly not compassion."

Teresa Battaglia, instead, accepted their true natures, unfettered by revulsion. She accepted everything about the people she faced as a matter of fact, even their most horrifying sides. That was why she was so good at her job. She didn't judge. She was never scandalized. She always tried to understand. But this came with a price: she suffered alongside them.

They were quiet for a time. "Romeo and Juliet" was playing in the background, telling its story of romantic and ill-fated love.

"We really must have some of that ice cream now," said Massimo to end the impasse, and got to his feet.

She reached for a cushion and placed it under her head.

"Not for me, thank you."

Massimo was already in the kitchen, fussing around with bowls and spoons.

"Oh come on, Superintendent. I got the sugar-free version for diabetics, just like you told me to. It took me a while to find that ice cream shop you mentioned. At least have a taste."

He walked back into the living room and realized immediately that something was off. He could have sworn it was fear he saw in the superintendent's eyes.

He placed the bowls on the table.

"What's wrong?"

She didn't reply straight away. She kept looking at him as if it were the first time she had ever set eyes on him.

"When did I tell you to bring me ice cream?"

Her voice, usually so purposeful, now quavered with a kind of unease Massimo had never heard in it before. Only then did he realize he'd committed a faux pas he might never be able to make up for.

"I meant that I knew this is the only kind of ice cream you eat. You must have told me about it . . ."

"When?"

"I don't remember. Ages ago, probably."

"Bullshit."

Yes, he was lying to her. He knew it, and she knew it, too.

He would never forget how her eyes looked in that moment: dilated and staring into nothing, unshed tears fixed in place. He watched them dart toward the kitchen sink, which could be glimpsed through the door he'd left open. She brushed her bangs from her eyes and straightened her back in a gesture that might have equally signaled pride, denial of what she had just realized, or dignified acceptance.

She cleared her throat.

"You know what I think, Marini?"

He didn't reply, his heart in his throat.

"That maybe I'm not such a good detective after all."

"Superintendent Battaglia . . ."

"Aren't you going to ask me why? You keep calling me superintendent, but if I were any good at this, I would have noticed that I'm wearing my silk kimono, even though I tend to dress much more sloppily when I'm at home. I rarely eat anything other than frozen ready meals, and even more rarely do I make enough pasta for two. The only explanation I can think of is that I must have forgotten I was expecting a guest for dinner."

She was showing herself no mercy. Her analysis was brutal, and she wasn't pulling any punches.

"There was too much pasta because I measured out two portions. And you brought me my favorite ice cream not out of some lucky coincidence, but because I asked you to—as recently as today. I even told you where to buy it."

She looked straight into his eyes and delivered the final blow.

"I forgot I had invited you for dinner, and you've been kind enough to pretend there was nothing wrong, even though it made you look like a fool. Isn't that right?"

Massimo would never have thought that a single syllable could be so difficult to utter. He managed to spit it out eventually, and that briefest of sounds was powerful enough to crush the woman in front of him.

"Yes."

"When?"

It was his turn, now, to find his voice again.

"At Parri's office. You told me to come by because I refused to let you leave, so you . . ."

"Ah, yes. A showdown. I must have been meaning to tell you the truth, but instead I've simply shown you."

He watched her gaze around the room, looking embarrassed and adrift. He hated himself for what he was putting her through.

"Well, Marini, I guess it's not quite going as I'd planned, but we're here now, so we might as well . . ."

Her face crumpled under the brute force of her anguish, and she couldn't continue. He was by her side immediately, putting his arms around her.

She was quite small, really, and so delicate. How thick and steely that armor she wore every day must be to make her into the virago she appeared to be, whose presence he couldn't even feel now.

She moved away, slipping out of his arms and curling up far from where he sat. Her hands, pressed against her chest, were shaking.

"Go home, Marini."

She had kept her eyes closed as she spoke, as if to keep him at arm's length, as if ignoring his presence might be enough to remove the problem.

"I won't tell anyone, Superintendent."

"Maybe they already know. God knows what I say and do when I get like that."

"No. If anyone had been talking about it, I would have heard."

She did not respond. She was completely still, her face turned away in what might have been shame.

Massimo gathered his courage and moved closer. He feared that this spirited, independent woman would not accept his help, but he was fully prepared to insist on it, to argue if need be, because he had no intention of leaving this place—where he could be right by her side.

He feared her and he cared for her. He loved her and hated her. He drew strength from her, and he wanted to support her.

That was how it had always been with her: a constant search for balance between wildly conflicting emotions.

He sat with his back straight, full of tension. Between the two of them, he was certainly the least courageous one.

He cast around for something to say.

"It happened to my grandmother, too."

"Jesus Christ, Marini. You're still here? Just leave."

Massimi didn't say anything. He didn't leave, either. He stretched out his arm toward her. He touched her shoulder, felt her retreat. He pulled her gently toward him, and Teresa let herself fall into his chest, let go of her fear of showing vulnerability.

She cried, finally, her shuddering sobs interspersed with what Massimo surmised must be muffled curses.

He felt like smiling, and crying, and screaming, but he didn't.

In the background, Mark Knopfler's voice and the sound of his guitar were chasing each other in the most magnificent live rendition of "Brothers in Arms" Massimo had ever heard.

Without even realizing what he was doing, he began tapping the notes out on her arm, and soon, those soft touches had turned into caresses. Little by little, her tears died down.

Her sobs gave way to a spine-tingling guitar solo, and to something between them that transcended their respective roles, ages, the masks they wore every day.

They were just two human beings now. Fallible, confused, clinging doggedly to life and to each other.

The final notes of the song faded into silence. She had stopped crying.

"You do realize you've just compared me to your grandmother, don't you?"

She was still curled up where Massimo had pulled her

close, her body relaxed and her head resting against his chest.

"She was quite a beauty, my grandma."

They laughed together, then said nothing at all for a long moment, until Massimo finally uttered the promise that had kept him awake for the past few nights.

"You won't be alone, Teresa. You won't be alone."

Her whole body shivered. Then, more laughter.

"That's *superintendent* to you, you little shit."

Massimo tucked her hair behind her ear and leaned a little closer.

"You can say whatever you want, but I'm not leaving. I'm staying right here."

There was silence again, and a sigh, but this time it signified peace.

"Thank you."

He kept holding her, cradled in his arms.

18

Twenty-seven years ago

PARRI WAS NOWHERE TO be found. His colleagues and various assistant staff in the forensics department had looked everywhere for him—even in the cellars—until they'd had to return to their posts.

He'd come into work as usual that morning. One of his colleagues showed Albert the stamped time card. He swore he'd seen Parri walk into his office not long after the time shown on the card.

"How did he look?"

A moment's hesitation.

"Still sober." But Albert's forbidding gaze would not let the trainee off the hook, until eventually the young man stopped prevaricating and capitulated. "Who can tell, when it comes to Doctor Parri? One morning we found him inside a broom cupboard. And we'd already looked in there a few times."

The trainee turned around to flee, and in a few brisk strides, he was just a lab coat fluttering at the far end of the corridor.

Teresa couldn't believe his impudence. She wanted to chase after him, shake him, shatter the relief he felt after having disavowed his mentor at the first opportunity.

Albert turned toward the public prosecutor and threw up his arms.

"It's up to you now, Doctor Pace."

Elvira Pace was reputed to be a tough and competent magistrate who also knew when it was necessary to make compromises. Always clad in tight-fitting suits and low-cut silk blouses, her face strikingly made-up, and black hair sculpted with spray, she had found herself with the nickname "Elvira the Witch." Rumor had it she didn't mind. Every time she met her, Teresa wondered if the shoulder pads, a ubiquitous feature in all her outfits, might in fact instill in her the strength required to navigate a world that required muscular and often subtle adjustments.

Doctor Pace had called a meeting with Parri at the forensics institute to discuss their findings so far. She wanted to *see* the evidence with her own eyes, not just read descriptions. She was the kind of person who had no qualms about plunging her hands—bright red manicure and all—right into the murky depths of a murder investigation. She would have been perfectly capable of rolling up her sleeves and doing all the dirty work herself, if needed.

The latest tests had confirmed that the blood retrieved from the first victim's dog matched its master's blood type. In the mud scraped from the soles of the man's shoes, they had found traces of concrete. This had led them to a building that was being restored not far from where the body had been left for them to find. Work on the construction site had been on hold for months due to a lack of funds. That was where the man had been killed.

Some progress, then, but Elvira Pace had made it clear to everyone that they must redouble their efforts and avoid another standstill.

Teresa admired her from afar, wishing she could work up the confidence and courage to ask her how she managed to hold the reins so firmly in her grasp while avoiding the inevitable traps that lay in her path. There was a ten-year age gap between them. How far would Teresa have advanced when she reached forty? She thought about the superintendents' exam she needed to prepare for, and how Sebastiano would react to the kind of career progress he kept saying was necessary, but which in practice he kept obstructing, as if her success might somehow mean the diminishment of his own.

Elvira Pace spun her watch around her wrist, nails ticking against metal, a bouquet of sweet, spicy perfume wafting through the air.

"I am not exactly pleased, but I can see no other solution than to postpone the meeting until Doctor Parri decides to show up."

Teresa couldn't resist.

"Doctor Parri is one of the leading lights of this institution."

Albert stifled a laugh, as did Pace's assistant. The coroner's alcohol problem wasn't exactly a secret. The forensics department was situated in the basement of the city hospital, a microcosm in which everyone seemed to know everything about one another, and where interdepartmental dinners were rife with quips about the state in which Parri would show up for work sometimes—so much so that the same jokes had taken hold in the offices of the police headquarters and down the corridors of the courthouse.

Prosecutor Pace gave Teresa a brief glance.

"Doctor Parri's expertise is not in question, Inspector Battaglia. That is why we will wait for him."

Everyone looked serious again. Elvira the Witch had restored order without even having to raise her voice. In the commanding silence that she wielded, the only sound was that of her heels clicking as she made her exit.

Before he followed her out, Albert paused for a moment to glance at Teresa.

"You look awful. Are you all right?"

She nodded, her mouth full of saliva.

He left as well. Teresa looked around in a panic. She couldn't remember where the bathrooms were. For several interminable minutes now, she had been fighting back nausea, but it wasn't just a feeling this time. When she finally managed to find the staff toilets, she sprinted inside, belly heaving as she crouched over a toilet bowl.

She did not experience the relief she had expected. She continued to retch even though her stomach was empty. She felt hot and cold, sweat beading on her skin, legs trembling. She would have fallen to her knees if not for a cool hand against her forehead. Behind her, someone who smelled of hospital-grade soap, the only scent in the world that seemed, in that moment, to have the power to calm her, and not turn her whole body inside out.

"Take a deep breath. It'll pass."

It was a man. Teresa pressed her hands against her thighs to steady herself, finding a position in which she was able to resist the nausea.

Eventually it seemed to go away. She gingerly straightened her back.

He let go of her forehead. Teresa heard him tear some paper towel from the automated roll, and open and close a tap.

He returned to her side and wiped her face in the manner of a person used to taking care of other people's bodies—his gestures functional, efficient, and as swift as possible.

He had one of those deceptive faces whose age is hard to pinpoint, light and golden, with smooth features. Nothing like Sebastiano's menacing beauty. He could have been twenty, or just as easily thirty. His reddish hair, spiky with gel, and his smooth, freckled arms, emerging from the short sleeves of his hospital uniform, all emphasized his youthful appearance, but his expression and build were those of a grown man.

Teresa held her forehead in her hands. She'd felt dizzy all of a sudden, as if she had gone for a ride on some infernal rollercoaster and was now back on the ground. When it was over, she smiled at him.

"Thank you."

"No problem." He smiled, too, throwing the paper towel in the trash. "Are you new? I haven't seen you here before."

"I don't work in the forensics department. I had to use the staff toilets because . . . well, you saw why."

He crossed his arms over his chest.

"It happens. It's nothing shocking."

Teresa ran a hand through her hair, which must have been

a mess. She caught sight of her reflection in her mirror. The makeup around her eyes was smudged, and the fluorescent lights shining from the ceiling accentuated the regrowth of the lighter roots from her scalp. Venetian blond, just like the young man's hair. She looked away.

"I was searching for Doctor Parri. We had an appointment, but he's late. Do you know where I might find him?"

"At his usual bar, I suppose." He pointed his thumb at a small window near the ceiling. Down there, light only filtered through the ground-level basement windows. "It's across the road."

He spoke without judgment or scorn, merely reporting the facts.

Teresa instinctively warmed to the transparent clarity in his words. She picked up her bag, which she had previously dropped in her haste.

"I'll be off, then. Thanks again."

He called after her. He put a hand in the pocket of his trousers, and offered her a packet of fruit-flavored sweets.

"My mother always said they helped with nausea. Here, have some."

Teresa was about to refuse, and he must have realized it, for he replied to the objection she hadn't even uttered.

"Go on, take them. I'm a nurse, even though we don't exactly heal patients down here." In the end he just took her hand and placed the pack in her palm. "Did you know that sometimes the people you meet can turn out to be all right?"

19

Today

THE ICE CREAM HAD already melted in the bowls. Neither of them had spared it another thought.

Massimo was still holding her in his arms, so that she wouldn't run away. Teresa was a little girl curled up against his chest, a frantic heart whose fluttering he could feel through her skin, as if that skin were somehow his own—a blood tie, a connecting thread of imagined kinship.

He wanted to tell her that people don't always get close just so they can use and abuse you, and he wanted to ask her what had happened to convince her of the contrary, but instead he just kept quiet. He had no intention of opening old wounds just so that he could peer inside.

She was the first to break the silence.

"Has anyone noticed?"

"No, I swear they haven't. I would have heard something otherwise."

Massimo asked her the question he had been pondering for some time now.

"Who else knows, apart from me?"

"Parri and Blue."

He nearly burst out laughing.

"As usual, I'm the last to find out. Why am I even surprised?"

She gave his knee a gentle pat.

"It's not a competition, Marini."

"I could say the same to you. You don't always have to appear indestructible, you know."

"I should have retired months ago, when I would look at you and have no idea who you were, and you would talk, and talk, and talk . . . But instead I've gotten to the stage where I'm touching evidence with my bare hands. Had you already figured it out?"

Massimo felt a lump in his throat.

"I've had my suspicions."

"Since when?"

"A while."

"Anyone else . . . ?"

"No, I told you. Just me."

She pulled herself up into a sitting position. Massimo loosened his grip, giving her the space she needed.

"You need to concentrate on the case, Marini, not waste time with me."

"I disagree, Superintendent."

"When will you ever learn to just say yes and not protest for a change?"

When she decided to trust him completely. Then that yes would be unconditional, both from his side and from hers.

"There's something I'd like to show you. Give me a minute."

He watched her disappear into the room that served as library.

They had all the time in the world, he told himself. And if time decided to be fickle and tried to take her away from him sooner than planned, he would find a way to reel it back. He quickly dried his eyes.

Teresa walked back in, leafing through a thick tome.

"Something's off. The timeline is just too neat. How did the man who presented him with his latest victim even know Giacomo? How did he find him?"

"Are we really going to talk about the case right now?"

She peered at him over the top of her glasses.

"I might forget by tomorrow, Marini."

"Do you have to keep saying things like that?"

She put the tome down on the coffee table.

"It's actually quite liberating. Who would have thought."

Massimo leaned over to examine the book.

"I know this might be heresy, but what if Lona is right? What if Mainardi's stories are just the fabrications of a twisted mind? Maybe there is no mystery caller. Maybe the caller is Mainardi's own psychosis."

He turned a few pages; she flipped them back to where she had placed her bookmark.

"No, Marini, no. You haven't understood."

"Of course not. When do I ever."

"Whoever picked Giacomo's victim for him had already been following his work. They were aware of the things he had done and knew not just who he is, but *what* he is, too. They knew exactly which strings to pull to get what they wanted from him. But even that's not enough. I think it's important that we ask ourselves this: How much mental strength is needed to bend another person's will like that? No coercion. Just the pure and subtle art of persuasion. Is that what's happened here?"

"In theory, anything is possible, but in practice, how many cases of this kind are we aware of?"

Teresa pointed at the pages she had opened the book to.

"Very few. They are rare. And you'll find them all in here. The first we know of involved Sigvard Thurneman, a Swedish psychiatrist. He would use hypnosis to induce his patients to commit homicides. And there's another case you must have heard of: Charles Manson."

Massimo saw the underlined passages, the notes penciled in along the margins.

"Mainardi is a serial killer who has confessed to his crimes. I can't imagine he would need much convincing to kill again."

"And you'd be wrong. Giacomo may be a serial killer, but he's not a hitman. He's not merely interested in killing. He's interested in killing *a specific victim in a specific way*. Yet according to what he has told us, all it took was a single conversation for him to welcome a new participant into his own personal liturgy. I've never seen that happen before. But something just doesn't add up. A mind as sharp as his, beaten so easily at his own game . . ."

"How did Giacomo not suspect a trap? What guarantee could this person or these people have given him?"

He watched her ponder the question, brow furrowed and with the temples of her glasses between her teeth, as always. There were bite marks on the plastic.

"I doubt there were any guarantees on offer, Marini. That

kind of reasoning doesn't tend to feature too prominently in the mental processes of a serial killer. In fact for the more experienced ones—Giacomo among them—the presence of risk adds to the excitement."

"But Mainardi seemed afraid."

"I think he must be a pawn in a much bigger game, and I think the caller must have offered him an opportunity he knew Giacomo could never pass up. Something deeply pertinent to the iconography of Giacomo's inner world, which must have paved the way for the most potent and unspeakable of his fantasies."

"He's told us that already: they presented him with the perfect victim."

"But he could have easily found one himself, no? Maybe this was the perfect target for reasons that go *beyond* the match with his usual victim profile. Perhaps there were *other* reasons—reasons even Giacomo himself hadn't considered, until that moment."

They spoke in unison: "He knew the victim."

Teresa stood up, took a few steps around the room, then sat back down. She was obviously agitated.

"He said he didn't."

Massimo had no choice but to correct her.

"That's not the question you asked him. You said: Can you give me a name?"

She looked stunned.

"Really? Is that what I said?"

"I remember it well because I thought it was odd. It's not like you."

"Not like the *old* me. How sloppy. That's all the opening people like Giacomo need."

"Even so, would you go so far as to rule out the possibility that he might just have lied to you?"

She took a moment to reply.

"No, but for manipulators like him, these little games and omissions are not the same as lying. That is how they absolve themselves."

"So what are we waiting for? Let's go and talk to him."

"It's not that easy. Evil doesn't just cooperate; you have to go and catch it."

"He won't tell us?"

"He won't tell us."

"He's toying with us."

"It's his fantasy, and now we're in it."

"Doesn't he scare you?"

"Who, Giacomo?"

"Yes."

"I don't know, Marini. No, I suppose he doesn't. It's hard to explain, but I don't believe he would ever do anything to hurt me."

"How can you be sure?"

She opened her mouth, then snapped it shut, as if she'd silenced herself with a slap to the cheek.

"I am much more concerned about the person who led him to it. A dangerous individual, capable of orchestrating a campaign of secret conditioning even Giacomo himself is unlikely to be fully aware of. A person of formidable power, mental and organizational, and with an overarching vision that is lucid and rational. And if he really did manage to infiltrate the prison to kill Giacomo's cellmate . . . well, then we have a much bigger problem on our hands than we think we do."

"What you're describing is a power with pervasive reach."

"You can't rule it out."

There was a silence. Teresa closed the book and offered it to him. Massimo took it, but not without stating his conditions.

"I will study this, Superintendent, but that doesn't mean I am willing to forgo your involvement in this investigation."

"You'll have to accept it eventually. Go home now. We both need our rest."

Massimo helped her lie down, and placed a cushion under her feet.

"You know I'm not going anywhere."

"Antonio will be back in a few hours."

"Then I'll go in a few hours. But . . ."

"But?"

"But there's two other people you should talk to about this, don't you think? You always tell us we're your boys, and the bane of your existence. Your affection is amply reciprocated. Don't you want to see them?"

She didn't respond.

"You should do it now, right away. It'll be easier than you think."

Her chest heaved with a sigh. She nodded.

Massimo sent Parisi and de Carli a message, and texted Elena so that she wouldn't worry. Then he took care of Teresa. He placed a plaid shawl over her, dimmed the lights, and put a new CD in the hi-fi. He sat back down among the cushions.

"You and Doctor Parri are good friends."

"Are you jealous?"

"No, just relieved. I'm glad he's part of your life. How did you meet?"

She turned to lie on her side, one hand under her cheek. She closed her eyes.

"Like all best friends do. We were both in some deep shit. We helped clean each other up."

20

Twenty-seven years ago

THE BAR WAS CROWDED. Late breakfasts mixed with early aperitifs, warmed-up croissants jostled with pints of beer turning lukewarm in front of the television. The screen showed a splash of green and lots of tiny, harried-looking figures running around the pitch.

Teresa waded through a variety of scents, some syrupy, others more sour. She recognized him right away, huddled over the counter. She quickened her step and plucked the glass out of his hand.

Antonio Parri glared at her.

"What do you want now?"

"I'll keep taking these away until you stop."

"Why even bother?"

"Because you're the best we have, and together, we can stop him."

He tried to take his glass back.

"The best we have? Fuck off, Inspector."

"I think he is refining his methods in an attempt to arrive at . . . *something*."

"Interesting. Completely meaningless, of course, but interesting."

Teresa grabbed a stool and placed it next to his. She climbed onto it, her jeans pulling at her legs.

"He's learning."

"What exactly is he learning?"

"That's what we need to figure out. Together."

"Sounds like you've reckoned without your host. That's me, by the way. And I'm thirsty."

He reached for the glass, but Teresa moved it away again.

"Any first-time jitters have faded now. He knows he can do it, and the second attempt went much more smoothly. Soon, he'll have another go. But there's one detail I can't explain. The modus operandi can vary at the beginning, and will gradually settle into a tried and tested routine—but the signature never changes. It's connected to the killer's personality. So why take the phalanges from the victim's hand on one occasion, and from the feet on the other?"

"At least it's seven bones in both cases."

"Yes, but . . ."

"Maybe it's the number that matters."

"They're *bones*. Think of the symbolism, the iconography . . . surely they must mean more than that."

He rested his forehead in the palm of his hand, looking drained.

"You should talk to Superintendent Lona about this, not me."

"But you actually listen to me."

"And he doesn't?"

"Albert doesn't listen to anything but the sound of his own voice."

"Have you noticed the way he looks at you?"

"The way he *treats* me."

"Clumsy, perhaps, but ardent, too."

"Misogynistic at best."

Teresa grabbed some nuts from a bowl.

"I've drawn up a profile."

"Just the one?"

"I think he must be around twenty-five years old."

"Now I'm curious. You did tell me you thought he must be young, but how can you be so precise? Assuming any of this makes sense, of course."

"Of course it makes sense. Violent fantasies will first manifest during adolescence. Statistics tell us that it takes an average of eight to ten years before such fantasies manifest as criminal acts. Hence the rule of thumb that the older the victim is, the younger the killer is likely to be: he needs to practice on frailer subjects first—as they will be relatively helpless, and easier to control."

"Any other maxims?"

"Well, since you ask: different perpetrators with similar personalities will commit similar crimes."

"Very impressive."

"Look, I know you don't believe me."

"Oh, really? Give me that goddamned glass."

"I think the killer has been off work for several months now. He's been placed on leave, or he's taken a holiday, or he might have been fired. If he's a student at university, then he must be falling behind in his studies. His attendance is erratic, and his grades are poor."

At last Parri looked interested.

"Why?"

Teresa picked her words carefully.

"He is completely focused on the hunt; there's no room for anything else. He *wants* nothing else."

Parri dropped his head onto the counter, and kept it there.

"He used surgical tape on the first victim; I was going to tell you in the meeting." He seemed to remember something all of a sudden, and glanced at his watch, wiping his hand over his face. "The meeting with Pace and Lona . . . That was meant to be an hour ago."

"Where can one source that kind of tape?"

"We'll have to wait for the latest test results to find out."

Teresa pulled a phone card from her pocket and pointed at the booth outside the toilet.

"Call Doctor Pace's office and apologize. Arrange another meeting as soon as possible."

"Must I?"

"You must."

Teresa popped the nuts into her mouth and nearly gagged. She spat them back out onto a napkin.

Antonio Parri looked at her as if his long-held theory had finally been confirmed.

"You're pregnant. That's why you've stopped smoking."

21

Today

THE CAR CAME TO a stop outside, its headlights shining onto the window. Marini became a black figure silhouetted against the glass.

"They're here."

He kept his back to her until the headlights went off and the quiet neighborhood echoed with the thud of car doors banging shut. Two thumps, one for each of the new arrivals. Only then did Marini turn to look at Teresa.

"Are you sure you want to do this?"

She had been expecting the question, almost felt it taking shape between them—so heavy was the atmosphere now. Marini was offering her one final escape route, ready to cover for her and come up with excuses for de Carli and Parisi, but the time for lies was well and truly over: illness can deprive you of many things, and particularly of the strength to run away.

Teresa was about to reveal all of her weakness and surrender to these young men who would measure what remained of her authority, of that credibility she had always enjoyed but which would be of no use to her in this final stretch of life. Widening her circle of intimacy was not something she normally did, as it was usually other people who welcomed her into their own, but now that the spell was broken, the illusion that she could always be the one to decide who she was and how much she would reveal had been shattered forever, with no way of putting the pieces back together. All she could do was accept the inevitable risk that comes with showing others who we truly are.

"Let them in, Marini."

Teresa remained sitting down, all her burdens still with her, back straight despite the aches, walking stick clasped in her hands and planted on the floor, as if to make the reality of her situation as clear as possible. Once upon a time, she might have thought of it as the sword of an aging warrior queen; now she wasn't even a policewoman anymore.

"I've never used the feminine 'policewoman' before—just 'superintendent.'"

The words came out in a murmur. Marini crouched in front of her.

"I'm one of those who's always called you just that." He smiled, feeling perhaps unsure if he should apologize, or if she had in fact been pleased.

There was a knock on the door, but neither of them took much notice.

"And I never corrected any of you. But I do wonder now . . . Maybe I should have done so. Maybe it was important."

"Important for you?"

Teresa shrugged and looked away, beyond the walls and beyond time. She looked into the past.

"For all the women who came after me. I was one of the first. I've had men serve under me who weren't particularly glad to be there. I suppose I felt the need to shout: 'I've taken what used to be yours alone.' And 'superintendent' seemed to tell my story better."

He touched her hands, which were still clasped around her walking stick.

"Then that's that. That's the way it should be."

"For whom?"

"For you."

"My time is over, Marini. You can tell from this sort of thing, too—which isn't exactly trivial, is it?"

He straightened up.

"Oh no, not this again!"

"You know you're allowed to swear sometimes, don't you?"

"It's not fucking over!" he yelled.

Teresa fell back onto the cushions, arms spread wide, a laugh bubbling in her chest.

"Finally!"

Another knock. This time Marini went to open the door.

"Try to be gentle with them."

"I will."

"Anyway, it's not the first time I've sworn, you know."

"Let's hope it's not the last, either."

De Carli and Parisi walked in.

"Have we interrupted an argument? Do go on; it sounds like fun."

Teresa propped herself up on her elbow.

"Marini was practicing how to swear."

"Why do you all think I'm such a goody two-shoes?"

"Because you are," they chorused.

Teresa took advantage of the carefree moment.

"Take a seat, boys."

They each grabbed a chair and sat down, a little tentatively.

"Is this about the investigation?" asked de Carli.

"It's about the team. Me and you."

"That doesn't sound too good."

She couldn't blame him for thinking that.

"I've probably had my fair share of melodrama, but never in front of an audience, so I'll cut right to the chase." She sat up straight, and muttered: "I have dementia."

They all stared at each other, motionless, in a state of immobility that offered a glimpse of their thoughts slowly crystallizing into shock.

De Carli cleared his throat.

"Did you say you've got influenza?"

"I have Alzheimer's!"

"Oh!"

They lowered their eyes, but not Marini: he was ready to carry the full weight of this with Teresa. She saw him wince, as if to say, *Is this what you call being gentle?* He had a point.

"It's bad, isn't it? I'm sorry to spring it on you like this, but I wouldn't know how else to do it."

Parisi was the first to react.

"I thought you said you had 'hortensia.' Which wouldn't be so bad. Something about the 'intelligentsia' would have been fine, too, come to think of it."

Teresa burst out laughing, and the others followed suit. Marini got to his feet.

"They would both make sense in connection with Superintendent Battaglia. Or should we say *Madam* Superintendent? Anyway, I'm going to make some coffee."

It was as good a way as any of giving de Carli and Parisi some space. Everyone deserved to have whatever time they needed to come to terms—and to blows—with the truth.

But that turned out to be unnecessary. Her boys—*her* boys—moved her to tears by demonstrating the strength she had nurtured within them. They didn't ask her about her illness. It would have been pointless. Perhaps they'd already known; perhaps they'd worked it out. What did it matter now?

"Madam Superintendent? Who came up with that?"

"It's just a couple of extra syllables, de Carli."

"Thank you, Parisi, I don't know what we'd do without your insights."

Teresa spoke again, her words drawing them closer.

"It just occurred to me that the terms we choose have the power to forge new paths. But I'm late to the party, as is often the case. I'm not a superintendent anymore, and no 'madam' superintendent, either."

Parisi stood up. Like her, he, too, seemed to find it difficult to sit still when everything around them was falling apart faster than they could keep up.

"Does that mean you're leaving us?"

"I will never leave you."

"But what about work?"

"I can't continue."

De Carli slapped his hands against his knees.

"So you're ditching us!"

"I'm not ditching *you*. I'm quitting my job."

"It's the same thing. We'll always be on your side. You should be on ours."

Teresa relinquished her remaining fear. She had to let go of some of her love, too, if she wanted to free them.

"I would put you at risk, and I would put potential victims at risk, too, when the whole point is that I'm supposed to protect them. I want to be present for as long as possible, and that means that everything needs to change; I can't just keep living the way I used to."

"Before long the violets will bloom by the crumbling wall," Georg Trakl had written. That was what she hoped for, if not for her present then at least for the future she was handing over to these young men. Her team, this team—they were her family. A family that could sometimes be problematic, and was certainly atypical, but also reliably tight-knit and supportive. She would always be part of it: she would survive in their memories, in their shared experiences, in the lessons she had taught them.

"This chapter of my life is over, boys. The sooner we all accept that, the sooner we'll be able to find a place from which to start anew."

Had she really said that? Did she really believe it? Even she didn't know. All Teresa wanted was to soothe the quivering anguish she could feel radiating from their bodies, and erase the confusion in their faces, which were flushed with the effort it took to suppress their emotions. They were afraid. Whether for her or for themselves, she did not know, but once again it fell to Teresa to guide them. So she armed herself with that matter-of-fact tone with which she usually tackled complications.

"Listen to me. This is important. You need to dig deeper into this case."

De Carli buried his face in his hands.

"I can't believe it! Are you really going to talk about the case at a time like this?"

"Yes. And so should you, if you want to spare me any further heartache, and if you truly want to help me. Got it?"

No one replied. Perhaps she was expecting too much too soon. That night, in this house, they had suffered a loss, and they were still grieving for it. But Teresa was still alive and breathing, and she would continue to do what she was best at until her last lucid moment.

"A serial killer uses symbols and rituals to paint an ideal tableau, but in this instance, someone else was also involved—and lo and behold, the killer's signature changed. Why? Why the tooth? For the first time ever, Giacomo did not just use tiles he chiseled himself. There must be a significance to that. Something must have changed in the story he's been writing in blood for nearly thirty years now."

Marini came in with a tray of coffee for everyone. He had been listening to the conversation from the kitchen.

"He's been in prison for twenty-seven years. Maybe that's what changed him."

"A picture of tranquillity, yes, but in his fantasies, he's never stopped killing."

Teresa took her cup of coffee and a bag of artificial sweetener. There was no way she was sleeping tonight anyway.

"From his point of view, he's told us everything we need to know."

"He's toying with us, Superintendent."

"True. But he's given us a great help. He could have easily said nothing at all."

"When will you stop defending him?"

"Sometimes we need to defend the Beast, too, Marini, and try to remember the child that every monster once was. I'm showing you an alternative perspective on the facts."

De Carli quickly downed the coffee Parisi had turned down with a shake of his head.

"Why did he help us, though? What's your read on it?"

Teresa had been wondering the same ever since it had all begun again.

"Some kind of twisted gamble? A yearning for vindication? A hypertrophic ego?" She looked down at the cup cradled in her hands. The spoon made a brief clinking sound. "An attempt to recompose the past, perhaps. A past I, too, was once part of."

"So this is how you leave us, with a riddle to solve?"

"I'm not going anywhere. I'll be right here whenever you need me."

"It's not the same."

Teresa put her cup down.

"I'm afraid we're going to have to get used to it whether we like it or not, de Carli."

Parisi had been the only one who hadn't said another word, standing with his back against the wall and his arms crossed over his chest.

The ensuing silence drew Teresa's gaze to him. He'd been watching her throughout. And they'd both just had the same thought.

"Are you going to tell them now, Superintendent?"

Marini snapped.

"Tell us what, exactly? I think I've had enough announcements for one evening."

Teresa already knew she would have to calm him down.

He was far too protective to take the news with any kind of equanimity.

"A few days ago, I asked Parisi to make some private inquiries. We will need a little more time to hear the full results."

Those few words were enough to transform Marini's expression.

"When you say *private*, I assume you mean unofficial."

"Let's just call it a preliminary investigation."

"On whom?"

Leaning on her walking stick, Teresa stood up and went to the window to stare into the night. The answer burned inside her; she let it out, a breath of fire into the shadows.

"On Blanca. She's not who she says she is."

22

Twenty-seven years ago

ON THE PAGES OF a calendar hidden in one of the drawers in her office at home, Teresa had mapped out her future in red felt-tip pen.

It had been a long time since that calendar had seen any daylight, so long that she could picture the red ink gradually fading away.

Once upon a time, those dates had sung of her triumphs, but what had once been an ode to victory had since faded into a torturous lament.

The superintendents' exam was imminent, but Teresa hadn't registered yet. She was nearly thirty-two; if she let another year go by, she would lose the opportunity forever.

She didn't feel ready. She would never feel ready. Her doubts increasingly felt like certainties. She did not believe herself capable of managing a team, of leading an investigation. She wasn't even capable of making her voice heard, of sounding authoritative. Sometimes she even doubted the effectiveness of the empirical methods she'd been testing out in the field.

And now there was the baby to think about, too. The new life growing inside of her was filling spaces that had been previously empty, and had already begun to change her, to smooth out her sharpest edges—those same edges she so desperately needed if she was to make her way in the world.

So much fear, and so much wonder. She was so nervous she could hardly breathe.

She had to protect her son and look after him; she had to tell his father about him, or else keep them apart forever. She had to run away, or stay and try—in vain, for she knew nothing would change—to bring the old Sebastiano back.

But maybe that "before" she thought she could return to had never existed in the first place. Maybe it had all been an illusion, and the evil in him had emerged from the heat of their marital bed even as she dreamed of a new dawn that would never arrive.

She was about to become a mother, but she also wanted to be a superintendent. She would have to rethink her daily routines, figure out how to welcome a baby into her life while she also worked on the report she intended to submit to Pace, with or without Albert's support. She needed to find a way to write about mutilated bones just as new bones were beginning to form in the dark, floating depths of her womb.

And what if this baby grew up to be like his father, with no light in his eyes? What if every time she touched him, her skin resurfaced the bruises she'd suffered, so that she couldn't help but keep the child at arm's length and deny him her love?

Teresa had to master her thoughts as she did her nausea, even though they sometimes merged into the same tangled mess.

She placed her palm on her belly, cupping her hand as if to bear a weight, or cradle it.

Soon she would be a single woman, and a single mother, with no family to stand with her. This was the moment to gather her courage.

All she had to do was take that first step out the door. A few more steps, one foot in front of the other, and she would finally be able to say she was "elsewhere," the past already behind her.

She picked up the handset and dialed a number from memory. Lavinia picked up after a couple of rings. Teresa didn't even give her friend the chance to offer the usual greetings.

"I need to see you, Lavinia. Could you come over, please?"

"Now? What's happened?"

"Nothing, but can you come? I need to talk to you."

Lavinia was the only person who had survived the scorching desert of human connection that Sebastiano had painstakingly created around Teresa. Lavinia was her friend and her sister-in-law. She had been the one to introduce her to Sebastiano. Like the rest of their family, she had embraced the medical profession, and like her twin brother, she had chosen to delve into the human mind; he had become a psychiatrist, while she was a psychologist.

Teresa had lost track of how many times she had asked herself whether Lavinia would be willing to help her. She still didn't know the answer, but something told her that her time was running out. She had to ask for help. If not for herself, then for Sebastiano.

"At least tell me what's the matter, Teresa. You don't sound like yourself. Are you unwell?"

"It's not me."

"Then who?"

"It's . . . Sebastiano."

"Sebastiano is sick?"

Yes. Yes.

"Teresa?"

Sebastiano was right there, staring at her. He'd arrived without a sound, as if moving at the farthest reaches of other people's perception were no longer merely a habit, but an unalterable aspect of his being. There was something predatory in his behavior—something nocturnal.

Teresa mumbled into the receiver.

"It's not urgent. I'll call you back." She hung up, ignoring Lavinia's questions.

"Who was it?"

"Lavinia."

"Was she the one who called?"

Telling him the truth was no longer a virtue, but a necessity. Who could say how much he'd heard?

"No, I did. I called her."

"Why?"

"I just . . . I just needed to talk to someone."

He spread his arms.

"Here I am."

Teresa felt a tingling in her belly, a gentle tremor running through her womb and making her skin quiver.

"So? Why aren't you talking?"

"I forgot my notebook in the office. I should go back and get it. I have to finish this report."

Sebastiano stood in her path.

"There's obviously something else you want to finish. Our relationship. Is that what you were about to tell Lavinia?"

"No!"

"No?"

"Let me through, Sebastiano."

"So this is how you talk to me now?"

He raised his hand in that gesture she had come to know far too well, its shadow falling onto her, corrupting her even before the blow.

Teresa said the only thing she thought might save her.

She spoke the words, and the moment she had uttered them, she realized she had made a mistake she would never be able to forgive herself for.

"I'm pregnant."

23

Today

MASSIMO LEFT TO GO home, feeling troubled.

He was returning to the warmth of his partner's embrace and to their plans for the future, but in doing so he was leaving *her* behind. Teresa Battaglia had barely spared him a glance when she had ordered him to go home to Elena, but he had learned by now that her tough exterior was her way of protecting herself, and that the indifference she affected was a symptom of pain. Massimo knew he'd already lodged himself in her heart—and he had no intention of letting go.

"I need to go now, but I'll be back."

"I know you will. I just can't seem to get rid of you."

Her comment might as well have been the world's greatest declaration of love. It was the perfect illustration of what their relationship looked like on the surface: a constant tug of war that might've worn anyone else out, but not them. So it was that their two lives, seemingly so different, could come within touching distance, each looking into the darkest depths of the other, and recognizing their own reflection within. Yet Massimo was afraid that he would not be able to keep her by his side, sharing everyday life. It was Parisi and de Carli who'd stayed behind with her—not him. It was Parri who was going to visit her later—not him.

A protective shield had been erected around her, and Massimo was not its strongest link.

He'd had to choose, and he had made his choice—but boy, did it hurt.

Then there was Blanca, who wasn't even Blanca, but a stranger who'd earned Teresa Battaglia's love and trust, only to turn around and betray her. A mystery within the mystery, this young woman who could trace dead people's final moments on earth. The past that needed revealing now was Blanca's own.

But yet again, the superintendent had soothed their fraying tempers. It didn't seem to bother her that she'd been deceived; who knew what backstory she'd already managed to glimpse in Blanca's lies about her identity? And so, prevented from doing what his instincts commanded him to do, Massimo remained on high alert.

When he got home, Elena flew toward him, her feet sliding over the hallway parquet.

Before she could even say a word, he picked her up in his arms and kissed her.

Instead of putting her back down, he carried her all the way to the living room. The lamp by the sofa was on, and the carpet was covered with the textbooks she persisted in studying even now that she had lost her once-in-a-lifetime job. Her hair was gathered in a chignon held in place by a pen. The knot unraveled in an auburn wave.

He put her down among the pillows.

"Isn't it dangerous to run around like that?"

Elena moved a tome from underneath her head, a volume entitled *Death and Burial in the New Kingdom of Egypt*.

"I've been sitting around all day. I might turn into one of these mummies soon."

But her belly was filling out, her cheeks were pink from the early summer sun, and to Massimo, she had never looked more alive. He lay on top of her, taking care not to crush her.

"I'd rather have some waxy old corpse than a fresh one."

Her eyes widened, but she did not let go.

"Now that's what I call poetry, Inspector Marini."

"You're missing your work."

"I've missed you."

"Seriously, though. Don't you miss the museum?"

"I'll find another job."

"Hmm. I may be wrong, but I don't think there's that many mummies around here."

"Apart from you, I suppose?"

Massimo slid to the floor and rested his face against her belly, listening for the sound of a second heart beating inside.

Elena stroked his shoulders.

"So? Did Teresa tell you?"

"I guess you could say she had no choice but to confess."

"*Confess!* What a terrible word."

"It was pretty awful, Elena. It's . . . it's what I thought it might be. She has Alzheimer's."

Her fingertips pressed into his flesh, but the tension in his muscles didn't seem to want to let go.

"I can't tell you how sorry I am. You want to be by her side."

"I want to be here, *and* I want to be by her side. That's the problem." He looked up at her. "Sorry."

"Don't apologize. I know how much she means to you."

Massimo kissed the palm of her hand, ran it over his face, breathed in her scent.

"She saved me from myself, Elena. Without her help, my father's ghost would still be haunting me. If there is an *us*, we owe it to her."

"And it's your turn to help her now. You need to do something concrete. There's no time to waste."

"She's got others with her."

"But she'll need everyone she has—especially you."

Massimo hoped it was true.

"Solving this latest case would be a good start. I know it would mean a great deal to her to be able to tie up all the loose ends before she makes her exit."

"So do it! Solve the case!"

Massimo rolled onto his back and started laughing, Elena's hand still firmly clasped in his own.

"I'll do my best, that's for sure."

She propped herself up on her elbow.

"How is the investigation going? I didn't get the chance to ask you on the phone, and you were in such a hurry when I last saw you."

He unbuttoned his shirt and kicked off his shoes. He could feel the weight of all the exhaustion he'd accumulated. He ran his hand over his face, his jaw still marked with bruises from the last case he'd dealt with.

"We've made some progress, but only because he wanted us to. It's maddening."

"You mean the killer wanted you to?"

"Yes. He told us where to find something he'd taken from the victim."

"Archaeologists work with corpses all the time, you know."

"Yes, but mummies aren't quite so gross."

"Oh go on, tell me. What did you find?"

"Mosaic tiles made out of human bones."

"How creative."

"You would have liked it, though. We saw this incredible crypt . . ."

She sat up straighter when she heard the word *crypt*.

"It was inside a church. In Aquileia. Just a random village. You'd never know there was . . ."

". . . the largest and oldest paleo-Christian mosaic pavement in Europe, previously buried for 1,500 years."

Her voice had nearly cracked.

"Indeed. And where did he go and put his tiles? Picture this place, some gloomy old crypt, light and shadows playing off each other, mosaics everywhere, and this massive bell tower sprouting out of nowhere and spoiling half the floor."

"Not half. A third."

"And right there, in the furthest corner, there's this little white rabbit, which has somehow escaped the belfry steps. There: that's where he put them."

"A *rabbit?*" She looked disgusted. "A *hare*, Massimo. A hare."

"Does it make a difference? Anyway, it's weird. It's all really weird. This guy turning himself in, confessing, confiding in Superintendent Battaglia and leading her all the way to that spot."

"Do you think the killer might have been studying the early Egyptian Christian community of Aquileia?"

"The what?"

"The path might not be accidental. He must have followed the Gnostic trail. Is that your theory, too?"

"What on earth . . ."

"You have to take me there!"

"Absolutely not. You need to . . ."

Elena straddled him and grabbed his shirt.

"Stay at home? Just because I'm pregnant?"

"No. *Obviously* not. But your condition is very delicate."

Massimo realized that he'd unwittingly raised his hands in surrender. He quickly brought them back down.

"Delicate my ass. I'm just pregnant!"

He saw her expression shift. No, that wasn't right: it was her strategy that was shifting. And she was about to land on a much better one.

Elena got back up and started tidying up her books as if nothing had happened.

"I suppose the hare is depicted in the act of eating a grape. An act, I should note, which does not occur in nature."

"How did you . . . Yes."

"And its eyes are red."

This time Massimo didn't even bother to answer. It wasn't a question, anyway.

Elena looked at him.

"Of course you already know that the hare you saw is the *Unnefer*, yes?" She placed her hand over her mouth in a show of surprise which could not have been more affected. "Oh. You didn't know. What a shame."

Massimo could hardly believe his ears.

"You've got me cornered, haven't you?"

"I have."

24

IV Century

THE LEGIONNAIRE'S CLOAK TRAILED across the polychromatic mosaic floor. The letters Chi and Rho formed the Chrismon, the seal of the new and only god, yet the monogram for Christ coexisted with effigies of beasts and mythical monsters hearkening back to a time when the smoke from sacred incense would rise toward a sky teeming with gods in the guise of animals.

In the torchlight, all those figures made of pearlescent tiles seemed ready to bare their fangs.

At the entrance to the second chamber, Lusius found Cyriac's servant, a poised young man with dark skin and dark hair, and the slender build and thick neck characteristic of the Samnites.

"Where is your master?"

"I have no master."

Christians. Specifically, it was the Gnostics that Lusius wished to reach out to. They, too, were concerned about the intransigence that some of their own brothers had begun to display in their insistence on the strictest observance of the rites. Sooner or later, the Fanatīcus would openly turn against every other cult there was.

"Cyriac is expecting me."

"Your weapon."

Lusius handed it over. The youth gave him an oil lamp, then nudged the curtains aside and gestured toward a dark corridor that led to the second chamber. His eyes were restless, darting away every time they landed on the gleam of Lusius's breastplate.

"Your hands are shaking, Christian. Does Rome frighten you?"

"I gave my cloak to Cyriac. He fears the chill of this land."

Lusius took the oil lamp and walked down the passageway. The toughened leather of his sandals clacked against the clay tiles and lime-based plaster of the opus signinum floor. Work on the new pavements had only just been completed, and the leftover sand had yet to be swept away.

A second curtain of pure-white wool stood between him and the mystic chamber. It looked like it had been cut out of an old toga. Roman norms required spotless garments, and clothing was washed so often that the fabric would eventually fray, its fibers acquiring a burnished sheen. Lusius recognized that sheen. But eventually, convenience had trumped decorum, and as the poet Juvenal had pointed out with caustic irony, no one in the Empire wore togas anymore except for the dead, who were buried in them.

He felt the urge to tear the cloth from where it did not belong, drape it over his shoulders, and bring Rome some measure of revenge against these calamitously changing times. But instead he merely pushed it aside with a gentle swipe of his battle-roughened hand.

The chamber welcomed him with the iridescent glimmer of flaming oil lamps. The path toward gnosis that lay at his feet, and which the ideal devotee was called upon to discover, struck him anew with the power of the mystery it had been created to depict.

Once more, he was being admitted into that sacred place normally reserved for the chosen few. Cyriac trusted him, and Lusius had learned to reciprocate the Christian's feelings. He believed in the dialogue this man from the Orient was seeking to establish with him and with those Lusius had been called upon to represent: a legion devoted to a faith which—like Cyriac's Gnostic Christianity—now constituted an engendered minority.

The chamber was empty, the incense unlit, the room half engulfed in shadows.

"Cyriac?"

A soft splash shook the waters of the baptismal font where Christians immersed themselves to be born again unto the light. A bronze polycandelon swayed above the basin, its rocking nearly imperceptible. Its twelve arms bore the symbols Alpha and Omega and the monogram of Christ, but the candles had been snuffed out, plunging the room into darkness.

Lusius stepped closer, raising his oil lamp. He saw red water and glassy eyes, and heard the last breath of a dying man.

He dropped his lamp, grabbed Cyriac by the shoulders, and pulled him out of the water. Cyriac's throat had been split open.

It was the night of Ceres, Lusius remembered—one of those dies religiosi when the goddess's pit was opened in ritual celebration, revealing the fearsome mundus Cereris, which served as a gateway between the worlds of the living and the dead, and through which the latter could drag the former down into their underground realm. And so Ceres became Mother of Specters, just as Isis was Mother of the Night.

Cyriac would not rise again.

"It's over."

Lusius turned around.

He recognized the man who had spoken and who stood before

him now, flanked by a pair of torch-bearing centurions. His chiseled bronze breastplate gleamed with power, and his purple cloak denoted his membership of the senatorial order. Lusius also knew the figure who stood further back, engulfed in shadows. He was a Christian priest who belonged to the Church of Clement. He was said to have labeled Cyriac and his people as the "sacrilegious" progeny of Mary Magdalene, and to have called the Jews "betrayers of Christ."

The tribune who seemed to be protecting the priest spoke again.

"Give me what you are hiding, Lusius, and you shall be allowed to return to your comrades."

Lusius rested Cyriac's head on the floor. His new friend was gone. He prayed that the god Cyriac worshipped might truly exist, and show the dead man mercy.

He stood up, the Istrian marble of the baptismal font pressing against the back of his legs and reminding him that there was no escape—though running away was not something he had ever contemplated.

"Do you speak for the Senate or for yourself?" he asked.

"I will not repeat my offer."

"When did Rome start killing its own sons to pander to the whims of others?"

The tribune smiled.

"We are all children of the same god now. Didn't you hear?"

"I am a son of Rome."

The tribune lifted his arms wide.

"And I stand before you, representing Rome, to welcome you back to the fold. As long as you give me what I want."

"What you want, or what the man standing behind you commands?"

The smile vanished.

"I didn't come here to negotiate, Lusius."

Lusius had hoped until the very end that Calida Lupa's fears and those of so many pagans would turn out to be unfounded, but that hope was disappearing now, mixing with Cyriac's blood in the baptismal water.

But he had also made sure not to face his destiny unprepared. He was a soldier of the Empire after all, and of the mighty-winged goddess.

The bundle was inside his armor, flush against his chest. He pulled it out and spread his fingers wide, presenting it to his audience. It was wrapped in the golden, impalpable fibers of the finest byssus.

At a signal from the tribune, one of the soldiers took the bundle and untied the knot holding it together.

The light from the torches illuminated a small, shapeless piece of wood.

Lusius's laugh echoed among the stones and marbles of the chamber, down the dead man's throat, and in the frightened viscera of those who had sacrificed his life.

The tribune unsheathed his sword.

"You will die."

"So be it."

Lusius would die, but his death would serve to uncover the true face of the enemy. Others would benefit from the revelation.

The tribune pressed his blade against Lusius's neck. The centurions pulled at the strings that held his armor together, and let it clatter to the floor.

"Where is the figurine?"

Lusius's stare pinned the tribune to the full responsibility of what he was about to do.

"She of many names is also known as Amentet, the hidden one. We have been expecting you, and you will not find her."

The blade pushed into Lusius's exposed ribs, then drew back, blood gushing in its wake.

Lusius fell to his knees, his eyes rolling up toward the arched, shadowy ceiling to find arcane constellations and godly designs which ordinary men could never comprehend. The mosaics absorbed the warmth of his ebbing life, and took on a bright vermillion hue.

He dragged himself across the floor, fingernails finding purchase on various mysterious figures until he reached the octagonal frame that held the one image he had recognized immediately, and interpreted correctly.

He brought his forehead close to the creature with a white coat and red eyes, handing himself over to death and to the god staring at him through the animal's dilated pupil. He had one final warning to the men who were responsible for his agony.

"The might of Solomon is nothing against the Hare. And you—you are all powerless."

25

———◦∞◦———

Twenty-seven years ago

AS SHE LAY IN Sebastiano's arms that night, feeling more alone than ever after telling him she was pregnant, Teresa realized that there was nothing more that could be done for him. He was made purely of darkness now. She had understood this from his reaction, from the glint of triumph she had glimpsed in his expression. There had been no signs of happiness, no tears of joy. Only smug satisfaction, and a comment that had chilled her to the bone: "You'll have to skip the exam and devote yourself completely to your new life."

What kind of new life could he possibly conceive for her, other than one of captivity and submission? And it would have been no different for their child, either.

Control. That was all he wanted. Sebastiano was so fragile that he had begun to fall apart the moment Teresa had set out on a path of her own, carving out increasingly wider swaths of autonomy.

Teresa was no longer the impressionable young woman she'd been at the start of their relationship. She had learned to see beyond his refined mannerisms, to look past the exceptional erudition he liked to flaunt so as not to let anyone glimpse what lay in the depths beneath. And that was something Sebastiano simply could not tolerate.

Whatever steps she took next, she had to be cautious. Sebastiano would rather tear her apart than let her go and admit he had failed.

At dawn, Teresa carefully nudged Sebastiano's sleeping form away from her own, making sure not to awaken the beast.

She went to headquarters first to pick up her notebook and jot down the report she had been thinking about all night, after Sebastiano had finally fallen asleep and stopped planning her future for her.

Teresa stapled the pages together, still warm from the photocopier. She'd have to make do without the usual cover sheet and binding. She placed the copies inside an envelope and tucked it into her shoulder bag. She stepped out into the corridor and nearly crashed into one of her colleagues.

"Is Superintendent Lona in?"

"I haven't seen him."

Teresa looked inside Albert's office. It was empty and extremely tidy, but his car keys were on his desk.

She stopped another officer.

"Lona?"

"You're always one step behind, Battaglia. He's already left."

Teresa checked the time. It wasn't even nine o'clock, and she'd been there since seven-thirty. Her colleague seemed to guess what she was thinking.

"While you were busy sleeping, he's been here all night working on the report for Pace."

"But the meeting's in an hour. We're supposed to go together."

She did not like the smile on the officer's face.

"Wake up, Battaglia."

Teresa felt a sense of foreboding. She ran toward the elevator, but when she saw that it was occupied, she sprinted down the stairs, the sound of laughter following her.

Another trap, another trick. Would she ever be able to shrug off the feeling that she could not trust these men—or any man at all, for that matter? Would the rage she felt ramming against her chest transform her into a different woman, and change her for the worse?

She went to the security cabin and requested a car. The guard didn't even look up from his logbook.

"Superintendent Lona took it."

"Then call for another."

He pushed a sheet of paper toward her through the gap in the screen.

"There was only supposed to be one car. You're going to have to fill out this form."

"Fuck the form! I need a car now!"

Teresa couldn't believe she'd actually shouted. She was even more astonished than the guard. Gasping for air, she scrunched up the form and ran out onto the street, nausea dogging her every step. She rifled through her pockets for some sweets and popped two into her mouth. The sour fruitiness did the trick.

She felt like crying, and cursing, and shouting again. She could call a taxi, but she'd have to retrace her steps to do so, and she had no intention of going back into the office and dealing with her colleagues' sarcastic remarks.

She hopped onto the first bus that passed, its doors huffing as they opened. She had to change buses twice before she finally managed to reach the courthouse, her stomach roiling from the smells and from the endless stop-starts along the way.

By the time she had climbed up the stairs to the public prosecutor's office, she was flushed and disheveled. As she pushed the door open, she realized she hadn't even knocked. Doctor Pace, Albert, and Doctor Parri were all staring at her. Albert was feigning calm. Parri looked concerned. Pace was inscrutable.

"I'm so sorry."

Elvira the Witch was sitting at her desk, looking even more elegant than usual.

"Is it your tardiness or your manners that you're apologizing for, Inspector?"

The prosecutor's tone was brusque, but Teresa thought she detected the hint of a smile in it.

She stepped forward.

"For both, Doctor Pace."

"Superintendent Lona requested yesterday that the meeting be moved to an earlier time. Were you not warned?"

Albert spoke up.

"I tried to reach Inspector Battaglia several times last night, but I could not get through. I would have left a message, but her answering machine didn't seem to be on."

Prosecutor Pace glanced at Teresa, who nodded in confirmation.

She had heard the phone ring as she lay in Sebastiano's

arms. Albert had called nine times before Teresa's husband had unplugged the telephone. All Teresa could do was silently cry for help, as if the vibrations of her fear could travel through the telephone line and reach whoever was at the other end.

Sebastiano hadn't touched her, but somehow the calmness in his demeanor had been more terrifying than any form of physical violence, for it had made her wonder what thoughts he must be turning over in his mind.

"It's true."

Pace motioned at Teresa to sit on the chair that had been readied for her.

"Perhaps next time you ought to drop by your colleague's house in person when an appointment with the public prosecutor is moved, Doctor Lona—don't you think?"

Albert blushed.

"Of course, Doctor Pace."

Elvira's gaze flashed toward Teresa.

"Though needless to say, we all hope that will not be necessary."

In that flash of a look, Teresa saw Pace's eyes pause on her cheek, where the bruise seemed determined not to fade, and instead turned more purple and more obvious with every passing day. It did not wish to hide, and it refused to be hidden.

Elvira had figured it out. She was telling Albert that he could help Teresa if he wanted to. She was telling Teresa that she could be saved.

Teresa watched her close the folder with the case file.

"Well, I suppose that's all. You'll keep me updated. Doctor Lona, do make sure to apprise Doctor Battaglia of what we have discussed."

Teresa gathered her courage and pulled out the file from her shoulder bag, ignoring Parri's silent admonition.

"I'd like to submit a report, too, Doctor Pace."

"I've already received a report."

"I've just finished writing it. You will find some considerations on the objective facts of the case, but with some new investigative methods applied—psychological and statistical. Here . . ."

"This is your work?"

"Yes."

Elvira held out her hand. Teresa gave her the stapled documents and thought of how the prosecutor's perfumed fingers, laden with rings, would spend the next few hours leaving their mark all over those pages. Prosecutor Pace did not seem to notice the unembellished presentation. Or perhaps she did notice, but didn't care. She skimmed through the report with rapid efficiency, her brow furrowed.

"Doctor Battaglia."

"Yes?"

Pace lifted her gaze—but it wasn't Teresa she was looking at. It was Albert. She kept her eyes fixed on him as she spoke.

"Doctor Battaglia, the contents and conclusions of your report are essentially identical to those Doctor Lona submitted earlier. I was very pleased to read those, and I am impatient to see them applied in the field."

Teresa was looking at Albert, too, now. Her bewilderment quickly turned to scorn. He had taken her notes and passed them off as his own work. With his back to the wall, and caught in the impasse of a difficult case, Albert had betrayed her, and sacrificed her professional reputation.

Teresa didn't say another word. She kept staring at him

even after Pace handed her report back and got to her feet, followed by the others. Parri leaned toward Teresa.

"I'll wait for you outside," he whispered.

The prosecutor said nothing more about the matter. She picked up her bag, mentioned something about needing her second cigarette for the day, and let them know they were dismissed.

The room emptied, but Teresa did not move from her chair.

She only realized she wasn't alone anymore because Elvira's perfume preceded her every step. She'd returned.

Elvira came to stand in front of Teresa, the backs of her thighs leaning against the desk. She tapped an unlit cigarette three times against her bag.

"You may have lost today, Teresa, but that doesn't mean you should just sit there and take it. Remember the rage you're feeling now: it'll help you fight any feelings of guilt you might experience when you are the one wielding the power. As I have no doubt you will someday."

Teresa looked up.

Elvira rifled through her bag and took out some foundation.

"The one you're wearing now is the wrong shade. It actually brings out the purple more." She placed the makeup in Teresa's hand. "Try this one instead. And then get rid of that bastard."

26

Today

ONCE AGAIN THE CRYPT of the basilica opened up for Massimo, but now it wasn't Teresa Battaglia standing by his side.

Elena squeezed his hand.

"This is unreal!"

She had tried to keep her voice down to a murmur, but it came out sounding more like a squeak, so much so that the watchman turned around to look. He sat down near the entrance to the crypt and shifted his attention back to his phone. After all, there was nothing much for him to keep an eye on, as the visitors weren't planning to touch the mosaic floor this time.

Dressed in a white cotton dress that grazed her ankles, Elena shivered, her feet nearly on top of each other.

"Are you cold?"

"It's not the cold."

There was something about the way she said it. It was

love—love for the past, for the people who had dwelt in it and sung in praise of their god, for the tiles placed there by hardworking hands, and for every trace of color that had remained stubbornly attached to its square of plaster over the course of so many centuries. Massimo encouraged her to step forward.

"It's all yours."

Elena lifted her hands in the air.

"Can you feel that wind? An underground current. To keep the relics well-preserved."

"I don't really know anything about it, I'm afraid. I don't have much to say, other than how pretty it is."

Elena turned around.

"That's because no one's ever explained it to you."

"Why don't you have a go?"

Elena was standing under a spotlight, her cinnamon-colored hair like a golden veil cascading to her waist.

She stretched out her arm.

"That way lies the Orient, the rising sun. The first light of dawn would filter through the windows and fall upon the faithful. Imagine their awe, the potency of that ritual, the water inside the ellipsoidal baptismal font glittering in the light."

The font was nothing but a pile of rocks now.

Elena took a few steps forward.

"But the real treasure, Massimo, lies beneath our feet. A path of initiation whose full meaning remains a mystery to this day."

"A path of initiation?"

"Every figure you see here relates to all the others, and together they compose a majestic vision. These mosaics are in part an iconographic representation of the *Pistis Sophia*, a Gnostic text written in the Coptic language, and dating back to the third century. The followers of the Gnostic faith were dissident Christians who probably came here from Alexandria to evade the censorship of the Church Fathers. The four volumes of the *Pistis Sophia* were later understood to form part of a much more extensive Gnostic library, after the discovery in 1945 of the thirteen codices of Nag Hammadi found buried in a jar by two shepherd brothers."

"What did the codices contain?"

"Revelations. The words Jesus Christ left behind for his apostles in the eleven years he spent with them after his resurrection."

"*After* his resurrection? That's a little alarming."

"It alarmed orthodox Christians, too. By the fourth century, Christianity had become a *religio licita*, made legal through edicts issued by Galerius and Constantine. This was before the ecumenical councils, so there were still several different currents within it, many of which—from a doctrinal point of view—were often in conflict with one another. There were those who argued for a simpler faith, fearing that sophistry could lead to cheap heresies. But others were eager to preserve the philosophic and mystic precepts they had also found in Alexandrian Hellenism and in various esoteric, astrologically inclined Egyptian cults. So it was that orthodox Christians, supporters of the Great Church, began persecuting not just pagans, but their own Gnostic brothers, too, whom they quickly labeled 'heretics.'"

"Were they seen as a threat to the Christian faith?"

"Gnostics were Christians who encouraged the study of philosophy, but also the pursuit of esoteric learning. In their view, it was *gnosis*, or knowledge, that led one to God—not passive acquiescence to dogma. They did not embrace faith blindly, but sought instead to investigate its mysteries. And what we have here beneath our feet is the path to that knowledge."

"I can't see it."

"Gnosis was all about exploring mysteries. It required serious study, and adherence to a path of initiation that would lead to illumination. You would have to undertake a lengthy catechumenate before you earned the right to be admitted to this chamber."

Massimo leaned over the balustrade, peering at the figures in search of a trail his thoughts might be able to follow, but he couldn't find anything, and immediately felt lost.

"Keep going."

"Alexandria of Egypt had been the cradle of Hellenism, but even that great city was soon aflame. Orthodox Christians began to practice the same persecution they themselves had endured. Numerous intellectuals were excommunicated. Near the end of the fourth century, the library was destroyed. Some years later, the pagan philosopher, astronomer, and mathematician Hypatia was killed and dismembered. Her remains were dragged through the streets. By the second century, the Gnostics had already begun to scatter. They crossed the Mediterranean Sea and reached the port of Aquileia. They were hoping for a new beginning. The Christian community in this imperial city described itself as descending from Alexandria, and had thus always been characterized by an atmosphere of unparalleled intellectual freedom. It was a commingling of peoples and faiths."

"I guess things didn't quite go according to plan."

"We can't really be sure, but what we do know is that there's no trace left of them outside of this room."

"So they were wiped out."

"Either converted, or exterminated."

Elena lowered herself to her knees and spread her hands over the transparent walkway.

"The Gnostic is the perfect Christian; through the path to knowledge, he is transfigured into Christ and turns to Light. *Returns* to Light, in fact, reconnecting with the origin of everything. And this happens not in the afterlife, but right here on earth, on this very plane of existence. Man *is* Christ. And the path of initiation that believers must undertake in order to rediscover man's divine lineage and transform into 'men of light'—gods within God—is laid out right here in front of our eyes."

Massimo moved closer.

"Here among these animals?"

"They are symbols. This is an initiation ritual. Nothing is as it seems. The orthodox Christians of the Great Church could never accept it. Gnostic texts like the *Pistis Sophia* rested on magical elements of Egyptian derivation—not to mention that as far as the Gnostics were concerned, the perfect apostle was Mary Magdalene, the seeker, and Judas was the only one who had actually fulfilled Jesus's wishes, helping him return to the Pleroma, the realm of divine totality. The Gnostics believed in the equality of men and women, in the futility of martyrdom, and in the reincarnation of the soul, which could thus return to complete a path left unfinished. The wrathful, selfish, vindictive god of the Old Testament was, to them, a minor deity, embedded in the material world: the creator and demiurge who barred

Adam from access to knowledge and thus to transfiguration. Ultimately it is Eve and the Serpent who free Adam from deceit—and are thus redeeming figures. Eve is the vessel for Zoe—Life itself."

Massimo peered into the universe Elena was illustrating for him, but he couldn't quite see it yet.

She kept walking, leaning forward as she went.

"In the outermost sphere, we find the Hebdomad. The demiurge and his three hundred and sixty archons oversee a shadow world in which they hold souls captive, barring their ascent to Illumination. Their battlefields are the planetary spheres which divide the visible world from the Pleroma. Above them are five great archons tasked with blocking the way for souls. Look, you can see them right here in the third nook, residing in that celestial sphere, which Jesus, speaking to Mary Magdalene after his resurrection, described as 'the Midst.'"

Beneath the walkway, a series of mosaics depicted a bright-red winged horse, a black donkey rearing on its hind legs, and a dark billygoat with a scepter, a horn, and a red cloak, symbolizing Jove. Several other figures were hidden underneath the foundations of the bell tower.

"Who is the donkey?"

"Typhon. He was usually depicted as having the head of a donkey, like the Egyptian god Seth."

"Egyptian symbolism in a Christian church?"

"I told you!"

"What about those birds?"

Each archon was flanked by a pair of birds—the soul and its dark double.

"The ancient Egyptians also believed that the part of the

soul known as *Ba* took the form of a bird. All souls must evade the tricks of the archons and of the material world if they are to continue in their ascent toward the Pleroma. This is where the fourth section begins, with the 'sphere of fixed stars.'"

Animals again, this time perching on what looked like palm trees: a gray goat and some kind of crustacean with a torpedo fish swimming above it.

"These stand for the constellations of Capricorn and Cancer. The paralyzing power of the torpedo represents the sun's apparent immobility during the solstice. We are now in the Treasury of Light, at the threshold of the First Mystery, the highest level of reality. This is where Jeu resides, master of the threshold, and father of the father of Christ."

Elena slid further along the walkway, still on her knees, her body following the soaring path to initiation embedded in that stone floor.

"According to the Manichean and apocryphal gospels, the five trees correspond to the five aspects of the awakened soul, no longer subject to reincarnation. But look at this little goat, Massimo."

He followed her gaze.

"They botched it."

Unlike all the other figures, this one looked somewhat ungainly, ill-proportioned, and placed in an unnatural position.

"They didn't botch it. The master craftsmen who created these treasures would never have failed so miserably. It was probably tampered with in later years. What we are looking at now is certainly not what was there originally."

"And what would that have been?"

"The clue is in this basket of bread beside it. As part of

their religious rituals, the Ophite and Naassene Gnostics worshipped the serpent, bringer of knowledge, and would have a snake curl up in a basket of consecrated bread. This contorted figure you see here is in fact a serpent: Aberamentho."

"Abera-what?"

"Aberamentho, Lord of Amenti. As described in the ancient Egyptians' *Book of the Dead*, Amenti was a place corresponding to the fifth hour of the Night, the territory Ra crossed to resurrect. Amenti was also one of the epithets of Isis, the Hidden One. Aberamentho, the constellation of the Dragon, the perfect serpent who twists around the axis of the world, is one of the incarnations of Jesus."

It was true. The little goat's body looked like it was twisted into a spiral. Perhaps someone really had tried to erase the original figure. Massimo couldn't believe it.

"All these pagan images . . ."

"Magic, in fact. What we see here is a mystery cult—a Christian mystery cult of Egyptian origins."

Elena kept moving forward until she was behind the bell tower, hovering right above the last figure.

"Here is the ram, symbol of Adamas, the original man. Also the rooster and the tortoise, animals sacred to Hermes, who later became Christ. The figures are placed within octagonal frames because the number eight is the symbol of the supercelestial region."

They had reached the end of the path. Elena stood up.

"The initiate would need to walk over these mosaics and know how to interpret each of them correctly, so as to blossom into the light like the lotus flower from which emerged Atum Ra, father of the gods. And finally, here is the symbol you are most interested in."

The white hare.

"The white hare appears in the cartouche of Osiris: it is the *Unnefer*, who triumphs over death. An epithet of the god reborn who leaps like a hare beyond death itself."

"So the Gnostics believed that Jesus was in fact Osiris?"

"It's not always easy to keep track of who was who over the course of several millennia."

"You said something about Isis, earlier. You called her 'the hidden one.'"

"The Amenti, yes."

"It must be a coincidence."

"What do you mean?"

Massimo smiled, feeling a little foolish.

"It's just that I've come across Isis before, in another investigation. Why hidden, though?"

"The persecution of pagans began around the year 100, and quickly intensified. The Romans tried to eradicate the cult of Isis. She was too popular, and her priests too powerful. Her statues were thrown into the river Tiber, her priests were butchered. Her devotees began calling her by other goddesses' names, such as Ceres, just so they could keep worshipping her."

Massimo couldn't seem to tear his eyes away from the hare's missing tiles.

"It's almost as if Giacomo knew," he muttered. "Everything you've told me leads back to this symbol. It seems unlikely the killer would have chosen it at random."

Elena made him turn around.

"There must be a reason he chose the hare, the most hidden of all the figures here. You should ask him."

"He would never tell me."

"Then you must insist. He's the only one who knows the answer."

"And what about the letter Tau?"

"Where's the Tau?"

"The tiles he removed and replaced with the bones spell Tau on the hare's snout, just like the one on the ram."

"The letter on the ram's brow is not a Tau. It is thought to be the Hebrew letter Kaph, as in the word Keter, meaning crown. The crowned, victorious Christ. That would certainly fit with the narrative unfolding in these octagonal frames. It might also be a reference to the Greek word *kyriakos*, meaning 'of the Lord.'"

"So you're telling me the symbol on the ram is not a Tau."

"It's not a Tau."

"That's what we thought it was, and so we assumed the letter the bones on the hare spelled out must also be a Tau."

Elena studied it for a moment. "I'm pretty sure that's just an ordinary *T*."

They looked at each other.

"An *ordinary* T?"

"Oh."

27

Today

MASSIMO HAD DROPPED OFF Elena at home and headed straight back out to the prison. He had decided to do what neither Teresa Battaglia nor police protocol would have allowed: meet with Giacomo Mainardi alone. He had decided to risk it all.

The killer agreed to see him. He wanted to play, and had evidently already foreseen this meeting.

Massimo found him in his makeshift workshop. Mainardi had covered his mosaic with a white cloth, perhaps a bedsheet. He was waiting for Massimo with his hands tucked between his knees, his wrists tied down with cable ties.

"Good morning, Inspector," he said, head bowed.

"I'm tired of this sadistic game of yours, Mainardi."

"It saddens me to hear you say that."

"I don't give a damn how you feel."

"Now you're just being mean. Where's Teresa?"

"Superintendent Battaglia's whereabouts are none of your business."

"She is exhausted."

"Stop talking about her as if she were your friend!"

"She is."

"*No.* She's a police superintendent, and you've confessed to multiple murders. You'll never be on equal terms, let alone friends."

The killer's eyes flashed toward him. Massimo felt a shiver, as if the contact had been physical, as if Giacomo had touched him with those fingers coated in marble dust.

"Maybe we were on equal terms, once upon a time. Maybe we still are. How would you know? You and your expensive suits. You're definitely not affording those on your ridiculous inspector's salary. It must be daddy's money. Ah, yes, I can see from your face that I've hit the mark. There's something unresolved simmering inside of you. I can feel it pushing. Sooner or later it'll have to come out, won't it?"

Massimo realized in that moment that the thing Teresa Battaglia had feared had already come to pass: Giacomo had taken an interest in him, in his emotional landscape, and with a few glances and well-placed remarks, he had already taken the measure of him—*understood* him, even. Now he knew exactly how to twist the knife. Giacomo was manipulating him, but it was too late to take cover. The answer Massimo was looking for was right here, where everything could come crashing down on his head.

"Why the basilica? Why the hare? Why the *T*? Does it stand for Teresa?"

"You're the detective who knows how to find all the answers. Or aren't you?"

"Does the *T* stand for Teresa? Yes or no?" Massimo shouted.

Giacomo lifted his hand, bringing thumb and index finger close.

"You've only got this far to go, Inspector. A small but crucial piece to put back in its place. Once you've done that, maybe *then* you'll understand."

Massimo placed his hands on the cloth that covered the mosaic. He felt the freshly laid tiles slipping beneath his palms. He wanted the monster to snap, to lunge toward him. Then he would have an excuse to punch him, as he'd dreamed of doing since the moment he'd walked into the room.

"Do it, Giacomo."

The killer's eyes blazed, but instead of exploding into a rage, he burst out laughing.

"You don't even know. She didn't tell you!"

"What didn't she tell me?"

Giacomo was crying with laughter now.

"Talk!"

The killer brushed a finger across his eyelashes to wipe them dry. He stopped taunting him, and looked at him with compassion, as if he really could perceive Massimo's sorrow, his fear, his despair—and make them his own. Massimo was impressed. Here was a chameleon, a perfect mimic of human emotions. Yet he was not quite human anymore—not fully so, at any rate.

"What you don't know, Inspector, and which you would rather not hear, is that in all these years, Teresa has never abandoned me. She has never stopped coming here. What happened back then is something that binds us, and always will. If you think I'm lying, go ahead and check the visitors' log. But if instead you're wondering why she never told you, I'm afraid you already know the two possible answers to that: either she didn't want you to be part of our story, or she forgot. Teresa isn't just exhausted, is she? She's sick." He sounded stern now. "I offered you a chance to tell me, earlier, and you didn't take it. And now you expect me to answer all your questions."

How Massimo wished he could dismiss it all as lies, but he could feel the serrated edge of the truth scraping at his heart.

He had to get out of there, and so he did, followed by that pair of eyes he could still feel boring into his back even after he'd shut the door behind him. He asked the officer who was waiting in the hallway to take him to the warden's office. What he learned there left him feeling confused.

"Has Superintendent Battaglia been visiting Mainardi recently?"

"They had monthly meetings."

"Of what nature?"

"Personal. The first Saturday of every month."

"Since when?"

"I've been the warden here for fourteen years, and as far as I can remember, they've always happened."

"May I check the logs?"

They went through the records together. In the last six months, she had skipped two meetings. On one occasion, she'd come on the wrong day. That was how Giacomo had figured out what was happening to her.

There was something between those two that Massimo couldn't quite figure out. He could just about glimpse its outline, but it wasn't enough. It couldn't just be compassion that moved her, and it couldn't just be loneliness that made him so receptive. They actively sought each other out.

He went back to Giacomo, but he wasn't there anymore.

A prison officer was checking the tools and ticking them off against a list.

"Where is he?"

The officer barely looked up.

"The prisoner asked to be taken back to his cell."

"I need to talk to him."

"You'll need to put a new request in, but Mainardi has already said he does not wish to see anyone else today."

"So he leaves messages now? What are we, his private secretaries? I need to talk to him now."

The man shook his head and closed the folder he was holding.

"You know the procedure, Inspector. It's not me you have to ask. Put your request through, and see if that madman will want to meet you again. We can't make him."

The officer left him alone in the room, which stank of cement and of things left half-spoken, there to torment and instigate doubt.

Had Teresa not told him the full story because she didn't trust him, because she wasn't interested in involving him, or because she couldn't remember what she had been doing?

He noticed that a little cube of translucent travertine had been placed right in the middle of the white sheet.

In Mainardi's imagination, it must be a pale imitation of human bones.

A small but crucial piece to put back in its place, he'd said. A tile.

He picked up the tile and lifted the sheet, and when he saw what Giacomo had made, he felt like he was about to die.

28

Twenty-seven years ago

ALBERT HAD PREPARED A memo for the district attorney and left photocopies on everyone's desks except Teresa's. She saw it by chance when she walked past the desk of a colleague who was out sick.

She picked up the report, filled with a destructive urge that miraculously remained confined to the realm of unrealized impulses. Her anger dissolved when she read it. The news was dispiriting: there were no matches with the prints that had been found on the crime scene; as for the surgical tape they'd discovered on the first victim, the clinics that used it were too many to count. It was also readily available for purchase at numerous pharmacies.

The second part of the report did not come as a surprise, as Parri had already warned her about it, but even so, seeing it spelled out like that on an official document—even one designed for internal use only—struck her like an admission of defeat.

Teresa sat down at her desk. She was tired and drained from the nausea, and all she wanted to do was close her eyes and lie down.

She chewed on yet another sweet (at this rate, it was becoming a vice), rested her head on her arms, and curled up on her chair. Just a minute's rest, enough to give the muscles in her back and legs a chance to relax.

At the sound of the fax machine, she jumped.

> I've been wondering: could opportunity be play-
> ing a more important role in this case than a
> deep-seated psychological motive?
>   Perhaps the killer made a compromise. They
> have to do that sometimes—more often than you
> might think. Knowing the answer to that would
> clarify a number of aspects.
>
>   R.

Teresa read the short message over and over again.

The question of opportunism. She hadn't thought about it, not as much as she should have.

Why did the killer target the elderly? Were they part of a specific fantasy, with a precise symbolic value, or were they just easy prey? Perhaps this second possibility played a more significant role than Teresa had previously assumed.

She had focused her attention on the psychological motive, but maybe there were other factors guiding the killer's hand. He'd had to adapt to circumstances, and he'd had to forgo some of the components of his ideal fantasies in order to be able to realize them.

There had to be a link between the victims, some practical point, though they had not been able to see it yet.

He had watched his victims, he had chosen them and followed them. What the police had to figure out was where it had all begun.

Teresa looked out into the hallway and flagged one of her colleagues. This time she did not ask after Albert. She was a police inspector after all. It was time to start acting like one.

"Lorenzi, are you free?"

Her voice came out sounding curt, so that her question was more of a command.

The officer flinched, glancing around the corridor.

"Yes."

"We need to dig deeper. There must be a connection between the victims. The killer may have taken advantage of some specific circumstance that saw them all involved."

"We've already established that they didn't know each other."

"We've not established a single thing. I'm not talking about personal acquaintance, but of habits. Pensioners' clubs, amateur sports associations, dance classes, activities they might have accompanied their grandchildren to . . ."

"We've combed through their lives already . . ."

"And we'll do it again. You *will* find something. Understood?"

He seemed to be taking stock of his new and wholly unexpected situation. Finally, he nodded, looking at her as if it was the first time he'd seen her.

"Yessir."

29

---·᠁·---

Today

DRIVING AT SPEED THROUGH the city's residential neighborhood, Massimo felt his phone vibrating in the pocket of his
blazer. Whoever it was would have to wait.

He skidded to a halt outside Teresa Battaglia's Liberty-
style house. The gate was open.

He sprinted down the driveway. Massimo had been
utterly distraught as he'd left the prison, insisting before he
walked out on verifying personally that Giacomo Mainardi
was locked up in his cell and couldn't hurt anyone. But even
so, after what he had just seen, his gut told him something
different. Teresa wasn't safe.

He furiously pressed the bell until the door swung open.
It was Parri.

"I was just calling you, Inspector."

Massimo walked in.

"Where is she?"

"In the library. I wanted to see you both because there's something important I need to tell you."

"So do I, and you're not going to like it."

His terror did not fade even when he saw her sitting in an armchair, holding a book, and with the temple tips of her glasses squeezed between her lips, as they always were whenever she was thinking about something. She looked unperturbed, slightly weary, perhaps a little older, and maybe even quite pleased to see him again—though she would never say that aloud.

"Massimo?" said a familiar voice.

"Elena?"

Elena had appeared behind Teresa, bearing a tray of pastries.

"What are you doing here?"

Elena placed the tray on the desk.

"I brought Teresa my books on Egyptian Christianity. I was telling her about our visit to the basilica. Don't worry, the pastry is for me."

Teresa Battaglia closed the tome she was reading, and placed it on top of a pile of other books.

"Your hair is all ruffled, Inspector. Between you and Parri, I'm not sure who's in a greater rush today." She took a closer look at him, and frowned. "What's wrong?"

The pile of books toppled over. Massimo would have liked to go down with them, knees buckling to the floor.

"I saw the mosaic Mainardi has been working on. It's a portrait of you. He's been making a portrait of you, Superintendent."

Teresa Battaglia stood up, Elena rushing to her side to help her.

"You went to see him? On your own?"

She seemed angry.

"Did you hear what I said? He's made a portrait of *you*."

"You have no idea what you're doing. You shouldn't have done that."

"Because I would have learned too much?"

Elena gave him a horrified look.

"Massimo!"

Teresa pointed her finger at him.

"And now you think you've won, while all he's done is show you exactly what he wanted you to see, and nothing more."

"Is that all you have to say?"

"Well, I'm surprised, but not exactly shocked. Giacomo has become somewhat fond of me, or at least he thinks he is."

"And rightly so, given you've been visiting him regularly for years now."

"Is it me you're investigating now, Marini?"

"I'm trying to understand. It's not an ordinary portrait, Superintendent. The face . . . the face is missing a tooth."

This time the blow found its mark. He saw her close her eyes and squeeze them shut, as if she'd been physically hit. Massimo hated himself for this, but he knew he couldn't give her time to let the news sink in. He had to understand what was going on so that he could keep her safe.

"Teresa, this man has thought about committing an act of violence against you, probably so many times that he has felt the urge to portray it in a mosaic."

"Marini . . ."

"Listen to me."

"You should all listen to me, actually," said Parri,

interrupting them. He seemed to be shaking. "Now I really *have* to tell you, though I have no idea how."

But whatever it was, he couldn't say it. His mouth seemed to be chewing on words that refused to emerge. Parri's uncharacteristic hesitance left Massimo feeling like a loaded gun, ready to shoot.

"This isn't helping, Doctor Parri."

"We have isolated the DNA from the tooth retrieved in the basilica. It's old, but we started with it because we figured it would be easier to extract genetic material from a tooth than from tiles. We were right. We will need more time to isolate the full sequence, but we already have a confirmed match."

Massimo could scarcely believe it.

"We have a match?"

"Yes. It's 'external' DNA that does not belong to Mainardi. I can also confirm with absolute certainty that the bones the other tiles were made out of do not belong to this same individual."

"So we're looking for two bodies now?"

"No. Two people. One of whom is still alive." He took a deep breath. "The tooth belongs to Teresa."

Massimo asked him to repeat what he'd just said.

"The tooth is yours, Teresa."

Nobody breathed a word.

"The DNA is a perfect match with the sample I took from you to identify any contamination in the evidence."

Teresa looked petrified. Massimo touched her arm and made her look at him. His head and his ears felt like they were stuffed with cotton wool. A thrumming in the background muddled every thought and every gesture.

"Is there a single goddamned reason why a homicidal maniac would have one of your teeth in his possession?"

Teresa's eyes had reddened, but she did not let a single tear fall.

"Yes."

"*Yes?* That's all?"

"It's a long story, Marini."

It may indeed have been a long one, but it was clear that she had no intention of even beginning to tell it. Massimo refused to let it go.

"We need to talk to Mainardi. We need to persuade him to meet with us so that we can figure out what he's been trying to tell us."

She turned her back on them and walked toward the window. Her footsteps were unsure again, her body hunched over.

"You could force him to see you, if you really wanted to. But you can't force him to talk to you. He won't tell you anything he hasn't already said."

"And what about you? Do you have anything else to tell me?"

The answer traced a silent arc over their heads, then plunged down upon them.

"No."

"Superintendent!"

"Stop calling me that."

"Let me help you."

She turned around. She was trying to smile.

"Telling you that part of the story wouldn't be of any use. Not to you, not to me. And certainly not in solving the case. Trust me."

Massimo looked at Elena and saw that she was in tears. He glanced at Parri in search of support, but the coroner motioned at him to let it be.

That was when he understood. Teresa's past was a tomb, and it must never again be opened.

30

Twenty-seven years ago

TERESA'S EYES SPRUNG OPEN in the darkness. The phone was ringing downstairs. Sebastiano was a silent silhouette on the other side of the bed, a curved form that was not to be touched. She carefully pulled the covers aside, and did not bother looking for her slippers on the floor. She moved in slow motion, and only once she had reached the corridor did she break into a run, bounding down the stairs barefoot, stifling a curse when she banged her little toe on a sharp edge and the pain shot through her like bolts of lightning. She hopped the rest of the way to the phone.

"Hello?"

"He's killed again."

It was Albert. Teresa squinted at the clock display. It wasn't even dawn yet.

"I'm coming."

"I'll come to you. I'm calling from a phone booth around a hundred meters from your place. Hurry up."

He hung up, leaving Teresa with the receiver in one hand and her eyes fixed on the ceiling, as if they could pierce right through it and check that her husband—her persecutor—was still asleep.

Once again, she would have to choose whether to be true to herself or surrender to his threats.

Leaving the house was a provocation.

Working was a provocation.

Having aspirations was a provocation.

Pretty soon, Sebastiano would come to see even her breathing as a provocation. And Teresa could already feel the air running out.

She put the receiver down and scribbled an explanation on the notebook by the phone. She forced herself to add a few expressions of affection and regret, offerings designed to soothe the wrath of a fallen god.

To avoid going back into the bedroom, she picked an outfit from the pile of clothes that still needed ironing. She shut the front door and vowed to her trembling self that she would not have to be afraid for much longer.

By the time Albert's car pulled up in front of her house, Teresa had banished all traces of sleepiness and dread from her face.

They were both quiet for a long time, until he finally worked up the courage to speak.

"Let's figure out how to stop him. Let's just focus on that. All right?"

What he was really saying was that it didn't matter how he'd treated her, it didn't matter that he'd gone through her possessions and stolen her ideas to pass them off as his own. He wasn't conceding anything at all, and he never would.

Teresa turned her head to look into the night.

"We'll stop him."

"Really?"

He sounded so hopeful.

"Yes. But you'll never change."

"What do you mean?"

"You are and always will be a scumbag."

Albert did not respond. He accepted the insult as the price he would have to pay so that he could use her again—and all things considered, it wasn't even that steep.

A gentle rain began to patter onto the windshield. It washed the asphalt clean and lifted fragrant scents from people's gardens, which turned into fields as the car drove on.

Death had risen like a rarefied mist from a cluster of acacias in bloom, among the odorous moisture of a verdant hollow traversed by a canal. It had climbed out of the silty bed like smoke, far from the lights of the city. In the blue dawn, as frogs croaked and trickles of water polished the fronds, the soil, teeming with bulbs, had become saturated with blood.

Teresa lifted her hood over her head, her long hair sticking like dark seaweed to her cheeks and chest. She zipped her parka over her belly to keep her baby warm.

It was so nice not to feel alone anymore. Wherever she went, there would be two of them now. It would never be just her again. She started walking, murmuring a soft, comforting lullaby. She was taking her child into hell, singing songs of love along the way.

"I'll protect you."

She would vow to do so every day for the rest of her life, to kiss him and cuddle him and never hold anybody else as tight as she held him.

The crime scene had already been marked off. There were officers at work combing through the area for clues. Teresa spotted the district attorney and Doctor Pace talking under an umbrella as dark as their clothes, and further along she saw Parri, who also had his hood up over his head and was crouching over a figure Teresa couldn't quite make out.

She huddled inside her coat, but not from the cold. It was that melancholy feeling of abandonment that always took hold of her every time she saw a corpse.

Albert had shown no inclination to make his way toward the district attorney. He stood right beside her, hoping, perhaps, to catch some suggestion she might let slip. He was groping desperately in the dark. He needed a scapegoat, someone naive enough to let their guard down and advance some kind of hypothesis.

Teresa was not naive, but she didn't have much to lose, either. The moment she told them about her pregnancy, she would be taken off the case anyway.

"How did the attack unfold?" she asked him.

"Exactly the same as the previous one. No signs of duress, and he cut his throat. Parri is still examining the body, but the cut is a neat one. He sliced the carotid artery wide open."

"So he's learning. What did he take away this time?"

A moment's hesitation.

"There is a laceration on the torso, along the flank. It's a rib. The tip of a rib."

"Which one?"

"Which one? I don't know which one."

Teresa turned to look at him.

"You've been here already, haven't you? How many hours has it been since you found him?"

"Don't get all edgy now."

"What's your excuse this time? Same as the last time? My phone didn't start ringing until half an hour ago."

Albert remained impassive, which for him meant assuming a glacial expression that turned his well-proportioned features into marble, lips sealed shut and rivulets of rainwater flowing from his eyelashes down his jawline and all the way to his chin.

"You're a woman, Teresa, and you need to accept that. Do you really want to be looking at scenes like this for the next thirty years of your life?"

He gestured at the body sprawled over the muddy ground not far from where they stood. Teresa's gaze did not follow his hand.

"I don't know, *Albert*. But I think I can make my own mind up about what I may or may not want to do."

She started walking, and he followed right behind her.

"You called me because you have absolutely no idea what to do."

"If they take me off the case, you'll be gone, too."

"You're making it sound quite tempting."

He grabbed her arm and spun her around.

"It's your husband you should be sneering at like this, not me!"

She stared at his hand. Albert let go.

"Superintendent Lona?"

It was Lorenzi.

"The victim's car has been found abandoned on the dirt road."

Teresa flinched.

"Where?"

"Over there, just past the turn. There are traces of blood."

Teresa was already heading for the vehicle. She slipped on a pair of gloves and shoe coverings in readiness.

The back doors were wide open, and the blue chrome Volvo looked like a beetle that had dropped dead just as it was spreading its wings to fly.

Teresa approached the passenger side. The seat was drenched in blood, a thick pool that the foam rubber and its velvet upholstery had failed to fully absorb.

"The killer drove the car."

The words had come out in a whisper. Teresa suddenly realized that everyone was looking at her. They had followed her there, and now they were surrounding her. Perhaps they were trying to understand her fascination, her passion for what she did; perhaps they felt it was inappropriate.

Instead of dismissing her, this time Albert gave her free rein.

"Keep going."

"I read about a similar case, once. The killer would drive around in his victims' cars for hours, even after he'd already slain them. He would later explain that this helped him create an even deeper bond with them."

"The body was found by a couple who came here in search of a private spot where they could fool around. They said they saw the car arrive, then someone dragged something out of it, stared at it for a while, and finally left the scene."

"On foot?"

"Yes."

There was something else he was about to blurt out. Teresa could tell from the tone of his voice. And she was right.

"Our findings so far indicate that at some point the killer must have driven past a police checkpoint on the state highway, not too far from where we are now."

That explained the weariness in his voice. It was fear. Teresa would not let it infect her.

"The photo from the victim's driver's license?" she asked.

"It's gone."

Another totem. Teresa often thought about the wedding ring they had retrieved in the nymphaeum. It was a detail whose precise significance she just couldn't seem to place. Why had the killer taken it from the first victim only to discard it?

She requested a map of the area, and used a pen to mark out where the three bodies had been found.

Albert watched from over her shoulder.

"What are you thinking?"

"That the theory of the geographical midpoint might apply, though we would need at least five different crime scenes to make an even remotely reliable estimate."

"We certainly can't afford five victims."

Teresa's eyes filled with lines, contours, and place names—the killer's hunting ground, where she could picture him marking his territory like an apex predator. And just like any predator, he must have a den where he would retreat to fantasize, plan, and bask in the afterglow of the kill. Wherever it was, they had to find it.

"When there are multiple homicides with similar characteristics, it is likely that the killer either lives close to the first crime scene, or has his center of main interests there. In time, he will tend to start moving around more, taking his victims—whether they are still alive or already dead—farther and farther away."

"What do you mean by his 'center of main interests'?"

"His place of work, for example, or the location of any other activity that takes up most of his time, though I continue to think that he must have long since abandoned his daily routine to devote himself entirely to his fantasies."

Albert did not dismiss her theories. He called the other officers over.

"We need to narrow the search perimeter; we don't have enough on-field resources."

"We need to be careful not to scare him away," said Teresa absent-mindedly.

She sat on her haunches, taking a closer look at the blood on the car seat while she waited for a chance to examine the corpse itself.

The smell reached her nostrils, muddled her thoughts, and stirred her gastric fluids.

There was something stuck in the clotted mess. She carefully pulled it out with a pair of tongs she'd brought in her pocket.

Albert saw what she was doing.

"What's that?"

Teresa brought it close to her eyes.

Lanceolate, turquoise, fleshy: she'd seen it before.

"A petal. From the water lilies at the second crime scene. He must have gone back there."

"Is that normal?"

"Textbook behavior. But I'm not sure what it means. Why a petal?"

It wasn't the only one, either. There were others.

Teresa summoned Lorenzi and gave him the tongs.

"Over to you."

She quickly stepped away, mouth full of saliva. She felt like she was about to throw up, and did not intend to do so over the evidence.

She hid behind an ambulance, knees bent, hand clutching a tissue she'd managed to pull out of its pack at the last moment.

She took deep breaths, the smell of silt mixing with the sweet scent of acacia flowers. She kept her eyes fixed upon the edge of the ditch, staring at a patch of wild violets.

The wave of nausea reversed down her throat, back toward her stomach.

"Everything okay?"

Teresa shook her head, reluctant to risk speaking. The voice did not belong to any of her colleagues, and it wasn't Albert's, either. Thank goodness for small mercies.

A hand massaged her back from her kidneys all the way up to her shoulder blades. She flinched at first, but the contact eased the tension in her muscles and helped her regain some measure of control.

"I told you, you should eat fruit candy whenever you feel it coming."

Teresa smiled, her eyes closed. She recognized him now.

"I've run out."

"Good thing you bumped into me. I happen to always carry a spare pack with me."

He helped her straighten up. He was wearing his nurse's uniform under a big waterproof jacket.

"What are you doing here?"

He put his hands in his pockets and nodded toward the crime scene.

"I'm here with Doctor Parri, though it looks like he'd prefer to do all the work himself."

"Is he sober?"

He grimaced.

"More or less."

Teresa stifled a curse, but felt a smile forming over her face. He offered her the pack of sweets, still unopened.

"Sweets from a stranger."

He bent down to pluck a violet, opened one of her hands, placed the sweets and the flower in her palm, and pushed her fingers closed again, his own hand lingering there for a moment that could have meant anything and nothing.

Teresa said the first silly thing that popped into her head.

"But what if you need sweets, too?"

They looked at each other, rain streaming down their faces.

"I'll wait until I meet you again. You'd better save me one. Actually, wait. I'll give you my number." He took the notebook he could see peeking out of her pocket, pulled out a pen, and looked for a blank page.

"Hey! What are you doing?"

He laughed as he quickly scribbled something down.

"What are you so afraid of?" He gave her the notebook back, immediately serious again. "You're looking at me as if I'd written down the devil's number."

Teresa was trembling. Sebastiano would be furious if he

found out about the stranger's attentions, and the looks and words they had already exchanged. She lowered her eyes, feeling the young man's gaze roaming over her face.

"I'm married. And I'm pregnant."

"I know."

The moment of unexpected intimacy was interrupted by the sound of thunder. He looked away.

"Parri is waving me over. See you later, Inspector."

Teresa did not turn around. She listened to his fading footsteps. She listened as the storm reached her and turned the soft drizzle into a raucous deluge. She thought of when she was just a girl, dancing under rain showers. She could feel it now, that same urge to turn her face up to the sky and drink.

She turned around only when she heard Albert calling for her. In the ensuing ruckus, she did not manage to catch sight of the young man who had come to her aid.

She hadn't even asked for his name.

31

Today

THE CAGE WAS FILLED with white noise. Gone was the silence that had come with the awakening of the monster inside his flesh. Prison had digested his fear, like an organism mutating endlessly, observing, cataloging, and commandeering every stimulus, and responding with a thousand staring eyes, hundreds of layers of skin, and perennially hungry throats.

Giacomo could feel it buzzing around him. In the language he had learned to speak ever since he was a child, it meant that there was a new predator roaming the corridors, searching for him in every cell.

The guard who watched his every move would not protect him. His job was to stop Giacomo from killing himself—not to risk his life saving him from someone else.

Every blow of Giacomo's hammer matched a thundering beat of his savage heart. He alternated between striking the marble and the tongs until the metal thinned—until it grew sharp.

Could a person be prepared to die in order to survive?

Yes.

Just as they could be prepared to be locked up forever behind steel bars. But that hadn't worked.

He kept time with every strike of his hammer. For most people, deciding when to kill themselves would be an unfathomable thought, but he was marking the seconds so that he wouldn't succumb to panic, so that he could shape this opportunity to his liking, and be born again elsewhere.

And when the moment came, when the guard—absorbed and comforted by a routine that dulled his senses—looked down at the screen of his mobile phone, Giacomo took action.

The sharpened edges of the tongs sliced the flesh of his wrists wide open.

Giacomo watched silently as his portrait of Teresa took on a dark red hue.

He bent down to kiss her lips. They tasted of blood, just as they had all those years ago.

32

---·∞·---

Today

THE POLICE HEADQUARTERS WERE beginning to empty as people left for their lunch breaks. Massimo had already tossed out the sandwich he had bought from the vending machine. It tasted like plastic and he wasn't hungry enough to eat it anyway.

He had been scrutinizing every single line of the final report on the Giacomo Mainardi case that had been drawn up twenty-seven years ago, and he still hadn't discovered what he was so desperate to find: that crucial piece of Teresa Battaglia's story, the keystone that could explain the bond she felt she had with the killer.

Their lives hadn't merely crossed. They must have been intertwined.

Massimo had rediscovered her words among the documents he had reviewed, and recognized her signature underneath the reports. She was a constant presence, her tone tenacious but her assumptions and her conclusions always impeccably balanced. No inaccuracies, not a single oversight. She was already the relentless hunter he had come to know.

But at a certain point, her presence seemed to disappear entirely, leaving behind only a surface trace of Albert Lona— who appeared even back then to be feeding off her energy. He was the superintendent at the time, and he had been the one to close the case. Inspector Battaglia had simply vanished.

"Marini? I need a word."

Massimo looked up from the stacks of paperwork. It was Lona, quietly ominous, and as unerringly punctual as the devil to turn up when summoned. The district attorney's expression changed when he saw the report Massimo was looking at.

"How can I help you, Doctor Lona?"

He sat on the edge of Massimo's desk.

"I wanted to know whether you had any news of Superintendent Battaglia."

Massimo leaned back in his chair. This was certainly an interesting development.

"Yes. I do have news of Superintendent Battaglia."

"How is she?"

"She's recovering."

"I heard you were with her when she found out."

"I was."

"Did she tell you anything?"

Massimo crossed his legs and surveyed the elusive, unknowable creature before him.

"About her tooth? What do you think?"

Lona's gaze fell on the old case file.

"She didn't, of course. Otherwise you wouldn't be here combing through the past."

Lona seemed tired, and not like a man busy with endless machinations.

Massimo took his chance, thinking he might be able to glean some information from him.

"I've deduced it must have something to do with the trail of bodies Giacomo Mainardi left in his wake. Was there a physical altercation, perhaps?"

"It wasn't a good time in her life."

"I know about her abusive husband and the child she lost."

"Good!"

"Good?"

"Yes. This way you'll have a better sense of how to . . . I can't think of the right expression. Handle her, I suppose. Yes, that's it."

"Handle her."

"Did I say something inappropriate?"

"What happened to the husband?"

Lona looked down, plucking nonexistent lint from his trousers.

"She reported him, of course. As soon as she was able to. He was arrested and later sentenced, but he never served the full term. He was released early for good conduct."

Massimo cursed. Even Lona seemed embarrassed about how things had gone.

"If you think about it, Marini, it had only been twelve years since the law on honor killings had been repealed. That mindset hadn't really changed yet."

"Things aren't that different now, either. They still let them out of prison far too soon, and they often go right back to their old persecuting ways."

"Not in this case. Her husband obeyed the restraining order that barred him from approaching her. He disappeared from her life." The district attorney looked at his watch. "The deputy prosecutor has called a meeting for this afternoon."

"I got the memo."

"We've moved it forward. We need to be in his office in less than an hour. Oh, and apparently the forensics team has found some camera footage that might turn out to be useful. It seems it caught Mainardi driving with his last victim. They are trying to trace the owner through the license plate. We'll be discussing it at the meeting." He felt his pockets for his phone, took it out and scrolled through the menu. "I want Superintendent Battaglia there, too. I've already sent a squad car to pick her up." He held out a hand as if to silence any objections before they could be raised. This exchange was only ever meant to be a one-way process, the kind Lona knew best. "We need to get her statement anyway, now that her tooth has appeared."

"I can do that. I'll just go over to see her, and . . ."

"No. We'll skip that step. We might as well hear the full story with everyone present and up to date on the latest news. We're already falling behind."

Massimo was beginning to understand what Lona was getting at, and he didn't like what he was hearing.

"And I'm supposed to *handle* the superintendent, be the lightning rod."

"It might not be . . . easy, for Teresa."

"Yet you're determined to saddle her with this anyway, aren't you? You won't let her take the easier path."

"Obviously not."

"Why all this acrimony, Doctor Lona?"

"Perhaps you should ask her, Inspector Marini. But if you want my side of the story, well, I said something unfortunate once, and she's been seeking her revenge ever since."

"Teresa Battaglia, seeking revenge? You must be joking."

"It depends on the angle from which you look at things. At me and her."

"There's only one thing that woman cares about, and that's justice."

"Justice . . ." said Lona, smiling as if Massimo had made a joke. "Do you think you can persuade her to return from sick leave sooner?"

Until that moment, it was all Massimo himself had wanted.

"No. You're on your own there, Doctor Lona."

"Wrong, Inspector Marini. *You're* on your own. I always land on my feet."

"And on top of everyone else."

"That's what hierarchies are for."

"Do you know what I'm thinking of? I'm thinking of violent men. Only some violent men are actually capable of killing people, but on an emotional and psychological level, all of them are murderers. Words can kill, too, and so can intimidation. You wanted to annihilate her. You didn't succeed. Now you've decided to start picking on me."

"Picking on you? I've been accused of much worse, Marini. I wouldn't have gotten to where I am by being easily offended."

"You seem pretty easily offended to me."

Lona made a face, as if to downplay the comment.

"No. I'm just vindictive. It's a different approach. Far more rational."

"What revenge could you possibly want, after nearly thirty years?"

"I'm sure you can work it out."

"I want to hear it from you."

"You're crossing the line now."

"Is there even a line, at this point?"

Lona shrugged.

"No, I suppose not. I suppose we've long since moved past it."

Massimo waited.

"I offered her my help. She refused it. I suppose I was . . . irked."

"Wounded. Rejected."

"I see. You already know what this is about. She's told you."

"Indeed."

Lona sighed.

"We can only do so much, no? And I did what I could. Regrettably, it wasn't enough."

"You seem sorry about it."

"How could I not be? She lost her baby."

Massimo believed him. He could see something there— not exactly anguish, perhaps, but some sort of mild sorrow which he couldn't quite bring himself to call guilt.

"Then why all this hostility toward Teresa?"

Lona stood up, looking irritated.

"Why, why, why. Because I'm difficult, that's why; because I made a mistake, and I can't ever make up for it.

When someone sees you as a monster, it's easier to just turn into one rather than spend your life trying to convince them otherwise, don't you think?"

Massimo kept quiet.

The district attorney indicated the case file. "You're looking in the wrong place, anyway. That's not where you're going to find the answers to your questions."

"Where should I be looking, then?"

Lona was already at the door, with his back turned, when he replied.

"I've just sent you an email with an attachment. That should satisfy your curiosity."

"Why would you do that?"

"To prepare you."

Massimo sat motionless before his screen. All he had to do was log onto his email, and the secret would reveal itself.

Did he really want that?

Would *she* really want that?

There are some truths about the people we love that we should never be able to access. Human beings are made more of mystery than of transparent matter, and that ratio is ingrained in their nature.

It wasn't Massimo's place—or Albert Lona's—to shine a light back where Teresa Battaglia had decided to extinguish it forever. But he did it anyway. He clicked on the attachment.

The photographs loaded first.

33

---·∾·---

Twenty-seven years ago

TERESA PULLED THE ZIP shut, sealing part of her life inside the suitcase. It hadn't been too difficult to choose what to pack. Anything could be useful, but nothing was truly necessary. Every object she took from this life would be a reminder of failure. Carrying it into her new life before it had even started would be like casting a deadly spell.

Starting again. It felt like far too bold an ambition, yet here she was, about to take that leap. Into the void, into the dark, on her own.

For Teresa really *was* alone, even though she'd briefly deluded herself into thinking the opposite.

She'd been packing her notebooks when she had taken the newest one from her bag and searched for the phone number that had been hurriedly jotted down in the rain by the same hand that had brushed fleetingly against her hips.

As she'd flicked through its pages, a violet had fallen out and fluttered to the floor.

She had felt like a fool as she'd dialed his number. What would she say to him? What would he think of her?

But her questions had immediately been swept aside by an automated message: *The number you have called is no longer in service.*

She'd felt so gullible—idiotic, even.

A disconnected number. What a marvelous metaphor for all her hopes.

She heard the front door open, and hurriedly hid the suitcase in the wardrobe.

She sat on the bed and grabbed a book from the bedside table.

Sebastiano called out from the floor below.

She heard him coming up the stairs in quick, heavy strides. She could picture him climbing two steps at a time.

He appeared at the door, beaming and disheveled.

"The dean has given me a new role."

He threw himself onto the bed, among the pillows. The mattress bounced beneath him.

"A more prestigious position, this time. They all came by my office to offer their congratulations. So many phoney smiles and greasy handshakes. God, what a thrill."

Teresa was silent.

"Aren't you going to say anything?"

She picked her words carefully. She chose the only salve that worked on him—and it was neither the love nor the pride of an admiring wife.

"Your colleagues will be so jealous they won't be able to sleep tonight. Congratulations."

Sebastiano burst into laughter and pulled her toward him, slinging his arm around her neck.

"Those fools won't be sleeping for *weeks*."

His grip was tight, robbing her of air. He looked euphoric, but with him it was hard to tell what was genuine and what was feigned, and his euphoria was as frightening to Teresa as his anger.

She tried to get up.

"We should celebrate."

He held her back.

"Are you in some kind of rush?"

He hadn't eased his grip, and soon her neck was straining against the muscles of his arm. The pressure reached all the way to her eyes, and as they fell, in that moment, upon the wardrobe door, she realized she must have left it ajar in her haste.

Had he noticed, too, with his predator's eyes?

"What are you talking about? I'm not in a rush."

The pressure eased. Teresa lay back and rested her head on his stomach. Sebastiano was taut and lean. Teresa wondered what kind of existence could find refuge there, curled up among the sharp spikes that covered his body inside and out. It wasn't easy to touch, nor was it easy to inhabit.

Sebastiano had stopped caressing her.

"I noticed yesterday that some of your clothes were missing from the wardrobe."

Teresa swallowed bile.

"I took them to the dry cleaner's. I'll be going up a few sizes soon, and who knows when they'll fit again. I thought I'd get them washed and ironed before storing them away."

"Really?"

"Yes."

"Which dry cleaner's?"

"The one at the crossroads near the park."

Teresa made a mental note to take some items there the next day.

A few petrifying moments later, his caresses resumed, though their true nature was clear in her body's instinctive reactions. Her reptilian brain immediately unleashed the full range of physical responses to an act of aggression. But Teresa remained completely still. She played dead so that she could stay alive.

Sebastiano wasn't caressing *her*. He was polishing the invisible chains he'd wrapped around her day after day, and had been tightening with ever-growing relish.

In that moment of outward calm, Teresa knew with absolute certainty that he would never undo those chains, nor would he allow her to break them.

The only suitcase she'd be able to take when she finally walked out of this marriage was going to be her own skin.

34

Today

WHEN TERESA'S DOORBELL RANG, it was Elena who answered. The two women had discovered a broad range of shared interests—including ancient history. Teresa could have listened to Elena's archaeological disquisitions for hours on end and never get bored. Elena had brought her several new books on ancient Egypt, all full of fascinating photographs. But Teresa suspected Elena was also there to ensure there was always someone by Teresa's side. Marini had figured out a way to be present even when he was busy elsewhere. When she thought about it, Teresa was quite moved.

Elena came back into the living room, looking concerned.

"There are two policemen here. They're asking for you."

Teresa went to the front door. The two officers looked familiar, though they had joined the force not long ago, and she hadn't had too many chances to work with them. Parked outside the gate with its lights flashing, their patrol car had been noticed by a few passersby, and by Teresa's neighbors, who were now looking out of their windows and balconies to try and figure out what was happening. Teresa couldn't find the words to ask the two men what on earth they'd been thinking. She stammered a half-sentence, then realized she'd switched the words around. She might even have thrown a completely unrelated term in there.

The officers exchanged a look, as if they might be wondering whether this woman who looked so lost could really be Superintendent Battaglia.

Teresa felt a growing sense of unease. She heard Elena calling out to ask what was going on, but she had no idea how to respond.

"You need to come with us, Superintendent Battaglia."

"Where to?"

"We're here to escort you to headquarters. The appointment with Doctor Gardini has been moved forward."

With so little warning, and no time to prepare for the prospect of a formal meeting designed to delve into parts of the past she never wanted to relive, Teresa's mind went blank. Or had the meeting been planned in advance—only for Teresa to forget all about it?

"I don't remember."

Elena put her arms around her.

"Is everything okay?"

"No."

Caught off guard, and pinned to her front door by the staring eyes of a pair of strangers, Teresa felt her agitation intensify. She looked down at her clothes, worrying that she'd worn things in the wrong order, or accidentally styled her hair like a little girl, or done her makeup like a twenty-something preparing for a wild night out.

All of this could certainly happen, and at some point, they probably would. She'd begun to notice that unexpected events could cause her tachycardia and anxiety attacks. Any deviation from her usual routine was irrationally and dispro-portionately distressful.

Elena nudged her gently aside and planted herself between Teresa and the two officers.

"Does Inspector Marini know about this?"

"We're here on the district attorney's orders."

"I will call the inspector now. Please wait in the car. You might consider turning those lights off. You're scaring the neighbors."

"We don't have time for that, ma'am. The district attor-ney . . ."

Elena smiled.

"I'm sorry, but that's not our problem."

She was about to close the door on them when another car rounded the turn at the end of the road, coming to a screeching halt next to the squad car. The driver pulled the handbrake with such force that they heard the sound all the way from the house, almost as if he'd wanted to tear it off. It was Massimo—and he wasn't alone.

Parisi and de Carli stepped out of the car and dealt with the two officers, sending them right back where they'd come from.

Elena walked to Massimo.

"I was just about to call you."

He took her by the hand, then looked at Teresa and shook his head.

"One of these days I'm going to give that Lona a piece of my mind."

He ushered them back inside and closed the door behind him, restoring some privacy, and calming Teresa's mind.

She realized then that she had been shaking.

"They told me about the meeting, but I don't remember anything about that."

"Lona decided at the eleventh hour to move it forward and to involve you. You couldn't have remembered that because it was never the plan."

"But now I have to attend, and I'm not ready."

"You can take all the time you need, Superintendent."

The calmness in his voice, both firm and soothing, seemed to have the power to help her breathe better.

"But you said they moved the meeting forward."

"They'll have to wait."

Teresa looked down again, running a hand over her clothes and smoothing creases that only existed inside of her.

"Am I dressed appropriately?"

Marini gave her one of those mischievous grins that made his eyes sparkle.

"Are you wearing any underwear?"

Teresa felt around with her hands.

"I think so."

"Me too. So I guess we're sorted."

"Really?"

"Really."

Both of them knew they weren't actually talking about underwear.

Marini gave Elena a kiss and handed Teresa her walking stick.

"Ready?"

"Let's pretend we are."

He led her all the way to the car and had her sit in the front passenger seat. Parisi and de Carli were already in the back. She waved goodbye to Elena, who was standing at the door. If she hadn't been there to help keep her anxiety at bay, Teresa would have been in quite a state by now.

"Another one of the district attorney's schemes, eh, Superintendent?"

"I've stopped trying to keep track, de Carli."

Teresa placed her walking stick and her bag between her legs.

"Good thing I wasn't supposed to get involved in this case. Marini, have we said hello already?"

Marini laughed as he reversed the car.

"A couple of times. Hang on . . . was that a rhetorical question, or have you actually forgotten?"

Teresa gave him a gentle thwack. *How typical*, she thought, *that we should both immediately go looking for the tragicomic side of life*. It was an activity they were well-versed in, and an approach that had saved them time and time again.

But that day, Marini's face was flushed and his eyes a little puffy.

Teresa looked away, letting her gaze roam over the city unfurling outside the window like stills from a movie.

"And now my tooth's popped out all of a sudden. As if we didn't have enough to deal with."

De Carli, who was sitting directly behind her, perched his chin on the back of her seat.

"Do you remember how he got it?"

Parisi grabbed his shoulder and put him back in his place with a punch to the ribs.

"Did you seriously just ask her that?"

Teresa turned around. It wasn't exactly an inappropriate question, in the circumstances, but she wasn't ready to bare her soul like that, either. In the end, she opted for a half-truth, which would affect neither the investigation nor her feelings.

"There was an . . . altercation." As she spoke, she glanced at Marini's face in profile, now a picture of unnatural still-ness. He was controlling his emotions, the immobility clearly a strain, but he already knew about the violence she'd suffered and that she'd had a miscarriage, given she was the one who'd told him about it—so what, exactly, was troubling him now?

Teresa's eyes returned to the road.

"To be honest, it wasn't until I got to the hospital and they patched me up that I started assessing the damage, and I certainly wasn't going to go back and look for the missing piece."

There'd been thousands of pieces to pick up, of course—not just the one. And it hadn't been as simple a matter as getting herself patched up.

But de Carli seemed satisfied.

"So you do remember."

This time it was Marini who turned around and whacked him, now in the knee.

"Ouch!"

"Idiot."

Teresa put her sunglasses on and called them to order.

"Behave yourselves. One case of dementia per team is more than enough. *Your* heads should be working perfectly fine."

35

Today

TERESA WAS STILL LEANING on Marini's arm when she entered the deputy prosecutor's office. She would have to get used to people's stares now, and learn to ignore the embarrassment of needing that support, and of struggling to put one foot in front of the other. She wasn't sure she could ever go back to being the person she had been before, not even physically. And this was only the beginning.

Gardini leapt to his feet and came around the desk to offer her a chair.

"Good afternoon, Teresa. Thank you for coming."

Teresa greeted him by lifting two fingers from the handle of her walking stick, then sank into the chair. Her sciatica had begun to bother her again. Marini sat behind her.

"I suppose it was inevitable, given we found a piece of me embedded in a crime scene. Greetings to you, too, Doctor Lona."

Albert responded with a nod.

"Are you feeling better?" he asked.

"No."

"Do you plan on extending your sick leave?"

"I don't think I have a choice, unfortunately."

Antonio Parri arrived, out of breath.

"Sorry I'm late."

Gardini returned to his desk.

"We hadn't started yet."

The coroner took a seat, an assortment of folders and papers strewn haphazardly across his lap.

"You'll have to excuse the awkward question, but at my age I think I can afford to ask one of those every now and then. Whose idea was it to move the meeting forward? It takes time to incorporate all the latest updates into an official report."

Everyone looked at Lona, but no one spoke.

"Right. I see. A pointless question."

Gardini opened the case file on his computer. There were slides for the overhead projector, too. It was a lot of information to summarize and sift through, and Teresa was already exhausted. One of the aspects of her illness was that it affected her endurance, both physical and mental. Irritation, impatience, and distress became harder to control. So essentially, Teresa was at an inherent disadvantage.

Gardini asked his assistant to dim the lights.

"Let's begin, then."

The first bit of news was that Giacomo had been truthful on at least one count: he hadn't been the one to murder his cellmate. The killer had yet to be identified, but it couldn't be Giacomo. The DNA retrieved from beneath the victim's fingernails did not correspond to his.

Albert was less than pleased.

"That doesn't let him off the hook," he noted.

Teresa's response was prompt.

"But it doesn't incriminate him, either. Such a pity, right?"

The deputy prosecutor proceeded to reel off the facts—old and new—of the Mainardi case, detailing all the latest findings, too. They began to discuss Teresa's tooth as if she weren't its owner, taking great care not to dredge up her past unless it was strictly necessary, and to refer to her personal involvement in only the vaguest of terms, making no explicit reference to the actors responsible for any given incident. It was a conversation in allusions.

"That was when the assault on Superintendent Battaglia occurred."

That was the precise formulation Gardini used. He also chose the word *item* to refer to Teresa's tooth.

It was the only time Giacomo could have taken it. Nobody said anything about when and where the attack had happened. And no one even dared speak of who had committed the act in the first place.

This was all that Gardini was willing to put on the table; the rest didn't matter anyway. Everything else was irrelevant, and beyond the scope of the meeting. Teresa was grateful to him.

Parri gathered up the expert reports he had just finished telling them about.

"It was obviously some kind of trophy."

Teresa hadn't said a word until that moment.

"That would be atypical, though not impossible," she remarked.

Everyone stared at her.

"Why would it be atypical?"

The question had come from Marini, who was still sitting behind her—not to distance himself from the proceedings, but to support her through them. This was his first contribution, too. He hadn't asked for a single clarification, not even when the exchanges had become too nebulous for someone who didn't know the full story.

Teresa turned her head a little, though not far enough to meet his eyes.

"Because a serial killer takes trophies from his victims, Inspector. But I was the one hunting *him* down."

Marini refrained from pointing out that she must have been a victim, too, given her tooth had fallen into the killer's hands. He did not take the step Teresa had led him to—her way of putting him to the test. He hadn't betrayed himself.

Albert used the projector to show them the recording that a bank's security camera had captured the night before the latest killing, whose victim was still unknown.

"We checked the plate. The car appears to have been stolen."

He replayed the magnified footage in slow motion.

"There he is."

Giacomo Mainardi was staring right into the camera. He knew it was there, filming him. Beside him was a seated figure. It was only a shadow, but it was clearly a person.

Giardini put his glasses on and leaned closer so as not to miss a single detail.

"Was the victim alive?"

Teresa replied without a moment's hesitation.

"No. Already dead."

Albert immediately questioned her assertion. "How can you be so sure?"

"You know how. He's done it before. You were there. He has a history of driving around with a fresh corpse in the passenger seat. He's also driven past a police checkpoint before. It's his modus operandi, the only way he knows how to experience the emotions he longs for. He's done all of this before."

Gardini called for a break.

"Right. We all need a coffee. Let's reconvene in half an hour."

The lights came back on. Teresa was the only one who didn't get up.

"If that's all you need from me, I think I'd prefer to go home."

The deputy prosecutor had no objections, and agreed that she could be dismissed.

"We'll keep you posted. You just concentrate on getting better."

If only he knew that she was never going to come back . . . Teresa watched them walk out, shaking Parri's hand when he nudged hers in farewell, and only then did she laboriously get to her feet, her jaw clenching with the effort. Marini helped her find her most comfortable position, which was more and more hunched, and less and less effective in keeping the pain at bay.

"Go with them, Marini. Make sure you're always there."

He made no move toward the door.

"When you said Giacomo has done this before, you meant something more, didn't you?"

Teresa did not reply. She wasn't sure whether this was just

normal curiosity on his part, or if he was purposely creating an opportunity for her to be honest with him.

Marini pressed on.

"Giacomo Mainardi went way beyond these . . . games," he said, gesturing vaguely toward the now-closed projector. "The day he was caught wasn't the only time you were in contact with him. And I mean before you started visiting him in prison."

Teresa made him hand over her walking stick.

"Go with the others, Marini. I can get to the elevator by myself, and Parisi and de Carli will be waiting for me down-stairs."

"Aren't you going to reply?"

Teresa laughed out of sheer desperation.

"You weren't asking a question."

She walked away with small steps, as steady as she could.

Marini didn't need her to reply. He needed her to con-firm what he already knew.

The day he was caught hadn't been the only time she'd been in contact with the killer.

Teresa had thought that she was right on his heels, so determined to catch him that she'd convinced herself she was within reach.

But he hadn't been ahead of her; he'd been right beside her. And if he'd held on to a piece of her for all those years, it wasn't so that he could fantasize about her, but because what had happened was something that would bind them forever.

The elevator arrived.

"Teresa, wait."

She stepped inside, pushed the button, and watched Marini disappear behind the sliding steel doors.

36

Twenty-seven years ago

WHEN SOMEONE DIES A violent death, any conversation with the people the victim has left in the land of the living is a knife-edge upon which investigators must carefully balance.

Those who are left behind maintain that they must be told everything there is to know, but too often, these details only serve to prolong their torment rather than help them come to terms with death.

They maintain that their minds are clear, but in fact they will spend months, if not years, suspended in a limbo of pain that can quickly escalate to rage, causing them to lash out even at those working to untangle the mystery of what happened.

The third victim's wife did not deviate from this statistical norm. They hadn't been able to interview her the night before, as the sedatives the hospital staff had been forced to administer had left her catatonic. But by the next morning, she was a torrent of words and questions, and of recollections that were unlikely to be of any use to the investigation but still found a patient audience in Teresa, though they soon annoyed Albert.

Teresa couldn't really blame him. Death had forged ahead, leaving them well behind. They had to do something to breathe new life into their chase, before the killer decided to dip his brush in blood again and turn three into four.

An irritable comment from the widow resulted in an equally stern rebuke from Albert. That was when the first tears began to fall.

The woman began mournfully retracing the past, reflecting on the lifetime she had shared with the man who had so suddenly and brutally been taken away from her. They had been an ordinary couple, with a well-established routine, no children, and no particular passions that might cause them to repeatedly and regularly frequent any particular location. Their only hobby was travel, which they loved, but for the time being, that did not seem like a viable lead in the investigation.

Patience was key now, but Teresa and Albert had already worn theirs thin—and Albert's was just about ready to give.

"How do you think you can catch him if you won't even listen to me!" the widow said.

"Ma'am, with all due respect, we won't find the solution to this case by letting you inundate us with fifty years' worth of memories."

"The solution . . ." More tears ran down her face, scrubbed free of makeup and swollen with the effort of holding in what desperately needed letting out.

"You're talking about this as if it were a game, some kind of crossword puzzle. I've lost my *husband*."

"Believe me, I understand."

"No. You couldn't possibly understand."

Albert wrote something down in his notebook, tore the page out, and passed it to Teresa.

We're not getting anywhere. Let's wind this down.

Teresa nodded, carefully folding the note up and slipping it into her pocket as if it contained instructions for some crucial next step in the investigation, while Albert tried to reassure the woman with words and a tone of voice that would have fooled no one, let alone a heart left as exposed as hers was now, so sensitive to every lick of air. And Albert blew ice-cold.

"I have just asked Inspector Battaglia to look into something that I believe will prove crucial to the outcome of the investigation. We will come back to you with further updates. Soon, I expect."

"We were supposed to enjoy our retirement. We were comfortable. My husband's never been ill, not even a cold."

Albert stood up. Teresa followed suit.

"I suppose that's life," he said.

"That's life, my ass!"

The woman's sudden movement knocked over the glass of fruit juice which Teresa had requested instead of coffee. The sugary liquid spilled over the embroidered tablecloth and Teresa's notebook, which she hadn't yet picked up.

One of the woman's relatives quickly sat beside her on the sofa, ready for the inevitable flood of tears. Another protested half-heartedly with Albert, pleading for a little more tact.

Teresa hurriedly patted her notebook dry with paper

towels. She regarded the widow with renewed compassion—this woman she had previously deemed to be fairly unremarkable, but who was clearly capable of fighting talk when necessary, especially if she felt she was being trodden upon.

She wasn't unremarkable. She was brave, though she didn't know it.

What was it about these people's unremarkable lives that had attracted the killer?

Opportunity. Robert's suggestion kept echoing in her mind. The killer had made use of an opportunity.

"What kind of monster could have done this to Filippo? We'd just been planning our next trip. He was so happy. His hip was finally fixed. The implant wasn't giving him any trouble. There was nothing to stop us anymore; we were ready to go."

Something inside Teresa clicked into place. It was the weight of a cold leg in her arms, and Parri's words of warning. *Don't rotate it.*

"Had your husband recently had a hip replacement?"

"Six months ago. They told him he had good, strong bones. A young man's bones at the age of seventy-two. They just needed to fix his hip and then he'd be good as new."

"Who did? Who told him that?"

The widow looked at her as if Teresa were the one who sounded a little unhinged.

"The doctors who looked after him in the orthopedics ward, obviously."

"Ma'am, I'm going to need to use your phone."

"Yes, of course."

Teresa was already dialing the extension for one of the

offices inside the forensics institute. Parri picked up almost immediately.

"It's Battaglia. The third victim has a prosthetic hip, too, doesn't he?"

"Yes, that's right. I was working on my report now, actually. I've just finished with him."

Teresa gripped the receiver a little tighter.

"So just like all the other victims, then."

"Hip replacement in the first victim, knee in the second. Fairly common operations, at their age."

So common that they created an opportunity.

"The operations determined the killer's selection. That's where he found his victims."

"Where exactly do you mean?"

"I'll call you back."

Teresa hung up.

Albert, the widow, the relatives who'd swooped in to defuse the argument, Lorenzi, and another officer were all staring at her, waiting for her to say something.

Now what?

Her voice came booming out of her chest.

"Lorenzi, do we still have the map we were consulting at the crime scene?"

Her colleague quickly pulled it out and spread it over the coffee table.

The marks Teresa had made were clearly visible.

"Is that where my Filippo died? Where it says number three?"

"That's where we found him."

Teresa used her hands to measure distances, drawing lines and midpoints which she then enclosed in a circle.

There it was, right at the center of it all. The city hospital.

She could sense Albert craning his neck behind her.

"Have we found him?"

Teresa nodded. No doubt, this time. She pointed at the spot.

"This is where he chooses them."

37

Today

WHEN THE DOORS OF the elevator opened on the ground floor of the courthouse, Teresa came face to face with Marini again.

He was standing there, panting from the exertion of rushing down the stairs, with his arms spread wide and planted like tree trunks against the metal frame. He must have flown down.

"Where exactly do you think you're going?"

She pointed her walking stick at him.

"Same place *you'll* end up taking me. To the madhouse."

Somewhere behind Marini, Parisi called out to Teresa.

"Do you have a moment, Superintendent?"

Marini relented, letting her through.

"What is it?"

"I have the information you wanted on Blanca. All of it."

He sounded unusually solemn as he handed her the

piece of paper on which he had quickly transcribed the girl's details.

Teresa read it, then looked around.

"I need to sit down."

They walked her to one of the chairs in the visitors' waiting area.

Marini's eyes kept darting between her and Parisi.

"Is anyone going to tell me what's going on?"

Teresa gave him the note.

"What's going on is that the girl is not who she says she is—but that much I'd already suspected. What worries me more is what she might want from me."

She spoke the words softly, as a warning to herself: *Be careful, Teresa, you're not in a state to be making promises to anyone. You're not fit to be anyone's hope.*

"Alice Zago? That's her real name?"

Marini seemed more surprised than angry. A good sign. But he didn't know the full story yet.

Behind the glass doors, Teresa could see Albert chatting with Gardini on their way back from their coffee break at the café across the road.

If the district attorney found out about this, if he learned that they'd been misled, he would find a way to unleash his fury—the wrath of an unhappy tyrant—on the young woman, on Teresa, and on the whole team, who'd placed their trust in Alice disguised as Blanca. A fragile Alice who'd been swallowed up by a hole in the ground and slipped down the muddy tunnel all the way to the bottom.

Teresa sighed.

"I know her story, and I'll tell you what it is eventually, but for the time being I have to ask you all once again to trust me and bear with me for a little while. Is that too much to ask? Just say if it is."

In the silence that followed, Teresa sensed a kind of resolve that seemed to transcend individual will.

With no more information than that, and without further ado, Marini handed the note back to Parisi with a meaningful nod, whereupon Parisi pulled out a lighter from the pocket of his jeans and burned the piece of paper to ashes, turning it around in his fingers.

Then, all of a sudden, something changed.

Through the glass, Teresa saw Albert seeking out her gaze, mobile phone at his ear, and an expression on his face that alarmed her.

There's a storm coming, thought Teresa.

The district attorney ran toward her. The magnitude of what he was about to tell her was clear in his eyes, but she didn't want to look.

She followed the motion of his lips as she would have followed those of a mime. There was no sound, other than background noise ringing in her ears.

Giacomo had slashed his wrists open—just as he had done with the pages of the old story Teresa was now forced to revisit.

3 8

———— ⚬ ————

Twenty-seven years ago

THE SPIDER EMERGED FROM his black hole and spun his viscous web with the thread spilling from his abdomen, where everything was warmer, and where even he felt incandescent. The spider's legs moved busily around his prey, weaving a cocoon where he could preserve them and make them feel safe.

He would drag them into his black hole well before he killed them.

It had happened at least three times already.

His victims would go on with their lives, waking up beside their wives in the same bed they'd probably shared for decades, eating, bathing, going outside to feel the sun shining on their faces, to watch it set, feeling happy, or sad, or dissatisfied, perhaps. But always oblivious. They would talk about day-to-day matters and complain about minor ailments, never once suspecting that they were, in fact, already as good as dead.

That black hole had very specific coordinates, foundations made of concrete, and wide windows of steel and glass. The city hospital. The orthopedics ward.

It had to be. Teresa was sure of it. And she kept repeating it to anyone who would listen.

"That's where he chooses them."

Albert was holding his head in his hands, still unsure, his face wearing the expression of a man who felt he was being dragged somewhere against his will. His eyes were fixed on the desk in the meeting room. Photographs, reports, diagrams, and expert analyses were all laid out before him, fanned out like tarot cards bearing symbols whose meanings remained a mystery.

"We have no evidence, Teresa."

"Then we need to hurry up and find some, because he can't wait to kill again."

Albert snapped, sending the papers flying.

"What would you have me do? Stalk the hospital corridors arresting people for looking at me the wrong way? And what if I were to step on the wrong person's toes? What would the press say then? That I'm casting aspersions on the medical profession?"

Teresa made no move to pick up the files that had fallen to the floor.

"Our *job* is to look for things, to be suspicious, to ask questions and demand answers. And to ruffle a few feathers, too, if necessary!"

"You know all about that, don't you?"

Albert had lowered his voice now, and for once there was no hostility in his tone. They stared at each other in silent challenge, and he muttered a curse. He began to pace the room, measuring its length in nervous strides, until he had finally convinced himself to make the round of phone calls that would authorize them to broaden the investigation to the hospital.

He didn't even look at her when he hung up.

"We have the green light. Now we just need to wait for the official warrant. It shouldn't take long."

Waiting was the hardest part. Teresa motioned at Lorenzi to tidy up the scattered papers, and he rushed to the task. She turned her attention back to Albert.

"We can use this time to go over the case again. Run through the facts, study the crime scene photographs. There are a few details I'd quite like to review."

Albert rummaged in the desk drawer for a pack of cigarettes.

"What's the point?"

"What's the *point*? Are you serious?"

"If you're right, and you seem sure you are, then all we need to do is go there and catch him, no?"

He walked toward the door.

"Go for a walk, Teresa. And try to calm down, while you're at it."

He left her feeling dismayed and silenced. Teresa's great fear was that sooner or later, the inchoate rage she felt inside of her would solidify, turning her into a completely different person. The thought scared her, but part of her yearned for that change, which felt a little like payback.

She closed her eyes. They were burning, either from exhaustion or unshed tears. She sometimes caught herself thinking that no matter what decisions she made, no matter what steps she dared to take, she would never get far enough.

Her colleague was still crouching over the scattered papers, trying to gather them together.

"Leave everything as it is, Lorenzi."

Teresa walked across the room and through the corridors with an old woman's gait, and when she got to the lobby, she headed for the phone she used whenever she needed to make personal calls.

She put her bag on top of the booth, and as she looked for spare change in her wallet, she spotted the note where her gynecologist had jotted down the date and time of their next appointment. Teresa would go alone, though strangely this didn't frighten her but gave her strength. She was about to become a single mother. She wasn't the first, nor would she be the last. Just one of many. There were others out there who were in the exact same position. It was a comforting thought.

She slipped a coin into the slot, dialed the number, and waited.

When Lavinia picked up, Teresa didn't say a word.

"Hello? Who is this?"

Teresa leaned her forehead against the telephone. Maybe she wouldn't have to go to the appointment alone after all.

"It's Teresa. Do you have a moment?"

This time it was her friend who remained silent.

In the background, Teresa recognized the sweet, crystalline notes of the *Clair de lune*. It was thanks to Lavinia that Teresa had discovered that piece. She had never listened to Debussy before, but in Sebastiano and Lavinia's family, classical music had always been the soundtrack to a perfect life. Teresa and Sebastiano had spent many a night clinging to each other to the sounds of that same melody, only to wake up the next morning as strangers.

"Lavinia, are you there? I thought I might come and see you, if you're free. I need to talk to you."

Which actually meant, *I need you, like some distant moon, like a light in the darkness, like a star I can cling to as it passes by so that I can fly away from here.* In the silence that followed, Teresa could hear her own heartbeat.

And the moon quickly revealed itself to be nothing but a hollow crater.

"You want to come here to air your dirty laundry, don't you?"

Teresa instinctively cradled her womb, as if it had suddenly been left exposed.

"What . . . ?"

"I did not appreciate that phone call the other night. Remember, it's my brother we're talking about."

"Lavinia . . ."

"If you're no longer interested in him, just leave him, but for God's sake don't drag me into your problems. What am I supposed to do when I see him?"

Teresa felt a teardrop fall from the tip of her chin all the way to her hand, curled around the metal telephone cable.

"I need help."

The words had come out in a whisper—the fading arpeggios in the background mirroring her dwindling hope.

"I'm sorry, but you're going to have to deal with this on your own."

The gods often argued with each other, Teresa thought. *They even clashed sometimes. But they never took mortal form just to rescue an insignificant human. No amount of love, compassion, or even basic pity was enough to make them truly forsake their own tribe. What dwelt in the heavens remained in the heavens.*

Lavinia hung up, and something in Teresa's universe, in the sidereal realm above her, suddenly ceased to shine.

"Battaglia!"

Teresa turned around, the now-quiet receiver still in her grasp, her ear refusing to register the silence at the other end.

Lorenzi's head was peeking out from the elevator, the rest of his body jamming the doors open.

"We've just received the warrant, Inspector Battaglia. We need to call the hospital to get them to send us their files on the staff of the orthopedics ward. Superintendent Lona said to ask you to do it."

Teresa dried her tears with the edge of her sleeve and picked up her bag.

"What, so that they're warned we're coming? Absolutely not. I'll go there myself."

She dropped the receiver, letting it hang from its cord.

39

Today

TERESA HAD WANTED TO see Giacomo alone. As soon as she walked into the room, she realized that she had always known, deep down, that someday she would find him right where he was now. Not in a morgue, not in a prison cell he'd never get out of, but in a hospital bed. Somehow, he'd found a way to return to where it all began.

She sat next to him. He was asleep. The brush against death—his own—had exhausted him.

She tucked the sheet in and fixed the elastic band of his oxygen mask so that it wouldn't cut into his cheeks.

"Oh, Giacomo. Did you really have to?" She sighed. She was exhausted, too. "I'm not sure I can bear it, you know."

She held his hand. That strong hand, capable of delivering both death and salvation, now lay calm and inert. Perhaps it had finally found peace now that he had used it to shed his own blood.

Giacomo had turned on himself, as was often the case in stories like his—generating a maelstrom of destruction before crashing back down into a heart that was often too tired to beat on, that had never come into its own.

Teresa ran her thumb over the dressing on his wrist. His veins had been repaired with stitches, and the bandages were straining to hold together the flesh of his tattered life. Teresa reflected on the bitterness that characterized certain cursed existences. She had once risked the same fate herself.

She rested her face in his palm. She could smell the same medical scent that had marked their shared history— a history that continued to torment them both. Shoved deep inside one of the two gashes, the surgeon had found a pearlescent marble tile. Teresa had no doubt that it was the missing piece from the portrait he'd made of her. Of all the leftover pieces that had been found, it was the only one that had been carved into any kind of shape: a hexagon, which symbolized their bond and fit perfectly in the empty spot.

Buried stories will always remain inside of us, tucked away in some cold recess, the dark room everyone avoids and where the lights are never on. But that means the dust can never settle. Everything remains exactly as it was.

Giacomo's cry for help was still there, twenty-seven years later. Teresa had never been able to untangle the knot of hurt he carried in his chest.

She reluctantly let go of his hand.

"I'll be back soon. Don't go anywhere."

As she walked out of the room, she kept her eyes fixed on his face, hoping to catch even the slightest trace of movement, and when she closed the door behind her, she did so very gently, as she would have done if he'd been a little boy, fast asleep and dreaming of his toys.

But who knew what Giacomo was actually dreaming of, or whether there was a place somewhere, in some other universe, where violence was not a curse destined to be passed on from generation to generation, and where he might get the chance to feel what it was like to be like other people—no better or worse than anybody else.

A TEAR SLIPPED out of Giacomo's eye and slid down his cheekbone, until it hung suspended from his jaw.

The nurse who had come in to check on his vitals quickly wiped it dry with a piece of rough gauze. Had he actually been asleep, this would have woken him up.

How careless the nurse's gestures felt—especially after how gentle Teresa had been.

Giacomo kept his eyes shut to the world.

He was suffering, but it was a different from the pain that made him kill.

It was a sad pain, but it was also kind.

40

IV Century

LUSIUS WAS DEAD, MURDERED by a fellow Roman in the temple of the Christian god. The news had traveled from mouth to ear in whispered breaths among the campfires outside the city walls of Aquileia. The soldiers bristled with fury and doubt, but their orders were to stay put. They must not show any signs of unrest, or else the enemy would strike again—not just against one man this time, but the whole legion.

"He might still be alive," the optio murmured to his commander. "Nobody saw what happened."

Claudius Cornelius Tacitus took his helmet from his assistant's hands.

"He's dead."

He stepped out of the tent, and the scent of ritual incense was quickly replaced by the smells of the encampment: leather and braziers, roast meat and male skin, sand, the metal of the soldiers' weapons, dried fish, and the sweet, heady fragrance of open wineskins. But the men's goblets were still full to the brim, and so they would remain. Any semblance of calm was a fiction.

The milites rose to their feet as he walked past. They beat their fists against their chests.

Claudius put his helmet on and tightened its leather strap. He was getting ready to leave behind the only life he'd ever known.

And for what? the fear inside of him asked. Did faith truly have the power to subvert all logic, and to solidify within a man's heart what had, in fact, no solid form at all?

He would soon find out.

Feronia and Mist were raring to go. The mare was stronger and wilder than Mist, and Claudius decided to ride her first. She was quicker, too, and would carry him far, while Mist's stamina would serve Claudius better during the daylight hours.

He slipped his foot into the stirrups and heaved himself onto the horse. Feronia absorbed his weight with a grunt. Claudius patted her neck. He could feel her energy quivering between his thighs.

"Calm down, now. You'll be running soon."

The encampment was an expanse of torchlight and quickened, agitated breaths.

Claudius gazed into the distance. It was getting dangerous to wait any longer than he already had.

"It's late. There isn't much time left until the changing of the guard," said the optio, voicing what many of the others were thinking. "The barriers . . ."

Claudius grabbed the reins and banished all doubt.

"The barriers will open."

Feronia was restless, causing Mist—who was tethered to her—to neigh in response. Claudius would only let her walk in circles, storing up the power that would shortly be released with thunderous, inexorable force at just a clip of her rider's heels. Meanwhile his own fervor was growing, too, matching the mare's.

One of the soldiers pointed toward the eastern edge of the encampment.

"There's someone coming!"

They could not yet make out the identity of the figure running toward them, but he was too slight to cause any kind of alarm. A young man, a boy, approaching alone.

"That's Lusius's servant."

Lusius was definitely dead; that was clear to everyone now. Claudius felt his insides churning.

Other figures were following in the young man's wake. A tribune and his centurions. They were still quite far away.

Claudius leaned toward the optio.

"Protect the boy. Find out who wished to see Lusius dead, and kill him in turn."

He maneuvered Feronia into the attacking gait that had brought them so many triumphs. The mare launched herself forward like an arrow from the bowstring, but Claudius did not direct her toward the barriers yet. He galloped instead toward the boy, but stopped the horses several yards short, ordering the young servant to throw what Lusius had given him for safekeeping.

The boy, well-trained and experienced in battle, didn't hesitate.

Claudius pulled at the reins, and Feronia reared on her hind legs. With one hand he caught the bundle out of the air, and with the other, he tugged again at the horse's harness.

Now he was racing furiously toward the barriers that sealed the encampment like sluices. The doors that faced north were supposed to open at his arrival. If they didn't, he would be doomed.

Behind him, the milites were busy slowing the advance of the tribune and his centurions, resuming their military community's

*evening activities as if nothing unusual had happened. They were
protecting the boy, recognizing in his loyalty to Lusius the spirit of
a true soldier of Rome.*

*Claudius was almost at the gates, illuminated by torches and
braziers. He was close enough to be able to look into the eyes of the
four sentries who'd been stationed to guard it.*

*The horse's heart was his own. Their courage, too, was shared.
The mare showed no signs of hesitation, and she would only ever
stop at his signal, even at the cost of her life. Mist did not pull back
either, keeping pace with their advance, emboldened by blind faith
in his fellow beast and their master.*

*Claudius spurred Feronia on. He was about to find out whether
the sentries' loyalty had also held.*

*The men recognized him. Someone yelled an order, and the thick
wooden bars that secured the gates were pulled aside.*

*Claudius crossed the border of the encampment through streaks
of torchlight and a flurry of dust, and in the cacophony, he caught
the sound of someone behind him calling out the name of the goddess—like a blessing, and a reminder that he must never betray her.*

*Claudius waited until darkness had engulfed him completely
before giving himself and the horses a break, and slowing their pace.
Only several miles later did he stop to turn and take in the distant
lights of Aquileia, the Empire's resplendent bulwark.*

*Before him lay a dark and silent hollow where the light of Rome
did not shine. Every day now, Roman blood was shed in that land
that stretched from Constantinople all the way to the Julian Alps.*

*He took off his helmet and placed it inside the sack that Mist
carried on his flank. He took out a black cloak and pulled it over
his military robes.*

*Separated from the rest of his legion, completely on his own, and
without the comfort of familiar symbols to remind him who he truly*

was, Claudius felt the uncertainty that came with the first stirrings of a new kind of freedom.

He stroked Feronia's head, rewarded her with the kinds of whispered words that would usually be reserved for a woman. The mare nuzzled his hand. Behind them, Mist let out a grunt.

Claudius opened the bundle he was still clutching in one hand and brushed his lips devotedly against the statuette, before tucking it safely away inside the bandages that stopped his breastplate from chafing against his chest. He picked up the reins again and prepared to face the unknown, his gaze alert.

Their faith must survive. It must be carried into new lands that still worshipped pagan gods. Beyond the castrum of Ibligine to the north, all the way past the Alps and into the Noricum; or east, past Forum Julii and across the forests, toward Illyria.

Claudius opted to head east, where the Light of the new day rose, where the Sun returned unvanquished every day after crossing through the most dangerous hours of Night.

It was his turn, now, to overcome that Night.

41

Twenty-seven years ago

ALBERT DECIDED HE'D VISIT the hospital's administrative department, too, as soon as he found out that was what Teresa intended to do. He couldn't possibly come second, not even in others' misguided ventures.

She made no comment, and practiced instead how to channel what few resources she had into moving forward—even when what she had was a narcissistic boss who would step aside for nothing but his own outsize ego.

But at this juncture, Albert represented the state, the team, the will to discover the truth. His presence mattered—as Teresa quickly realized from the behavior of the hospital director, who gave them free access to the personnel records and wasted no time in helping them sift through all the documentation. He seemed to respond particularly well to the embodiment of male authority who stood before him, addressing Albert even when it was Teresa who asked a question. Had she turned up on her own, he probably would have ignored her, and everything would have taken that much longer.

"We've come here because a few lines you drew on a map happened to intersect somewhere," muttered Albert when they were invited to wait in a conference room for the rest of the files they'd requested. "What if it's all a mistake?"

He was clearly apprehensive about the process he'd set in motion. Scared of damaging his reputation—and consequently his power—because of a misstep that wasn't even his own.

It was a problem Teresa didn't have.

"Albert, we've come here because our hypothesis aligns with the clues we've gathered so far, and because we certainly can't expect the killer to come to us himself. You have to be willing to take a risk, otherwise we'll never see the end of this case—at least not the kind of end we're all hoping for."

"What you're hoping for is to see me end up in the stocks."

"You're wrong. Anyway, knowing you, you'd probably find a way to send someone else there instead of you."

But she wasn't going to let it be her again. She was getting more pregnant by the day; there was no time to lose.

The director and his secretary had returned, carrying the files for several employees.

Out of all the staff in the hospital, those whose characteristics and positions were the closest match for the parameters Teresa had identified were two surgeons, three female nurses, one male nurse, four female orderlies, and two male orderlies, all from the orthopedics department.

Teresa immediately set aside the files corresponding to female personnel. For the first time, the hospital director actually spoke to her.

"Why are you ruling them out?"

"The killer we're looking for can't be a woman. And not just because of his physical build, which we can deduce from the handful of footprints we have identified."

Albert interrupted her.

"Though those could, of course, be easily altered with oversize shoes."

"So if that's not the main reason, then what is?"

"Statistics, and psychological profiles." Teresa pressed a finger on the stack of files. "Female serial killers are very rare, and more importantly . . ."

"More importantly, you're basically harmless."

So much sloppy thinking, cheapening a science that had already achieved so much, and had made such a significant contribution to their cause.

"*We* may be relatively uncommon, but more importantly, our approach is more targeted," she replied. "Female serial killers tend to choose their victims from among a narrow circle of family and loved ones. They take advantage of relationships of mutual trust and care. They do not like to resort to physical violence and bloodshed, but tend to develop more sophisticated methods—which are consequently more difficult to spot. They are equipped with an exceptional capacity for camouflage, and they hardly ever get caught. And so they keep on killing, for years and years. That doesn't exactly sound *harmless*, does it?"

Albert glared at her.

"Shall we proceed?"

Teresa leafed through the two surgeons' files. They were both middle-aged, with spotless and fairly straightforward professional records. Albert leaned in to take a closer look.

Teresa was doubtful.

"The age range isn't right."

"But they would have access to the training and the tools needed to remove the bones the victims were missing. Besides, you haven't got some kind of crystal ball. You might be wrong."

"The amputations performed on the first two victims were a mess."

"But the third was clean."

"He could have learned along the way. He must have, in fact."

"Though according to Parri, the killer was already using a scalpel by the time he got to the second victim."

But they still hadn't figured out what the murderer was looking for in those bodies, why he removed fragments from a different bone each time. What did he do with them? What did they represent? Why did he always carve his victims' chests open?

They moved on to the file belonging to the male nurse. His CV was also impeccable. He had a year left until retirement. Teresa glanced at the photographs that came with his file.

Again, the age wasn't right. Teresa set the file aside.

"This one's too good."

They moved on to the orderlies, younger men whose professional records were equally unblemished.

Teresa turned to the director.

"Is this all? Don't you have any other matching profiles?"

"We do, but they were all on shift during the dates and times you've indicated."

Albert was getting irritated. He gathered all the papers together and tucked them under his arm.

"What's your objection this time? They're the right age, aren't they? We'll study their profiles and look into their alibis."

Teresa did not get up.

"That would be a waste of time."

Albert sat back down.

"Why?"

She almost felt sorry for him. He looked exhausted.

"Because we're looking for an individual who is devoted solely to the fulfilment of his twisted fantasies. Devoted to evil, Superintendent Lona. Until the first murder, he might have still managed to pretend otherwise and continue to lead some kind of double life, but by this point, psychosis will have taken hold. He is not interested in showing up for work on time, he is not interested in earning a salary. Work is actually an impediment. Everything is an impediment to his one and only goal: finding new victims to murder. He probably forgets to eat sometimes. He needs time to come up with his plans, he needs time to exercise his imagination. And murder is tiring; it takes up all his energy." She gestured toward the files. "These service records are impeccable. We won't find the killer's name in here."

Albert gave her a look that seemed almost hateful.

"You're exaggerating."

"Actually . . ." began the director, clearing his throat. "Actually there is someone who matches your description. I hadn't brought his file out for you because he's been on leave for the past three months, but the first murder was committed just over a month ago. The kid requested some time off after the death of his mother." He whispered a name to his secretary, who hurried out of the room. "But even before that, his mother's illness would regularly take him away from work, and he was frequently late and often distracted. He's been issued with two written warnings due to mistakes he made when treating patients."

Teresa felt her heart speed up. *That* was the profile she was looking for.

When the secretary returned with the file, the director made as if to hand it over to Teresa, but Albert was quick to intercept it.

"Twenty-three years old," he said, reading from the folder. "Lives not too far from here."

Teresa leaned across the table to see if she could glean any more information, but Albert tilted the folder upward like a screen.

"There isn't much else in here."

The director turned to Teresa.

"The personnel office tried to contact him around ten days ago, as there were some forms that needed updating. But they never managed to get through to him."

Teresa didn't even need to read the file. If it was true that his mother had died so recently, the premature death of such a fundamental figure in his life could well have been the event that triggered the violence.

She had a sudden thought, which took on immediate urgency.

"We need to contact every patient who has passed through this ward in at least the past six months. They must be tracked down and warned of the danger."

Albert looked up at the director.

"How many would that be?"

The man threw up his hands.

"At least a hundred."

Teresa had to act fast. *Close the circle around the killer*, Robert would have said.

"We can start by filtering for age, gender, and type of operation to identify those whose profile corresponds to the victims so far. We narrow the search. And no one speaks to the press. It would be like warning him that we're coming."

The director nodded. His arrogance had vanished.

Albert slid the young man's photo across the table.

Teresa stopped it with the palm of her hand, then flipped it around.

Her other hand went instinctively to her womb. Her throat filled with bile, scalding her like lava.

"Teresa?"

"I've seen him before. He's the nurse who was helping Parri at the third crime scene. I've seen him at the forensics institute, too. I've spoken to him."

"Are you sure it's the same person?"

"Yes."

The director picked up the photograph.

"But that's impossible. Giacomo Mainardi had already requested to go on leave, and as far as I know, he has no connection to the forensics institute at all."

He had requested the time he needed to kill.

As for his visits to the crime scenes, his presence at the morgue, and his proximity to the investigating officers, Teresa knew exactly what they meant.

"He's been keeping tabs on us. Gathering information. And now he knows we've gotten this far." She stood up and looked at the park outside the window. He might even be out there. "I want to see where he worked."

42

Twenty-seven years ago

SO HIS NAME WAS Giacomo. They had never properly intro-
duced themselves, but the killer already knew who she was.
He had been watching her as she studied the trail of corpses
he left in his wake. He might even have been carrying pieces
of those bodies when he approached her. And he had come
so close to her baby.

Teresa stifled the urge to vomit, pressing a tissue against
her mouth.

She felt a hand on her back—Albert's hand.

"Are you all right?"

She nodded, but didn't risk opening her mouth.

The suspect's locker had been cleaned out weeks ago, but
Albert still put a pair of gloves on before opening it.

"There's no point bringing anyone in to collect fingerprints."

Teresa tried swallowing a few times before she spoke
again.

"Let's give it a go. We might find a trace in a corner somewhere."

"You're hoping for a miracle."

She was well aware of that. Albert took his gloves off and looked around for a bin to throw them in.

"We'll need a warrant to search his house, and who knows if and when we'll get that. And before we can even apply for one, we'll have to find some fingerprints that match those from the crime scene. You can't have one without the other—it's like chicken and egg."

Teresa's eyes instinctively veered toward her notebook, which was peeking out of her open bag. The disconnected phone number the killer had given her was still in there, written in one of those pages—but she had probably wiped his fingerprints off with her own hands. She pulled the notebook out from one of the bag's inner pockets.

"The last time I saw him, he gave me a phone number that didn't work."

Albert looked at her as if she had gone insane.

"You *flirted* with him?"

"No! He just grabbed my notebook and wrote it down."

Albert muttered a half-strangled curse.

"At least we might get some fingerprints from it," he said.

"I wiped the cover clean when we were visiting the third victim's widow and all that juice spilled over it. But we could still try."

"We'd be wasting our time."

"We have to wait anyway."

Albert had sent four plainclothes officers to stake out the suspect's residence, but they hadn't yet sent any alerts back to headquarters. They had taken a neighbor's statement, who told them that the shutters had been closed for days. Mainardi must have left to go on that trip he had mentioned. The neighbor had described him as an elusive but polite figure. Not exactly nice—just polite. The neighbor had always sensed that there was some kind of distance separating their respective worlds.

Teresa hadn't believed the story about the trip, not even for a second.

"Where could he be?" she muttered, eyes fixed on the locker whose metal surface those hands must have touched countless times.

"How should I know?"

"I was talking to myself, Albert."

A nurse walked in, greeting them with a nod. She opened her locker, unpinned her employee badge, and placed it inside, then took off her cardigan and hung it up. Between every gesture, she turned around to look at them, until finally her eyes crossed with Teresa's.

"That's Giacomo's locker. He doesn't work here anymore."

Teresa had been waiting for her to make the first move.

"We're aware, ma'am. Do you know him well?"

"Not exactly. We were just colleagues who saw each other maybe every other week, when we happened to be on the same shift. Sometimes we'd have a quick coffee together and chat about the weather, or at most about the patients here. Nothing more than that. Did something happen to him?"

It was the way she asked that caught Teresa's attention. The woman was afraid, either for herself or for him.

Teresa pulled out her badge.

"We're with the police. When was the last time you saw Giacomo Mainardi?"

"He was here a few weeks ago. I turned around and found him standing right behind me. I hadn't even heard him come in. He asked me how I was, how work was going. I thought it was strange."

"Why?"

"He'd never really opened up to me, but there was something different about the way he was looking at me that day. He told me: 'I'm here for you, because you've always been kind to me.'"

"How was he looking at you?"

"This might sound crazy, but there was almost something romantic about it. Of course I'm old enough to be his mother. He'd brought me a gift, too . . . A ring—a wedding band. He told me it had belonged to his grandmother, and he wanted me to have it because I was a special person. I refused to even touch it."

"How did he react?"

"I got the impression that I'd hurt his feelings, and I did try to clear the air, but he didn't give me the chance—he just left. I was so scared I didn't sleep for days. I suppose he hadn't exactly done anything wrong, but it just seemed like such a crazy gesture."

"Do you remember when this happened?"

"I could never forget it."

She pointed at a calendar hanging on the wall. It was the day before the second victim was murdered.

Teresa rummaged through her shoulder bag, extracted the case file, and showed her the photograph of the wedding ring that been taken from Giovanni Bordin. It was a gold torchon band, worn and a little dull. An old-fashioned design.

The woman wrapped her arms around herself, her face taut.

"Yes, that's the one."

Giacomo had taken the first victim's wedding ring and tried to gift it to this woman. But she had rejected his gift. And he'd started killing again.

It was typical of serial killers to present people who mattered to them with objects that had once belonged to their victims, but if that was what had happened here, then Teresa did not understand why the killer would have left the same ring behind in the pond by the nymphaeum.

She stepped away to look for the photograph that showed the ring on the finger of the marble arm they had found among the cerulean water lilies at the foot of the mutilated statue. A shiver coursed through her.

If in the killer's imagination that ring was meant for a woman, if he had been following the progress of the police investigation, if the contact he'd made with Teresa had not been accidental, then perhaps that ring . . .

She remembered the cerulean petals that the killer had left behind in the third victim's blood. Gifts and more gifts. All for her.

"Why have you come here? Has Giacomo done something?"

The woman had sensed Teresa's panic, glimpsed in it a reflection of her own, and asked whether the fear they both felt was justified.

Teresa turned around and smiled at her.

"Nothing you need to worry about."

And she meant it, too. Perhaps the killer had identified her with his late mother, or with a girlfriend he'd never had.

Love and romantic relationships were confusing to him, but he did not take his frustration out on female victims. In his mind, women represented detachment and rejection—not anger and revenge.

But if she was to truly understand him, Teresa had to discover the full story of Giacomo Mainardi.

She gave the woman her card.

"Should he reach out to you, buy yourself some time, arrange to meet him in a public place, and call us immediately. Do not meet him alone."

The woman took the card, her hand shaking.

"You said I had nothing to worry about."

"That's right. We're looking for him in connection with an investigation into a gambling ring, but even so, you shouldn't meet him alone."

The woman placed a hand over her heart.

"I definitely won't. Not a chance."

They were about to walk out of the room when she called out to them again.

"Giacomo told me something strange when he tried to give me the ring. He told me he carries his mother's surname, Mainardi, because his biological father never accepted him. And when she got married again to an older man, her new husband refused to give Giacomo his surname, even though Giacomo was only two at the time. He told me he would never be able to give his future wife a normal family surname. I've been thinking about that a lot. Maybe what he meant is that he feels different from everyone else—because of that double rejection. At least I think that might be the case."

"I think so, too."

It was as if the surname on all his personal documents certified that he was only half a son—a woman's child alone.

"He also told me he has a hole in place of a heart, and asked if I would be able to accept him anyway. I felt sorry for him, and I was scared of him."

Teresa was gripped by the same sensations. She felt pity, and she felt fear.

43

Today

IT WAS MARINI WHO escorted Teresa home after she had gone to visit Giacomo. He turned the key in the lock and pushed the door open, then stepped aside to let her through.

She limped inside and didn't even turn the lights on. The sunset was filtering through the curtains, casting melancholy shadows. She threw herself onto the sofa.

"There's definitely nothing poetic about old age."

He picked her bag up from the floor and hung it on one of the hooks by the front door.

"You're not old, you're just a little worse for wear."

"I can feel every single one of my years. In fact, I think I can feel at least twice as many."

"It'll be three times the amount soon, if you're not careful. Are you sure you want to do this?"

Teresa let her head drop back among the cushions.

"The alternative would be to pretend, and I don't want to do that anymore."

But before she could forget about the world, there was one final thing she had to attend to: the small matter of the girl who'd entered her life under another name. She had turned to Teresa under false pretenses, precisely at a time when Teresa simply couldn't afford to leave anything to be dealt with in the future.

Marini turned the table lamps on (he'd learned by now that she detested the aggressive glow of ceiling lights) and sat in front of her, his hands intertwined and elbows resting on his knees.

"So, are you going to tell me the truth about Alice now?"

"I suppose the second part of her life, the one that comes after the carefree childhood, must have begun ten years ago. There was a flood somewhere in the north, close to the Austrian border. The river swelled during a torrential downpour, destroying a bridge that connected a village to the state highway and causing part of a hill to collapse. In that chaos of mud and water, a woman disappeared. Alice's mother."

"My God."

"A few witnesses had spotted her walking along the river path, but no one could say for sure that they had seen her carried away by the currents."

"Why is that significant?"

"Because the body was never found. The local search and rescue teams and the police were both called to the scene, as per normal procedure."

"Wait—is this going where I think it's going?"

"I was the officer who led the police investigation."

Marini swore.

"And now that little girl has grown up and decided to come back into your life to torment you."

"Everything's always a tragedy with you, Marini. I don't think her objective is to torment me."

He stood up and walked to the window. A bolt of lightning framed his dark silhouette against the half sapphire, half ash-gray sky. The sunset had faded. A storm was coming.

"So what is it that she wants?"

"To solve a mystery that's become an obsession. That night ten years ago, we found two packed suitcases and a large sum of cash inside her mother's wardrobe. Where was she planning to go? Who was she going with, and why? We never found out the truth about what happened to her. Did she run away? Was it a freak accident? Or something worse? There was one little girl left behind who just couldn't stop thinking about it. It was Alice."

"Could the father have been involved?"

"We investigated the woman's husband, too, as you'd expect, but quickly ruled him out as a suspect. If I'd had even the slightest doubt about him, I would have left no stone unturned. I would never have left that little girl in his care. None of the witnesses we interviewed—including his daughter—mentioned any incidents of domestic violence in their statements. By all accounts it was a harmonious family, and yet the hours leading up to the incident were and will always remain a mystery. Alice wants to know why her mother was preparing to abandon her, and that's a question I will never be able to answer for her."

"Only her mother could. Do you really think she's dead?"

"If she wasn't swept away in the mudslide, then she must

have decided to be as good as dead to her family. Of the two possibilities, the second seems worse to me, though Alice felt otherwise. Sometimes we cling on to illusions. But now I'm wondering: What if she's right? What if her mother's still alive? That would mean I failed."

"No. It would only mean that woman was a liar. A liar who took advantage of a natural disaster to tweak a plan she'd already made, and disappear forever."

A flash of lightning, followed moments later by the roar of thunder. Teresa counted the seconds in between, just like she used to do when she was little.

"Can an obsession take physical form, Marini?"

"It can happen—as we both know."

"And it was right in front of our eyes all along: Alice has become an expert at tracking human remains—the best around, in fact—because she wants to bring her mother back."

"With the power of sheer desperation."

"Perhaps she can still sense her mother's living, breathing body beside her—not buried somewhere along the river. Who knows how many times she must have combed through that riverbed with Smoky."

Marini stepped away from the window.

"She can tell us herself. She's just arriving now."

He opened the door before the young woman even had time to start looking for the doorbell.

Alice stepped inside, still wearing her Blanca mask. She seemed to sniff his presence out.

"Perfect timing, Inspector. Thank you."

Smoky weaved his way through their legs, tail wagging. As soon as he spotted Teresa, he started barking and skipped toward her.

She ruffled his fur and petted him until he'd settled down.

The young woman took off her jacket and backpack.

"There's a storm about to break."

"You've made it just in time."

"I left as soon as you called me. It sounded urgent. What's going on? More remains to search for? Or is it a body this time?"

"Sit down, Alice."

The girl did as she was told. She chose the armchair and sat still with her hands squeezed between her knees, the smile plastered on her face crumbling as she struggled to maintain composure. She had heard the name Teresa had used. Her real name. She blushed.

"Who told you?"

"I had begun to suspect something. There was too much mystery. You never talked about yourself. And you never turned around when I called you Blanca." Teresa smiled at the memory. She'd briefly wondered whether the girl was deaf as well as blind. "You kept ignoring the forms you needed to fill in order to work with the police—even though you were so eager to join the force. What could possibly have held you back, if not some secret you couldn't reveal?"

The girl lowered her head, wilting like a flower under Teresa's gaze.

"Hey. It's all right."

She did not reply.

"I know why you did it, Alice."

"I lied to you."

"We all lie. Every day. Sometimes with words, sometimes with kisses and unspoken thoughts."

"But I did it to you."

"I remember your story."

The girl lifted her head back up.

"Really?"

"I never forgot it."

Alice's eyes filled with tears.

She quickly wiped them off with her arm, then started rummaging inside her backpack. Her fingers ran over its contents as if they could read each item's name inscribed on its surface. She picked out a bundle of photographs held together with blue ribbon, and shakily offered it to Teresa.

"My father always took lots of pictures of me after Mom was gone. They weren't for me, obviously. They were for him. He says that in these ones, there's a mysterious woman standing somewhere in the background behind me. He says she's in disguise, but it's definitely *her*."

Her mother—or an unshakable obsession with her absence.

Teresa took the bundle, untied the ribbon, and studied the images. Marini came to stand behind her so that he could take a look, too. Teresa went through them all once, then again.

"Have you ever shown these to anyone else?"

"No."

She must have been too scared to hear the truth.

The girl couldn't stop wringing her hands. Smoky must have sensed her distress, for he leapt up next to her on the armchair and started licking her face.

"Is she there?"

Teresa had to choose the lesser of two evils, however crushing it would be: the truth.

"No, she isn't."

There was nobody standing behind little Alice—only the world and all its colors, all those shapes she couldn't see, and a father who had decided to lie to her out of love.

That physical distance Teresa had glimpsed between father and daughter was occupied by falsehoods. It was possible that Alice had sensed she was being deceived, but had chosen to believe him anyway. The alternative was to succumb to the gnawing suspicion that her father might have started lying to her even sooner, back when her mother's disappearance could still have been solved, but which—thanks in part to him—had remained a mystery.

Teresa got up, went toward her, and wearily lowered herself onto her knees, opening her arms wide just in time for Alice to fall into her embrace.

Teresa absorbed Alice's tears as if the young woman were the brave but frightened little girl Teresa had met ten years before. She comforted her with the words a mother would have used with her child—a mother who had decided to stay rather than run away.

When the tears stopped falling, Teresa pulled away from their embrace, got a tissue from Marini, and patted Alice's face dry.

Alice clung to Teresa's sweater.

"I'm sorry. I'm so sorry."

Teresa tucked Alice's blue locks behind her ears.

"We're not angry at you. None of us are—right, Marini?"

"That's right."

"But I have to be honest with you, Alice: although I think I know the reason why you've sought me out, I can't give you what you've been hoping for. I will never be able to find your mother. I couldn't find her ten years ago, and I can't find her now. And you know exactly why."

Alice took Teresa's hand in hers. Her last tear fell onto Teresa's palm.

"I'm not asking for any promises, but please don't tell me it can never happen."

Someone rang the doorbell, then started banging on the door. Teresa and Marini looked at each other. They had recognized the voice calling Teresa's name.

"What could he possibly want now?"

They went to open the door together.

They found Albert Lona standing before them, soaking wet and visibly distressed. Behind him stood Antonio Parri, who looked like he'd been crying.

44

Twenty-seven years ago

You must maintain a safe distance, Teresa. Don't
slow the rhythm of your steps, but don't let yourself be swallowed up by his story, either. Or by him.

R.

The warning in Robert's latest fax echoed inside Teresa's
mind.

Her mentor had sensed her unease more clearly than she
had, that unsettling tremor coursing through her body. His
mind had seen just how far she had gone.

He hadn't used the word *killer* because he realized that
Teresa saw something else in him.

She had dug into that young man's life, so deep that she
could hear his heart beating in the darkness. She could
almost see it, flesh and blood battling to survive, to carry the
breath of life all the way into those depths.

No matter how many victims he'd left in his wake, he himself was the first victim—though in what way exactly, she hadn't yet been able to work out.

She had just scrunched the fax into a ball and thrown it in the bin when Lorenzi walked into the office.

"We have some news on the suspect. He wasn't lying. His mother . . ."

Albert, who'd been following behind him, shoved Lorenzi aside and took the conversation over.

"Giacomo Mainardi. Born out of wedlock, father unknown. Rejected by his stepfather, too, who refused to give him his surname." He sat on the edge of the desk. "Mainardi's mother died three months ago. I suppose you'll be pleased to hear that all your theories have been confirmed."

If he could have spoken in a growl, he would have. Teresa took the dossier from Lorenzi's hands.

The man who had raised Giacomo Mainardi, and whom Mainardi called "father," had worked at the time as a sales representative, traveling across Italy and Switzerland. It was in Switzerland that he met the woman he'd eventually left his wife and Giacomo for. One day, out of the blue, he simply didn't come home.

Teresa skimmed through the file but didn't find what she was looking for.

"Does the stepfather still live in Switzerland?"

"We're looking into that now. He seems to have left there, too. His most recent partner says she hasn't heard anything from him in at least two months."

Teresa could scarcely believe it.

"And she didn't report him missing? It's not that easy to disappear."

"No report. The man had done the same with his first wife and was an unrepentant libertine, whose behavior was facilitated by the nature of his job. He was rarely home. They argued constantly, and had broken up several times before. He always did the same thing. He held a separate bank account, keeping only the bare minimum of funds in the joint family account. But even those transfers stopped after he disappeared. The woman describes him as a controlling partner and father, but says he was never physically violent with her or their two kids. Our inquiries seem to confirm she is telling the truth."

"Those kids are his. Giacomo was another man's son. That changes things, and quite drastically, too. Anyway, there's more to abuse than physical violence. Can we access his personal account? Check for any recent activity?"

"Yes, but it'll take time and patience. We're dealing with a Swiss bank. We'll need an international rogatory. We've already alerted the gendarmerie. All we can do now is wait."

But they were running out of time.

"Albert, the profile we've drawn up suggests that the killer is likely to go after men much older than he is as a way of punishing his own father figure. So it's not just a matter of opportunity."

"Yes, we get it, thank you. It's not exactly rocket science."

Teresa leapt to her feet.

"If the killer really is Giacomo, then it's his stepfather he's trying to murder—don't you see? The man is in danger."

Albert's expression curled into a grimace of disgust. "Do you realize you keep calling him by his first name?"

"So what?"

His face relaxed, the trace of a smile playing on his lips as it always did right before he was about to strike. He smirked.

"So, Teresa, you just can't bear to stay away from violent men, can you?"

She vaguely noticed Lorenzi flinch behind Albert, looking mortified. She couldn't even react.

The phone on Teresa's desk started ringing, and Albert was quick to answer. He muttered something to the caller, then hung up.

"The widow of the third victim wants to talk to us. Someone's bringing her upstairs. Are you still with us, Teresa?"

She was standing with her arms hanging by her sides. She pulled herself together only when the widow walked into the room, accompanied by an officer. The woman was clutching a shopping bag tight against her chest. She looked pale and haggard; her bloodshot eyes indicated both that she had not slept, and that she found being awake utterly unbearable.

Teresa walked toward her and offered her the chair she had been sitting on, helping the woman lower herself onto it.

The widow clasped Teresa's hand.

"It was horrible. That look."

"What do you mean, ma'am?"

"That young man who came to see me at home. I've already told this officer here about it."

"Would you mind telling us, too?"

"He rang the doorbell. He looked familiar, though I couldn't quite place him. I still can't. I opened the door anyway; there were people outside, the neighbors were mowing their lawns. I asked him what I could do for him. He told me he'd found this on the pavement and wanted to return it to me." She handed Teresa the shopping bag. "I told him thank you, but inside I was so afraid I thought I would die, and I just wanted him to go away. He couldn't possibly have found it on the pavement. And even if he had, how could he have known to return it to me?"

Teresa exchanged a worried look with Albert and opened the bag, a wave of dread coursing through her and leaving goosebumps in its wake.

It was a cap. A dark blue cap made of synthetic fabric and lined with leather.

The woman burst into tears.

"It's Filippo's. He was wearing it the day he was killed. He was wearing it when he left the house and never came back."

Teresa closed the bag shut without touching its contents, and handed it over to Lorenzi.

"Have this cataloged and analyzed for fingerprints."

She turned back toward the woman.

"I'm going to show you a photograph now. You need to tell me whether or not you recognize the man in it. If you have any doubts at all, please don't be afraid to say so."

She took the picture of Giacomo Mainardi out of the file and placed it in front of her.

The woman screamed, covering her eyes with her hands.

"It's him! It's him!"

Albert signaled to the officer to come and look after her, then took Teresa aside.

"Tell me what I need to do."

She glared at him with every ounce of contempt she could muster, but when you were in a race against death, there was no time even for hate.

"This is typical behavior. I'm not surprised. I would expect the killer to show up at the cemetery, too."

"At the cemetery?"

"The first victim has already been interred, and tomorrow will be the three-month anniversary of his mother's death—which, incidentally, falls on the same day he killed the first victim, the sixteenth day of the month. If you ask me, I think he'll visit the grave to see if he can relive the experience."

"His mother's grave?"

"No, Albert. The first victim's grave."

"Are you thinking of a surveillance camera? You know better than I do that we don't have the resources for that. Nor do we have any men to spare."

"Bullshit. And you might not have any men—but you have a woman."

45

———

Today

ANTONIO PARRI HAD BEEN crying. Teresa took note of this fact with a rush of anxiety. She had seen him like that only once before, and would have preferred to never think of that day again. Albert stood beside him, deathly pale.

"What's happened to you?"

The two men kept exchanging looks, silently daring each other forward. *What a strange pair they make,* Teresa thought. They often sized each other up from a distance, trading menacing growls that never escalated into proper clashes. The fact that they had both come rushing to her house was a bad sign. She felt her apprehension grow.

"So?"

It was Albert who managed to say the words the other couldn't.

"Giacomo Mainardi has escaped from the hospital. He knocked out the nurse who was supposed to change his dressing, stole his uniform, and climbed out of the window. The officer stationed at the door says he didn't hear a thing. Another nurse discovered what happened when she noticed that her colleague hadn't yet emerged. Mainardi had all the time in the world to walk across the hospital gardens and leave the premises. We are looking for him now, but I wanted to make sure you knew."

Teresa stared at him, lost for words. Marini stepped toward the district attorney.

"Do you think he might be coming here?"

Teresa managed to find her voice somehow.

"No. It would be foolish of him to do so, and he is anything but that."

Albert looked at Parri again, then back at Teresa.

"That's not the only reason we're here, Teresa."

So he'd been the one burdened with the task, whatever it may be. Why not Antonio? Why did her friend's mouth seem to be sealed shut?

"Antonio?" she said. "Whatever it is, just tell me."

When he finally lifted his eyes and looked at her, Teresa understood that someone must have died.

"I've finished analyzing the tiles that were retrieved in the basilica along with your tooth."

"And?"

His voice was so hoarse that it didn't even sound like his own.

"They've been cut from the victim's breastbone. The tissue is spongy and highly vascularized, rich in red bone marrow. Fairly typical. One of the tiles is made from the victim's xiphoid process—the lower tip of the sternum."

Teresa turned to look for a chair. Marini, who was

holding her elbow, grabbed one for her, and she fell onto it like a dead weight. A marionette cut off from its strings.

After twenty-seven years, Giacomo had finally taken what he had so desperately yearned for, kill after kill. The perfect tiles. The perfect death. The final revenge on pain.

I have a hole in place of a heart, he'd said. After all this time, he'd finally claimed a sternum—an echo of the misshapen one he had been born with, and which had cursed his entire existence. Teresa wondered why he hadn't done it sooner, why he'd always kept his distance from that particular bone even though he liked to cut his victim's chests open. Perhaps he was scared of it. Perhaps it was too powerful a symbol for him to handle.

After so many years, Giacomo must have felt ready. All his previous attempts had prepared him for this moment, leading him to that cathartic, horrifying, liberating thrust.

But Antonio was playing for time. So there was more. Teresa could already hear the deafening roar of the shock wave forming among the unspoken words he kept turning in his mouth.

Albert seemed to sense Antonio's distress, and so he did something Teresa would never have thought possible.

He kneeled before her.

"Teresa, the victim's DNA matches one of the entries in our database. The man was a repeat offender. He nearly killed a woman. He served his sentence, but was arrested again a few months later for assault and threats. His sister had taken him in, and it nearly cost her, too."

The feeling of his hands resting on hers was disorienting, as was the searing surge of compassion she felt rising from her stomach all the way up to her heart.

Another battered woman, she thought to herself. *It kept happening every day, over and over again. All the time. When would it end?*

"What happened to first woman? The one who almost died. Who was she? I mean . . . the wife. The . . ."

Albert squeezed her fingers.

"It was you, Teresa. The remains belong to Sebastiano."

46

Twenty-seven years ago

AS SHE WALKED AMONG the tombstones with a baby in her womb, Teresa was beset by an underlying sense of melancholy. She felt as if she had taken him out for a stroll in some strange limbo she should never have brought him to, among stone angels who had descended to earth to tear someone's love away, rather than announce new life.

She kept stroking her belly, even though she'd read somewhere that it was better not to do so. But it was too soon to start worrying about that kind of thing. Her hands kept finding their way there of their own accord, cupping that new life like a cradle, creating a bridge between two hearts. Teresa could picture it, that baby bird's heart beating furiously like a pair of tiny fluttering wings.

The encroaching sunset lengthened the shadows cast by the cemetery's colonnades, stretching their blackness and framing the remaining patches of light on the cobblestones, which seemed desperate to evade the forward march of time.

The ceiling of the pedestrian path was an archway whose colors and decorations changed at almost every step.

Teresa paused underneath a navy blue vault brightened with golden stars. A whole family was buried inside the wall. A full-size sculpture of an angel had been positioned as though it was about to let itself fall off a cliff, swept away by the wind, its massive wings unfurling.

Teresa turned her back to it so as not to let herself be dragged down by the harrowing beauty of that final farewell.

She leaned against a column, out of sight. She had no intention of putting her baby at risk. She'd already come perilously close to crossing the line; she had no intention of going anywhere nearer. She was only there to discover whether the theories she had based her work on would actually apply to real life.

The sun sank lower and the sky flared crimson, bathing the marble all around her in pinkish hues. The cemetery's votive candles began to flicker in the twilight.

There was beauty in this place, too—an earthbound firmament of fragrant blossoms that could almost make you forget what lay beneath them.

It was nearly closing time, though there were still some visitors lingering and talking in the footpaths between the graves. A mother holding a boisterous little boy by the hand, two old ladies leaning on each other as they changed the water in the vases, a handyman repairing a lamppost.

Maybe Giacomo wasn't going to come. Maybe she'd gotten it wrong. Maybe dates weren't as important to him as Teresa had assumed, and he was going to spend this anniversary away from here, far from death. Or perhaps his plan was to go chasing after death again—just not in a cemetery. Teresa's stomach lurched. If she had made a mistake, if it turned out that his intention was to mark this date not with rituals of remembrance but by pursuing a fresh victim, that would mean Teresa was in the wrong place, and someone else was about to die.

Albert and the rest of the team were keeping watch over Mainardi's house in case he showed up. Another squad car was waiting for Teresa outside the cemetery; she'd successfully argued for two other officers to be dispatched with her.

She checked the time, then pulled out the suspect's file from her bag. They'd managed to get in touch with one of his relatives, a second cousin who'd given them what little information she had. Everything else they knew, they had learned from the family doctor who'd known Giacomo since he was a little boy, and from the teachers who'd taught him at school. By now the picture was clear.

Giacomo had been born with a malformation of the sternum. His chest caved in at the center. The deformity had shaped the course of his life, so that he'd ended up feeling—and ultimately being—different from everyone else.

I have a hole in place of a heart.

Teresa couldn't get those words out of her head, that confession which, until that moment, had been impossible to fully comprehend.

She leafed through the file, as if hoping for a different ending.

His stepfather had repeatedly refused to let Giacomo get the operation he needed. The reason why Giacomo's mother hadn't spoken out against this act of sadistic cruelty was simple enough to understand, and utterly banal, just as evil usually is: she did not want to be abandoned again. And so she had offered up her own offspring as sacrifice.

In doing so, she'd effectively told her partner that he was the most important thing in her life—that man she had let into her home, and who would go on to take all his frustrations out on a little boy, forcing him to bare his chest when they went to the beach in the summer and making him take swimming classes in winter. Just as the new dominant male in the pride goes hunting in the high grass for his predecessor's cubs, this man, too, sought to annihilate what the man before him had left behind—marking his territory at the expense of a boy's childhood.

Until finally, a little piece of Giacomo—situated right in the middle of his chest—had died forever.

Perhaps it was the influence of her own unborn child speaking to her through the force of life, nurture, and connection, but in any event, Teresa felt a growing affinity for the unloved son that Giacomo had been. And yet Giacomo, like every other child in the world, had never stopped loving his mother.

A tear fell from her eyes onto the case file, but it wasn't enough to dissolve the toxic ink with which this story had been written.

Compassion. Teresa wondered if she'd be cursed with that feeling forever, all the way into the future that awaited her.

When Giacomo's stepfather had walked out on the family, mother and son had lost everything they'd ever had, including their home, but the woman had finally felt free to get Giacomo treated. By then he'd grown into a teenager. It took numerous operations and a metal plate to lift up the sunken bone and cartilage, as well as an orthopedic corset he'd had to wear day and night for seven long years. Seven—like the phalanges he'd removed from his victims. He'd probably divided the rib into pieces, too. Teresa understood now: in the hospital, this young man had found a family. It was there that, in spite of everything he had been through, and with his mind already crawling with violent fantasies, Giacomo had found the strength to make a fresh start and become a nurse, working in precisely the same department that had repaired his own life.

But though his body had been fixed, his mind and his emotional universe would never be the same again.

By the time Teresa had finished reading the report, twilight had already taken over, and the last traces of gold had fleeted from the faces of the statues and the crosses perched atop private chapels.

She looked up and realized she was alone. There was a quarter of an hour left until the gates would close.

She put the file back in her bag, picked up her walkie-talkie, and tried to contact the officers stationed outside the cemetery gates. No reply. They hadn't even turned theirs on.

She glanced at her watch again, deciding she might as well head out.

She started walking at a brisk stride. At the end of the footpath, the caretaker was moving the ladder he'd used to climb up to the lamppost. He leaned it against the dovecote and headed straight for Teresa.

She quickened her pace. Was he going to tell her off?

"I was just leaving!"

But the man walked right past her without saying a word,

his face hidden by the brim of his hat. The smell of his body clawed at her stomach, and she pulled away instinctively. It wasn't unpleasant in the ordinary sense of the word; rather, it was feral.

Teresa turned around to look, and realized that the man wasn't wearing a blue work uniform, as she had originally assumed, but gym clothes.

She turned around again and fought the urge to start sprinting away, her arms cradling her belly protectively.

It was him. Teresa could feel it on her skin. Her subconscious was screaming at her to run.

She hid behind a row of cypress trees to look for him.

Giacomo had headed in the direction of the newer graves, and was now standing before a tombstone with his back to Teresa, though she could see that his face was in fact turned toward the grave right next to it—where the first victim was buried. He was studying the freshly dug earth, and the temporary wooden cross with the name tag.

He showed no signs of movement. He appeared to be absorbed in prayer, but in fact, he was allowing himself to be watched. He had recognized her. He must have been feasting his eyes on her, and filling his thoughts, for a very long time.

Teresa couldn't breathe. He was communicating with her through the stillness of his body, through his profile exposed to her gaze, but she couldn't understand what he was trying to say, didn't have the tools she needed to decipher the message he was sending her.

Giacomo bent down toward the tombstone.

The sudden movement alarmed Teresa, who ducked behind a nearby chapel. She rummaged through her bag, grabbed her walkie-talkie, and tried again to reach her colleagues.

"Do you copy? He's here."

She was whispering, but she would have liked to shout.

"Do you copy? *He is here!*"

She looked up again, but Giacomo had vanished. The walkie-talkie slipped from her grasp and fell to the ground. A rustling sound from among the graves, frighteningly close, made her skin crawl.

Teresa started running, though she had no idea where she was going. All she could see were black crosses silhouetted in the blue night, tombstones, and funeral candles. There were no lights on. He hadn't been pretending to repair the lampposts; he'd unscrewed the bulb from every single light in that section of the cemetery. The marble angels seemed to be commiserating with her, not falling from the sky but rising from the earth to announce her death.

Teresa thought of her unborn child, of the danger she'd put her baby in. She started crying, looking for an exit she couldn't find, oblivious to the noise she was making and how exposed she was to anyone's sight. Panic had turned her into easy prey, and now she kept knocking against the sharp edges of a trap she herself had walked right into.

Somewhere on the cypress-scented gravel, her walkie-talkie began to crackle. Teresa could hear her colleagues laughing. They had been playing a prank on her while she was attempting to flee from a killer.

All the footpaths looked identical, like a maze without walls, but Teresa finally spotted a gate. She sprinted toward it and started pulling, but it was locked.

That was when she felt his presence.

A few steps away, close by, and right behind her.

Teresa turned around, her face wet with tears. She thrust her hand underneath her parka to take her gun out its holster, but he was quicker than she was; he grabbed the weapon and threw it into a flowerbed.

Now that he was standing so close, Teresa recognized the face beneath the hat as belonging to the young man who had been so kind to her, who had helped her in her time of need.

She also recognized the animal whose presence she'd detected in his scent. It glittered in the blackness of his pupils.

Giacomo brought his face right up to hers, so close that they were breathing the same air.

Teresa couldn't help but lower her eyes to his chest, where his clothes covered up the scar that had cut right through to his soul.

He followed her gaze. Perhaps he understood that Teresa knew.

He looked up toward the sky, and she saw anguish on his face, a glimpse of his shattered but enduring humanity. Giacomo let her go, turned around, and walked back into the night.

Teresa sank to her knees.

"I called you. I dialed that number."

She spoke this into the darkness, after she had managed to still her chattering teeth, hurling the words out from her heart. They came out a mere whisper, but she knew, beyond any doubt, that he had heard.

47

———— ❦ ————

Twenty-seven years ago

GIACOMO'S HOUSE SMELLED LIKE a coffin. Teresa recognized the scent the moment she stepped foot inside. It reeked of wilting petals and rot, of ribbons soiled with grief-colored earth.

The latest developments in the case had finally persuaded the judge to issue a search warrant for his home. The fingerprints from the third victim's hat, which Giacomo had returned to the widow, matched the prints found on the crime scene as well as the prints taken from Teresa's service weapon, and Teresa had also confirmed that the man who'd grabbed her gun at the cemetery was indeed Giacomo Mainardi.

Albert chose to interpret these events as proof of his own supremacy.

"He's lost his head. He no longer has control of the situation."

Teresa took them as a sign of what they really meant: the

whirlwind of death and ruin was beginning to implode, spiraling into a self-destructive epilogue.

Some of the other officers had just completed the various formalities that preceded every search, presenting the search warrant to a terrified neighbor. The court-appointed lawyer had just arrived. Teresa let him enter first. None of the relatives they had tracked down had wanted to attend. As an orphan, and an only child whose mother had also been an only child, Giacomo was alone in the world. Any remaining ties had been severed by the news that he was being investigated for murder.

Teresa had come this far by following the trail the killer had made with his victims' bones. She pictured them spinning around her like cogs in a mechanism whose workings remained obscure. Teresa was aware that every step she took was one the killer wanted her to take, so she considered every detail and every possible scenario before her with the knowledge that things were exactly where and how he had intended.

Your mind must be a clean slate, Robert had urged her. She went further than that. She turned herself into an empty chalice, so that she could receive whatever morbid gift might be awaiting her.

That scent she had smelled came from dried flower petals strewn across the floor. Black, shriveled, and malodorous, they spoke of abandonment and of lives disfigured.

His apartment was tidy, the neatness covered in a layer of dust. Its owner had clearly been busy attending to other matters over the past few weeks.

Every room was photographed, and every object closely examined. In a wardrobe, taped inside one of the doors, they found newspaper cuttings relating to the murders, the passport photos he'd removed from the drivers' licenses, and an assortment of women's costume jewelry hanging from a nail.

Albert called Teresa over.

"What do you think these mean?"

Teresa brushed a gloved hand against the necklaces and bracelets, making them jingle.

"Perhaps they belonged to his mother. Or perhaps he stole them. These types of killers are usually voyeurs, too. They watch other people's lives and steal the occasional object to put their skills to the test. They don't necessarily intend to kill—not always."

Albert studied the glittering trinkets as if they were voodoo fetishes.

"What am I supposed to do with them?"

Teresa stepped away from him in irritation.

"Log them as evidence, and see if you can find their owners among his neighbors and colleagues."

"Will you take care of the annex?" said Albert, gesturing toward a door that opened into the backyard. "There's a greenhouse in the garden."

Teresa walked up to the window. The branch of a desiccated tree grated against the glass with every gust of wind. That little patch of soil had become stuck in a perennial winter. Unlike the triangle of green that greeted visitors at the entrance, back here the grass appeared not to have been mown in months, perhaps even years. It looked like hay folding back in on itself in heavy tufts, smothering any new growth until it all turned to rot.

There are some places in this world that seem to be seeped

in mephitic vapors, and such was the case with the iron and glass edifice, which towered over that backyard moor.

The portable floodlights were positioned and lit. A flock of crows took flight with a series of shrill caws.

The windows had been taped up from the inside with old newspaper pages, yellowed by their exposure to the sun until the ink had been all but erased. Some were stained with moisture, thickened by leaks. Others were home to the downy nests of large spiders retreating from the glare of the officers' flashlights.

Ever since an incident in her childhood, Teresa had been terrified of spiders. She had accidentally knocked a nest over while playing one day, and found herself covered in spiderlings—dozens and dozens of them. She swept the memory away now, and brushed her hands over her arms and face to get rid of the physical sensation she could still feel there.

The moment her fellow officers opened the door, the choreography of evidence gathering commenced around her. Someone found a switch and turned it on. A lone light bulb dangled from an exposed cable that hung from the ceiling.

Teresa could not sense any imminent danger, other than that which faced her psyche.

The greenhouse was pervaded by the same smell as inside the apartment, only more intensely. On the clay floor, next to vases full of shriveled plants and rusty gardening tools, they found the funeral wreaths sent by the first victim's friends and family to mark his burial. The victim's name spelled out in gold left no room for doubt. Here was yet another collection of totems, romantic reminders of a love affair with death.

The far end of the greenhouse was occupied by fitness equipment: benches, weights, resistance bands, pull-up frames. The walls in that part of the building were covered with posters and calendars showing nude male figures. Teresa's colleagues interpreted these as a declaration of homosexuality they derided with crude and vulgar innuendo. Teresa whipped them back into line with a barked command none of them dared disobey, and which even Albert didn't question. The superintendent had joined her in the search now, though he was standing a few steps back and limiting himself to watching her movements.

Teresa strode up to the posters. There were finger marks on their glossy surfaces. Giacomo must have caressed them so many times that his thoughts had left lustrous furrows in their wake.

In those hairless, perfectly sculpted chests, Teresa saw the unattainable ideal that tormented Giacomo. That suggestive display of open nudity signified, perhaps, that he had never had the courage to give himself over to anyone that way, man or woman. And yet he'd always wanted to.

Teresa had sensed as much in the darkness of the cemetery. She'd scented a kind of naivete in him, an animalistic attempt to be in the world, and to be close to her, though he was still experimenting with it. The clumsy overture with his colleague at the hospital was proof of that. He was learning through imitation.

This young man still felt the presence of that hole in his chest, underneath the metal plate which had fixed the quirk of nature he'd been born with; he could feel the void that had replaced his heart, and tried desperately to fill it with flesh and muscle strong enough to reclaim his sunken self-esteem.

Everyone had stepped away from Teresa now, as if her colleagues were waiting for whatever it was that might be

simmering inside of her. An idea, a gesture, maybe an indica-
tion that she was ready to step out of that place. They would
have followed her without batting an eye.

She made a half-turn where she stood. She was looking
for a sign, knowing Giacomo must have left one behind.
That was how creatures like him always communicated. Yet
the sign seemed to be missing this time.

Albert interrupted her musings.

"Well?"

"I don't have a crystal ball."

"But so far you've always acted as if you did."

Teresa tried to maintain her focus. One of the other officers tore a few pages of newspaper down from the windows.
The floodlights illuminated the greasy panes from the outside. Albert started berating him, shouting something about
protocol, but meanwhile, Teresa thought she had glimpsed
something reflected in the glass.

"Turn those lights off!"

The greenhouse was plunged back into darkness, pierced
here and there by the bright rays of the floodlights outside.

Albert cursed under his breath.

It was an eye. An eye staring at them, drawn straight onto
the glass with a finger. Wide open and terrified. Or perhaps
mesmerized.

Albert began tearing more pages down, revealing a second
eye in the next windowpane.

Everyone seemed to have stopped breathing. Teresa collected herself.

"We need to tear them all down."

She made them turn the lights back on, and asked for
more lamps to be brought in. They set about individually

numbering the newspapers so that they could later be restored to their original positions, and thus allow the investigators to search for any hidden messages. Then they put them on the floor, stacked in a corner of the room.

But they did not find any other drawings. Only that pair of enchanted eyes staring at something straight ahead, at something that perhaps existed only in Giacomo's mind.

Albert dropped the last batch of newspaper pages to the floor for Lorenzi to pick up, then scrubbed his hands on his trousers with such alacrity that it was as if he wanted to get rid of the appendages altogether. Finally he returned to Teresa, ashen-faced.

"Now what?"

She had not stopped looking around her.

"He wants us to *see* something. Something that matters to him."

"The wreaths he stole? The half-naked men? What?"

She didn't know. The message could be hidden anywhere, embedded in any given object—or in nothing at all.

Albert voiced the question she herself had been trying to answer.

"Where do we start digging? We don't have all night. He may have already chosen his next victim. If we get it wrong and waste more time . . ."

It was only when Teresa stepped up onto a bench that she saw it. A patch of ground just a shade darker than its surroundings, and right in front of the eyes traced on the windowpanes.

Decomposition. The soil there must be teeming with fats and nutrients. It was just a corner of the room, half hidden by a rubber mat on which he had placed a pull-up frame.

Teresa stepped off the bench and found a shovel.

"That's where we're digging."

Albert took the shovel from her and handed it to another officer.

"Dig."

They rolled up the gym mat and put it to one side. This released a smell which some of them had learned to recognize from past investigations. The grave must be a shallow one. They put on their face masks.

Teresa got down on her haunches.

"Be careful, now."

She helped them dig with her hands until she felt something through her latex gloves.

The first thing that surfaced was the fabric, a strip of white cotton with a light-blue floral pattern. They removed all the loose soil above and around it until the full outline of a human body was revealed.

They had unearthed a corpse in the advanced stages of decay.

It was wrapped in a sheet from the neck down. The air inside the greenhouse had dried it, darkened it, molded leathery skin onto bone. It looked like a mummy lain to rest in a pagan tomb. Its folded clothes and personal effects had been placed beside its feet and femurs.

Teresa asked for the file the Swiss gendarmerie had faxed over at her request.

She ran through the list of personal effects belonging to Giacomo's father, supplied by his partner just an hour ago—particularly a small gold medallion she had gifted him, inscribed with his initials. There it was, still in place around the withered neck.

Teresa handed the fax back to her colleague.

"We'll run the usual tests, but I don't think there's any doubt here. It's him. Has anyone called Parri?"

"He's on his way."

Teresa grabbed a pen and scraped the soil off the skull. It was broken. She carefully lifted the edge of the stained and darkened fabric. The rib cage was shattered, too.

Albert hid his nose under the lapels of his suit. The face mask wasn't enough.

"He looks like he's been hit by a train."

Teresa pointed at the limbs and abdomen.

"Everything else is intact. What we have here is a different kind of fury."

"You think his son did all this damage?"

"Stepson. I'm sure of it."

"You've probably just made us use the murder weapon as a spade, Inspector. Good job. I'll be putting that in my report."

But Teresa was barely listening, too busy trying to catch the lingering echoes of what might have happened.

Where had Giacomo met up with his stepfather? How far had he convinced him to go, and where had he finally struck? How had he managed to get him all the way here? Or had his stepfather come of his own free will? Perhaps Giacomo had carried him—already dead—in the trunk of a car the police had yet to trace, despite the license plate number that the vehicle licensing office had already transmitted to all the units on patrol.

Teresa feared that most of these questions would remain unanswered, like a void that could only be filled with their imagination, with conjecture, and with the shapes and physical contours of their innermost fears.

Albert looked around. He seemed tired but satisfied.

"We need to dig through the whole garden. There might be more."

Teresa stood up and wiped the dust off her jeans. She decided there and then that she would get rid of them; no amount of washing would ever be able to cleanse them, not after what they had touched.

"There could be, but it's unlikely. There may be no blood tie, but this is still his father's grave—Father with a capital F. The Father who inflicts suffering, and then abandons the family. It's highly symbolic. For Giacomo Mainardi, this wasn't simply about hiding a corpse, but a way of burying the pain this person had caused him. He left all the others outside of this burial circle, out on the street and or in some field. But not him. He wanted to keep him in sight, every single day. He's the first victim. Giacomo killed him after the death of his mother—the event that first triggered his destructive spiral—but *before* all the others."

"So should I have the garden dug up or not?"

He hadn't been listening.

"Yes, I suppose so. After the coroner has finished his work."

"But you just said no!"

"I said we probably won't find any other bodies there."

"Then what are we doing?"

Teresa didn't know, but something told her there must be more.

Once the search zone had been marked out for Parri's arrival, the officers began to trickle out into the starry night looking for fresh air to breathe.

Teresa was left alone. Albert called after her, but was immediately distracted by other matters, orders to hand out, reports to compile.

That was when Teresa saw it. It was just a plant, but amid all that death, it stood out like an interruption to the normal order of things.

Teresa walked right up to it.

The stand was made of steel, like the kind found in plant nurseries. The earth inside was damp, and home to a family of wild violets. Pale lilac petals, a white bud, heart-shaped leaves. A patch of recently changed soil.

Her thoughts went immediately to the third crime scene, to that thicket of flowering acacias far from the city lights. A mist had been rising from the murky canal bed while frogs croaked all around them. There, too, the soil had been black and rich with humus, thick with bulbs and blood, and covered in violets. Teresa remembered the fragrant rain, her nausea, and the touch of that hand on her back, which seemed to say, *You are not alone.*

She had wanted to tell him the same, in that cemetery lit with flickering candles.

"I called you," she'd said, which was tantamount to promising him that a different life was possible.

Those flowers were meant for her. They weren't dried, they weren't cut. They were alive.

Teresa sank her hands into the earth to pull the roots from the fresh soil, but she found something else. She brushed the dirt off and wiped the surface clean until it glistened under the floodlights, revealing a magnificent, malevolent object of ivory-hued splendor.

A stab of pain in her abdomen brought her to her knees, her cry for help smothered in her throat.

48

—◦—

Today

TERESA BATTAGLIA DID RETURN to police headquarters after all, but she did it in the middle of the night, when the hallways were silent and the offices mostly empty. Those who recognized her leapt to their feet as she walked past, while the rest went looking for her later, heads peeking out of doorways as the news traveled inexorably from floor to floor.

She was escorted by Massimo, who did his best to shield her from curious stares—which could easily become a nuisance or even prove hurtful. She had come there that night to look at herself, to look at her face reflected in a portrait and either come out stronger, or utterly defeated.

Massimo was also scrambling to gather the fragments of her failing memory, trying desperately to piece them back together, but they were like hot coals, destined to dissolve into ash and slip through his fingers. He knew he had to come to terms with the decline that her illness inevitably entailed. But although he was willing to let the *superintendent* go, he was not prepared to give up on the woman Teresa Battaglia still was—not until she'd been fully vindicated.

As they stepped into the office, Massimo pulled the door shut behind them. He'd been working there on his own for the past couple of weeks, and every time he walked in, he would ask himself what was going to become of him, of the team, and of Teresa's legacy, and whether they were strong enough to gather the ashes and fashion them into something new.

Parisi and de Carli had been waiting for them, and sprung to their feet as soon as they walked in.

"Superint—"

She didn't even let them finish.

"There's no superintendent here. Is that it, over there?"

Massimo switched on the desk lamp, illuminating the details of the mosaic that had been sent from the prison. The reason she was so abrupt sometimes was because she was afraid of getting hurt. It had taken Massimo months to understand that.

"Yes, that's it."

She kept her distance, as if standing by the doorway could ensure she had an easy way out in case of emergency. But unfortunately there was no way out.

Massimo had put in an urgent request for the portrait to be confiscated and brought to the police headquarters because he knew that eventually, Teresa would have no choice but to confront the feelings that still bound her to the killer—murky, suppressed emotions that had been frayed but never completely severed by the passing decades. He wanted to make sure he was right beside her when that moment came.

Finally, Teresa moved closer, her gaze fixed on the portrait.

"May I touch it?"

"Yes."

Teresa tried to pull a chair up; Parisi quickly came to her aid. She sank into it with a sigh.

But she still resisted running her fingers over those tiles, which had come together to create an astonishingly accurate portrait of her face—immortalizing her at an age that was nevertheless difficult to determine. Not young, but not exactly old, either. It was unmistakably her, but at the same time, she was eternal, unconstrained by terrestrial coordinates.

Massimo felt a sense of awe every time he looked at it.

This was a Teresa with sparkling eyes, hair rippling in the wind of life, head proudly raised. Her mouth was half-open, and there it was: that gap, that void between her teeth that had all the gravitational pull of a black hole.

Massimo crouched beside her. He wondered how much more this woman could handle before she finally fell apart. As if life hadn't already taken enough from her, she was now expected to look for the corpse of the husband who'd tormented her, and to do so, she had to inhabit the mind and understand the urges of a killer with whom she shared a pact of reciprocal silence.

Massimo realized his thoughts were heading into dangerous territory, and quickly brushed them away.

He watched as she stretched out a finger—just one—and ran it over the tiles.

"He's always had an eye for detail."

Massimo felt the urge to place his hand over hers.

"He's certainly been very precise," he agreed, "and true to his fantasies, too, no doubt."

He saw her shake her head almost imperceptibly.

"This is not his imagination at work, Marini."

"Then what?"

"It's simply what happened."

"And that's something you'd rather not tell us about."

"Oh, Massimo. Haven't I suffered enough?"

He rested his forehead on the desk, heartbroken. He was still tormented by the photographs he had seen. Her devastated face. Her body, violated.

"Forgive me."

"Come here, all three of you."

They folded themselves around her, as if in an embrace. De Carli was tearing up; Parisi couldn't look anyone in the eyes.

"It wasn't easy admitting to being a serial killer's favorite. I was meant to be hunting him down. But that's how it was, and that's how it still is. Figuring out who you're supposed to fear is not always obvious, boys. Sometimes we're so in love we refuse to see it. We run headfirst into tragedy without even realizing what we're doing."

Massimo lifted his head.

"Do you think you're in danger?"

"No. He's not going to kill me, if that's what you're worried about. Giacomo never made portraits of his victims."

"Then what?"

She pulled her hand away from the tiles, as if the contact had suddenly become unbearable.

"We never did manage to decipher his message. The images in the mosaic we found in the greenhouse back then were all fairly explicit, displayed openly before our eyes . . . and yet impossible to describe. Perhaps it was supposed to be hell."

"Hell. And what exactly *was* hell, for Giacomo?"

Teresa's eyes shone with the spark of someone who'd just been struck by an idea.

"Not what, but *where*."

49

Twenty-seven years ago

THE GYNECOLOGIST WHO WAS on night shift at the public hospital was quick to reassure her. The baby was fine, and so was Teresa. There was nothing to worry about.

Teresa's guilt dissipated. Her baby's heart was beating.

She had just seen it for the first time on the ultrasound screen. It really did look like a little bird's heart, perhaps even tinier than that—yet so strong, and so stubborn.

"You should get some rest. Try to avoid stress, and take some more time for yourself. The first three months of a pregnancy are always the most delicate."

That was the advice the doctor gave her as she left the examination room to continue her rounds, and Teresa decided to take it to heart. It was time to give up the chase, and let someone else catch the prey. She put her clothes back on, finally feeling like she knew what path to take.

Someone knocked on the door.

"May I?"

"Come in."

Antonio Parri stepped inside, looking awkward. He'd been the one to persuade her to get herself checked up, after he and Albert had found her on her knees in the greenhouse, staring in horror at the mosaic that had terrified them all. A kind of darkness had emerged from that soil, taking on a form none of them would ever forget.

"Everything okay?"

"Yes. Did the doctor tell you? I'll need to take some time off, just as a precaution."

He leaned his back against the wall.

"Would you like a second opinion? I agree with her. You can't go on like this."

Teresa finished tying her bootlaces and stood up.

"But you're a doctor for dead people."

"Yes, but I'm also interested in making sure the living stay alive, you know? And in one piece. And that you're happy."

Teresa started laughing, but her laugh faded almost immediately. He interpreted it as a sign of bitterness.

"They'll catch him, Teresa. They're practically breathing down his neck, and he definitely won't strike again now. He knows he's surrounded. You're not worried, are you?"

She nodded, but letting go of the reins wasn't that easy.

"I'm going to go home now and . . ."

Teresa fell silent. She'd been out for hours. She hadn't warned Sebastiano. As soon as she went back, he would unleash his fury on her, and she could no longer allow that.

Parri understood straight away.

"I'll take you to mine." She must have looked perplexed, for he quickly put his hands up. "I swear I'm not looking for romance, or any other kind of adventure. I'm only offering friendship."

Teresa wrapped her arms around her chest. Here it was, the new road she was supposed to take, but what she'd failed to account for was the terror that always accompanied those first few steps.

"I've been sorting out my parents' old apartment. I've taken some stuff over already, but it's not ready yet. Sebastiano doesn't know."

"If it isn't ready yet, then surely it's not fit for a pregnant woman."

Teresa studied him. He seemed genuinely worried about her, but it made no sense to her that a stranger would care so much.

"What's wrong, Inspector? What hidden recesses are you sounding out?"

"I'm trying to understand why you're doing this."

"Oh, I see, you're not buying the whole friendship thing. I do appreciate your frankness in calling me a liar."

That brought out a small smile. She had to bite her lip to hide it.

"Well, Teresa, since you're so fond of statistics, think about this: What are the chances of you meeting a violent egocentric, a serial killer, and a pervert, all at the same time? Considering you've got the first two down already . . ."

This time she couldn't help but laugh out loud, surprised by his brazenness.

"Fairly slim, I suppose."

Parri gave her a wink. "I can assure you we'll both be sleeping like logs tonight."

"All right, then. Thank you."

"Well done, young lady. I'll come with you so you can pick up what you need."

He helped her put her coat back on, and picked up her bag. He was swaying a little. Teresa helped him regain his balance.

"Have you been drinking tonight?"

"Well, it's after midnight now, so technically this counts as a whole new session."

"Why do you do it?"

"Don't worry, it's already fading."

"Yes, but *why?*"

He stood up straighter. Disheveled, eyes puffy, he looked like he'd just been in a fistfight. But he was smiling.

"I have no excuses. No trauma, no drama. Just boredom."

Teresa took the keys from his hand.

"I'm driving."

50

Today

THE DOORS OF THE courthouse archives swung open. Teresa had submitted the request herself. She was convinced that somewhere in that room, kept inside a wooden box and cataloged as evidence in a murder investigation, was the map that would take her right to Sebastiano's body.

It had been drawn with the tiles of the same mosaic she had discovered in that greenhouse twenty-seven years ago.

That night, she had seen a vision of hell. Hell was what Giacomo had had to walk through when he was a little boy, reemerging into the world as a monster. It wasn't a landscape of the imagination, confined to the psychic realm: it was real.

As the district attorney's staff carried the box toward them, Teresa began to perceive the telltale signs of something beginning to crack. It was the past itself; frozen for decades, but with its lid about to be lifted, suddenly on the verge of exploding.

The box was placed before them, and opened up.

Marini and the others leaned over as if they were standing at the edge of an abyss.

De Carli moved away almost immediately.

"I feel sick."

Even Parisi had started to look a little queasy. He didn't last very long, either.

Among the folds of a cliff whose walls looked like vertebrae, a red-haired boy, somewhere on the threshold between childhood and adolescence, sat with his back to the viewer, legs crossed, naked, arms raised toward a crucifix that glistened in the distance against the backdrop of a purple, apocalyptic sky. The boy had died and risen again in hell. His body was stripped of its flesh. He had none of the gleaming splendor of a creature brought back to life by a merciful god—only the gray pallor of a corpse, and dried-up skin that looked like it had melded with his skeleton. Flesh and bone fused together, like life and death, or love and hate.

On the flat rocky surface there was an open tomb, a canopic jar that had tipped over, rivulets of blood, a skull, the scythe that harvested life, and the ruins of an ancient civilization, represented by a handful of crumbling columns.

All of this had been skillfully portrayed with marble tiles measuring one centimeter on each side. The only exception was the principal figure. Part of his back had been rendered using small flat pieces derived from the victims' bones. The fragments still bore the tags the police had used to mark them as human tissue.

Giacomo had tried again and again until he'd found the most fitting combinations, the most malleable bones, the most perfect proportions. He was a master craftsman of horror, a maker of nightmares.

Marini did not give in. Face to face with that aberrant tableau, he held his nerve.

Teresa was proud of him.

"What we didn't take seriously enough at the time," she began, "is what's in the bottom right corner of the mosaic. Take a look."

"What's that?"

"You tell me."

He leaned closer, despite the smell that reminded Teresa of a greasy, rancid soup.

"It looks like an old phone receiver."

The object emerged from the bottom edge of the portrait, a gray and black arc with just enough space below it—before the metal frame began—for a glimpse of numbers on a dial.

"It is a telephone, yes. A seemingly incongruous addition, though back then it was assumed the whole thing was the product of the ravings of a madman. It appears to be connected to the Lazarus figure, raised from the dead, by a trail of blood. A red thread."

"That's true. So is it some kind of symbol?"

"Yes, and more. While I was working the case, I met Giacomo. Or rather, he found a way to meet me. He pretended he was on Parri's team. On the third crime scene, before the body had even gone cold, he came up to me and gave me his phone number. And I called it."

"Who picked up?"

"Nobody. It wasn't operational. An old account. He had given me a phone number that no longer existed. So I asked myself why he might have done so."

"And what was your answer?"

"That he just wanted a normal life. He wanted to be able to court a woman, give her the phone number of a house he wouldn't be embarrassed to show her, ask her out, maybe even kiss her. But instead all he was able to do was kill."

"You still talk about him as if he were a victim, too."

"Because nothing has changed: he still is a victim. We are all victims of someone, and at least once in our lives, we have all been someone's executioner. Some manage to save themselves, or find someone to save them. Others succumb. Thankfully very few become what Giacomo is. And *this* is what he is: a boy who already felt like he was dead while his peers were thinking and dreaming of their futures. With this mosaic he showed the world what he saw when he looked at himself in the mirror. The language used by the kinds of people we call monsters is almost always profoundly rooted in childhood. I was never able to understand where his language came from, or what its source was. I never had the chance to dig deep enough into his story to find out."

Giacomo was still on the loose, though he was being hunted with every resource at the authorities' disposal. There had been no sightings so far, and with every hour that passed, the chances of finding him diminished. It was like he'd handed himself back over to the night from which he had so briefly emerged. He could be anywhere, he could be stalking anyone. No longer prey, but predator. Would he kill again? Maybe, but Giacomo had already reached his zenith, or the nadir of his darkest self. No fresh murder could ever measure up to the perfection he had tasted in killing Sebastiano.

"Are you still convinced that someone was threatening him?"

"You're asking me as if you no longer believe it. Maybe you never did."

"What do *you* think?"

"I can only tell you what I know, because I witnessed it: as a boy, he experienced true fear, the kind that can absolutely petrify. I saw it; I felt it inside of me. I heard him calling for his mother, for help that never came, not until it was too late. But one day, as he grew up, he stopped feeling fear— forever. From that moment on, he became the danger. And he couldn't wait to put his newfound power into practice."

"He killed his stepfather."

"After he was captured, Giacomo confessed to every murder he committed. He collaborated with the authorities and walked them through every one of his crimes. Not all killers do that. I always thought it was a disturbing detail."

"Why is that?"

"Because he was honest. He did not wear a mask, which meant that when you looked at him, you saw exactly what he was."

"That's why you've always been sure he was telling the truth."

"Right. But it seems things have changed. In any case, it wasn't a pleasant experience for those who had to collect his statement. Giacomo started by explaining how he had lured his stepfather into the trap, with a simple phone call. They hadn't been in touch since he and Giacomo's mother had divorced. Giacomo found him through the company where his step-father worked as a sales representative. He still traveled across northern Italy for work, and would have covered this city, too. Giacomo pretended to be a potential buyer. He didn't just kill him and end things there. The whole thing was something of an initiation."

"What about those old men? What did they represent?"

"They all stood for his stepfather, who kept coming back to haunt him in his obsessive-compulsive thoughts. It was as if Giacomo had to kill him afresh every time to keep the pain at bay. But his relationship with those men was different. He didn't butcher them like he did his stepfather. He tried, at least, to kill them quickly. The trolling and wooing phases were based on persuasion. He would look after them in the hospital, gaining their trust and respect, even a kind of gratitude. It wasn't difficult to learn their habits, stage a fortuitous encounter, and convince them to follow him or give him a lift somewhere. When my colleagues on the case found Giacomo's car, they discovered a list in the glove compartment with the names of thirty-two men he'd attended to in the ward. He'd already killed three of them."

Marini ran a hand over his face.

"What are you hoping to find in this mosaic now?"

"I've already found it. I just needed to confirm my shaky recollections. I needed to see for myself that the telephone receiver was actually there, somewhere in his hellscape. Back then we didn't bother too much with the phone number he'd given me. We had the bodies, we had the killer, and we had even managed to find the parts he'd removed from the corpses. There was nothing missing." Teresa started motioning at the archive staff. "We made a mistake. An enormous mistake."

"Why?"

"Because it wasn't over. But it will be today."

Teresa tore her eyes away from the disturbing, melancholy tableau and slid to the floor, her back against the wooden box. She could almost feel that figure pressing against her spine, wrenching her vertebrae apart so that it could reach between them and pluck her heart out. Soon the mosaic was covered up, plunged back into the darkness whence it had come. Teresa hoped that this time, it would stay there forever.

"Have that phone number checked. It was disconnected, but I want to know what address it was registered to."

51

---·∞·---

Twenty-seven years ago

PARRI HAD FALLEN ASLEEP in the passenger seat. Teresa covered him with the jacket he'd put on his lap. She'd parked in the courtyard, where nobody would bother him. She wouldn't be long anyway; she just needed to pick up some extra clothes, enough to last her a couple of days.

The garden was like a storage depot. The light from the streetlamps shone over piles of rubble and wooden planks that had been thrown over the ground as makeshift walkways across the construction site.

It would take another couple of weeks for the refurbishment work to be completed, but once it was done, the house that had watched Teresa grow up would be transformed into a cozy nest for her and for her baby.

She turned the key in the lock and left the door open to let the light in from outside. Work on the electrical wiring was still ongoing, but the plumbing and the phone line were done. Soon she would be able to start working from there for a couple days a week, studying the case files and calling the office for the latest updates. Preparing for the exam, and planning her future. There was a nice light in there, morning to evening. Silvery from the northern side. Thick and warm from the south-facing windows.

Teresa climbed the stairs to the second floor, grabbed the bag of clothes that she had put inside the wardrobe, and stuffed a few more items inside. When would she stop feeling so rootless? Her hope was that the foundations of this house would become her own—just as they had been when she was a child.

"Did you really think I wouldn't notice?"

Teresa felt her blood drain into a prickling fear. *The boiler room*, she thought.

I haven't had the locks changed yet.

She turned around.

A fist smashed into her mouth. Splinters of broken teeth cut into her tongue. She stumbled, but managed to stay on her feet.

Sebastiano grabbed her hair. He forced her onto her knees, and began punching her head with his other hand.

"Did you really think you could leave me? Are you trying to humiliate me? Make everyone think I'm worthless?"

He was hitting her temples so hard that she started seeing double.

"Whose baby is it? *Whose baby?*"

He let go and Teresa fell to the floor. But not even the sight of her body lying inert was enough to placate the fury of that sorry excuse for a man. Sebastiano hit her face, her abdomen. Teresa fainted, then came to, mouth full of blood, and broken teeth strewn over her tongue. She tried to slither away from him, but Sebastiano snatched her hair again and smashed her head against the wall. The impact ignited a burst of white lightning inside her head.

I waited too long.

Teresa could think of nothing else.

I waited too long. It's my fault.

He grabbed her by the wrist, pulled her out of the room and down the stairs. Every step was a blow to her ribs. She could feel her bones breaking.

He dragged her into the living room and left her on the floor. One last kick. Wrong—the next one was the last. Three in all, until finally, the monster stopped hitting.

She heard him light a cigarette, his breathing heavy, then sit in the armchair that had once belonged to Teresa's father.

Between each slow drag, his fingers covered in her blood, his knuckles probably scraped, Sebastiano listened to her wheezing in agony as her throat struggled for air. He was watching her die.

There was shouting on the street, followed by laughter, and a metallic sound that might have been an empty can being kicked down the pavement. A group of young men and women, out on a lukewarm night. Was it a Saturday? Teresa couldn't remember.

Sebastiano stood up. She imagined him peering out of the window.

More laughter on the street. Then Sebastiano's footsteps again, now right in front of her, where he dropped to his knees. He touched her lips, put a finger inside her mouth, pushed it all the way into her throat.

He's trying to take my soul, she thought.

But really, he was just enjoying the feeling of suffocating her. Soon there were two fingers in her throat, then three. They tasted terribly bitter. Sebastiano was wearing latex gloves.

"Not talking much now, are you? I'd like to see you try."

Teresa gagged, her body shaking as she coughed up blood. Sebastiano cursed, and put the cigarette out on her lips.

One of the young men outside had started singing the first verse of a song. The sound soon began to fade into silence. The group was walking away.

Teresa had heard somewhere that when you were on the verge of death, hearing was the last of the senses to be extinguished. She would find out soon enough, and when she did, she hoped she could take with her the untroubled lightness of those vagabond youths, rather than the rasping lament of violated flesh. She wanted to rest her hands on her abdomen, but she couldn't feel them anymore. She couldn't feel the rest of her body, either.

Sebastiano brought his face close to hers. His breath carried the smell of a putrefied existence. The perfection he liked to surround himself with could do nothing to counteract the rottenness at his core.

"You know what's funny? That whether you live or die, everyone's going to blame that killer you're so obsessed with. It's just you and me in here. And you never told me about this place. If you try to say anything to the contrary, I'll find a way to destroy your credibility just as I have destroyed your bones. *You* are nothing. Nothing."

Teresa's body was jerked by a series of spasms, then finally fell still.

He held her wrist between his index finger and thumb, and waited. He touched her neck, too, checking her pulse.

He let out a sigh, which could have been one of regret or of relief.

"So you've finally given up."

He walked away, breath still heavy with the feat he'd accomplished, leaving her lying on the floor like a toy broken by a child's fury.

The sky outside thundered, heralding a storm.

But she was still there. *I'm still here. I can hear it.*

A door banged against its frame, over and over again. It was the wind.

It's here to fly us away, she thought to herself. Her and her baby. She knew she was crying tears of blood, and her lungs struggled inside her broken rib cage, grasping for air.

The door slammed again. Someone was running toward her. Parri.

Parri was coming to save her, but it was too late. Teresa felt herself being torn away, felt the chill that always lingered whenever life slowed to a standstill. She could sense it so clearly, like a vacuum in the middle of her chest. Her heart buckled, and finally stopped beating.

52

Twenty-seven years ago

THERE WAS A TREMENDOUS pressure on her chest. Teresa regained consciousness and returned to the world under the weight of two hands, which seemed intent on crushing her. They kept pressing on her breastbone, all so that they could pull one more breath, one more heartbeat, one last moan out of her. Any sign of life would do. And finally, they managed to bring her back.

Then they stopped, caressing the shapeless mush that seemed to have replaced her face, and rolled her over onto her side. Two fingers cleared the blood and broken teeth out of her mouth, and Teresa finally felt like she could breathe again.

She lay that way, momentarily alone. From the room next door, she heard words she couldn't comprehend. Snatches of a call to emergency services. The pain had come back and it was unbearable, obscuring everything else.

She felt like she had been smeared onto the floor, her bones scattered like astragali dice.

Parri returned and held her hand. Teresa tried to squeeze it, then he kissed her on the lips—those same lips another man had branded with fire only a few moments prior.

A long kiss, a slow unfurling of his body against hers.

Something her friend would never have done.

Teresa tried to open her eyes, but they were too swollen.

That smell. That savage, feral essence she had smelled on him before, and which was now mixing with the scent of her own blood.

She tried to scream with all the air she had in her lungs, but the only sound that came out was a gasp.

The sirens wailed, closer and closer.

Giacomo reluctantly pulled away.

53

THE HOUSE WHERE GIACOMO had grown up was in a state of neglect. The shutters were faded, and the plaster had started to come off the walls. The whole place was covered in weeds, even along the gutters and between the cracks that many cold winters had made in the tiled terrace floor. Part of the roof looked worryingly concave.

After Giacomo and his mother had been forced to leave, the house had gone through several owners. No one had stayed for very long. At one point the estate agents who had been tasked with selling it had forgotten it even existed. It had remained empty for the following thirty years, until it had finally been bought by a property development company. A billboard on the perimeter fence bore an image of the small block of apartments that would soon take its place.

The owner of the company handed Marini the keys.

"Everyone around here calls it the Haunted House. I used to live at the end of the road, I must have been twenty years old already, but on my way home at night, if I was on my own, I would still avoid driving past on my moped. I'd go the long way round instead."

He told them that there always seemed to be something that pushed people to leave. The sound of disembodied footsteps on the gravel in the yard, terrified pets scratching at the front door to be let back in after dark, weird symbols on the windows of the children's bedrooms. The most recent ones to appear were still there, so Teresa asked to see them: wide-open eyes, watching the youngest members of the household and the families that were trespassing on that territory. They seemed to be issuing a warning: leave this place.

They all ran away in the end, some unashamedly open about the reason, others refusing to say why, but all of them wholly convinced that the house was cursed.

They weren't too far off, though it had nothing to do with dark magic. It was the power of suffering, inflicted and endured, which kept Giacomo tethered to this place, like the fibrous internal scar tissue that forms inside a body in pain.

He was just a boy, a boy who spied on other families, who harassed them, who bothered them until they left. This house belonged to him.

Some creatures can grow fond of certain locations, returning even after they have been driven away either to die there or to give birth to their young. Giacomo was no exception.

Teresa nudged a tuft of grass aside with her foot. There was a FOR SALE sign lying on the ground, its colors long since faded. Perhaps it was Giacomo himself who'd knocked it down, over and over again. Teresa pictured some hapless estate agent refusing to let the matter rest, retrieving the sign and putting it back up after every incident.

Another few months and the house would be demolished to make way for the new building. Teresa hoped she could find what she was looking for before that happened.

The search area was marked out, and a handful of officers dispatched to gather statements from the neighbors. Someone might have spotted Giacomo roaming around recently.

The moment had come to look for the thing Teresa most feared she would find, as if the ghosts that had already risen from her past weren't more than enough to deal with. She was going to see Sebastiano again, but this time as a dead man—years after he had battered her all the way to within an inch of her life, and left her for dead.

Teresa had no idea how she was supposed to feel, and her instincts were refusing to come to her aid. They had taken refuge in some hidden recess, choosing to remain silent.

She called Alice and Smoky over. The pair had been familiarizing themselves with the search perimeter, aided by Parisi and de Carli.

Albert, who was standing beside her, quieter than usual, furrowed his brow.

"Alice? Wasn't she called . . ."

"You're misremembering."

"Is anything you've told me about her actually true?"

Teresa fished a sweet out of her pocket. It was the last one. She unwrapped it and popped it into her mouth. She had never tried any other brand.

"Do you have any complaints about their work?"

"No, but the rules ought to be clear from the start, and I don't know what game we're playing anymore."

Teresa would have burst out laughing if she hadn't been standing on what was probably a tomb, and the body they were searching for did not belong to the man who had killed her baby. "Albert, you're always changing the rules when you like. Trust me, this time you're better off making do with what you've got."

He did not seem convinced, but there were more urgent matters to attend to.

The girl and her dog walked over. Inspector Marini joined them, too. He'd been leading the search inside the building.

"Zilch. Looks like there's nothing of interest in there. However, someone seems to have set fire to one of the rooms. You can still smell the kerosene in the air. There's a half-burned mattress on the floor." He looked at Teresa. "Mainardi had mentioned a fire in our first interview with him. He said someone tried to kill him by setting fire to the hut he'd been sleeping in."

Teresa studied the house. Giacomo may have sought shelter there while he was on the run.

"He told us a half-truth."

And at least one lie. He had never told her he'd taken one of her teeth. And if they found Sebastiano's remains in the garden, then there would be two lies, and she would no longer be able to say who Giacomo really was. Maybe she had been crazy all along, but she had always trusted him.

She reached for Alice, guiding her closer.

"Giacomo's victims always had multiple wounds. If there is a body here, it should be no exception."

Alice pulled her hair up in a ponytail and patted her hand against her thigh. Smoky immediately came to her.

"We'll start in the garden."

They led her to the boundary marked out by police tape. The area had been divided into various sections. Marini grabbed a handful of soil in his fist, then let it trickle back down between his fingers.

He gently spun Alice toward the direction the wind was blowing from. This way it would be easier for Smoky to locate the scent cone.

They began their search.

Smoky was trained to sniff out death, whether whole or in fragments, buried or exposed to the elements. Keeping pace with his human, he scanned the ground and the sky. All the odor molecules he detected formed a web of coordinates that guided him to his goal as clearly as a set of visible signs.

Ever since she had first seen Smoky at work, Teresa had begun to picture smells as if they were filaments floating across the surface of the world. Right now, they were all immersed in a vortex that the human olfactory sense was not capable—or perhaps *no longer* capable—of catching and identifying. If Teresa's theory was right, then in that moment a miasma of cadaverine, of blood and broken bones, must be hovering somewhere inside the house or out in that wild, unkempt garden. It was the same smell that clung to Giacomo's hands. Those airborne compounds floated on currents of air and spiraled toward the ground, swirling around their feet.

Teresa did not stay to watch the pair of trackers at work. She walked away, leaving the others to attend to whatever they might need. She was afraid that the theory that had brought her here would turn out to be true. If there really was a body buried here, she was sure she knew whose it was. But that would also mean that Giacomo had lied to her when he'd said that someone else had hidden the body. She searched her memories for details of that interview, for Giacomo's expression, the tone of his voice when he'd told her that, the way he'd looked at her. But she couldn't find anything. It was as if the meeting had never happened, and his remarks had been delivered to her by an intermediary. And if that particular conversation was already shrouded in mist, how many other interactions had she already lost without realizing? What had she and Giacomo said to each other in all those years of encounters in the prison meeting room? She didn't know anymore.

She shifted her gaze toward the garden. Patches of weavers broom had sprung up among the tall grass and vines. Smoky and Alice appeared and disappeared from view among box-wood hedges and rosebushes. Parisi was following one step behind the girl, making sure she didn't get any scratches.

There was one last thing to do before Pandora's box was opened, freeing all the evils—the last ones left—nestled within that story.

Teresa took her phone out of her bag and opened her list of contacts, trying to remember the name of the person she'd been meaning to call. It had been in the back of her mind since the moment Albert and Parri had shown up at her front door to announce that Sebastiano had died. "His sister had taken him in, and it nearly cost her, too," Albert had said, before Teresa had even realized that he was talking about her ex-husband.

His sister. Lavinia—that was her name. She'd been the one to report him to the police for a second time, thereby paving the way for her twin brother's renewed incarceration.

She was a psychologist by training, working for the regional government to help coordinate social services between different departments. Teresa had needed her help on a case she had been investigating a few months ago, but the encounter had been a frosty one, and her former friend hadn't said a word about her brother or the violence she herself had suffered at his hands. Albert had done some research: it seemed Lavinia had cut all ties with Sebastiano years ago, just like the rest of their family.

Teresa stared at her phone screen until it went dark again. She just couldn't bring herself to make the call.

"How are you feeling?"

It was Marini, who had come to join her where she was standing.

"What about you?"

"A bit weirded out."

He was looking at her as if wondering how to fix her, how to heal the wounds that still haunted her more melancholy days.

"There isn't," she told him.

"What?"

"There's no way to undo what's happened, if that's what you're obsessing about. Stop worrying about it."

"I don't think that's possible."

She took his face in her hands.

"What do you see when you look at me?"

"A lady who's always pissed off?"

"You might as well have called me an old woman."

"Calling you a lady doesn't mean you're old."

"Come on, Marini. What do you see? A face disfigured by all those punches?"

"Jesus. Stop doing that."

"Or by the kicks?"

"Enough."

She let him go, the palm of her hand holding a caress that never reached his face.

"Well, you're wrong. The woman standing before you is a woman who managed to get back on her feet and move forward with her life. *That's* what you should see."

He shook his head, a faint smile playing on his lips.

"Do you really think I don't already see you that way? I've *always* seen you that way, even before . . . even before I knew about all this. But you can't stop me from feeling compassion for you, not after you taught me what that is."

De Carli ran toward them, interrupting their brief moment of mutual surrender, the kind that freed the spirit rather than destroying it.

"They've found something. We're still digging, but it looks like it's quite close to the surface."

Marini held her elbow.

"Would you like to go closer?"

Teresa nodded, but managed only a few steps forward. Her legs didn't seem to want to follow her commands. They stopped, observing silently from a distance.

There was a corpse down there, somewhere behind the screen of bodies crowding around the excavation site.

Smoky was never wrong. There was no hope of a false positive to cling on to.

Marini let go of her arm.

"I'm going to go and check."

Teresa noticed Parri slipping through the throng of officers.

She exhaled, expelling the tension that had been eating away at her.

When Marini returned, Albert was there with him, which was how Teresa knew that the verdict was precisely the horrifying one they'd been expecting.

She caught Marini's eyes.

"Well?" She wanted him to be the one to tell her.

"Parri has identified him using the photographs we have on file, though he said he would have known even without."

Sebastiano. The last image Parri had of him was probably of his icy expression at the final court hearing. Teresa leaned even more heavily on her walking stick.

"Is it him?"

"Yes. I won't ask whether you'd like to see him."

That would have been too much, even for Teresa.

"I don't."

"Is there anyone who could identify his personal effects?"

"His sister, Lavinia Russo. Have we . . ."

"Yes, we reached out to her a few hours ago to tell her about the DNA match." Teresa didn't remember. "I'll deal with it. It won't take long, and I'll drop you at home when I'm done."

"Thank you."

Marini walked off again. He was trying to relieve her of as many burdens as he could, but all she wanted was to turn back time to a few days, a few weeks ago.

Albert approached her, hands in his pockets. It almost looked like he wanted to give her a hug.

"It's over."

"He escaped."

"We'll find him. There's an international warrant out for his arrest. He can't hide forever."

"You don't sound angry."

"With you? Why would I be? It's not your fault."

"Well this is unexpected."

"Oh come on, Teresa. You've always been more prepared to give murderers the benefit of the doubt than show me any kind of understanding."

It wasn't a question of being understanding, or of forgiveness.

"I just don't trust you, Albert."

He shrugged.

"What's new? Everyone knows I can't be trusted."

Teresa didn't know whether to laugh or shout at him. She decided to go with the former; she could certainly do with some mirth, even if it tasted a little bitter.

"You're always so completely yourself, Albert."

"Surely that's a good thing. At least you always know what to expect of me."

"I suppose so."

"Do you think it was meant as an act of revenge? Giacomo finally found a way to avenge you. It would be the perfect ending to a nearly thirty-year-old story, wouldn't it?"

"*Perfect?*"

"You know what I mean. Of course it's a tragedy."

But his offhand tone suggested the opposite. None of those who *knew* could really consider it as such.

Giacomo had sent Sebastiano straight back to hell—that was what Albert was thinking. That was what Teresa herself had thought, before she'd managed to get her emotions back under control. She didn't want to hate him. It had taken half her life to leave that hatred behind. As for the guilt, she'd held on fast to that—though soon she was bound to forget about that, too, along with everything else, her broken bones, the baby she had lost.

Albert checked the time on his phone.

"Gardini should be here shortly. I intend to propose that we consider the preliminary investigation closed."

"What did you say?" Teresa snapped.

"The deputy prosecutor has more than enough material to take to the judge. Now the pretrial phase can begin."

"Absolutely not!"

"Teresa . . ."

"We need to find out who guided Giacomo's actions. This case is far from closed. This time there's someone else behind the murder."

"They're just the fantasies of a twisted mind. There's no mystery man behind Sebastiano's death. There's only Giacomo; *he's* your mystery man. Why do you refuse to admit it? You're still trying to save him, to redeem him in your head. But he *chose* to kill your ex-husband, just like he chose to kill all the others. Except this time he probably thought he was doing you a favor."

"I don't think so."

"I do. And I'm the district attorney."

Parri whistled to catch their attention. He was waving his arms about, signaling at them to come toward him. Teresa stayed put.

"I don't want to see the body."

Albert pushed her in the back, nudging her along.

"I don't think it's the body he wants to talk about. That's at the opposite end of the garden."

They found Parri waiting for them with the rest of the team.

"There's something I'd like to show you, Teresa. Don't worry, it's nothing too awful. It's a room of some sort."

"Of some sort?"

"Well, I nearly fell into it."

The ground here had been hollowed out. The mouth of the pit was covered by a few wooden slats overgrown with moss and grass and held together by rusty nails. The lid was slightly dislodged, offering a glimpse of bare brick walls. There was no sign of concrete or any other structural elements. It was impossible to see what was at the bottom.

Marini leaned over.

"It looks like one of those makeshift pits they used back in the day to repair vehicles. My grandfather had one in his garage on the ground floor. This one looks like it hasn't been touched in decades."

Teresa craned her neck to look inside.

"They're used in the countryside, too, for the maintenance of farm vehicles."

Marini lifted one edge of the lid.

"Give me a hand, Parisi."

They moved it aside until the hole was filled with light and glittered with myriad multicolored reflections.

Teresa sat down on the grass. She could hear the boys talking, but there was a buzzing in her ears growing ever louder. That pit was built, above all else, out of the emotional walls with which young Giacomo had sought—in his own way—to protect himself.

"Superintendent Battaglia? Teresa?"

Marini had had to raise his voice to catch her attention.

"Did you see what's at the bottom?"

She had. Raw wooden boards on which little Giacomo had found some way to glue pebbles, shards of glass, marbles, and tiny plastic objects. The light shining onto them now brought out stunning aquamarine hues and enduringly vivid reds, shapes and figures that were childlike and yet astonishingly full of life.

This was where his obsession must have begun—in this attempt to retain some kind of humanity, to see beyond his suffering. An attempt that had mostly failed, but which had also saved him in some small way, transforming him years later into the corpse brought back to life and depicted in the mosaic they had found in the greenhouse.

"Looks like a prison," said Albert. "Maybe his stepfather used to lock him up down there. It would certainly fit the profile."

Teresa thought to herself that Albert would never be able to see what simmered beneath the surface of things, nor hear the song of creatures lost.

"You don't understand, Albert. It was Giacomo himself who chose to shut himself away down there. So that he could survive."

Parri approached her.

"There's something else I'd like you to look at, Teresa."

He handed her two see-through bags with items from the scene he had already examined.

"I found these mosaic tiles in the corpse's mouth. There's eight of them in total, and based on their size, color, and state of preservation, I would suggest they might be the ancient tiles missing from the crypt in Aquileia. Then there's this object."

He showed her an alabaster statuette no more than five centimeters in height. The figure, who had female features, was wrapped in a cloak that had been painted black and designed to open up like a miniature sarcophagus. There was nothing inside, except for an inscription. Teresa read it out loud.

"*Mater larvarum.*"

Teresa felt Marini's chin brushing against her head.

"What does it mean?"

"The Mother of Specters. One of the epithets of Ceres, a nod to her nocturnal side." Teresa spun the statuette around in her fingers. "It must have contained something."

When Alice and Smoky rejoined the group, the dog immediately began to show signs of excitement again. He kept barking and spinning around in circles. Alice did nothing to stop him.

"He's trying to tell us something."

Teresa brought the bag up close to his nose and he immediately sat down, suddenly calm.

"Can he smell the body?" Teresa asked Alice.

"No, he's already signaled for that. This is a new scent."

Which must mean the scent of a different body.

Teresa looked at Parri.

"Whatever used to be in here came from a human."

"A relic, perhaps? Do you think the statuette might be of ancient origins?"

"We'll have to get it looked at to find out. And we'll need an archaeologist's report as well."

Her friend's expression turned uncharacteristically dark.

"There's one thing I can tell you myself. Whatever this might mean, I think it's intended as a gift for you. And I don't like it. I don't like it one bit."

54

IV Century

ANOTHER DAY HAD PASSED since his escape, and it was still the night-time paths that Claudius relied on to keep him safe, resting during the day in the cover of ever-thickening forests. His body covered in dust, he was like earth upon earth, like moss rolling green into the distance.

The lights of Forum Julii flickered at his feet, in the hollow among the hills that led toward the mountain passes, the gateway to the east.

Claudius avoided the city and its commercial roads, keeping away from Roman insignia. He was walking near the edge of the meadow, where the vegetation was thinner, leading Feronia and Mist by their bridles and walking a few steps ahead of them. The horses were jittery, sensing the absence of protective shelter and the safety of the encampment.

Claudius wasn't used to acting alone, to being the master of his own destiny. He felt, at times, like a flame, flickering helplessly in the wind. The kind of wind that called out to him from the dark depths of the forest, in clicks and murmurs.

Mist started neighing. Claudius had to work harder to calm him down than he'd ever had to before, even on the battlefield.

He remembered an old saying: "The night has the ears of a fox."

He could have sworn the night had eyes, too. He had felt them following him ever since he had crossed into that now-contested territory. He wasn't alone.

The moon surfaced from behind the clouds, illuminating a pair of thick antlers among the leaves. A deer emerged from the tangle of branches, unafraid, and they stared into each other's dark eyes. Claudius could almost hear the beating of its formidable heart. The beast huffed, its warm breath condensing into white vapor.

Claudius knew that this was a sign. Diana was speaking to him through the appearance of the celestial body in the sky, and by sending her sacred animal to him. Yet the message from the goddess of the hunt was enigmatic; it was not for Claudius to know whether he was the hunter or the prey.

The deer swelled its throat and released its call into the sky. A gust of wind tore down a smattering of leaves.

That was when Claudius spotted them, swaying in the shadows: mysterious objects hanging from the branches of linden and oak trees. He walked toward them and held them in his hands. They were made of vertebrae bound together with tendons. The voice he had heard calling out to him as he passed was the sound of their clinking.

The deer bounded off into the night.

Claudius looked up at the moon. What was Diana's will? He did not know.

A sound like creaking wood caught his attention. His hand went to his hip, but he did not draw his weapon. It was too late. It would be of no use, except to hasten his death.

The shadows had moved around him, until he was surrounded.

The men stepped out of the forest. Their facial features were flat, like those of the barbarians Claudius had encountered in the lands beyond the river Tanais, on the shores of what was known as the dark sea, the Pontus Euxinus.

They were just as Herodotus had described them: strong, amber-skinned, blond-haired, imposing. Their breastplates were carved out of the bones of their mares, smoothed, polished, and scrubbed until they were nearly transparent, then placed side by side like feathers. The tips of their weapons were also made of bone. They did not know metal.

They were Sarmatians, a people of horsemen, accomplished livestock farmers, and spear-wielding warriors.

Fighters so fierce that the great Marcus Aurelius had enlisted them into various Roman legions. And now they had ventured all the way here.

One of the warriors approached Feronia, feeling her thigh muscles and examining her hooves. The mare neighed and reared on her hind legs, displaying her full splendor. The barbarian started laughing, caressed the horse, and said something to the other men, throwing the Roman a defiant look. Claudius approached him, careful not to display any fear. He showed the stranger the things they had in common, and which brought them closer than any shared language could: the stirrups, an innovation these horsemen had brought to the Roman armies; and the rope that tied both horses, as was the Sarmatian way.

The barbarian seemed to understand. Feronia and Mist had spoken for Claudius, declaring that their master, too, was a horse-rider, and their presence living proof of the respect he had for his horses—and which, by extension, was owed to him.

But one could easily end up respectfully killed.

The Sarmatian grasped his shoulder and forced him onto his knees, while another took his gladius from its sheath. The gleam of the naked blade was a reminder of Rome, of the Empire, of a life and a man who no longer existed.

Seeing these symbols of Rome seemed to stir the Sarmatians into a state of frenzy. Some began to pace in circles around him, bringing their torches right up to his face. Others thumped their spears on the ground, inciting their comrades with animalistic howls.

Claudius kept them all in his sights, his senses attuned to their movements even when they were behind him. Feronia and Mist were but a few steps away, untied. It would take but a few quick leaps to get back into the saddle and attempt a getaway. It was only a matter of deciding when to act, and if and how to recover his gladius.

The excitement around him suddenly waned, the crackling of the torches distinctly audible in the ensuing silence. At the sound of rattles, the circle around him opened. A woman stepped through, carrying an instrument similar to the sistrum. She was elderly, her slender frame wrapped in linen, face and eyes painted with white lead. On her bare arms and shoulders he saw glimpses of tattoos of deer with flaming antlers and swans in flight. Other women soon appeared behind her, faces concealed by pale masks with sharp beaks and enormous eyes.

Their masks symbolized the birds used in scarification rituals by the bone-worshippers. Devotees of the bird goddess, theirs was a northern faith inherited from the ancient inhabitants of the Altai mountains. The Roman generals who had served in those territories still talked about it.

Maybe everything that Claudius and the legion had hoped to find was standing right here before him, ready to take his flesh. Here was a faith that was still very much alive, and a cradle to which he might entrust his own.

Claudius took off his grimy cloak. Beneath it, the pristine tunic of the warrior-priest of the goddess Isis gleamed in the torchlight, as white as the bones these people worshipped.

He bared his chest to show them the tattoo of the winged Egyptian goddess spanning his sternum and collarbones. From within the bandages wrapped around his ribcage, he retrieved the statuette he'd protected with his life. He pushed it open, revealing another object concealed within its hollow core, a winged, diaphanous figure carved from the mortal body of Isis herself.

The old shaman woman, whose fingers were dyed black like the claws of an eagle, took the figure and brought it up to the flames for a closer look, then sniffed at it, seeming to recognize in its scent the smell of bone.

She looked at Claudius, and he did not know whether it was his salvation he saw reflected in her light eyes, or his end.

Silhouetted against the flame, the statue of the goddess looked like it was burning.

It occurred to Claudius that perhaps it had to happen if she was to be reborn.

The Christians thought they had turned her to ash, but from the ashes she would rise again in different form.

55

Twenty-seven years ago

TERESA FELT HER WHOLE body burning. Every part of her was consumed, with a flameless, smoldering, all-consuming ember. The void inside of her was expanding. Someone kept breathing near her boiling skin, triggering a wave of shivers. They insisted that she try to move her fingers, her hands, her feet.

"Just try, Teresa. Give it a go."

What did that voice know of the effort it took? Still, she did her best to satisfy its request.

"Looks like you've regained some feeling. Welcome back."

Who was this person? She opened her eyes, but everything looked blurry.

The sound of wheels, the creaking of metal, footsteps beside her. She smelled disinfectant, felt the roughness of a bedsheet tucked all the way up to her chin.

Soon she had also regained her sight. Yes, she was back. But where exactly had she landed?

On a bed, being rolled down an excessively bright corridor. Teresa could see everything streaming past, a nurse's face hovering above her. Her eyes followed a narrow tube attached to an IV drip until it disappeared into the folds of the bedsheet. She pulled at it and felt a stab of pain. It was attached to her.

"Calm down. Stop fidgeting."

The nurse smiled, but when his eyes fell on her face, he couldn't quite hide his dismay.

She raised her other hand and touched her cheeks, her nose, her eyelids. She couldn't feel anything; it was as if she had no face at all. There was a bitter taste in her mouth. Her fingers were stained with iodine. The skin on her arm was purplish. She tried to say something, but her jaw was locked. She had no idea what day it was, if it was night-time or morning. She was confused, struggling to stitch her tattered memories back together.

The nurse pushed the bed into an elevator. The walls and the ceiling were made of steel. Teresa turned her head, her vertebrae creaking with the effort. She looked for her reflection, but did not recognize the woman looking back at her. Destruction and annihilation had trampled all over her. The lower half of her face—imprisoned in a metal brace—had been recomposed, pieced back together, but she did not know how, and did not know if her flesh would be able to forget or if it would forever carry the mark of violence. Who could know whether the body remembered?

She retched, but managed not to vomit. Her skin pulled,

held taut by the metal. The nurse dabbed at her lips with a paper towel.

"Don't worry, it's just the aftereffects of the anesthesia."

What did anesthesia have to do with anything? She was pregnant. She was nauseous because she was expecting.

The elevator doors slid open.

On the other side was Albert, and behind him, Antonio Parri. When they spotted her, Albert immediately averted his gaze as if he'd been slapped in the face, while Parri began to cry like a child.

Teresa reached for her friend, but it was Albert who took her hand and placed it back on the sheets.

"Don't worry. Don't worry."

He seemed to be directing the words more at himself as he escorted the bed—and the vaguely human lump upon it—to their destination. He couldn't bring himself to look at her. All in all, he was not very reassuring. Perhaps he didn't know how to be.

Teresa wondered if he was telling her not to worry because she was sure to get her working body and her old face back, or because he had finally managed to stop Sebastiano.

Suddenly, she remembered.

The thought of the man who had broken her was like a gut-punch. She tried to tell Albert, pulling at his jacket, but he just kept staring straight ahead.

Sebastiano was free. No one was out looking for him because no one knew he was the one who'd done this to her. Teresa tugged at Albert's sleeve again, and again he pulled his arm away.

Unlike the previous corridors she had passed through, this one was not deserted, but full of medical staff carrying patient files, people visiting their sick relatives, and orderlies pushing trolleys about. Once Teresa's head had started working again, she was able to deduce that they had moved her from an operating room into the ward. So it was true that she'd been through surgery of some sort.

The orange light of the sunset filtered through the windows in her line of sight. Pitch-black clouds were piling up on the horizon, long and slender like striations on the earth's back. And still she did not know what they had done to her, nor how many hours, or days, or weeks had passed.

Sebastiano was free. That was all she could think about.

They stopped in front of a room. Another nurse came to help her colleague squeeze the bed through the door. She opened the other panel, too, and they tried to find the right angle. They were soon joined by a doctor, who asked to take a look at Teresa's charts. Teresa had the feeling she'd met her before.

Another stab of pain in her abdomen, but more powerful this time, enough to elicit a groan. Teresa gripped the bed rails until it passed, leaving her breathless. Was this what going into labor would be like? She tried to reach for her stomach, but the doctor took her hand and crouched over her.

"We're going to give you something to help you sleep, now."

Teresa remembered where she had seen her. She was the gynecologist who had checked her over in the ER. Teresa squeezed her hand as hard as she could and tried to tell her about the pain, but the woman eased herself out of Teresa's grip with little trouble, and started giving the nurse some instructions.

Teresa didn't want to sleep. She wanted them to listen to her.

She looked for Parri among the people who were passing her by, sometimes bumping into her as if she weren't even there.

She thought she had recognized him in a figure clad in blue who had hovered at the edges of her vision all this time, the same man who had followed her hospital bed since the moment it had emerged from the elevator.

Teresa tried to focus on his face.

Wearing his blue overalls, and with his hat pulled low over his face, Giacomo looked up as if he had been waiting for this moment all along. He didn't even attempt to run away; he just stood staring at her—eyes bloodshot with madness, perhaps, or from sleepless, anguished nights—as if this were the only thing that mattered.

Teresa tried to sit up, but the nurse pushed her back onto the pillows. She struggled against him, pulling at Albert's sleeve. Albert frowned.

"I don't understand what you're trying to tell me."

Giacomo took a few steps backward, then turned around and left.

Teresa threw herself off the bed. The IV drip came off her arm, but she didn't feel anything anymore. She managed to stand up, elbows digging into the bed rails. Everyone started shouting.

For once in his life, Albert seemed to grasp what was going on. He followed her gaze all the way to the man making his way out through a crowd of people who had all scattered at the commotion—but the version of the story he was telling himself was not the right one.

He pulled his gun out and chased after him, keeping the

weapon trained on Giacomo. He ordered him to stop, or he would shoot. The corridor had emptied out.

"He came back to finish her off!" he yelled at Parri, who had meanwhile arrived and taken cover behind a trolley.

Giacomo stopped with his back still turned, but he did not raise his hands as Albert had commanded. Perhaps he had never really meant to leave, or perhaps he didn't want to—or simply couldn't—stray too far from her.

"Put your hands where I can see them, or I will shoot!"

Albert was shaking. It would not have taken much for him to accidentally pull the trigger.

Lorenzi arrived and crouched beside Teresa, struggling to catch his breath. He'd spilled coffee all over his shirt and trousers. He tried to lift her up and drag her away, but Teresa wriggled free.

They hadn't realized.

Giacomo turned around, his face lined with tears. He took a step toward her, eyes locked on hers.

No. Teresa wanted to stop him.

Albert cocked his gun.

"Stop!"

Giacomo took another step forward.

Teresa tried to articulate the words to explain that he hadn't come to kill her or anybody else, but that what had brought him here was probably nothing but the pain he had witnessed, and which would not allow him to leave her side. Perhaps he had felt something then. Something human.

Albert took aim. Teresa grabbed the gun from Lorenzi's holster, then used him to pull herself back toward the bed and onto her feet. She took aim, too.

Lorenzi cried out in warning. Albert glanced over his shoulder, and understood. He lowered his weapon, suddenly disoriented, then gestured with his arms as if to say, *What on earth are you doing?*

Teresa was pointing the gun at him.

She had no idea where she'd found the courage to do it, nor what consequences awaited her.

Parri got back to his feet and yelled at Albert to stop.

"She's trying to tell us it wasn't him!"

Teresa dropped the gun and slid to the floor. Her legs had gone numb. The medical staff sprang back into action all around her, touching her, trying to help her up, calling for assistance. Albert was still shouting at Giacomo to surrender.

Teresa lifted her hospital gown. It was stained with blood. Her bandages were damp and had turned crimson. She ripped them off.

They had sliced her belly open and patched it back up like an old sock, coarse black thread plunging in and out of her raw, reddened flesh.

She realized why she had felt that void inside when she had first returned to the world. It was because she had returned alone.

They had opened her up and emptied her out. And it didn't hurt, because her body was still numb from the anesthetics. The pain that was consuming her was something else entirely, something that came from her soul—which knew everything and had seen it all happen without being able to do anything, because there was nothing that could be done.

Teresa had lost her baby. There would never be another baby.

She screamed so loud that she startled the staff who were trying to restrain her—and all around her, strangers with stricken expressions, trays laden with medical equipment clattering to the floor, and Albert calling for security, pointing his gun with the force of fear.

Teresa kept screaming, so much that the sutures on her jaw popped, a wail that told the story of a grief that would never fade, of the guilt that would forever go with it.

That was when Giacomo ran toward her.

He managed to brush his lips against her forehead before Albert and the security personnel pinned him to the floor.

"I was too late," he whispered, his eyes full of despair. "I came too late."

56

Today

IT WAS SUPPOSED TO be the end of her old life, but as far as epilogues went, it was pretty eventful.

The desolation Teresa had expected to find waiting for her at home was absent. Instead, Marini and Elena, Alice and Smoky, Parri, de Carli, and Parisi were all there. They'd spent the day rearranging things around her house to better accommodate her illness. They'd covered up all the mirrors, put name tags on any objects that hadn't been labeled yet, set up a new induction stove in the kitchen, and found a nice cornflower blue with which to paint Alice's new room. Teresa had persuaded her to move out of the modest apartment she'd been living in and come and stay with her instead. She wanted to help Alice as much as she could—though she suspected it would be the other way around, and the young woman's vitality would end up helping her.

"You know I'm not asking you to stay so that you can be my live-in nurse."

"You know I'm not agreeing so that I can persuade you to look for my mother."

While the others put the finishing touches on the house, Parri made dinner. He'd drawn up a calendar with the dates and times he would spend at her home. Teresa had stared at him as if he'd gone mad.

"It's been twenty-seven years, Antonio. When will you stop feeling like you owe me some kind of debt?"

"It's not about debts. I'm just fond of you. And anyway, I'm so lonely that this is actually perfect."

"It's actually perfect that I'm sick?"

"Well, when you put it that way, it doesn't sound so good."

"That's the way you put it."

"I'm a doctor, not a poet."

Every now and then Teresa would stop to take their pictures, and photograph herself with them, too. She was capturing flashes of joy, and they weren't just going to stay on her phone. She was going to print them all out and wallpaper the house with them, so that even in her moments of deepest confusion, she would be able to look up and see the familiar faces of the strangers who cared for her. They would be like clues that she had left behind for herself, so that she would know she could trust them. It was all she had left to cling on to, though the fear was that one day, she would no longer even recognize herself.

She walked back into the room that served as her study and library. She had been trying to reorganize it, but it seemed an impossible task to handle efficiently. There were so many memories tucked away between the pages of those books, so many dreams and sleepless nights. That was how she had rebuilt her life.

She pulled one of the desk drawers open. Inside was the last of the notebooks she had carried every day of her working life, singed around the edges, and thick with scribbles. She hadn't expected to find it there, and didn't even remember putting it away. Seeing it now caused her pain. It was a symbol. She had spent so many years identifying with her profession.

And yet she was heartened by the sound of cheerful chatter breathing new life into her home. She had managed to make a family after all—not one bound by blood, perhaps, but by strong and at times surprising ties. Not all change is catastrophic. Things always settle down eventually, and life goes on somehow.

She picked up the notebook. It was time for one last farewell.

"No more regrets."

She walked out into the garden. The driveway was full of boxes of old paperwork to dispose of.

She stood there holding the diary, unable to let it go. It was the tiniest of gestures, yet so difficult to make. A small personal sacrifice, an offering to fate in the hope that it might prove just a little bit merciful—for there was no doubt it was going to be cruel.

All of a sudden, the crickets stopped chirping.

It seemed crazy, but in that burst of unannounced tension, Teresa recognized the same feeling she'd experienced years ago in a lamplit cemetery. Or perhaps she had simply been expecting this to happen.

Her eyes bored into the night.

"I know you're there."

Nothing moved, not even a leaf trembled, and for a moment she felt silly, but then Giacomo stepped out of the shadow of a flowering wisteria. He must have rehearsed that step in his mind a thousand times. Hands thrust in the pockets of his jeans, a leather jacket over a T-shirt. He looked almost boyish.

He leaned against the metal gate.

"Always these bars between us."

Teresa did not approach him.

"I used to think there was honesty between us, too, but instead you've been lying to me."

He didn't reply, but just kept watching her.

Teresa felt a mixture of anger and hurt that she had been made to feel like a pawn in someone's game precisely when she had been at her most vulnerable.

"You've had your fun, Giacomo."

"Listen to me."

"No."

"Why?"

Teresa strode forward and grabbed the bars.

"Because I wouldn't believe you." She could feel her eyes stinging. "You forced me to go looking for Sebastiano's body without ever stopping to ask yourself how I might feel on discovering it was him."

"He nearly killed you. What could you possibly have felt?"

She gasped for breath.

"Certainly not happiness, nor any kind of satisfaction."

Giacomo was looking at her as if he might disavow her.

"It's true that I lied to you. But not about everything."

"You knew where the body was buried all along. No one ever moved it."

His lips tightened into a smile.

"Have some pity on me, Teresa."

"*Pity*? I've given you plenty more than that these past twenty-seven years. I've given you my trust, and you tried to play games with me."

"It was never a game."

"Then what was it?"

He looked up at the stars, eyes wet and gleaming with tears.

"A way of keeping you close, perhaps. Of going back in time. As if these twenty-seven years had never passed. I just wanted a different ending this time."

Teresa lowered her eyes for a moment, then collected herself enough to push her emotions away.

"What's the statuette about, Giacomo? What does it mean?"

"I don't know what you're talking about."

"Bullshit! I'm tired of your riddles."

"I would solve it for you if I could."

"So it wasn't you who thrust a two-thousand-year-old statuette into Sebastiano's throat."

"The only thing I put in Sebastiano's throat were mosaic tiles. And he was still alive when I did that."

"Spare me the details, please. Why the hare, why Aquileia? It can't all be random."

"It isn't. I was following the steps of a path to redemption someone told me about—you can probably guess who."

"The person who got you to do this."

The stranger had leveraged Giacomo's imagination, the vision of that Lazarus-like figure—risen from the dead in the form of a corpse—that he had always felt himself to be. He had returned from the afterlife wearing the colors of death, just like Osiris, that ancient god who was always depicted in the greenish hue of putrefying flesh.

"You can trust me, Teresa."

"Really, now."

"Come on, don't use that tone with me. I'm trying to help·you."

"And who's helping *you* right now?"

"I'm managing on my own."

Teresa muttered a curse, and threw a quick glance over her shoulder.

"Why are you here, Giacomo?"

"To warn you. The person who told me to commit this murder wanted to send you a very specific message. They know your past, and they know mine. By the time I figured out that their real target was you, it was already too late. I couldn't help myself."

"I know."

"The person who used me knows you well; it's their way of telling you that they are very close to you, and know what matters to you most. This time they made you step back into your past, but next time . . ."

"It'll be my team's turn? This isn't helping, Giacomo. You need to give me more."

He looked melancholy.

"That really is all. And this is goodbye." He touched her face. "I feel sad."

"I can't let you go."

"What exactly are you going to do? I promise you I'll never kill again."

"You know that's not true." Teresa spoke the words in a whisper, turning again to look at the house.

"If you really care about them, you won't call out. There's a pregnant woman in there. You've seen what I'm capable of. An animal is always an animal."

Teresa looked at his hands. She knew what they could do. She didn't even want to think of them touching her boys, who had come there to help her—unarmed and unaware.

"The day you caught me, twenty-seven years ago . . ."

"You made that one mistake. I've never understood how it could have happened."

"It wasn't a mistake, Teresa. There was only one reason why I did it, and it's the same reason that makes me stand here right now, with three cops just a few meters away and one right in front of me. I was totally, magnificently attracted to your power. I couldn't stay away from your light."

Teresa felt tears gathering in her eyes.

"You were so fascinated that you took one of my teeth as I was dying, and kept it for thirty years."

He shook his head.

"How can you think that? I didn't take it. It was your husband. He carried it with him. I told you: an animal is always an animal."

A totem in Sebastiano's possession. All this time, her executioner had kept it as a symbol and reminder of the power he had exerted over her. The symmetry with Giacomo was astonishing, but there was one fundamental difference. Sebastiano had retained his role within society for as long as possible—he had been the husband, the brother, the irreproachable colleague. Giacomo, on the other hand, was a serial killer who had always lived and been kept at the margins of the world. The former had tried to erase her. The latter had saved her life.

Teresa was shaking, and when Giacomo saw that, he took a step back.

"Keep shining, my darling Teresa. I won't be the one to extinguish your light."

He turned around to go, but she stopped him.

"If you really want to help me, tell me more about the man who wanted Sebastiano dead."

There was a pause.

"I never said it was a man. You just assumed it was."

Teresa went cold. Had she really made that mistake?

What else had she forgotten?

A terrible thought began to enter her mind. She gripped the metal bars tighter.

"Was it me? Was I the one who asked you to kill him?"

He returned to her, stroked her face through the bars, and saved her for a second time.

"No, Teresa. It wasn't you."

As she watched him walk away, she couldn't decide what to do.

She was still holding her notebook. She could jot down all that he had revealed, or she could throw it away. She could ask for help, or she could keep silent.

But what did she *want* to do?

It was always the same question whirling in her mind: Could she ever be anything other than a cop?

No.

She opened her notebook in search of a blank page, and saw the last words she herself had written down at the end of a case that had left her with an enigma to decipher. *Mother of Bones. Be careful.*

That was the warning the strange man gave her before vanishing into darkness, as the blaze that she and Marini had escaped still burned behind her, scattering ashes and sparks into the night. The man who had rescued her notebook from the flames and smuggled away an ancient icon whose power extended well beyond its artistic beauty. He was a friend she didn't know she had.

But in the meantime, Teresa's life had unraveled: her body verging on collapse, Giacomo's escape and return, Sebastiano's death. She hadn't given the nameless man's warning any further thought, or perhaps it was her illness that had decided to remove the memory from her—only for it to resurface now.

She had interpreted it at the time as a tasteless joke, an inconsequential attempt at an ominous sound bite, but the discovery of the *mater larvarum* changed everything. Or did it? This was no time to be swayed by the power of suggestion, or to succumb to confusion and doubt.

Marini joined her outside. She could tell from the way he was smiling that he had no idea what had just happened.

"Everything okay?"

Teresa didn't reply.

"Is something wrong?"

Two mothers: one of bones, and the other, leading a progeny of specters, retrieved from a dead man's throat—a dead man who used to be her husband. Teresa didn't believe in coincidences.

The Mother—whoever or whatever she may be—would soon come looking for her. The statuette must mean

something very specific, and it was Teresa's task—hers alone—
to discover and interpret what that was.

Mother of Bones. Be careful.

"Do you have a pen?"

He found one in his pocket and handed it to her. Teresa
crossed the sentence out.

She chose to protect her boys. They had come just within
reach of something that was better to let go of, something
that was stalking *her*—not them. Her heart was beating furiously in her chest.

Marini leaned against the gate and looked up at the sky,
just as Giacomo had done moments before. The scent of
wisteria was sweet and peppery.

"On a night like this, death feels very far away, like I can
almost shake it off."

A breeze shook the fronds, and a petal floated onto his
shoulder before slipping to the ground. Maybe there was
something else moving in the darkness.

There was a disparity in the flow of emotions that connected Teresa and Giacomo. She was compassionate; he was
obsessive-compulsive. In the eyes of a killer, Marini could
easily be construed as a rival.

Teresa closed the notebook.

"Massimo, get away from there."

He turned around.

"That's ominous!"

But his smile vanished when he saw the look on her face.
He stared into the night, senses on high alert, as if he had
guessed what was going through her mind. He let go of the
gate and took a few steps back.

"What just happened here?"

"Don't get agitated."

"I'm not agitated."

This was Marini. He was already agitated.

"Who did you see, Superintendent?"

Teresa told him the truth. All she had done was let enough time pass to ensure her boys were safe.

"Giacomo. Call Lona."

57

IV Century

THEY HADN'T KILLED HIM. *That was enough to thank the gods for,* Claudius thought—not so much about his own life, but for the sake of the mission he'd been entrusted with.

The Sarmatian witch—the statuette with the relic inside still in her painted fingers—was leading a procession of women and warriors that Claudius had been forced to join. They were escorting him into the depths of the forest, where not even trained assassins would have ventured. The darkness that seemed to be breathing all around him could well have contained the whole cosmos—the Mundus. Perhaps these strangers with their faces painted white were nothing but the dead, risen from the grave to drag him down into the chasm of chasms.

But when they reached their destination, it wasn't the grave of specters that opened up before his eyes. In the moonlit clearing, the camp seemed asleep. Sarmatians knew how to hide from any looks they wished to evade.

The old woman slipped into a tent guarded by two younger women and returned with a basket in hand. There was something moving inside it.

The circle of warriors opened and Claudius saw her walking toward him with outstretched arms. She placed the basket at his feet. There, displayed like a relic, and draped in silk and garlands of feathers, was a baby girl. The old woman took her in her hands and lifted her up, naked, presenting her to Claudius. The baby's tiny form was covered in arcane symbols traced with white lead. Her birth had been protected with magic spells.

Claudius could not understand why they had brought him to her until the old woman turned her around. The baby's shoulder blades jutted out like the wings of a newborn bird. She was the embodiment of their faith. A living goddess.

He wondered whether to prostrate himself before her, or if the symbol of the winged Isis that adorned his chest was enough to declare his true nature to the tribe: warrior-priest, and custodian of the divine.

The baby stretched her arm out until her hand brushed against his nose.

The old woman wordlessly encouraged him to do the same. A reluctant Claudius took her in his arms. The torchlight reflected in her irises, which were the color of light stone.

Claudius made as if to hand the baby back to the old woman, but she waved her hands in a gesture of refusal.

The elderly shaman then led the way through a path that penetrated even deeper into the forest, where the trees tangled into a wet womb, and at the end of which was a cart with no horses or oxen attached to it.

The bird women stepped away from the procession, lit a fire, and threw some powder into the flames, making them burn light blue.

Upon the cart was a wooden sarcophagus inlayed with figures of intertwined dragons.

The old woman took the baby back, returned the statuette to Claudius, and invited him to step onto the cart.

He jumped on. The wind had picked up, a northerly wind that carried the scent of ice and left a cascade of falling leaves in its wake.

He looked inside the open sarcophagus and felt his knees buckle until they fell upon the wooden slats.

The statuette seemed to be throbbing in his palm, but perhaps it was just his blood, the blood of a warrior-priest, flowing faster.

Isis herself had led him here. She had found a way to save herself. Claudius felt absolutely certain now that the statuette would survive through the centuries, bearing her message and perpetuating her worship, because everything he had ever kneeled before, everything he had ever venerated, the earthly incarnation of his faith, was right here in front of his eyes. In bones with no flesh.

58

---◦◦◦---

Today

JUDGING BY THE SHEER number of officers he'd deployed in the hunt for Giacomo Mainardi, Albert Lona would have happily mobilized the army, too, given the chance.

Massimo had never seen such a massive use of resources. Lona was taking the matter personally, and for a moment Massimo almost caught himself rooting for the killer just to see the district attorney struggle.

Lona had arrived at Teresa Battaglia's house with four other police cars in his convoy, with the surrounding area already cordoned off. The flashing lights and the presence of armed officers in her yard had set Teresa's phone ringing without pause. She'd ended up reassuring the whole neighborhood, and every now and then a curious local would pretend to be casually walking past her house just to see what was happening.

If there was any way of gifting Giacomo an escape route, then this confusion was surely it.

Meanwhile the district attorney wouldn't stop pestering Teresa, who hit back with retorts that only he would find reassuring, incapable as he was of detecting the traces of irony in her tone—or anyone else's, for that matter.

"Do you think we'll catch him?"

"Of course, Albert."

"It's been two hours already. If only you'd managed to keep him from leaving."

"I did wonder whether to invite him inside, you know."

"Do you think he would have agreed?"

"I don't know, but now that you ask . . ."

He huffed. "You could have at least tried." He studied them all one by one. "I need all the resources we have. I want you all on the next shift. Marini, we are meeting with the deputy prosecutor tomorrow morning."

He stood up to go, but no one seemed inclined to see him out. Everyone remained seated: Teresa, Parri, Massimo, de Carli, and Parisi. Elena and Alice had pretended to go upstairs, but Massimo was willing to bet they were hiding somewhere on the stairs, busy trying not to laugh.

Only Smoky followed him to the door, trotting behind him. Even the dog wanted to make sure Lona was definitely leaving.

Massimo eventually got up, too, though somewhat unwillingly.

"I'll be back soon."

He caught up with the district attorney on the driveway.

Lona turned around before Massimo had even called his name. He must have been expecting this—a terrible sign.

"What is it, Marini?"

Far too polite.

"I wanted to ask if at tomorrow's meeting you were planning to discuss the possibility that there might have been someone else behind the murder."

"Someone else?"

"Oh Christ, you're not going to do anything about it, are you?"

"And what am I supposed to do? Take a serial killer's word for it?"

"Teresa Battaglia believes him, and I believe her."

"And by extension you believe Mainardi, too. Yes, I see how it is between you, this little . . . pact," he said, waving his hand dismissively.

"There is no pact. It's just a question of trust and loyalty."

"How sweet."

"If you won't do anything, then I will."

"You would be ill-advised to go down that route, Inspector Marini," said Lona, pulling a cigarette case from his jacket pocket.

"Are you going to stop me?"

Albert laughed. It was the first time Marini had ever heard him laugh so heartily.

"See, Marini? You're biased. You think I'm doing it out of spite."

"Then why?"

The district attorney lowered his voice. All traces of amusement in his manner had completely disappeared.

"Why? Because if there really is someone else behind this murder, as Mainardi claims, then it can only be our very own Teresa Battaglia."

Massimo froze.

"What a perfect motive, Marini. And what a sublime strategy. Sebastiano was killed on May 20, Teresa's birthday. What better gift than that?"

"This is nonsense."

"I've not said anything that shocking, have I? Think about it, Marini. It could have happened during one of her prison visits. Remember when you found out about those? She might have let slip some seemingly innocuous remark, which someone like Giacomo would have taken as an order. I'd like to see him dead; he deserves to die; the world would be a better place without him." He cupped a hand, lit his cigarette, and exhaled. "Does that really sound so outlandish?"

He did not wait for an answer. He signaled at another officer and started walking toward the car. The sight of his cigarette smoke against the blue twilight and the blinking police lights seemed to Massimo like an omen of war.

Massimo had learned by now how to interpret the district attorney's words. The point of Lona's suggestion was not to protect Teresa. He was telling Massimo that he had him in his grasp, and sooner or later, he would collect his dues.

But today was not that day, and when it did eventually come, Massimo would be ready to face him. He'd be waiting at the breach, and he would not be alone.

He went back inside the house, where Teresa immediately caught his eye.

"Is everything all right?"

There was no point upsetting her.

"Everything's under control."

De Carli made one of his usual quips about Massimo and his need for control; Parisi took the opportunity to fire back with a joke of his own; Alice was helping Parri out in the kitchen; Smoky growled when Massimo dropped down onto the sofa and pulled Elena close. Everything was perfect.

Life resumed its course almost as if nothing had happened.

Massimo called out to Teresa, who was busy setting the table.

"Will you tell us the story of how you became superintendent?"

She paused, holding the cloth with which she had been polishing the cutlery, and seemed to seek approval from Parri, who had stuck his head out of the kitchen when he'd heard the question. Parri shrugged, giving her a smile.

Teresa returned to her polishing, wiping a little harder this time.

"Let's see . . . How did I become superintendent . . ." She was searching for the right words, indulging in memories that were more valuable now than ever before. "Well, to start, I had to walk down a very long corridor where everyone was staring at me. That was actually the hardest part. It was all downhill from there."

EPILOGUE

———⟨∞⟩———

Twenty-six years ago

TERESA'S COLLEAGUES WATCHED HER as she walked down the corridor. Their chatter would stop abruptly at her passage, only to pick up moments later as a sort of background hum where she could occasionally distinguish the sound of her name and perhaps the killer's, too. They were talking about her and about the case that had just been closed. They were commenting on her lopsided gait and on the brace that was still holding her jaw in place after it had been bolted back together.

During their last acupuncture session, Mei Gao had called her "Superintendent," but Teresa was here today to face the examination panel who would decide whether she had earned that title.

She still couldn't speak properly, slurring the odd word. Her pain was compounded by the unease of feeling as if she were being judged for the way she looked: like a woman who had been massacred by the hands of a man.

And yet those vicious hands had also shaped her, made her ready to become what she was now preparing to be.

The scar on her belly burned. It would never stop burning. Blood had flown from her heart all the way down to between her legs. She had been born again, and not from the ribs of a man who believed himself to have been made in the image and likeness of some god—but from her own broken, aching, twisted bones.

Sebastiano was now behind bars, where he had begun to serve his punishment for all the evil he had thrust upon her, but no sentence would ever suffice—and his was particularly lenient.

The whole system needed changing.

As soon as she had been able to stand again, Teresa had lodged a complaint with the human resources department, reporting the mistreatment she had endured, the sidelining and professional sabotage, and the psychological pressure she had been subjected to just because she was a woman. There was currently an internal investigation in progress, targeted also—and primarily—at Albert.

He had called her once in the middle of the night, when Teresa was still recovering.

"Don't turn against me. You'll regret it."

But it wasn't war or a personal vendetta that Teresa was after—only justice, and a fairer and more limpid way of existing in the world. She wanted to pave the way for all the other women who would follow, and for anybody—regardless of their sex—who might be vulnerable to being victimized by people in positions of power. From now on, those who held that power would have to think twice before they abused it.

Albert's last words to her had been stark: "You'll never pass the exam. You're not ready. You'll never be ready."

It was the backward blessing of a man who was clearly afraid of the strength of a woman who was capable of challenging and undermining his power.

But Teresa was no longer disposed to bending to anyone else's will.

Parri was waiting for her outside the room where the individual examinations took place.

Teresa stopped a few meters away.

They hadn't seen each other since that day in the hospital. Teresa had kept her distance from him and from those memories.

The day she was discharged, it had been someone else's smiling face that had greeted her at the door of her hospital room. Elvira Pace had taken her in during the first few weeks of her recovery. She had helped nurse those wounds for which medicine knew no remedy, and had taught Teresa the true meaning of solidarity.

Parri's eyes filled with tears as they roamed over her face. They were both thinking the same thing.

If only he hadn't drunk so much and fallen asleep that night, Teresa would not have lost her baby, and Antonio would have been able to save her.

But life cannot move forward when it is mired in regrets and recriminations; it will only stall and turn to rot.

Teresa took a few steps forward, closing the distance between them. He seemed to have aged disproportionately— or perhaps in proportion to his remorse.

He was the one who spoke first.

"You look different."

He was studying her short hair. Her flat fringe fell over her eyes, and her bob just about reached her cheeks. Teresa had dyed it the color of lava, like the kind she felt seething inside of her.

"I *am* different."

She watched him avert his gaze, and felt sorry for him.

"What are you doing here?"

A silence had descended around them.

Her friend finally found the courage to look her in the eye.

"I'd rather never leave your side again, if you don't mind. If there was a way to fix things . . ."

The doors of the examination room opened, and an assistant stepped out, holding a list. He was scanning it for the next candidate's name.

Today would also have been Teresa's due date. *Perhaps I'll give birth to myself*, she thought. The pain she felt now was just as fierce.

She looked at Parri again.

"There is a way to fix things: stop drinking. You and I will do great things together."

They called out her name.

Congratulations, dear Teresa!
Those "monsters" will have to watch their backs now.

With much respect and affection,

R.

AUTHOR'S NOTE

———◦◦◦———

IN RESEARCHING MY NOVELS, I always learn things I never knew before—or had only superficially glimpsed—about the place I am from. Like its predecessors, *Daughter of Ashes* also has its roots embedded in memory and origins. For me, it has been a thrill to journey into the ancient past of Aquileia, to follow the dissolving cult of Isis and the dawn of Christianity, and trace mystic revelations, which have filled me with wonder.

I have used History to write a story. I've adapted it, transformed it, filled it with new suggestions and with my own imagination, and always treated it with love, all in an attempt to re-create some of that wonder through the medium of words.

I list below some of the works that served as a starting point in my research:

De Clara, L., Pelizzari, G., Vianello, A., *Dalla salvezza di pochi alla salvezza universale. Breve guida ai mosaici della Basilica di Aquileia* [From salvation for the few to universal salvation. A brief guide to the mosaics of the Basilica of Aquileia], Forum, Udine, 2016.

Fontana, F., *I culti isiaci nell'Italia settentrionale. 1. Verona, Aquileia, Trieste* [The cult of Isis in northern Italy. 1. Verona, Aquileia, Trieste], with a contribution by Emanuela Murgia, EUT, Trieste, 2010.

Giordani, C., *Il cristianesimo egiziano di Aquileia* [Egyptian Christianity in Aquileia], Gaspari editore, Udine, 2020.

Various authors, Circolo Culturale Navarca, edited by A. Bellavite, *La Basilica di Aquileia. Tesori d'arte e simboli di luce in duemila anni di storia, di fede e di cultura* [The Basilica of Aquileia. Artistic treasures and symbols of light in two thousand years of history, faith, and culture], Ediciclo editore, Portogruaro, 2017.

ACKNOWLEDGMENTS

TO JASMINE AND PAOLO, who give me strength even when it feels like there isn't any left.

To my family, who are always there.

To the fantastic team at Longanesi, who continue to be by my side in this beautiful journey in the best way possible. Stefano Mauri, Cristina Foschini, Raffaella Roncato, Diana Volonté, Ernesto Fanfani, Alessia Ugolotti, Patrizia Spinato, Lucia Tomelleri.

A heartfelt thanks to Fabrizio Cocco and Giuseppe Strazzeri for their unwavering belief.

To the irreplaceable Antonio Moro.

To the extraordinary Viviana Vuscovich, Elena Pavanetto, Giulia Tonelli, and Graziella Cerutti: you give me so much energy.

A special thanks to Claudia Giordani for her invaluable

help on Aquileian mosaics and on the practice of Egyptian Christianity.

To friends old and new, who support me and help defuse doubts and anxieties.

To the journalist, bloggers, and booksellers who help my stories soar: I will be forever grateful.

To my readers, who surround me with so much warmth: you are the ones who have made this possible.

To each and every one of you: thank you, from the bottom of my heart.

Other Titles in the Soho Crime Series

STEPHANIE BARRON
(Jane Austen's England)
*Jane and the Twelve Days
    of Christmas*
Jane and the Waterloo Map
*Jane and the Year Without a
    Summer*
Jane and the Final Mystery

F.H. BATACAN
(Philippines)
Smaller and Smaller Circles

JAMES R. BENN
(World War II Europe)
Billy Boyle
The First Wave
Blood Alone
Evil for Evil
Rag & Bone
A Mortal Terror
Death's Door
A Blind Goddess
The Rest Is Silence
The White Ghost
Blue Madonna
The Devouring
Solemn Graves
When Hell Struck Twelve
The Red Horse
Road of Bones
From the Shadows
Proud Sorrows
The Phantom Patrol

The Refusal Camp: Stories

KATE BEUTNER
(Massachusetts)
Killingly

CARA BLACK
(Paris, France)
Murder in the Marais
Murder in Belleville

CARA BLACK CONT.
Murder in the Sentier
Murder in the Bastille
Murder in Clichy
Murder in Montmartre
Murder on the Ile Saint-Louis
Murder in the Rue de Paradis
Murder in the Latin Quarter
Murder in the Palais Royal
Murder in Passy
Murder at the Lanterne Rouge
Murder Below Montparnasse
Murder in Pigalle
Murder on the Champ de Mars
Murder on the Quai
Murder in Saint-Germain
Murder on the Left Bank
Murder in Bel-Air
*Murder at the Porte de
    Versailles*
Murder at la Villette

Three Hours in Paris
Night Flight to Paris

HENRY CHANG
(Chinatown)
Chinatown Beat
Year of the Dog
Red Jade
Death Money
Lucky

BARBARA CLEVERLY
(England)
The Last Kashmiri Rose
Strange Images of Death
The Blood Royal
Not My Blood
A Spider in the Cup
Enter Pale Death
Diana's Altar

Fall of Angels
Invitation to Die

COLIN COTTERILL
(Laos)
The Coroner's Lunch
Thirty-Three Teeth
Disco for the Departed
Anarchy and Old Dogs
Curse of the Pogo Stick
The Merry Misogynist
Love Songs from a Shallow Grave
Slash and Burn
The Woman Who Wouldn't Die
Six and a Half Deadly Sins
I Shot the Buddha
The Rat Catchers' Olympics
Don't Eat Me
The Second Biggest Nothing
*The Delightful Life of
    a Suicide Pilot*

The Motion Picture Teller

ELI CRANOR
(Arkansas)
Don't Know Tough
Ozark Dogs
Broiler

MARIA ROSA CUTRUFELLI
(Italy)
Tina, Mafia Soldier

GARRY DISHER
(Australia)
The Dragon Man
Kittyhawk Down
Snapshot
Chain of Evidence
Blood Moon
Whispering Death
Signal Loss

Wyatt
Port Vila Blues
Fallout

Under the Cold Bright Lights

PETER LOVESEY
(England)
The Circle
The Headhunters
False Inspector Dew
Rough Cider
On the Edge
The Reaper

(Bath, England)
The Last Detective
Diamond Solitaire
The Summons
Bloodhounds
Upon a Dark Night
The Vault
Diamond Dust
The House Sitter
The Secret Hangman
Skeleton Hill
Stagestruck
Cop to Corpse
The Tooth Tattoo
The Stone Wife
Down Among the Dead Men
Another One Goes Tonight
Beau Death
Killing with Confetti
The Finisher
Diamond and the Eye
Showstopper

(London, England)
Wobble to Death
The Detective Wore
 Silk Drawers
Abracadaver
Mad Hatter's Holiday
The Tick of Death
A Case of Spirits
Swing, Swing Together
Waxwork

Bertie and the Tinman
Bertie and the Seven Bodies
Bertie and the Crime of Passion

SUJATA MASSEY
(1920s Bombay)
The Widows of Malabar Hill
The Satapur Moonstone
The Bombay Prince
The Mistress of Bhatia House

FRANCINE MATHEWS
(Nantucket)
Death in the Off-Season
Death in Rough Water
Death in a Mood Indigo
Death in a Cold Hard Light
Death on Nantucket
Death on Tuckernuck
Death on a Winter Stroll

SEICHŌ MATSUMOTO
(Japan)
Inspector Imanishi
 Investigates

CHRIS McKINNEY
(Post Apocalyptic Future)
Midnight, Water City
Eventide, Water City
Sunset, Water City

PHILIP MILLER
(North Britain)
The Goldenacre
The Hollow Tree

FUMINORI NAKAMURA
(Japan)
The Thief
Evil and the Mask
Last Winter, We Parted
The Kingdom
The Boy in the Earth
Cult X
My Annihilation
The Rope Artist

STUART NEVILLE
(Northern Ireland)
The Ghosts of Belfast
Collusion

STUART NEVILLE CONT.
Stolen Souls
The Final Silence
Those We Left Behind

So Say the Fallen

The Traveller & Other Stories
House of Ashes

(Dublin)
Ratlines

GARY PHILLIPS
(Los Angeles)
One-Shot Harry
Ash Dark as Night

Violent Spring
Perdition, U.S.A.
Bad Night Is Falling
Only the Wicked

SCOTT PHILLIPS
(Western US)
Cottonwood
The Devil Raises His Own

That Left Turn at Albuquerque

KWEI QUARTEY
(Ghana)
Murder at Cape Three Points
Gold of Our Fathers
Death by His Grace

The Missing American
Sleep Well, My Lady
Last Seen in Lapaz
The Whitewashed Tombs

QIU XIAOLONG
(China)
Death of a Red Heroine
A Loyal Character Dancer
When Red Is Black

NILIMA RAO
(1910s Fiji)
A Disappearance in Fiji

MARCIE R. RENDON

(Minnesota's Red River Valley)

Murder on the Red River
Girl Gone Missing
Sinister Graves

JAMES SALLIS

(New Orleans)

The Long-Legged Fly
Moth
Black Hornet
Eye of the Cricket
Bluebottle
Ghost of a Flea

Sarah Jane

MICHAEL SEARS

(Queens, New York)

Tower of Babel

JOHN STRALEY

(Sitka, Alaska)

The Woman Who Married a
*   Bear*
The Curious Eat Themselves
The Music of What Happens
Death and the Language
*   of Happiness*
The Angels Will Not Care
Cold Water Burning
Baby's First Felony
So Far and Good

(Cold Storage, Alaska)

The Big Both Ways
Cold Storage, Alaska
What Is Time to a Pig?
Blown by the Same Wind

LEONIE SWANN

(England)

The Sunset Years of Agnes
*   Sharp*
Agnes Sharp and the Trip
*   of a Lifetime*

KAORU TAKAMURA

(Japan)

Lady Joker

AKIMITSU TAKAGI

(Japan)

The Tattoo Murder Case
Honeymoon to Nowhere
The Informer

CAMILLA TRINCHIERI

(Tuscany)

Murder in Chianti
The Bitter Taste of Murder
Murder on the Vine
The Road to Murder

HELENE TURSTEN

(Sweden)

Detective Inspector Huss
The Torso
The Glass Devil
Night Rounds
The Golden Calf
The Fire Dance
The Beige Man
The Treacherous Net
Who Watcheth
Protected by the Shadows

Hunting Game
Winter Grave
Snowdrift

An Elderly Lady Is Up
*   to No Good*
An Elderly Lady Must Not
*   Be Crossed*

ILARIA TUTI

(Italy)

Flowers over the Inferno
The Sleeping Nymph
Daughter of Ashes

JANWILLEM VAN DE
**   WETERING**

(Holland)

Outsider in Amsterdam
Tumbleweed
The Corpse on the Dike
Death of a Hawker
The Japanese Corpse
The Blond Baboon
The Maine Massacre
The Mind-Murders
The Streetbird
The Rattle-Rat
Hard Rain
Just a Corpse at Twilight
Hollow-Eyed Angel
The Perfidious Parrot
The Sergeant's Cat:
*   Collected Stories*

JACQUELINE WINSPEAR

(Wartime England)

Maisie Dobbs
Birds of a Feather
The Comfort of Ghosts